A GIFT OF TIME

BOOK THREE IN THE NINE MINUTES TRILOGY

BETH FLYNN

A Gift of Time
Copyright © 2016 by Beth Flynn
All Rights Reserved
Edited by Jessica Brodie
Cover Photo by Tara Simon
Cover Design by Sommer Stein with Perfect Pear Creative Covers
Cover Model: Lasse L. Matberg

ISBN-13: 978-1535168670
ISBN-10: 1535168676

AUTHOR'S NOTE AND READING ORDER

A Gift of Time is the third installment in the Nine Minutes Trilogy. It is not intended to be a stand-alone novel, but could be read as one. Still, I highly recommend that you read my first two novels, *Nine Minutes* and *Out of Time*, to be able to understand the background stories of the main characters. There are many twists and turns in both books that can best be connected if read consecutively. Recommended reading order:

The Nine Minutes Trilogy
Nine Minutes (Book 1)
Out of Time (Book 2)
A Gift of Time (Book 3)

The Nine Minutes Spin-Off Novels
The Iron Tiara (Book 1)
Tethered Souls (Book 2)
Better Than This (Book 3)
Tarnished Soul (Book 4)

Thank you for your support and readership!

This book is lovingly dedicated to

The Niners

Not one single day has gone by where I haven't felt your unconditional love and support for me and my stories. Thank you from the bottom of my grateful heart.

and to

The little boy I met on a playground in 1974. The real Tommy.

TIMELINE

1975
Ginny / Kit's abduction

1985
Grizz's arrest
Ginny marries Tommy / Grunt
Ginny and Grizz's daughter, Mimi, is born

1990
Ginny and Tommy's son, Jason, is born

1999
Moe's remains found

2000 Summer
Grizz's execution

PROLOGUE

Ginny, 2007, North Carolina

A very old and wise friend once told me, "It's not by coincidence that everything comes full circle, back to the way it was meant to be."

I remember holding her bony and gnarled hands in my own. Her strong grip had a strength that belied her age. Intelligent blue eyes met mine as she gave me those words. I saw a challenge in them as if she was daring me to defy or question her wisdom.

Looking back at that moment, almost six years past, I have to concede she was right.

The memory washed over me now as I sat on the cool grass, inhaling its sharp, crisp scent. I'd always loved the smell of freshly cut grass, which would hang in the humid air like a wet blanket during the hot summer days in Florida. That's where I grew up and spent most of my life—Fort Lauderdale, Florida. But I was a long way from there now. The sun warmed my shoulders and felt good on my face. I grabbed another weed, tugging it softly. It came up easily, and I tossed it to the side.

I glanced around the tiny cemetery and sighed as I looked at the gravestones. Some were bigger and newer, standing erect in tribute to a lost loved one. Some were worn and slanted, fighting to stay upright out of respect to the person or persons that lay beneath them. One thing they all had in common: Not one grave was bare. They each displayed some form of remembrance. Flowers—fresh and artificial. Flags, banners, personal mementos. Regardless of the dates, some going back to before the Civil War, each grave was cared for with high respect.

My eyes settled on a headstone two rows over that always caused an ache in my heart. It simply read "Our Children," then listed seven names with a set of dates beside each one. Each child hadn't lived past the age of two years old, the last one having passed away in 1932. I was fascinated enough about that grave to do some research when we'd first moved here. After all, they were family, and I was very curious to know what had happened. Actually, they weren't exactly my family, but they were distant relatives of my husband and children, and even though I wasn't their blood ancestor, I still considered them my family.

I returned my gaze to the dark granite gravestone I sat before and found myself fighting back tears. Another ache in my heart. One that would always be there.

But along with the tears came acceptance. Acceptance of the gift we call life and all it brings, including death. His death.

I never expected to be sitting on a mountaintop so far away from the hustle and bustle of Fort Lauderdale. So far from the ocean and the feel of the sand between my toes. So distanced from everything that had been familiar and safe to me. But I'd more than willingly traded it for this existence, this new beginning. And I wouldn't have it any other way.

I traced my left hand over the gravestone, over his name. In spite of the sun's warmth, the hard granite was cool beneath my fingertips. My nails dug into the crevice where his name was etched, and almost unconsciously, my eyes focused on my ring finger. Two rings. One of ink and one of gold. Not too many women would ever know the blessing of being loved so deeply by more than one man.

Blessed to still have one of them in her life now.

Just then I heard them, and I quickly turned my gaze to the tiny white clapboard church adjacent to the cemetery. The majestic Blue Ridge Mountains served as a backdrop to the picturesque scene. As I watched, my husband walked down the wooden deck steps, a child clinging tightly to each hand. It was a Wednesday morning, and we had the old church and family cemetery all to ourselves. Our four-year-old daughter, Ruthie, stopped and looked up at him.

"Pick me up, Daddy. Pick me up!" she insisted.

I watched as he smiled down at her and effortlessly scooped her up, wincing when she accidentally kicked a tender area. He'd suffered a serious wound years ago, and it still caused him some pain and probably always would. It was a reminder of our old life. The life we'd finally put behind us.

Ruthie's twin brother had already let go of his father's hand and ran to me, plopping himself down hard on my lap. I buried my face in his hair and inhaled deeply. He smelled like soap, sweat, and maybe even some dirt. I smiled. I remembered telling my husband when I'd confirmed my surprise pregnancy, "I'm too old for this. We're too old for this!" He'd just laughed then, and reminded me I was always the one talking about unexpected blessings, fresh starts, and new challenges. I can say for sure having twins at our age was and still is a challenge. But I've never been so invigorated and optimistic about the future—in spite of certain things I've learned. And I'm loving every single minute of it. I didn't love the extra stretch marks that came with having two babies in my belly, but there is even beauty in those. I feel like they speak to me: Look at the beautiful children you've made. Job well done, Ginny.

I watched as my son lifted his hand to the headstone and put his tiny finger in the name engraved in it, spelling it out loud and clear as he followed the grooves. When he was finished, he tilted his head back and looked up at me.

"Just like my name, Mommy. His name is the same as mine."

"Yes, it is, sweetheart," I answered him, smiling softly. "Yes it is."

PART I

"You can't start the next chapter of your life if you keep rereading the last one."

U_{NKNOWN}

1

Ginny, 2000, Fort Lauderdale (Three Months After Grizz's Execution)

I don't remember how long I sat on the hot asphalt of Carter's driveway and just stared at the ground. After a while, I lifted my hip and pulled the blue bandana from my pocket where I had stuffed it just minutes ago. Or had it been an hour?

Thirty minutes ago, my childhood Bible was returned to me along with a letter from my mother, Delia. The letter revealed some sad truths about her past and mine. I'd read about a twin sister who died in the hospital after Delia abandoned her and I found out I was actually older than what I'd always believed. And now, having just discovered the missing motorcycle and Carter's unspoken confirmation that he was alive, Grizz was still alive, I could do nothing but sit and stare at the empty spot in the garage. It was all just too much.

I quickly looked back over my shoulder to see if Carter was close by. She wasn't. I held the bandana to my face and started to cry again, this time with small but soulful, gut-wrenching sobs. The kind of sobs that come from a place so deep within your chest you didn't know they existed until they confronted you with a ferocity that caused physical pain. The kind of sobs that if you stifled them, caused your ribs to hurt and your back to ache. I hadn't even cried this hard after his execution.

I tried to fathom why that was. Was it because his death was final?

Or so I had thought. I could neatly tuck my love and grief in an imaginary box and label it "In the Past." Where was this new grief coming from now? What was I actually feeling? Betrayal? Hurt? Love?

No. I wouldn't do that to myself. I couldn't let myself believe, even a tiny bit, that I was still in love with him. I loved Tommy. I was in love with Tommy. Our love was real and not a consolation prize after Grizz's arrest, incarceration, and supposed death. Yet...what was it? I wouldn't let myself finish the thought.

I had to battle the urge to get Carter and insist she tell me everything she knew. I had to fight the instinct to dig for answers. Something bigger told me I shouldn't do any probing, that Grizz's secret was large enough to have repercussions should I decide to investigate —which was what my flesh wanted me to do, but my spirit knew better. No, I wouldn't question. I wouldn't ask. I would do what he apparently wanted and just file away the knowledge he was out there should I need him, but move on and live the life he insisted I have.

I sat up a little straighter then and resolved to do just that. *You want me to move on, Grizz? You got it.* Shoving the bandana back in my pocket, I picked myself up. I avoided glancing at the empty spot in the garage where his motorcycle had been—the spot where he had recently been—and I headed around the side of the building. I charged up the stairs to the guesthouse with a determined resolve I wasn't feeling. I reminded myself that I was the master of illusion. I could and would act fine until today's revelation eventually made its way to the back of my subconscious.

Yes, it was time to start convincing myself he was dead and gone. For good.

I swung open the door and let myself into the guest apartment. I strode to the windows, opening up the blinds, unlatched the window locks, and hoisted them open. They were still in good condition but stiff from years of disuse. I inhaled the hot, thick air as it floated in and thought about turning on the air conditioning.

A plan formed as I worked: First, I would assess how much cleaning out I would need to do. I swung around, and with my hands on my hips surveyed the tiny living space. It was clean and neatly but sparsely furnished. I walked over to the small alcove that served as a kitchen. I started opening up the cabinets and found the bare necessities—plates, cups, and silverware. I knew I wouldn't be cleaning out these things, but I was stalling for what needed to be done.

I walked to the only bedroom. The light was dim, but I couldn't miss the small cardboard box sitting on top of the bed. I stood staring at the box that had suddenly become the size of a mountain in my head. I'd told myself cleaning out the guesthouse and garage was going to be a huge physical task that would require lots of sweat and muscle.

But it wasn't huge. There would be no lugging things up and down the stairs. It all came down to that box. The box sitting on that bed.

We'd made love on that bed.

Don't go there, Ginny. I eyed the room. The bed was stripped bare of its linens. Two small nightstands with matching lamps flanked each side. It was all outdated but in good condition. They could stay. The telescope I'd given Grizz as a gift sat in a corner. I pretended not to notice it. Carter should be using this space for when she and Bill had friends in town. It was time for the garage and guesthouse to be used again. I wasn't following his rules anymore.

Slowly, I approached the bed. I wasn't the one who'd packed his things up all those years ago. It had been Carter. She'd been living with me then and suggested we start moving some of his belongings out. I'd resisted it at first until Grizz told me to do it. I shook my head as realization dawned. Of course. Carter had probably been in touch with Grizz and told him I wasn't moving on and then, voila! I hear from Grizz telling me to do exactly what Carter had suggested. Stupid and naïve. I clenched my fists at the memory.

I'd been so devastated then that I couldn't bring myself to part with his things, so I'd spent the day away from the house and asked Carter to do it. I knew she would have donated his clothes and shoes to charity, which meant I was going to find even more personal items in this box. Mementos she, or Grizz, thought should be kept. I couldn't blame either one for what I might find. I'd wanted no part of it. I remembered tasking Chicky with packing up Moe's belongings many years earlier. Clearly, I had a difficult time staring at tangible reminders of painful events.

But there would be no escaping it today.

I swallowed the lump that was beginning to form in my throat and opened the box. The cardboard at first resisted but then opened easily. I peered into it and inhaled deeply, making a conscious effort to release my breath and inhale again. My hands shook as I pulled out the first item. Clutching it tightly I had to loosen my grip so I didn't snap it in half. It was a record album still encased in a pristine cardboard jacket. My Barry White album.

Memories bounced around my brain, attacking my senses. I could feel the hot water as my hands stiffened in the motel's tiny kitchen sink all those years ago. I could smell the clean, fresh scent of the soap coming from the sponge I'd been using. I could see Chowder's homemade strainer sitting on the drain board. I could feel the gentle and feathery kiss Grizz left on my temple. And I could hear Barry White crooning to "Never, Never Gonna Give Ya Up" as I led Grizz back to the bedroom. I gulped and heard myself whisper out loud, "You saved it."

No, stop it, Ginny! Don't do this to yourself. I laid the album to the side and reached in for the next item. I couldn't tell what it was at first but immediately recognized the soft plushness of a stuffed animal. Grizz had a stuffed animal? I stared at the small toy for a second. It was a little gorilla, and I was transported back to a happy memory. On one of our many midnight dates, Grizz had taken me to a zoo. The night caretaker, who owed Grizz a favor, told us we only had two hours to ourselves before other employees would be reporting to work.

We had wandered through several parts of the zoo when we stopped at the gorilla exhibit to read the names and histories of some of the primates. One stuck out. Apparently, the silver back, or alpha leader of the group, was a big nasty gorilla named Grizz. I'd teased him about it for months after that date. As we were leaving the zoo, Grizz had jumped over a railing to get to a beautiful rose bush. He snapped some off, not even noticing the thorns had drawn blood from his hands. He had quickly removed his T-shirt and wrapped the roses in it. I remembered holding those roses and smelling them in the car during the drive home. The memory was so fresh I felt like I could still smell them. I looked down now, noticed something dangling from the stuffed toy's wrist. It was a card with a picture of a gorilla cradling a tiny kitten to its chest.

I carefully opened it and read what was neatly printed inside. "Happy Birthday. I love you, baby." It was signed, "Grizz."

I was holding a birthday gift he'd never given me because he was arrested. I felt my chest tighten. There was more handwriting at the bottom, but it was smaller and hard to see in the dim light of the little bedroom. I squinted. "I'm taking you to our special place tonight. Please wear them for me."

Wear what? I knew our special place. It was a little dive down by the docks called Vincent's. But what was I supposed to have worn? I looked back at the little gorilla and couldn't tell if I was missing something. Then I noticed them. The gorilla had a diamond stud earring in each ear. I'd almost missed them because of the thickness of the fur. That's what he'd wanted me to wear to my birthday dinner. Diamond earrings. Oh, Grizz. Why would you do this to me? Or rather, why would I let you do this?

With a trembling hand, I laid the toy down and swiped at the tears that were starting to form again. Without looking, I reached into the box and latched on to the first thing my hand came into contact with. I pulled it out and stared. A slingshot. It wasn't the store-bought kind. This one looked like it was handmade out of wood, some kind of tree branch, and a heavy-duty rubber band. I'd seen Grizz teach some kids how to properly use a slingshot once. Tommy had told me the story about how Grizz had been out squirrel hunting the day his little sister had died. Maybe he'd used a slingshot that day. Had this been his? Why had I never seen it?

I gently laid the slingshot on the bed next to the album and stuffed animal. One more item was at the bottom of the box, and this one I recognized immediately. It was a small black bag with a zipper running up the center. It was familiar because I'd bought it for him. It was a shaving bag. I'd presented it to him one Christmas and stocked it with necessities. His favorite— or rather my favorite—cologne that he always wore, razors, shaving cream, deodorant, scissors, and other manly items. I started to unzip it and hesitated. What if his cologne was in it? I didn't think I could handle remembering how he smelled right then. Don't open it.

But I knew I had to. I sat down on the bed and reached into the worn leather bag. I took out the single item it contained. And even though I didn't remember the incident, I knew exactly what I was seeing.

It was a box of bandages. They were old and sported an outdated logo. The box was dented, yellowed and worn, but it was recognizable.

They were the bandages I had given Grizz back in 1966.

2

Grizz, 1988, Prison, North Florida

I t was almost two o'clock in the morning. Grizz carried himself in a sure and confident manner through the prison's dimly lit halls, not noticing as the janitor and laundry attendant, also inmates, avoided eye contact with him.

He was the only man on death row who was given free rein to take a stroll through the maximum-security prison in the middle of the night. He rarely took advantage of this privilege during the day. He didn't like calling attention to himself. But at night, he needed to get out of his cell. To stretch his legs; try to feel a little normal. In the short time he'd been here, he'd discovered the library was his refuge. He usually visited it sometime between eleven and midnight, but tonight he had been so engrossed in the book he was reading he hadn't realized the time. Eleven? Two? It didn't matter. The room was always empty after hours, and he liked taking his time perusing the bookshelves. He'd recently discovered he loved to read. Shit, what else was he going to do in this place? Blue was handling things on the outside and usually called him or made the trip for a face to face for any important issues. He had no pending responsibilities, so he needed an occupation—reading it was.

It was getting harder and harder to get messages to Blue unnoticed. Even with his clout, Grizz didn't like to be obvious about some things. Communicating with Blue was one of them. Carter would have her animal ministry set up soon enough, and he would use the dogs to get messages to her, and she would, in turn, get them anonymously delivered. She was a smart one, and he was glad he'd stepped in all those years ago and helped her with the man who'd been stalking her. He'd done it for Kit, not realizing then how useful it would prove to be.

He quietly let himself in the library and immediately noticed he wasn't alone. He silently ducked behind a shelf and peered between them to see another inmate who sat behind a large glass window in the tiny library office and typed on a computer. Grizz could hear the keys clacking as the screen illuminated the man's face. Grizz looked closer and recognized him as a kid from the chow hall. Grizz didn't know his name. "Pretty" is what the other inmates called him. Grizz could understand why. He had very soft, feminine features. He was tall and slender and had eyebrows that seemed more naturally arched than most females, and he had very little, if any, facial hair. He also had a full head of brown hair that curled on the ends as it framed his youthful face. Yeah, he was a real beauty by prison standards.

One of Pretty's jobs was to stand by the garbage cans to sort and dump the trays after the inmates were finished and headed out of the chow hall. He never spoke to or looked anyone in the eye. Grizz wondered what he was in for, and now wondered what he was doing in the library in the middle of the night. Grizz swiped a hand over his smooth head, mourning the long locks he'd purposely shaved, then tugged at his beard. Didn't matter why the boy was here. After tonight, he would belong to Grizz.

He left the library as quietly as he had entered and returned to his cell.

The next day, Grizz was sitting in the chow hall. It wasn't his habit to eat with the general prison population, but he had on a few occasions. Today he used the time to sit back and observe. It was his prison, his turf, and he liked to watch, to listen, to be a presence. It didn't take him long to establish himself as the penitentiary's new inmate authority. He sat at a table that was close to Pretty but kept his back to him. He listened to the comments from the other inmates as they handed Pretty their trays. Some were engaged in conversations with each other. Some didn't say anything. Others used the opportunity to taunt the young prisoner.

Grizz observed through his peripheral vision as the line started to build up. It was time to make himself known. And he wanted an audience.

Purposely, he went to the back of the line, then wordlessly made his way to the front as the other men stepped aside and let him pass. As he got to the front, he listened as two men who hadn't noticed his approach spoke to Pretty.

"You still taking care of that rodent you call 'Buddy'?" One of them, a heavyset dark-haired guy, leered at Pretty.

No answer.

"Awwww, Pretty is embarrassed that he doesn't have any friends, Psycho. He's like that weirdo in that movie. What was it called? The one about a kid who fell in love with a rat."

There was some snickering, and Psycho crossed his arms. "Ben. The movie was called Ben. You sing your little rat buddy lullabies like Michael Jackson did?" He took a step forward. "You can sing 'em to me when I get you in the shower later."

Still no answer.

Grizz had heard enough.

"Move the fuck out of my way," Grizz said slow and low, shoving the two inmates out of his path.

Grizz tossed his tray at Pretty and purposely took his time perusing the young guy from his head to his feet. He noticed Pretty's name tag read "Petty." So that was his last name. Grizz could understand how it had eventually turned into Pretty.

In a voice that made it clear there would be no challenges, he said for those within earshot, "He's mine now. Only mine."

Pretty's face turned pale.

Without making eye contact with any of them, he headed back to his cell.

3

Mimi, 1997, Fort Lauderdale

Mimi sat back on her bed, the plump pillows cushioning her against the sturdy headboard.

"Done!" she exclaimed out loud to herself.

She had just put the finishing touches on a poem she had written for her parents. They had an anniversary coming up, and she wanted to surprise them. She had recently discovered she had a knack for writing, which she loved. Her teacher had encouraged her after she wrote an essay that focused on a poor migrant family who'd overcome insurmountable odds and found a new life in the U.S. Mrs. Horan had been impressed when she'd read the level of detail Mimi delivered in the essay, and she questioned her about her research. Talking with Mrs. Horan, Mimi had realized she not only loved writing about the family, but she thrived on the research, on digging in to find details someone else might've missed. Her teacher suggested she think about going into journalism. "You're still young and can change your mind, but when you have a passion for something, it shows in your work," her teacher had told her. "I see that passion in you, Mimi."

Mimi tucked the poem for her parents into her nightstand drawer, slipped off her bed, and bent down to pull something from under her mattress. It was her secret journal, another something she could credit to Mrs. Horan. Earlier in the school year, Mimi had taken Mrs.

Horan's advice and started writing down her thoughts and dreams. She even had some short stories in her journal. She was still too shy to share her words with her family. Her newfound love of writing was her secret. She was going to present the poem to her parents for their anniversary and gauge their reaction. She loved and trusted her parents, and even though they encouraged her in every way possible, she was still not confident enough to share something she considered so intimate.

Absently, she tugged at her earring and smiled as she tried to envision their response. "Mimi, we didn't know you had this talent in you! Why have you been hiding this for so long?"

She daydreamed about what she wanted her parents' reaction to be, but because she couldn't be certain, she decided to keep her journal and her dreams of writing to herself. At least for now.

She took a few minutes to write some thoughts down about how excited she was to present the poem, but she had something else to do. And since she only had the house to herself for another hour, she had to work fast and make the time count.

She closed her book and slipped it back between her mattress and box spring, tidied her bedspread, and walked to her bedroom door. Before opening it, she kissed the Titanic poster that was hanging on the back.

"When I'm a famous journalist, Leonardo DiCaprio, you'll be begging me to interview you!"

And with the innocence and excitement of a twelve-year-old on the brink of a future with endless possibilities, she headed for her parents' bedroom. She had some research to do.

INSIDE THEIR DARKENED BEDROOM, SHE HUNTED. WHERE WOULD IT BE? They had to keep it somewhere, and she'd had no luck at all going through her father's office.

She stood in the center of her parents' walk-in closet and surveyed the shelves. There were boxes on each one, but they were labeled neatly with their contents. Not a single box referred to personal papers or anything similar. Think, Mimi. You want to be an investigative journalist. Investigate. A marriage certificate is personal and something to treasure. Where would you keep something you treasured? Maybe with something else you treasured? She allowed her mind to wander while she imagined presenting her parents with this special gift and her poem.

When she'd noticed a silver-plated teaching certificate on Mrs. Horan's wall, she'd gotten the idea to have something made for her parents. Her teacher was only too happy to help her. She'd saved her allowance and babysitting money for years with the plan to spend it on something special. Now she knew what it would be. Mrs. Horan told her the personalized plaque would be expensive, and Mimi was thrilled to know she had enough to cover it. But she had a hurdle. She had to bring her parents' Marriage Certificate to Mrs. Horan so she could have the plaque made.

Where, where, where? She came out of the closet and slowly scanned the master bedroom. Her eyes landed on her mother's night-stand. A lamp, alarm clock, hand lotion, and a book. The Bible. Her mother's most cherished possession. Maybe it was folded up in the Bible.

She sat on the edge of the bed as she lovingly ran her hand over the front of the holy book. She smiled when she saw the initials that had been embossed on the bottom right-hand corner. G.L.D. They were so small they were barely noticeable and hard to see against the deep brown leather unless you were looking for them. She knew the history behind this Bible. Her father had told Mimi how he had presented it to her mother for her sixteenth birthday and how the printer had made a mistake. It should have read G.L.L., but Ginny wouldn't let Tommy have it replaced back then. Maybe she knew she was going to marry him one day. Mimi hugged herself. It was fate.

Mimi smiled as she brought herself back from the romantic memory and softly fanned through the pages of the Bible. Two cards fell out, each containing Scriptures in Ginny's handwriting. She hoped they weren't marking anyplace special and returned them to where she guessed they went. She noticed her mother's neat handwriting in some of the margins on the pages she was flipping through. Almost every single page had a notation. She turned back to the beginning and noticed the first few pages. It was where you could fill in your personal information. Marriages, births, deaths. She smiled as she saw where her and Jason's names had been recorded, along with the day they were born. Her mother also had notations of when they made First Holy Communion and other important dates.

Her parents' names were written in with their wedding date, and beneath it was a verse from Scripture. It was Matthew 11:25. Maybe it was a Scripture someone had read at their wedding. Mimi had been to weddings and knew people did that all the time. A backup plan began to form in her mind in case she wasn't able to find their marriage certificate. Maybe she could do something with this Scripture. Surely they would remember a Scripture that had been read at their wedding. She quickly flipped to the New Testament and, finding the page she'd been looking for, read the words out loud: "At that time Jesus said, 'I praise you, Father, Lord of heaven and earth, because you have hidden these things from the wise and learned, and revealed them to little children.'"

She looked up from the Bible and was puzzled. What in the world could her parents' marriage have to do with Jesus telling God about things He'd kept hidden? What could this Scripture have to do with anything? There was no reference to marriage that she understood, unless she just wasn't getting it. She reread the Scripture slowly and this time noticed some numbers in the margin next to it. 23-07-15. Her eyes darted back and forth from the Scripture to the numbers. The numbers, the Scripture. The words. One word.

Hidden.

She broke into a wide grin when she realized what she'd discovered. She couldn't be positive until she tried it out, but she was pretty sure she knew what she was looking at. A lock combination. Or in this case, she hoped, a safe combination. Was this her mother's way of remembering the combination to the safe in her father's office downstairs? She'd heard her mother claim many times she could be forgetful. Mimi heard her father telling her mother one time she purposely forgot about his business dinner because she subconsciously didn't want to go. He said something about how she had a mental block about things she didn't want to deal with.

Yes, her mother admittedly had a bad memory, and this was her way of making sure she didn't forget the safe combination. Writing the Scripture reference in an important place in her Bible was her mother's attempt to not make it obvious, but Mimi knew. She had a locker at school. She could only hope her father's safe worked the same way.

Mimi laid the cherished book back on the nightstand and made sure everything looked like she'd found it. Yes, Mimi decided. She would make an excellent investigator. Maybe I shouldn't be a journalist. I could probably be a detective or a secret FBI agent or something.

She strode to the bedroom door. She still had some time to see if she could get the safe open. She was certain she would find her parents' marriage certificate in it.

And because it probably wasn't something they looked at often, maybe even never, she could safely return it without anybody even knowing it was gone.

4

Tommy, 1976, The Motel, Fort Lauderdale

"You've got it. You're doing fine, Kit!" Grunt grinned at her from the passenger seat. "Just let up on the gas a little bit. You don't need to hit the brake to slow down. There's not another car in sight. Ease your foot off the gas pedal, and the car will slow down on its own. And remember, don't use your left foot at all. I can see you're struggling with that. Believe me, you'll get used to it, and you're doing great."

Ginny huffed out a breath. "I know. I know. It just seems like this car is so powerful. I'm not sure if I can drive something that seems so aggressive, Grunt. Of course, I've never driven, so I don't have anything to compare it to, but it just seems maybe he could've given me something a little more my style. Maybe something more like Moe's car."

Grunt glanced at her. He wanted to tell her she had a style all her own, and he couldn't think of any mold—or car, for that matter—that she would ever conform to. She looked so serious with her hands at the ten and two o'clock positions on the wheel.

"You need to relax," he said. "You look too stiff and uncomfortable. There's nobody around. Enjoy the ride."

She smiled at that and chanced a quick glance to her right.

"It'll be so nice being able to drive myself around, Grunt. I can't wait to pick up Sarah Jo and just head to the mall or the movies or the beach, or even the library. Well, not really the mall. You know how much I hate shopping, but it'll be fun to get out, you know?"

Grunt smiled back at her, but there was no sincerity behind it. He'd thought at first she would shun the over-the-top birthday present from Grizz. She wasn't the type to be impressed with fast and fancy cars, and Grunt had been right about that. But she didn't see the sparkling new Trans Am as a toy to be flaunted, to make herself feel good. She saw it as a means to return to some semblance of an average life. Having time with a girlfriend, doing what other girls her age were doing. And he didn't like that one bit.

They were quiet as ABBA serenaded them with "Dancing Queen." It was coming from a state-of-the-art stereo sound system that rivaled even his own.

"I hope you don't think I forgot about your birthday, Kit," he said after a few moments. "I ran out and got you something as soon as I realized that this," he motioned with his hand around the interior of the car, "was a birthday present. It took me a couple of weeks because I was having it personalized, but I brought it with me and thought I could give it to you over lunch."

He wasn't being absolutely truthful. Of course, he knew when her birthday was. He just couldn't let her or anybody else know, so he acted like he learned it for the first time when Grizz presented her with the car.

He reached down with his left hand and retrieved something from behind her seat. She peered over at the neatly wrapped package he held in his hand.

"You got me a birthday present?" She smiled as she moved her eyes back to the road and, without giving him time to answer, added, "I can't believe you bought me a present. Thank you."

"You don't even know what it is, and you're already thanking me?" His tone was light, teasing.

"It doesn't matter what it is. Just the fact you thought to get me something and wrapped it means so much." Then she added shyly, "I've never opened a present before."

He felt a stab of pain in his heart for her. He knew what that felt like. He'd never opened a present before, either. He quickly regained his composure.

"Get over to the right so we can get on 95. How about we head down to Miami for some real Cuban food? Does that sound good for lunch?"

She hesitated for a second, and he knew what she was thinking.

"Don't worry about Grizz, Kit. I told him I would spend the day giving you driving lessons. He knows I'm smart enough not to take you to familiar places. We're heading far enough south. It'll be fine."

She nodded and smiled as she gave the car a little more gas. He could sense she was feeling a little giddy. Was it the sense of freedom that came with driving her very own car, the T-tops off and the air blowing her ponytail around? Or was it the anticipation of opening a present? It didn't matter. He could tell it stemmed from a deep-rooted happiness or perhaps just a sense of belonging, and it warmed his heart to witness it.

Forty-five minutes later, they faced each other in the tiny booth at the little restaurant that offered the most authentic Cuban cuisine in all of South Florida. The tantalizing aromas teased their senses as the warm breeze caressed their faces through the open window. They could hear the drone of traffic through the window screen. They had just ordered their meals, and Grunt tried not to smile as Ginny practically bounced around in her seat. She was excited about his present, and it made his heart swell.

Kit, he corrected himself. He had to catch himself many times in the past several months when he'd started to call her Ginny and not Kit. He wasn't supposed to know her real name, and he hated the nickname Grizz gave her. She wasn't Kit. She was and always would be Ginny. He couldn't wait for the day when he could call her by that name to her face. A day when they would be free from what he considered a barbaric lifestyle.

He shook the thoughts aside and reached for the package next to him.

"I guess you're ready to open this." He grinned, handing the gift over.

She took it from him and held onto it, gazing at it with an expression he couldn't read.

"Happy birthday, Kit. I hope you like it."

She looked up at him, and he tried to decipher the expression on her face. She was turning red. Was she embarrassed?

"Open it!"

She didn't say anything, just looked at him then at the package and back at him again. She was hesitant, and he quickly realized why. She was savoring the moment. He let her. He didn't say anything for almost a full minute.

"It's okay to open it, Kit," he said finally. "I promise you, it won't be the last one you'll ever open." He smiled at her then, a sincere and genuine smile that came from the heart. He wanted to give this woman the world. And one day he would.

He watched as she carefully undid the tape on each end and then in the middle. She did her best not to rip the actual wrapping paper. After gently removing her present, she just stared at it, tears welling up in her eyes.

"You shouldn't have, Grunt, but I'm so glad you did." Her voice was a whisper. "It's beautiful, and I'll treasure it forever."

She lovingly stroked the dark leather cover. Clutching it tightly to her chest, she looked up at him with the most beautiful brown eyes he'd ever seen.

His breath caught in his throat as he imagined her looking at him that way for a different reason. Looking at him with eyes that cherished him as much as she cherished her gift. He cleared his throat and added in a voice gravelly with emotion.

"There's something else. If you look closely at the bottom right, I had your initials embossed. I had them made small enough so they wouldn't be noticeable unless you were looking for them."

He immediately saw the question in her eyes.

"It wasn't hard to figure out your real name, Kit. I'm not stupid, and Sarah Jo recognized you as the girl from her rival school that supposedly ran away. But," he quickly added, "they goofed at the printers."

She looked down at the Bible and squinted to see the letters.

"G.L.D," she said quietly.

"I can send it back and get you another one. I just didn't want to wait so long that you thought I forgot, so I chanced giving it to you now."

He reached across the table as if to take it from her, but she pulled it out of his reach and held it to her chest again.

"I want to keep this one," she told him.

He breathed a sigh of relief. Good. He wanted her to keep it. The printer hadn't made a mistake when embossing the Bible. It had been his intention all along for it to have the initials that would represent her future name. Guinevere Love Dillon. He even imagined them laughing about the happy coincidence after they'd been blissfully married for years. Relief washed over him.

"Besides," she added with a big grin. "It's not what's on the outside of this book that's important."

He looked at her with a raised eyebrow.

"It's about what's on the inside. Just like people. Don't you think? It's what's on the inside that really counts."

5

Carter, 1981, Fort Lauderdale

"Ann Marie! Ann Marie! Wait up!" Carter yelled as she ran toward her friend.

Ann Marie O'Connell continued to walk through the hallways of Cole University. She went out the door and headed to the parking lot, lost in thought about the class she'd just left. It was Introduction to Psychology. She found the class interesting, but if she was honest with herself, she didn't like it that much. She especially didn't like the part about labeling and assigning personality types to people. It made her squirm, and she didn't know why. If it weren't required, she would drop it in a heartbeat.

"Gosh, you must have earplugs in!" she heard from over her shoulder and realized her new friend, Carter, had come up behind her.

She smiled at Carter as she let her catch up and they walked toward their cars. Darn it—she still wasn't used to her alias, Ann Marie. Between Guinevere, Gwinny, Ginny, Kit, and now Ann Marie, she'd almost driven herself nuts with confusion. But maybe that's what Grizz's intentions were with the gang names. Confusion. She could understand it a little bit. But truth be told, she didn't really care that much anyway. She would even have gone back to being Priscilla Celery, the silly name from her first fake I.D. if it meant she could go to college. Thank goodness she didn't need to. She was now in her second semester at Cole and was thriving. She loved college.

"Do you have plans for the weekend?" Carter asked. Before she could answer, Carter added, "I thought you might like to come to my place and study. We have that big test coming up, and I could sure use the help. This isn't exactly my favorite subject. Interesting enough, but just not my thing."

Ginny—Ann Marie—stared hesitantly at Carter. This wasn't the first time she was invited to Carter's house, and she hated to refuse her again. She'd had a million excuses as to why she could never get together during the weekend or the evenings. She was always available to grab lunch after school or even meet at the library to study with Carter and their other friend, Casey, but she was careful to never socialize beyond school and most definitely never on a weekend. Studying at Carter's home seemed too intimate somehow. She was always concerned about letting down her guard and possibly slipping up about her past. She didn't want to draw unwanted attention to herself.

She looked at Carter's hopeful expression and had a change of heart. She decided that, yes, she would accept this invitation. She didn't think Grizz would care. She was certain after mentioning Carter and Casey a few times that Grizz probably had them investigated. She was positive that if he hadn't already done it, he would after hearing she had accepted this study invitation. It was a good thing, having a friend. She'd been lonely. Sarah Jo was still upstate attending school, and Ginny wanted this. Needed this.

Two nights later, Ginny found herself sitting in Carter's small apartment. Carter's little home resembled a tiny zoo. Three cats, two dogs, and assorted birds, gerbils, mice, and other small critters called this one-bedroom apartment home. Ginny had to compete with the sounds of the birds squawking from their cages.

"So, before we get started, tell me why that hot guy I've seen you with—what's his name again, Sam?—tell me why he calls you Kit," Carter said as she handed Ginny a glass of soda.

"Yes, his name is Sam." Ginny shifted uncomfortably in her chair. Maybe this wasn't such a good idea. She decided to change the subject.

"You go first, Carter. Tell me how you came to be here and about all of this." She motioned around the room. Just then, an orange cat jumped up on her lap and snuggled in. Ginny looked down and smiled, then up at her friend. "I've known you a couple of months, but I really don't know a lot about you. I mean, I know you go to school at Cole, and you work at the grocery store, but what else? Tell me something I don't know."

Carter giggled. "Sure, as long as you promise to introduce me to Sam. He is so damn good looking!"

Ginny sat back and listened—and learned there was more to her new friend than she could've ever imagined. Carter Coulter had been born with a silver spoon in her mouth. A child of wealth and privilege, she'd grown up in a real honest-to-goodness mansion on Cape Cod. She discovered when she was very young that she couldn't live up to what her wealthy parents expected of her, so while her sister and brother were being privately tutored in classical piano, foreign language, and sailing, Carter could be found in the kitchen with the servants or in the stables with the horses.

"I realized at a young age that I wanted nothing to do with that lifestyle." Carter shrugged and took a sip of her drink. "I can't explain it, Ann Marie. It's like I was born into the wrong family. Where my sister and brother thrived on the things that type of lifestyle afforded and expected, I shunned it at every opportunity. My mom was a socialite, and I was a chore for her. She wanted children she could parade before her snooty friends. It—it's like we were all in competition with each other, and the child with the most store-bought skills won. We were trophies. Ignored unless it was showtime. I barely knew my parents. Still don't know them and don't care to. I've been on my own since before I graduated from high school."

"You gave it up? Your family, love, security—all to do your own thing?" Ginny's mouth hung open as she glanced around the small but clean apartment.

Carter snorted. "Financial security, maybe. Love? There was no love. Like I said, I barely knew my parents. I was raised by nannies. And when my mother realized firing them because they couldn't control me didn't work—I was going to do what I wanted anyway—she just gave up. When I got kicked out of the umpteenth prestigious prep school for raising a family of rats in the kitchen..." Carter gave Ginny a wide smile. "Let's just say my mother developed a case of the overdramatic vapors and told my father to handle me. He only knew one way to 'discipline' me—" She used her hands to air quote, then continued, "By telling me that if I didn't graduate from Uppity Upperson's School for the Overprivileged and Short on Conscience

Academy for Snobs, he would cut me off. Which he did, and which is why I'm here. I took what little money I had of my own, got myself to Florida, got my GED, and enrolled at Cole. You already know I work full-time at the grocery store, and I go to school almost full-time, and every spare minute I get I use to come back here and take care of my animals. They're my family, and they're all I need." She paused before adding wistfully, "I do miss my horses, though."

"So you don't miss your family?" Ginny looked at her.

Carter smiled. "I was born into the wrong family. There was nothing to miss, Ann Marie."

Ginny sipped her soda and decided she had been right about Carter, right to come here. She had wanted so badly to trust this new friend, but had had a hard time letting Carter warm up to her. She was still so guarded about her own roots. To hear about someone who came from almost the exact same background, with the exception of all that money, gave her hope. She wasn't entirely alone. They'd both come from homes where they were not wanted, were used for ulterior motives, and were virtually ignored. Ginny had been used by Delia to keep her household running. Carter's parents had tried to use her by making her into a show ornament for their wealthy friends. It was different, but the same in a sense. She couldn't explain it, but suddenly she felt an almost kindred spirit with Carter.

"I've never met a girl named Carter." Ginny's brows knitted. "Actually, I've never met a guy named Carter, either."

Carter grimaced. "I have my parents to thank for that one. Does the name Carter ring any bells?"

Ginny looked thoughtful, shook her head, "No. I mean, that's our president's name, but other than—" Her eyes widened as Carter nodded at her.

"Let's just say my parents are very politically connected." Carter rolled her eyes. "They've been friends a long time. Who would've guessed one of my father's childhood friends would end up in the White House?"

"Wow," was all Ginny could think to say.

"So, your turn," Carter said, bringing Ginny out of her thoughts. "Start with Sam. Will you introduce me, and why does he call you Kit?"

Carter wiggled her eyebrows, and Ginny smiled. "I will absolutely introduce you to Sam. He is cute, isn't he?"

"No, he's not cute. He's adorable. Dimples and all. And quit avoiding the question. Why Kit?"

"Oh, that's just a nickname," she answered casually. "My husband calls me Kit. You know, it's short for Kitten." She blushed.

"I like it. You don't look like an Ann Marie." Carter leaned way back in her chair. "So when can I meet your husband? You don't strike me as the marrying type. I guess that tattoo on your finger, which I've never quite been able to read 'cause I haven't gotten close enough, is your wedding band. Am I right?"

Ginny subconsciously tucked her left hand beneath the cat on her lap.

"My husband isn't really the social type. He's a little older than me, and because of that, we find it hard to socialize. It's difficult to find friends or couples in our age group that like the same things as us. You know what I mean?"

Carter smiled kindly at her new friend. She could tell Ann Marie was struggling with something. Carter didn't mean to come off as nosy, but she was just so excited to have made another friend, one that she could sense was the real deal, she was a bit overzealous in her questioning. She wanted Ann Marie to trust her. And more important than that, she wanted it for the right reasons. She had grown up around so many phony people, and she wanted friends she could genuinely connect with. She would have to figure out a way to let Ann Marie know she was sincerely interested in her life, that there was no need to put on false pretenses. Carter could be trusted with whatever it was Ann Marie couldn't bring herself to share.

"So, Kit." Carter grinned and gave her a level gaze. "Has anybody told you that you are one lousy liar?"

6

Grizz, 1988, Prison, North Florida

After discreetly asking one of the guards on his payroll, Grizz discovered the young inmate, whose name was William Petty, had been given special privileges by another guard who had taken pity on him. The man allowed Petty a couple of nights a week to visit the library after hours. It was really the only time the young prisoner had to himself.

Less than a day later, a note was delivered to William. It read simply, "The library tonight. Midnight. Don't make me wait."

It was 11:30 p.m. when Grizz slipped into the library and realized William was already there. Just like the first night Grizz noticed him, William's face was illuminated by the computer screen. His eyes were wide with fear as he looked at whatever the screen held.

Unnoticed, Grizz made his way to the open doorway of the small library office. He casually leaned against it and just watched. When Petty sensed his presence, he stopped typing and slowly turned toward the large man looming behind him. He was visibly shaking.

Grizz looked past him and stared at the computer screen. To his surprise, it was Grizz's face staring back at him. Petty had been looking at his mug shot. He didn't say anything, just gazed at the young man, who was now very intently studying a spot on the wall.

Petty spoke first. "I know who you are. Every—everybody knows you."

"Then why were you looking me up on the computer?" Grizz asked in a low voice.

Still without making eye contact, the young man answered, "Just wanted to see how much was true." After a brief pause, he asked in a quivering voice that was laced with fear, "Wha...what...what do you want? What do you want with me?"

Grizz pulled his T-shirt up over his head and tossed it, his eyes never leaving William's face. The young man caught the shirt and, closing his eyes in recognition of what was to come, laid it on the desk. William heard the unmistakable sound of a zipper being lowered. T-shirt and jeans in prison. He knew this guy was important, and just the fact that he was in the library in the middle of the night wearing whatever he damn well wanted to told him he shouldn't try to fight what was coming. He'd read the guy's rap sheet. He knew he'd kidnapped a teenage girl, guessed he liked them young and pretty. Most of them do, he thought, as he quietly resigned himself to what was going to happen.

William opened his eyes and gasped when he saw the size of the man's cock. There was no way. Absolutely no way. This guy would tear him to shreds.

Grizz yanked him to his feet. William decided it was time to lose himself inside his own head. To block out what he knew was coming. To pray that there wouldn't be a mess left to clean up and if there was that he wouldn't be too incapacitated to do it.

He took a big breath and decided that maybe he was wrong to pray for those things. Maybe he would be better off if he prayed for a quick death.

7

Ginny, 2000, Fort Lauderdale (After Grizz's Execution)

I removed the diamond earrings from the little stuffed gorilla and carefully placed them in the pocket of my jeans. I would never wear them, but maybe I could give them to Mimi one day. It didn't require an immediate decision.

Thinking of Mimi brought to mind Perry, the therapist Tommy and I had been seeing. We knew we needed to tell Mimi that Tommy was not her biological father, not to mention figure out what to say in case she wanted to know who he was. Perry was walking us through that, and we were making some positive headway during our sessions. But while a part of me felt it was good to consult an expert, I still had reservations as to whether we needed someone to advise us.

It had only been a few weeks, but Tommy had been doing some bonding of his own with Mimi recently, which seemed to be helping. When she was younger, they used to go on daddy-daughter dates the second Tuesday of every month. Tommy would take Mimi out, just the two of them, and they would do whatever she wanted. I have to give him credit—he saw the inside of more skating rinks, movie theaters, and clothes stores for little girls than most fathers. And, of course, he always let her choose her favorite restaurant for dinner. I think Tommy ate enough fast food over the course of the years to last him a lifetime.

But a few years ago, she'd started making excuses not to go. We chalked it up to the dreaded teenage years; not sure if she suddenly found it embarrassing to be seen going out with her father or if it was the same withdrawal I'd experienced from her. But whatever the reason, it didn't matter now. Tommy was insistent that they spend time together, and we were relieved she'd been willing. Now, when I'd ask him how their recent "date" had gone, he would tell me they were getting to know each other again. He was trying to build trust for what we needed to tell her.

I could only pray this wouldn't be shattered when it was finally time to reveal the truth.

Shutting the door to the guesthouse, I marched down the steps and saw Carter on the side of the main house fiddling with the hose. She turned it off and approached me, her smile fading as she came closer and noticed a change in my posture. I approached her stiffly, the resolve in my eyes obvious.

I met her halfway and said evenly, "I'll call the paper to run an ad for the cars and bikes. I'll probably get some people who'll be interested. If I can't make it over to meet them, would you mind doing it?"

"Of course, I don't mind, Gin." She absently brushed her hair away from her face and peered at me. "I'm here most of the time."

I thrust my chin in the air. "Listen, I think it's time for you to start using the guesthouse again. I know you always have your activist friends coming and going, and sometimes you limit the invites because you can't accommodate them all. So, feel free to start using the garage and the guesthouse, okay?"

"Yeah, sure. That's great. Thanks for that." Her voice was quiet, and she hesitated. "Are you okay, Gin? I mean, the Bible, Delia's letter, knowing he's...I guess it's been one rough morning for you."

I didn't answer her as we both stared at each other. I looked down when I realized what I was holding, then roughly shoved the small cardboard box at her.

"And another thing—I need a favor. Can you make sure this goes out with tomorrow's garbage? There's nothing in there that I need or want. I'll get my Bible next time I see you."

Giving her no time to reply, I made a beeline for my car. I drove off without giving Carter or my old home a backward glance, all the while trying to convince myself that any feelings I may have still had for Grizz would be tossed in the garbage along with the box of mementos.

I GOT HOME EARLIER THAN EXPECTED AND DIDN'T KNOW WHAT TO DO WITH myself. For the first time in a very long time I felt listless, without purpose. Maybe it was because I'd put most of my activities on hold while we were getting our lives back in order after Grizz's execution. Hmph. Execution.

I could take a look over some of my new accounting clients' books. I was caught up, but I always found myself diving in to check and double-check myself. I loved working with the numbers. But not today. I wasn't in the mood.

I could work on my Sunday school lesson. Preparing the children's lessons always brought me calmness and peace, especially when I was upset about something. Not that I was upset. I was just so organized that I'd scheduled more time than needed to clean out the garage and guesthouse, and since that hadn't taken long at all, I had some free time on my hands. That was all.

I paced the house. I could call Sarah Jo to see if she was up for a quick lunch, but something held me back. Every time I'd tried to get with Sarah Jo in the past several weeks, she was tied up trying to arrange her move.

I changed the kitty litter, unloaded the dishwasher, wiped down the refrigerator, and swept the kitchen and back patio. I was putting the broom and dustpan away when I looked at the clock on the kitchen stove and realized it wasn't even lunchtime yet. I could surprise Tommy at the office and take him to lunch. Or, I could surprise him with something else. Something really special. Yes—that was it.

I headed upstairs to take a quick shower and change. I could only hope he didn't already have plans. Of course, I knew when he saw me, he'd know exactly what I had in mind and would immediately cancel any plans he may have had.

Less than an hour later, I walked through the doors of Dillon & Davis Architects. Eileen wasn't at her desk, so she must've already left for lunch. Good. That's what I'd hoped. I'd seen Tommy's car in the parking lot, but his office door was closed, so I knew he might be in there with clients. I was approaching his door to tap lightly and peek my head in when I heard a long, low whistle.

"Looks like my man Tom is going to get lucky this afternoon. What are you doing here, Gin? And isn't it a little warm for stockings and stilettos?"

I recognized the voice immediately and grinned as I turned to see Alec Davis, Tommy's partner. Before I could answer him, the phone on Eileen's desk rang, and Alec reached for it, mouthing, "Excuse me."

Alec was a nice guy. A good guy. We'd been friends with Alec and his wife, Paulina, for a couple of years. I'd never really warmed up to Paulina. There was something just a little off about her that I never could quite tap into. She was pleasant enough when we had a rare business dinner, but it seemed whenever we'd tried to socialize outside of work, she had some excuse. There were many instances when Alec would show up with his two little boys in tow for a barbecue or other activity that Paulina had begged out of at the last minute.

I'd wondered on more than one occasion if something was wrong. By all outward appearances, they seemed like the perfect couple. Alec was extremely handsome, successful, charismatic, and by all accounts a great husband and father. He had light brown eyes, dark brown hair that was long enough to cover the back of his shirt collar, and a prominent dimple in his left cheek. He was tall, about Tommy's height, and slender but not too thin. I knew he was a runner—not a jogger, like me, but a serious runner. He also must've spent some time with weights at the gym. It was obvious the first time I saw him at the beach. The tattoos running up and down both arms and covering his chest had surprised me. They did little to hide the fact that he had some amazing abs and heavily muscled biceps. I hadn't expected that beneath the formal work attire I'd always seen him wear. I hadn't drooled over someone as handsome as him since the first time I'd laid eyes on Anthony Bear all those years ago.

Paulina's coloring was in sharp contrast to Alec's. She had dark brown eyes and light hair. Her creamy skin only highlighted the deep chocolate of her eyes, and she kept her naturally curly hair short so that it framed her perfect oval face. She had a body that most women would envy, especially after having two children, and a beautiful and wide bright smile framed with naturally pouty lips. Sadly, her smile never seemed to reach her eyes.

I sat in the empty seat beside Eileen's desk and recalled a conversation from that first family beach trip. I'd been sitting in the beach chair by myself, watching as Tommy and Alec roughhoused in the water with my Jason and Alec's two boys. Mimi wasn't with us. Paulina had noticed a friend a few blankets down and had gone over to say hello. Alec had left Tommy in the water with the three kids and approached me with a smile.

"These kids are wearing me out. Don't know where your husband finds the energy." He reached for a towel and stood next to me, drying off. He squinted over at Paulina, and we both saw she and her girlfriend were taking a walk down the beach away from us.

Alec's swim trunks were heavy with the weight of the water, and they were slipping down below his waist. I'd started to look away when I noticed strange-looking scars on his right hip. He caught my glance and answered my unspoken question.

"Bullet wound," he said matter-of-factly.

He must have read the expression on my face because he quickly added, "Don't worry. I didn't rob a bank and get in the middle of a shootout or anything like that. Can't even claim to be a war hero and injured in the line of duty. Nope. My brother and I found my grandpa's shotgun in his barn when I was about ten years old. I'm lucky it didn't actually take my head off."

"I thought it looked serious." I sat up and took my sunglasses off to get a closer look. "Looks like a lot of little scars around it."

"Shrapnel from the blast." He towel-dried his hair. "Still bothers me sometimes. Even after all these years."

"I had a friend once who was shot. Grazed his rib cage and ended up in his side. I remember him occasionally mentioning that it bothered him."

I was referring to the time Grizz got shot. We'd been living at the motel then, and he'd come home with a bullet in his side. This was about six months before he got stitches in his head for smacking into one of the planters I'd hung outside our door. Yes, I was familiar with serious wounds and had seen Grizz stitched up on many occasions, though I didn't tell Alec any of this.

"Not unusual," Alec said casually as he bent over the cooler to get a drink. "I asked my doctor once if it was a phantom pain. He told me it was more likely the nerves that got damaged didn't heal correctly. The doctors did all they could do to repair them, but it's not a guarantee. Sometimes they kick in and do their own thing. It's not really painful anymore, more like I'm aware that I was hurt there. Is that how your friend described it?"

I didn't answer him, saved by the rest of the troop who had made their way out of the water and were asking for towels.

The sound of the phone being returned to its base brought me out of my daydream, and I stood up. Self-consciously, I tugged at my skirt, as if pulling on it could bring it closer to my knees. I hadn't given any thought to running into someone other than possibly Eileen at Tommy's office. I knew my response sounded lame, but I came up with the best excuse I could think of.

"I'm supposed to meet a new client later. Thought I'd stop in to see Tommy first...since my new client is near here and all."

I looked at the floor. I was the worst liar in the world, and I knew it, and obviously Alec did too. I could see in his eyes he knew exactly the reason I was there. I was certain I turned beet red.

He shook his head. "The lucky bastard is out with Eileen. She was having some car trouble, and he offered to ride along with her to some repair shop. That's why his car is still outside."

"Oh. I guess I'll just be heading out then. Can you tell him I came by? I wanted to take him to lunch before my meeting." I didn't mention that before taking my husband to lunch, I was going to lock his office door, pull the fancy blinds closed and give him the hottest sex he'd ever experienced.

My cheeks flushed, and I struggled to sound normal as I secretly prayed my carnal intentions weren't so obvious. I didn't know what was wrong with me. Just that I had a burning need to seduce Tommy, an insatiable need to feel him inside of me. For lack of a better or more eloquent description, I was there to bang his brains out and then take him to a restaurant, where I wanted to convince him over a quick lunch to check into a motel for another hour instead of going back to work. It could all be wrapped up in time for me to be home when Jason got off the school bus.

Alec stood there with his hands in his pockets and looked at me sideways with a grin.

"I'm no replacement," he held up his hands, "but I would be more than happy to take a pretty lady to lunch. That is, if she would do me the honor of her company."

I smiled and relaxed. This was Alec. Our friend. A happily married father of two.

"Of course. I'd love to have lunch with you. Thank you for asking me."

He held his arm out to me. "But if he shows up and sees your car, you won't be able to surprise him later."

I agreed to drive and steered him toward my parking spot.

At Alec's suggestion, we ended up at Bella Roma's, a small but excellent Italian restaurant on the ocean side of A1A just a little north of the office.

"We don't need to go someplace so fancy for lunch, Alec. Seriously. I'd be just as happy with Denny's."

"I invited you. And besides, we can't let you be all dressed up with nowhere to go."

I knew he was teasing about my overdressed state and laughed along with him. Lunch was pleasant and friendly until it turned serious.

Alec confided that Paulina had recently left him and the boys. She hadn't been happy for years and had been on a series of antidepressants.

"I guess she just couldn't find her happy place." His normally cheerful expression looked downright melancholy. "I think she was looking for it in all the wrong things. You know what I mean, Gin?"

"No." I frowned. "What do you mean 'the wrong things'—the medication?"

"She thought happiness could be bought. New car, bigger house. When that didn't make her happy, she thought children would be the answer. They only depressed her more and gave her a sense of responsibility she didn't want. You had to have sensed it, Ginny. I've seen you with your children. They're your life. Paulina considers our children the end of hers."

"Oh, Alec, I'm just so sorry. Tommy hadn't said anything to me. And I guess you probably know we were having some problems of our own."

I looked away uncomfortably, not knowing how much, if anything, Tommy had told Alec.

"Don't be sorry. I haven't told him a lot. I knew you two were dealing with some issues of your own, and I didn't want to burden him."

"So where is she? Does she come around to see the boys? Are you on friendly terms?"

I was curious about their situation but also trying to turn the conversation away from my and Tommy's recent problems, subconsciously kicking myself for mentioning it in the first place.

"She's out 'finding herself.'" His voice was casual, and he was momentarily distracted as he handed the waitress his credit card.

"So there's a chance she'll find herself or whatever it is she's looking for and come back to you, then. Right?" I had to be careful how I treaded here. It wasn't too long ago that I'd left Tommy to do some thinking of my own. I was reminded of a Bible verse: Judge not lest thou be judged.

He looked down. "I'd take her back, but she's never coming back." The waitress returned, and he signed the receipt.

Before I could decide whether or not it was polite to ask why, he answered my question for me. "She's out finding herself with her yoga instructor."

I was shocked—another man was involved. I had to admit I was surprised. I couldn't imagine Paulina finding a man who could come close to replacing Alec. In my opinion, he seemed to be the epitome of everything a woman could want. But I didn't live inside their marriage and had no right to speculate, I quickly reminded myself.

"Have you met him? Do you know his name or anything?"

"Yes, I have met him," Alec said drily. "He's a she, and her name is Sherry."

I didn't know what to say so I didn't say anything. I'm sure I just stared at Alec with my mouth open.

He smiled warmly at me then. "We need to get back to the office so you can see Tom and then meet your client."

I looked at my watch and realized we'd been eating lunch for over two hours. Where had the time gone?

"Oh, no! I won't have time to see him. I have to get going so I can be home when Jason gets off the school bus."

"I'm sorry, Ginny. I hadn't realized the time either. I hope this doesn't look bad for that client you were supposed to meet." He looked at me with a knowing expression, a playful smile on his lips.

I gave him a sideways smile. "You and I both know there's no client, so stop being a smart-aleck."

We both laughed at my pun. His eyes grew serious then.

"I hope Tom appreciates what he has. You are definitely a rare gem, Ginny."

There was something in his look and the way he said it that sent a small thrill through me, but I told myself it was nothing. What forty-something woman doesn't want to hear herself compared to jewels?

I brushed it off as lighthearted banter between two friends and let him walk me out to my car.

After hastily dropping Alec off in the parking lot at Dillon & Davis Architects, I sped home as fast as I could so I could change into clothes that wouldn't have my son questioning where I'd been.

I'd have to surprise Tommy another time.

8

Mimi, 1997, Fort Lauderdale

Mimi told herself if the safe didn't open on the third try, she'd just have to ask her parents for a copy of their marriage certificate. But she really didn't want to do that. Her heart was set on surprising them, and they would know something was up if she asked to see it. Not just see it—she'd have to borrow it to have the plaque made.

She sat cross-legged on the floor and breathed a sigh of relief when she heard the telltale click of the safe releasing. She turned the handle slightly and tugged. There was a suction that grabbed for a split second, but gave way when she applied more force.

After seeing its contents, she hesitated. She sat up straight and resolved to handle this as professionally and maturely as possible. After all, she was almost a teenager. If you want to be an investigator, Mimi, you're going to have to probably see things worse than this. She memorized how everything looked so she could be sure to put things back exactly as she found them.

Inside the safe were some dark tan envelopes stacked on top of each other. She was certain they contained what she was looking for. But it was what was on top of them that had her swallowing hard. Two handguns and several stacks of cash.

She tried not to think about why her father had guns and cash. It was probably something all fathers kept hidden away from their families. He was their protector, and he was responsible enough to keep the guns locked away where a child couldn't get to them. And the cash she was certain was for emergencies. There were also some small boxes, she realized. Probably some of Mom's more expensive jewelry.

With surprisingly steady hands, she removed the guns one by one and set them to the side. She did the same with the cash and small boxes. She reached in for the first envelope and smiled when she noticed her brother's name written on the front. Jason. The one below it had her name written on it. She set them both down.

The final envelope didn't have anything written on it. It was thicker than the other two. She turned it over in her hands and decided to undo the clasp. She opened it and pulled out the stack of papers. There was a large cluster held together with a big paperclip. It looked like the deed to the house. She fanned through the rest and saw what she thought were life insurance policies. There was a Last Will and Testament with both of her parents' names.

It has to be in here somewhere. She rifled through the papers, found her parents' birth certificates and laid them aside.

"Found you!" she exclaimed out loud as she saw the marriage certificate. She held it carefully and read slowly.

Her smile faded when she got to the date. According to this document, her parents' anniversary was off by almost two months. This can't be right. Unless...

No. Not her parents. Especially not her mother. There was no way her mother was pregnant with her before she married her father.

Mimi let out a sigh, her shoulders slumping. So her parents weren't perfect. That was okay. It might've even been a bit of a relief. They got married and stayed married, and that was more than she could say for a lot of her friends' parents. Unfortunately, she wouldn't be able to surprise them with a silver-plated marriage certificate without letting them know she knew their secret. She harrumphed out loud when she realized her surprise wouldn't have worked anyway. They would surely know where she'd found their marriage certificate —and they'd know what kind of snooping she'd have done to find it.

"Sometimes you don't think, Mimi," she said aloud.

Carefully, she put everything back in the envelope, closed the clasp, and laid it at the bottom of her father's safe. She reached for the envelope with her own name and started to put it away, but stopped herself. What kind of things were her parents keeping for her? She'd come this far. What was a little more investigating going to hurt?

She undid the envelope and pulled out the contents. The first item gave her pause. It was the deed to a house. It looked like the same type of paperwork she'd seen in her parents' envelope, except this deed was in her name. Miriam Ruth Dillon. And the address on the paperwork was in the Shady Ranches subdivision. She recognized the address immediately. Why was her name on the deed to Uncle Bill and Aunt Carter's house?

She shuffled through her immunization records and First Holy Communion and Confirmation certificates, then came to her own birth certificate. She smiled to herself as she held the document and realized she really didn't care if her parents weren't married when she was conceived. One thing she knew for certain—she was a baby made out of pure and sheer love. She sometimes watched how her parents looked at each other, and it was obvious even to a twelve-year-old how completely devoted they were. Their little secret was safe with her.

She picked the stack of papers up and shuffled them, banging them slightly against her knee to straighten them so she could fit them back into the envelope neatly, when a smaller white envelope fell out and landed on her lap. She picked it up and studied it. It was sealed and didn't have anything written on the outside. What could this be?

Carefully, she broke the seal. It was so old that it came loose easily. She took out the paper folded up inside and squinted as she tried to understand what she was seeing.

It was her birth certificate. Again. Wait, hadn't she already seen this? Why was there another copy folded away in an unmarked envelope? This was identical to the one she'd just read, so why...

Her eyes widened. Was she reading this right? There must be some mistake. This was her name—well, part of her name. They got her first and middle name right, but not her last name. Her birthday was correct. Her mother's name was clearly written. Guinevere L. Lemon Dillon.

But where her father's name should have been was a name she didn't recognize, and one she was certain she'd never heard before.

Who the heck was Jason William Talbot?

9

Grizz, 1988, Prison, North Florida

G rizz grabbed William "Pretty" Petty roughly by his arm and yanked him out of the small library office. He half dragged, half pushed the reluctant inmate around a large bookshelf and into a small alcove.

"Are we away from the camera?" Grizz asked quietly as he shoved Petty away from him.

"Yeah, we can't be seen," the young man mumbled. He looked at the ground and said in an even voice laced with resignation, "What are you going to do to me?"

The sound of Grizz's zipper caused him to look up.

"I'm not going to fuck you if that's what you're worried about," Grizz whispered.

"You—you're not?" Petty cocked his head. "So what is it that you want? Something else?"

"Yeah, I want something else." Grizz let the pause hang. "I want to talk."

Petty ran a hand through his hair. "I—I thought you were going to rape me. You looked um ... ready." His voice was shaky, the doubt still obvious.

Grizz rolled his eyes. "That boner wasn't for you. I never had to make myself think about my woman before while yanking on my dick in front of a guy. I did it to make it look a certain way in front of that camera in the office. After announcing to the entire prison in the chow hall that you were mine, I couldn't not do something about it in case they're watching us on the security camera, which I'm sure they are. They'll think I'm back here porking your brains out. I had to make it look real."

"Actually, no they won't." William rushed on. "They won't be watching. I've had that camera rigged on a timed loop for whenever I'm in here. I'm given special privileges by Officer Headly to have some time in here every week, but he thinks it's to read. He doesn't know I get on the computer, and I don't want anybody knowing it, so I hacked the camera and used a prerecorded feed from when I was in the library reading in that chair."

He pointed to a table with chairs visible through the big window in the small office, and just in line with the camera.

"If anybody thinks to look at the camera feed, they won't see me sitting at the computer, they'll see me reading over there at the table. It's not perfect, but they haven't noticed yet."

Grizz nodded. He'd stayed away from anything involving technology. Maybe he shouldn't have. After learning about *them* so many years ago, he knew technology would play an important role in how they accomplished a lot of what was in the foreseeable future. He preferred to stay away from it personally, but just because he didn't use it didn't mean he shouldn't have let himself be more aware.

"How did you pull up my mug shot? Is it on the library computer?" Grizz asked.

"No, not the library hard drive. I had to hack the prison's mainframe. Which I did easily." William looked at him. "You know, your mug shot, from when you were first arrested, doesn't look anything like what you look like now. You had long hair and no beard. Now you have no hair and a long beard. I almost didn't recognize you."

"Yeah, I did it on purpose. I want to look different. So let me ask you something."

"What?"

"Can you go into other agencies' computer systems and swap out my mug shot? Can you hack into the police department where I was arrested?"

"What do you mean? Do you have another mug shot?"

"No, but I can get one. I want my mug shot to resemble what I look like now. I want the longhaired, clean-shaven mug shot gone. For now. But one day, I'm going to want all of it to disappear. Can you do that?"

William nodded. "Yeah, if you can tell me the names of the agencies you think have them, I can access them individually. There isn't a way to do a general search—you know, with a search engine—but that's coming in the future. For now, I have to go to each one independently."

"So if somebody, maybe even the newspaper, has articles about me or pictures of me in their computer files, you can delete them or replace them?"

"Like I said, tell me the names of the places you think have you in their systems, and if they have a modem, a way to dial to the outside, then I can dial in. What I can't do is erase any evidence that might be on a microfiche machine or in hard files. You know—how libraries will take actual pictures of newspaper articles and store them on microfiche? One day physical copies of everything will be sent to the shredder, though we're not there yet," he shrugged. "But, yeah, if it has to do with computers, I can help you."

A slow smile spread on Grizz's face. This was good. This was very good. He wanted to start erasing any information that might be available about him and his past. He couldn't erase all of it, but he could certainly make a dent in it. When Grizz got out in a couple of years, he didn't want any chance, even remotely, that he might be recognized by someone. Besides, he never wanted his daughter, Mimi, to be able to run across anything from his past.

"You help me out, and I'll make sure nobody bothers you in here again," Grizz said. "We got a deal?"

William smiled broadly. "Oh, yeah. We got a deal."

Grizz turned very serious then. "You even think about betraying me, you will suffer and die. You understand that? I don't fuck around. With anybody."

"You keep Psycho and his crazy friend away from me and my rat, Buddy, and you'll have my loyalty and all the help you need."

Grizz nodded and motioned toward the small table and chairs.

"Now sit down and tell me about yourself."

William told him everything—how his parents had died when he was young, and he'd gone to live with his elderly grandfather. He had no siblings or aunts and uncles. It was just him and his grandpa. He was raised in Miami, and they lived in a small apartment over his grandfather's appliance repair shop. William could fix anything by the time he was ten. He didn't have many friends, but he didn't mind. His grandfather was his best friend. He told Grizz how his grandfather's favorite television show in the sixties had been Star Trek and how that show had influenced his interest in technology.

"My grandpa used to tell me that anything we see on TV, anything we think is pretend, will actually be a real thing in the future. If a man can dream it up, he'll eventually be able to do it. Anyway, even before computers started becoming popular, I was already learning about them."

"And that's what you do for a living? Did for a living, before you ended up here? Computer repair?"

"No. Computers are my hobby, not my job. And nobody knows about my hobby. I think it's in my best interest to keep what I do with computers to myself. Nobody needs to know what I can do. What they can do."

His last comment caught Grizz's attention. "They?"

"I didn't mean anything by it." William sighed. "You wouldn't believe me anyway." He looked at Grizz sideways, shook his head. "My grandpa was big into conspiracy theories and shit. Studied JFK's assassination and other crap like that. Forget I mentioned it. He was a crazy old man. He died believing that our first walk on the moon was shot in a movie studio. Lovable and kind, but a little nutty."

Grizz nodded in understanding. He would save the rest of this conversation for another time.

"You asked me what I did. I took over my grandpa's appliance repair business. If it was broken, I could fix it."

"So you were an appliance repairman who dabbled secretly with computers. How the hell did you end up in here? Hack a bank or something?"

"No, nothing like that. I was framed."

Grizz laughed. "Yeah, everybody in here was framed, myself included."

"No, I really was framed. And it had nothing to do with computers. I was in the back of a bar fixing the dishwasher when the place was robbed. They caught the guy, and I identified him." William's jaw tightened. "I later found out the robbery was a gang initiation, and I was warned not to get involved. Even the bartender said he couldn't remember what the guy looked like, but I was stupid. I honestly thought I was doing the right thing by helping to get the bad guys off the street. I was their sole witness, and the guy was convicted. Less than a month later, I got pulled over for a routine traffic stop. Cop said my taillight was out. Found drugs in my car. A lot of drugs. They weren't mine. Florida is tough on drug offenders, even non-violent ones. I have no prior arrests or convictions, not even a parking ticket, but I have to do ten years."

"Ten years." Grizz shook his head. "And you've only been in a short time, so you have a long way to go."

William looked away.

"What aren't you telling me?" Grizz cocked his head. "There's something else, isn't there?"

"Yeah. I have to do some time to not make it so obvious, but I won't be doing the full ten." He looked sheepishly at Grizz. "I fixed the records so I get out in a couple years. I can only hope nobody actually remembers what I'm in for and how much time I have left. If somebody digs into it, they could figure it out, but I'm counting on a nobody like me just slipping through the cracks."

Grizz broke into a grin. Fuck. He wished he could get away with something like that, but it would never work for him. He was too well-known. Jason "Grizz" Talbot getting released from prison wouldn't go unnoticed, especially with a death sentence hanging over his head. No, he'd have to play this out for the next couple of years. At least.

"Can you look something up for me?"

"Yeah, what do you need?" William's eyes brightened at the prospect of a new project.

"Can you hack into government agencies? See what's going on with the Florida Death Conviction Laws? I'm trying to find out where they are with passing the law on death by lethal injection instead of the electric chair."

"Yeah, sure, man. I can see what I can find. I'll work on that, and you let me know where you want me to search for data on you—you know, erasing or swapping out what you mentioned earlier."

Silence fell between them, and Grizz could hear the wall clock ticking. "So, the inmates refer to you as Pretty?"

William turned red, looked away. "Can't help how I look."

"I don't like it. What's your real name? Your whole name?"

"William Franklin Petty," the young man answered, looking Grizz in the eyes. "But I've always gone by Willie."

Grizz thought carefully for a minute. He didn't want Petty going by Willie. That name might be turned into something almost as degrading as Pretty.

"From now on, you're Bill. Anyone who calls you otherwise will answer to me."

Grizz rose from his chair then, retrieved his T-shirt from the office, and headed for the door.

"Same time next week, Bill," he called over his shoulder. And he was gone.

10

Ginny, 2000, Fort Lauderdale (After Grizz's Execution)

"Y ou did what?" Tommy asked me, as I lay wrapped in his arms that night. The look of disbelief on his face was almost comical.

"I showed up at your office all ready to seduce you and went to lunch with Alec instead. You were out with Eileen," I told him, laughing and trying not to blush at the entire situation again.

He pulled back to look at me, a knowing glint in his eyes. "You haven't done that since my birthday! What made today so special? And before you answer that, remind me to kick myself in the ass for taking Eileen to have her car fixed."

He got serious then as something dawned on him.

"Oh Gin, I didn't even ask you how today went. You were supposed to clean out Carter's garage. Did you do it? Are you all right?"

I sat up in our bed then and faced him. I crossed my legs in front of me, resting my elbows on my knees and told him everything. From the moment I arrived at Carter's until I got home from my lunch date with Alec. I told him about my childhood Bible and the letter and other paperwork it contained. I told him about the box I found in the guesthouse. About the earrings I'd put away for Mimi. I told him everything except for the fact that one of Grizz's bikes was missing. I had no intention of ever wearing that bandana so it made absolutely no sense to let Tommy worry or think about something that would never happen. No. Grizz was dead and gone as far as I was concerned, and I would not allow him to drive another wedge between my husband and me.

I suddenly felt lighter as the emotional baggage I'd carried all day evaporated. It felt good to get everything off my chest. At least until I looked at Tommy's creased brow. He looked worried.

"Are you okay, Ginny? I mean, the letter from Delia has to be messing with you. Especially after we've put so much behind us. To dig something like that up from the past. To know how your father died. Why Delia treated you the way she did. And the fact that you had a sister that died, too. It just seems like a lot to digest, honey. Do you want to talk more about it?"

The love in his eyes was so genuine, and I couldn't help but notice the little spark I saw when I told him I'd asked Carter to throw away the cardboard box of Grizz's keepsakes. I leaned over to kiss him.

"No, Tommy. I don't want to talk about it, and truthfully, I don't need to."

"You're okay, Ginny? You're really okay? You'd tell me, right?"

I gently kissed his neck as my hand made its way down his flat stomach in search of his manhood.

"Yes, I would tell you. I'm fine. I'm really fine," I whispered in his ear.

I could feel his body relax as he exhaled loudly, his growing erection evidence that he wanted me as much as I wanted him. He started to turn me on my back, but I stopped him.

"This is my night, and I'm in charge." Quickly, I straddled him. He smiled as I reminded him of Delia's note and the discovery of my real birth certificate. "So you see, you're actually married to an older woman."

Our lovemaking was hurried as I was again fueled by the burning need from earlier that day to have Tommy inside of me. My knuckles turned white as I gripped the headboard tightly while Tommy's fingers expertly matched the pace I'd been slowly building. My breaths came in short, quick intervals, my head was thrown back and my eyes were closed. I slowed my pace and opened my eyes. I saw the want, the desire, the absolute need in his eyes. And giving him a slow sensual smile, I went back to the rhythm I knew would signal his release.

After, I collapsed on top of him and laid there until our breathing returned to normal. I eventually scooted down by his side, and he pulled me close.

We started sharing more about our day, and he asked me if I wanted to do anything about my legal birth certificate. Did I want to change my name or go to some authority and have myself legally declared as Josephine Dunn?

I sat up and glared down at him. "Absolutely not! I am Guinevere Love Lemon Dillon, and I'm never changing it. I've had enough of the aliases and false identities, Tommy. Do you want to change your birth certificate to your real name, Thomas Talbot?"

We both knew his birth certificate had been falsified years earlier to make him think he was Blue's brother. Blue's real first name was Keith, but his surname, Dillon, was an alias. And Tommy's falsified birth certificate reflected that alias surname, Dillon.

We both looked at each other then, and I knew that we were thinking the same thing. Thomas Talbot still wouldn't be Tommy's real name. Grizz was raised by his stepfather and apparently had never even known his own father's real name. Trying to go back and figure out Grizz's true identity would be like dropping ourselves into a dark abyss, and both of us had worked too hard to make forward progress. Not go in the opposite direction.

No. We would remain Tommy and Ginny Dillon.

But maybe there was something we still could do.

"You know what I think we should do?"

He shook his head and his eyes widened as he waited for my reply.

"I think we should say to heck with the falsified birth certificates that we've used all these years. To heck with it all." I paused to see if he would reply, but he just stared at me. "I think we should do whatever we need to do to make our names—the names we're used to and have been using—made legal."

I raised my eyebrows, giving him a hopeful expression. He didn't say anything at first. Then he smiled, nodded in understanding.

"I think our attorney can discreetly file whatever paperwork is necessary to have our names legitimately and legally changed to Thomas Dillon and Guinevere Lemon," he said.

He yawned then and rolled over on his side. His eyes were getting heavy, but I saw him notice the wide grin I gave him, and he acknowledged it with another yawn followed by a small smile. I could tell he was relieved we were moving forward in a positive way. After all, we'd renewed our marriage vows with those names. That's who we were, and that's who we would always be.

"Another thing—the cars and bikes," I said. "Now that I've given it more thought, I really don't want to deal with selling them. Do you think it would be wrong for me to get in touch with Axel? I mean, he's legit now, and I know he'll take them and give us a fair price."

"I can call him for you," he answered in a sleepy voice.

"I've handled everything up until now, Tommy. I can handle one more phone call."

"That's good, Gin. I have a lot on my plate at work," he barely answered.

He was right. He'd missed a lot of work during our separation, and even though he didn't have to, I knew he wanted to make up for it. He was feeling somewhat guilty for putting the extra work on Alec when Alec had been going through personal problems of his own.

"I'm not tired. I think a hot bath will help," I said as I softly kissed his cheek. I wasn't sure if he heard me or not. I could hear his quiet snores as I got myself out of bed and headed for our bathroom.

I loved to take long hot soaks in my bathtub. I started the water and tossed some vanilla bean bath salts in. I lit some candles, dimmed the lights. No need to take my clothes off. I was already naked. I grabbed a hair band and put my long brown hair into a high ponytail.

I started to climb into the tub when my eyes rested on my blue jeans that, after I'd carefully removed and stowed the diamond earrings, I'd hastily discarded on the closet floor after returning from Carter's earlier that day. I glanced at the bathroom door and noticed I'd locked it behind me—a habit from years of being barged in on by the kids.

I walked to the closet and picked my jeans up. I started to toss them in the hamper but found myself reaching into the back pocket instead.

I pulled it out.

The blue bandana.

I don't know how long I stared at it. I don't remember walking to the tub or climbing in. I don't remember pulling my knees to my chest as I gently rested my face against them and quietly sobbed. The flood of water filling the huge tub drowned out any sounds I was making.

And for the first time, I understood why both Grizz and Tommy had lied to me for so many years about so many things. There were just some secrets we had to keep hidden in our hearts to shield those we loved. I didn't agree with everything they'd kept from me, but I could now relate. They'd justified it because they thought they were protecting me. Isn't that what I'd done just before making love to my husband?

I could never tell Tommy that Grizz was alive because it would destroy him.

I looked up from my bowed position and caught my reflection in the mirror on the back of the bathroom door. Silent tears streamed down my puffy red face.

I stared at the blue bandana that I'd hypnotically, unconsciously, wrapped around my ponytail. And I realized that a part of me still loved Grizz. Somewhere, buried deep within my heart, the memory of that love tried to claw its way to the surface.

But I knew to maintain my sanity, I would have to keep it locked away—or make a conscious effort to throw it away. For good.

With my arms still wrapped tightly around my legs, I laid my forehead back against my knees and whispered to myself, "Of course I need you, Grizz. I'll always need you. But I need Tommy too. And I'll never sacrifice his heart to get back a piece of my own."

11

Grizz, 1988, Prison, North Florida

I t had been more than a week since Grizz's last meeting with Bill in the library. The last time they'd met, Bill had informed him he'd been doing his best but couldn't tell where the State of Florida was going with the death penalty.

"It seems like it's been put before the State Legislature a few times already, and it keeps getting voted down. There are a lot of people who want to see lethal injection passed since it's a more humane death than the electric chair. It's fucking weird. A lot more people are for lethal injection than against it. Seems like it would be a no-brainer, but it keeps getting squashed. Somebody doesn't want it passed. Sorry, man. I can't tell you any more than that."

Bill looked at Grizz with concern. He almost felt sorry for him. This guy was facing the electric chair, and rightfully so. He deserved it. He'd read what Grizz had done. But Bill could also understand why Grizz didn't want to die that way. It was barbaric.

Grizz nodded his head in understanding and told him to keep an eye on it. He asked him then if the other inmates had left him alone. Bill told him yes. Psycho and his friend, Bender, had stayed far away from him.

That conversation had been more than a week ago. This was the third night Grizz had been in the library expecting to see him. What was going on?

Just then he heard the door open and saw Bill make his way quietly to the table where Grizz sat. His eyes were red. It was obvious he'd been crying.

"What's wrong?" Grizz stood.

Bill wouldn't make eye contact.

"Are they fucking with you again?"

Still no answer or eye contact.

"They know better than to touch you." Grizz clenched his fists.

"They haven't touched me," Bill said quietly.

"Then what the hell is wrong with you?"

Bill looked him in the eyes then. "They didn't defy your orders not to touch me. They haven't come near me, so you can't retaliate."

"What the fuck did they do? And don't tell me what I can and can't do. Now fucking spill it!"

Bill sighed. "They got ahold of Buddy."

Grizz knew about Bill's rat, Buddy. He sat down. It was an unusually large rodent and had been hand-fed and cared for by Bill since it was a baby. A rat wouldn't have been Grizz's first choice for a pet, but he'd always held a soft spot for any animal, especially since his baby sister, Ruthie, had cared for a family of mice in their old barn. It was why he'd been so reluctant all those years ago to follow his stepfather's orders to put out the poison—he hadn't had time to relocate Ruthie's pets to a safe place. It hadn't mattered anyway. He'd made good use of the poison.

"What did they do to Buddy?" But Grizz was certain he knew. They must've killed it. Stupid sons of bitches.

"They killed him and…and…" Bill's voice was laced with emotion.

"And what?" Grizz demanded.

"They must've paid somebody off in the kitchen or something," Bill said as he tried to stifle his sobs. "They told me he was in the hamburger I ate that day. It was set aside just for me, and when I went through the chow line, Joker made sure it was the one given to me." He balled up his hands, pressed them to his eyes. "I didn't know it. I ate it. I ate my pet."

The thought of what Bill was telling him made bile rise in Grizz's throat. The musty smell of the library mixed with the heavy aroma of disinfectants used by the cleaning crew caused his stomach to roil. He shifted in his chair, wondered how this news hadn't reached his ears already.

"Maybe it's not true," Grizz said. "Maybe they're just fucking with you. Maybe Buddy will show back up."

"Parts of him already did," Bill said. "I keep finding a different piece of him every day since then. Under my pillow. Floating in my toilet."

Grizz's fist came down so hard on the table it caused Bill to jump.

"Those motherfuckers should know better. They may not be touching you, but they are fucking with what they've been told is mine. And nobody fucks with what's mine!"

Bill gulped and gazed at him.

Grizz looked at Bill evenly then. "I'll find out tomorrow how much of what you told me is true, and I'll find out why I'm hearing it first from you—and not from my brothers."

This conversation was over, and Grizz was ready to move on. He'd been curious about something and had never gotten around to asking Bill.

"Tell me why that guard, Headly, lets you use the library. I never asked you."

"I helped him with his daughter's hospital bill."

"How?"

"I used to empty the wastebaskets in his office, and I heard him on the phone with his insurance company trying to get them to pay for a procedure. She's only twelve and pretty damn sick. I told him if I could use the library computer just the one time, I'd be glad to send my uncle, who just happens to work at that insurance company, an email and ask him if he could do anything to help."

Grizz's eyes blazed. "You told me it was just you and your grandfather."

"It was just my grandpa and me. I don't have an uncle. I made it up. I used the computer time to hack the insurance company and have the claim approved. Headly thought my imaginary uncle helped. It was the first time I had access to the library computer, and Headly made sure the camera was turned off so I couldn't be seen using it. Prisoners aren't allowed to use it. It's for the librarian only. But I wasn't just hacking the insurance company. I used the time to set up the camera feed so I could go back in later and use the computer unnoticed. When the claim was approved, he asked what he could do for me, and I told him I'd like some reading time by myself in the library after hours. He arranged it."

Bill swiped his arm across his face and sighed loudly. With slumped shoulders, he looked at Grizz. "Of course, you know I'm not in here reading."

Grizz nodded. He'd wondered how Bill had arranged this special privilege and was surprised they hadn't run into each other before that first night, but then he remembered he hadn't been visiting the library during his usual time.

Bill then filled him in on the progress he'd made hacking the different law enforcement agencies that might have had Grizz in their systems.

When they were done, Grizz stood to leave. He retrieved the book he'd selected to take with him.

"See you in here Thursday night," he told Bill.

The next day, Grizz sat with his men in the chow hall. He never held court in public, but this was something he wanted to get to the bottom of immediately, and he didn't have time to use their coded form of communicating. Not one of them had heard anything about the rat incident.

Grizz looked over at the chow line. "Which one is Joker?"

After they pointed Joker out, Grizz got up and headed toward the food line. As was the norm, the other inmates in line cleared a path for him. When he got to Joker, he whispered, "In the kitchen. Now."

In an attempt to impress Grizz and without missing a beat, the man behind the food line with Joker piped up, "Go ahead, man. I can handle this alone."

The guards turned the other way as Grizz followed a shaking Joker back to where the meals were prepared. As soon as the kitchen inmates realized who was following Joker, they looked away and went back to their work. It behooved them to not show any curiosity.

Joker stopped at the walk-in freezer and turned around to look up at Grizz. Before Grizz could ask or say anything, Joker spoke up, his voice low.

"I know why you're here, man, and I can explain."

"Talk," was all Grizz said.

"They came to me because I owed them a favor. I told them assholes not to do it. I know that just by messing with Pretty—uh, I mean, Bill—they were asking for trouble."

"Did you or did you not cook his rat and put it in his hamburger?" Grizz narrowed his eyes.

"They wanted me to, but I didn't. I knew better, and I can prove it."

Grizz raised an eyebrow at this.

Joker turned around and opened the big freezer door. Grizz watched as he walked to a shelf and retrieved a brown paper bag. When Joker came out of the freezer, he opened the bag and showed Grizz what was left of Buddy in an airtight freezer bag. No head. No limbs. Just a rat torso.

"This is what they brought me, man. I'm not stupid. I've been in here long enough to know you'd find out and come looking. This is the guy's pet. I never put it in his burger. Psycho and Bender don't know it; they think I did it, but I didn't."

Joker could still be lying. The prison was full of rodents, and the man could've gotten a hold of one just for this very purpose. Grizz would need proof. He told Joker to wait in the kitchen while he went out to ask Bill something.

Grizz returned minutes later. "If that torso doesn't have a missing patch of hair where the rat was burned on its left side, then I'll know you're lying."

With trembling hands, Joker turned over the clear plastic bag containing Buddy. Just where Bill had said, Buddy was missing some hair. Joker's sigh of relief was audible.

"Pack it back up," Grizz told him.

Joker put Buddy's remains back in the brown bag and handed it to Grizz.

Grizz nodded, and without saying anything else, left the kitchen.

LESS THAN A WEEK LATER, THE PRISON WARDEN SAT AT HIS DESK AND reviewed the prison coroner's report for the two inmates known as Psycho and Bender. He laid it on his desk and reached down and opened his lower left-hand desk drawer. Was it too early for a shot of whiskey?

After pouring himself a jigger, he leaned back in his chair and closed his eyes as the burning liquid made its way down his throat. It soothed his belly that was jutting out almost reaching the desk. Maybe one more.

After his second shot, he pondered these last two prison deaths. He shook his head as realization seeped in that he was no longer running this prison. He'd thought this might happen after Jason "Grizz" Talbot had received the death penalty and was sent here to sit on death row. In the almost two years Talbot had been at the prison, he'd managed to do something unheard of. There were several gangs in this prison, each one with their own boss. Talbot had not only wrested the prostitution and contraband business away from the inmates who'd been running them, but he'd managed to establish himself as the authority over all of them.

He was basically the bosses' boss.

The fact that Talbot had kidnapped a teenager and married her should've meant isolation and mistreatment from the other convicts. Instead, the man commanded with authority and demanded respect—and he got it. The warden shook his head.

And it was no mystery as to who was behind the canine and prisoner rehabilitation program. The warden was certain that Talbot was going to use the dogs to transport some of the smaller, but more potent drugs. He was a smart son-of-a-bitch. And to make matters worse, if the warden shut down the dog ministry, he'd look like the bad guy to all the human rights activists. They'd accuse him of depriving the inmates a chance for rehabilitation.

As far as the warden was concerned, nobody in this prison deserved a chance at rehabilitation. Damn, even more than half his guards were being bought on a daily basis.

Eighteen months until retirement, the warden told himself. Less than two years left in this dump, and I'll retire with a pension that will make me comfortable for the rest of my life. Hopefully, that bastard will hit the electric chair soon.

His thoughts were interrupted when Officer Headly entered the office without knocking.

"Have you signed off on the report, sir?" Headly asked the warden.

The warden reached for a different set of papers that had been sitting on the right side of his desk. He sighed as he handed them to Headly.

Without saying anything, Headly started to leave the office. He was almost out the door when he turned around to look at the warden.

"I'm sorry, sir, but I think you gave me the wrong report."

"No, I didn't, Headly. It's what you'll turn in."

"Sir, this says that it was a murder-suicide. That's not—"

"I know what the report says, Headly. I signed the damn thing, and it's what you'll put on file. Understand? Psycho got a hold of a shank and stabbed his boyfriend, Bender, in the shower. He then went back to his job in the laundry and hung himself with a sheet in the back room. A murder-suicide. Got it?"

"But, sir, the families will want to see, and have the right to review the medical examiner's report."

"And they will see one, Headly. They'll see the one you're holding. They just won't see this one," the warden replied as he picked up another set of papers from his desk and swung his chair around so his back was now facing Officer Headly. The high-pitched whine of a shredder resonated through the small office as the warden reflected on Talbot's brutality. He didn't know exactly what had happened, but this was extreme. If anybody in the prison had ever thought about crossing the death row inmate this would surely cause them to think twice.

Headly just shook his head as he took the falsified coroner's report and quietly left the warden's office.

Maybe it was better this way. After all, what next of kin wants to hear their loved one died from choking on pieces of a rat carcass?

12

Tommy, 1999, Fort Lauderdale

Tommy just stared at his daughter as she left the den. Then he looked at Ginny.

"She took that better than I thought she would, Gin," he said quietly. "I have to be honest, I wasn't sure I agreed with you that we should tell her about our early years with the gang. I think we could've kept it to ourselves until she was older. Maybe she never had to know about our past at all."

They had just returned from the police station, where they'd spent more time waiting to speak to the detective than they'd spent being interviewed. Moe's remains had been recently unearthed, and after positively identifying her through DNA testing, police had called in Ginny and Tommy for another discussion. It was uneventful and lasted less than an hour. They told the detective the same thing they'd told the authorities so many years ago when Grizz was arrested. Moe died from an overdose.

Tommy reluctantly agreed on the way home that maybe they should tell Mimi a little bit about their past. They didn't go into details about Ginny's abduction or her life with Grizz, just that they had been part of an unsavory crowd in their younger days. They wanted to prepare her in the unlikely event it was brought to the attention of the media. So far, nothing had surfaced, but Ginny felt it was time to start filling Mimi in on some of their history. But the teenager hadn't seemed fazed at all by what her parents told her.

After Mimi's nonchalant departure from the den, Ginny sat up straighter and faced Tommy.

"Just the fact that they found Moe's remains has made it obvious to me that we can't ignore our past." He started to say something, but she held her hand up to stop him. "Besides, if finding Moe doesn't bring the reporters out, Grizz's execution next year certainly will. And we need our children to be prepared. She now knows we were part of it. I'm a little surprised she doesn't seem to care, but she's a teenager and completely absorbed in her own life. She has finals next week. She has her piano recital coming up. She wants to learn how to drive, even though she's not even old enough to have a permit yet. I don't know, Tommy, you heard her. She thought what little we shared about our past was the coolest thing she'd ever heard. But that's today. Tomorrow, it'll be something else. Maybe we aren't as interesting as we thought we were. I mean, to her, we're boring old Mom and Dad."

Tommy sighed. "I guess you're right. Usually, I'm the one telling you you're reading too much into her behavior. Maybe we've both been wrong. Maybe we've built it up in our heads to be this monumental, horrible secret past, and yes, it is horrible, but it is our past. And it's so far removed from how we live our lives now that it's almost as if it never existed. And another thing—what about Jason? With Grizz's execution scheduled for next year, should we tell Jason anything? Do we need to prepare him?"

Ginny had to ponder this for a minute. She was certain the lack of interest Mimi displayed would be the total opposite of how her son, Jason, would react. He was nine years old and curious about everything. And heaven only knew how much he'd want to tell his friends.

"I think I'd like to take a chance on the press leaving this alone," she said finally. "Finding what was left of Moe hasn't seemed to have drawn a lot of attention. That gives us a year to decide if we need to tell Jason anything. And you're right. Grizz is scheduled for death next summer, but he's received so many stays, there's no telling how long before he's actually put to death. This could go on for years."

She shifted uncomfortably on the sofa and wouldn't meet Tommy's eyes. She didn't like this subject. Never had. Never would.

She stood. The conversation was over.

"I have to get started on my baking for the church cakewalk tomorrow night, and I told Carter I'd stop over later to help her exercise her horses. I was going to bring home takeout for dinner. Do you have a yearning for anything? Chinese? Mexican?"

Before Tommy could answer her, she quickly added, "Why don't you come with me? It's Denise's day to get Jason after school and take him to practice with Max, and she's taking him along to her mother's for dinner." Denise was the mother of Jason's best friend, Max. "Lindsay is supposed to come over and do homework with Mimi. Come to Carter's with me. Let's go now and I'll make the cakes after we come home later."

Tommy made a face.

"Oh, c'mon, Tommy. I know you don't have to go back to work for the rest of the day. Come with me. It'll be fun."

"It'll be fun for you, maybe," he said. "Last time I went, I got stuck shoveling the stalls."

"That's because you said you didn't want to ride last time."

"And I said I didn't want to ride because the time before that when I did help exercise the horses, I had to come home and put a bag of frozen peas on my balls."

"You're just not used to riding. You have to give it some time," she said with a smile.

"No thanks, Gin. I'll pass this time. I'm leaving tomorrow for Chicago, and I don't want to have sore balls. I need to pack, anyway."

"Chicago? I thought that was next week."

"No, it's been on the calendar. I leave tomorrow morning. I have an eleven o'clock flight."

"But the church dinner. You're going to miss the church dinner tomorrow night. It's our biggest night of the year. We're having the auction and mini-carnival. I invited Alec and Paulina and the kids. We're all going."

"Ginny, I can't help that my biggest client set this meeting up with me six months ago. This is a big deal, and you've known about it. It's been on the calendar forever. Don't act so surprised. And before I forget, I need to tell you it'll just be Alec and the boys. Paulina has some big yoga thing she's doing."

"Yoga thing? You know what, don't even tell me. She's even busier than me with all of her activities."

"Truthfully, I hadn't planned on telling you because I don't know anything other than it's a yoga thing."

Ginny stood over him and, bracing both hands on each of his

shoulders, she planted a kiss on the top of his head. He looked up at her, and she got very serious.

"I think I'll leave for Carter's now, Tommy. Instead of baking. I need to…to…you know."

She was trying to tell him she needed to escape their earlier conversation. She needed to be on the back of a horse, the wind in her hair, the sound and smell of horse and leather attacking her senses and obliterating her thoughts. She may have sounded brave and tough when she talked about not being able to bury their past, but her insides told a different story.

Sensing his wife's delayed reaction to the conversation about Grizz, Tommy stood up and hugged her.

"I'll come with you. I'm not getting on that beast Carter calls Comanche, but maybe I can play with the dogs or something."

She looked up at him with a grateful expression. "Thank you, Tommy. Thank you for coming with me."

LATER THAT NIGHT, AFTER WATCHING HIM FOR A FEW MINUTES, GINNY poked her head in Tommy's office. He was sitting at his desk and hadn't realized she was there.

"When are you coming to bed?" she asked, yawning. "It's after midnight."

He looked up. "Oh, hey, Gin. I just have a few more things, and then I still have to pack. Go to bed. I'll try not to be too loud when I come up."

"I know you're sitting here now because you came to Carter's with me. You didn't tell me you had to do some work for your trip."

"It's not your fault. The unexpected visit to the police this morning to talk about Moe threw me off schedule."

She leaned against the doorjamb and cocked her head. "But you'd be finished if you hadn't come to Carter's with me. Why didn't you just tell me you had more work?"

He stood up from his desk then and walked toward her, pulling her close and resting his chin on top of her head.

"Because I knew you were trying to be strong and that talking about what's supposed to happen next summer was weighing on you. I just wanted to be with you, Ginny. It's all I've ever wanted. No matter where you are or what you're doing. I love you, Gin."

"I love you too, Tommy."

She looked up at him then, and he kissed her gently on the mouth.

What started out as a small gesture of affection quickly turned into something more. It wasn't obvious which one of them deepened the kiss first, but before either one of them knew what was happening, they found themselves naked. Ginny was bent over the leather sofa as Tommy thrust himself inside of her from behind.

He reached around and found the spot that caused a loud moan to escape her lips. He brought her to a quick and powerful orgasm.

The moment he felt her softness clenching him in spasm, he found his own release.

"Oh fuck, Gin. I didn't expect you to come that quickly."

"You're not complaining, are you?" she asked him breathlessly as she started to put her nightshirt back on.

He watched as she retrieved her panties and started to slip into them. If he wasn't mistaken, she was avoiding eye contact.

"Ginny, look at me."

"What? What's wrong?"

He smiled at her. "Honey, I think you're blushing."

"I am not blushing, Tommy. For goodness' sake, we've done that a million times. Why would I be blushing?"

"I don't know, but your face is all red," he said grinning even more.

"Maybe all the blood went to it because of how I was hanging over the back of your couch with my butt up in the air."

He started laughing then and told her she'd just drained him of his last ounce of energy.

"I'm almost finished here. I'll be up soon, and I'll just pack in the morning."

"You don't have to get up early. I already packed for you. Goodnight, Tommy."

THE NEXT MORNING, HE WAS AWAKENED BY THE SOUND OF STOMPING IN the hallway. The bedroom door flung open, and Jason and Mimi stood there looking at him in bed.

"Mom told us to make sure you were awake before we left for the bus stop," Mimi told him from the doorway.

Jason had moved past his sister and ran to the edge of the bed where Tommy had started to sit up.

"Where's your mother?"

Jason wrapped his arms around his father. "Dexter had another seizure and Mrs. Winkle was too upset to drive him to the vet, so Mom drove them."

Dexter was their neighbor's dog. Mrs. Winkle was an elderly widow who lived across the street. She'd lost her husband in the Korean War and never had children or remarried. She was completely alone except for her dog, Dexter. This wasn't the first time Ginny had driven Mrs. Winkle and Dexter to the vet.

Tommy nodded in understanding.

"Have a nice trip, Dad," Jason said. "Will you be back in time for my game Sunday night?"

"Sorry, buddy, my flight doesn't get in until Monday afternoon, but you call me as soon as it's over. I'll want to know all about it."

He ruffled Jason's hair and looked up to say goodbye to Mimi, but she'd already left.

"Mom said to tell you the coffee is fresh, and there are some buns or something in the warming oven," Jason called over his shoulder as he chased his sister down the stairs.

Tommy looked at the clock on the nightstand and realized it was only 6:55 a.m. He had plenty of time before he had to leave for the airport.

Soon he found himself sitting at the kitchen table sipping on his coffee and reading the newspaper. There was nothing about Moe in the local paper. Good.

The recent unearthing of Moe's remains and the technology used to positively identify her had been on his mind. He thought about his past and what he'd found out after Grizz's trial—and all the research he'd done on the woman he suspected was his mother, Candy. Everything pointed to him being Grizz's son, but he'd never confirmed it with DNA testing.

He took a big sip of coffee and remembered how he'd tried a long time ago to see if he was related to Grizz. It was back when they all still lived at the motel, years before Grizz's arrest and trial. Long before Tommy had even heard the name Candy. At that time, Tommy had suspected Grizz was his older brother, not Blue. Grizz had come home with a gunshot wound, and Tommy used the opportunity to sneak a blood-soaked bandage to a friend at the school's science lab. The test confirmed he and Grizz shared a rare blood type.

It wasn't a DNA test, but it was the closest you could get back then. That had been in the late seventies when tests could only determine blood type since DNA profiling was still years away. He'd confirmed in his mind that Grizz was indeed his older brother, not Blue. But now, he wondered whether it was possible to get a DNA sample from Grizz to compare to his own. He supposed he could just visit Grizz in prison and ask him for one, but he wouldn't do that. As far as Grizz was concerned, Tommy was still living under the ruse that he was Blue's younger brother. Grizz had no way of knowing that Tommy suspected he was his father.

Then it occurred to him. If his suspicion since Grizz's trial so many years ago was true, Mimi was his half-sister. There was no doubt in Tommy's mind that Mimi was Grizz's biological daughter. If Tommy was Grizz's biological son, then he and Mimi would share similar DNA patterns.

He stared at the sticky bun that sat untouched on the plate in front of him. He downed the rest of his coffee in one healthy swig. He looked at the clock on the stove. He still had time before his flight.

Less than twenty minutes later, he stood in the bathroom that Jason and Mimi shared and stared at the countertop. A cup held a green toothbrush. That was most likely Jason's. Where was Mimi's? He quickly spotted it. A bright pink toothbrush off to the side, almost hidden completely by a carelessly tossed hand towel. He carefully placed it in the clear plastic bag and promptly headed downstairs and out to his car.

Less than thirty minutes later, he pulled into the parking lot of a grocery store. He spotted his friend, Dale, standing next to an SUV with a surfboard strapped to the roof.

"Hey, man, long time no see. How've you been, Tom?" Dale asked as Tommy got out of the car.

Tommy smiled at his old friend and gave him a quick man hug with the obligatory slap on the back.

"It's been too long, Dale. Things have been good. How 'bout you?"

Dale was the youngest son of one of Tommy's first clients when he'd started out at the Monaco, Lay & Associates architecture firm all those years ago. They were close in age and had hit it off immediately. They didn't really stay in touch, but Tommy knew Dale was someone who could be trusted. Not because he'd shared secrets with Dale. No,

Dale could be trusted because he basically didn't give a shit. Besides, he was too busy chasing waves and women to care about anybody else's business.

"I'm good. I'm busy," Dale answered with a sheepish grin. "Still a lab rat. Haven't felt the desire or inclination to move up the corporate ladder. Happy to do my nine-to-five in my sanitary cubicle and hit the waves on weekends."

"So not much has changed since you graduated college?" Tommy gave him a grin.

"Nope, and I don't want it to. I know you said you were in a hurry. You have the stuff?"

Tommy reached into his pocket and pulled out two plastic bags. One held a pink toothbrush. The other held a cotton swab, which he'd used to swipe the inside of his own cheek. He handed them to Dale.

"I just need a simple DNA test. I need to know if these two items contain DNA from biological relatives. That's all."

"Yeah, man, I get it." Dale held up the bag with the pink toothbrush. "You want to know if this is your love child. You're not the first guy to ask for this test, man."

"No," Tommy snapped. "Listen, I know for certain I'm not this child's biological father. I just want to know if we share the same father. It's that simple. Will you be able to tell me that?"

"Yeah, sure, that's easy enough. I'll call you."

"Don't call me, Dale. I'll call you. Is a week enough time?"

"Yeah, a week should be good, Tom."

"I really appreciate this, Dale." Tommy reached for his door handle. "I have to catch a plane. And thanks, man. I owe you."

Tommy watched as Dale climbed back into his car. He turned the key to start his, and headed for the airport.

Seven days later, Tommy sat in his office and dialed a number. Just when Dale picked up, Tommy saw his next client waltz into the office and approach Eileen's desk. *Damn, he's early.*

Dale has answered on the first ring.

"Hey, Dale, it's Tom. Wondering if you got those lab results?" he whispered.

"I did, my man, and I have your answer," Dale said.

"Well?"

"Yes. The two samples you gave me share the same DNA. You are most definitely related," Dale said. "And I think you should—"

"You're sure. No doubt?" Tommy asked, his voice low but urgent as his client, obviously ignoring Eileen who was following him, approached the office door.

"No doubt at all, man. As a matter of fact—"

Disappointment weighed heavily. Grizz was his father. Mimi was his half-sister. He didn't have time to dwell on it.

"I owe you, Dale. I'm sorry, man, gotta run. Thanks, though. Like I said, I owe you," Tommy replied, hanging up before Dale could comment.

On the other side of town, Dale sat in his cubicle and reviewed the test results for the second time. He'd wanted to double check because he distinctly remembered Tom telling him, "I know for certain I'm not this child's biological father."

"Well, my friend," Dale said to no one as he shook his head. "I know for certain that you are this child's biological father, but you probably already guessed that."

13

Leslie, 2000, Fort Lauderdale (Seven Months Before Grizz's Execution)

Leslie Cowan's head pounded as she squinted at the mailboxes in the rundown neighborhood. It was New Year's Day, and she had celebrated last night with a combination of too much cheap wine and watered down beer. Her stomach churned as the bright Florida sun burned a hole through her windshield and caused her head to ache even more. Not even her darkest sunglasses could ward off the brightness that served as a glaring reminder of last night's debauchery. She'd woken late this morning to find herself in an unknown bed with an unfamiliar and extremely heavy arm draped over her.

She shook her head as if to erase the disgust she felt with herself. What was his name? She couldn't remember and realized it didn't matter. She would never see him again.

The neighborhood she now drove through was old, and most of the homes had seen better days. She could see some residents still made an effort, but unfortunately, most of their attempts at a neat and tidy yard were thwarted by the person living next door. Overgrown lawns, junk filled porches, and cars on blocks must be sinking these home values. Why doesn't somebody call code enforcement?

Oh, well, not her problem. She thought back to last week, and how a friend had casually mentioned that her boyfriend's father knew some guy who used to belong to a motorcycle gang. Leslie had heard about a big magazine that would be dedicating an issue to celebrity bikers later this year. That rumor, combined with her friend's knowledge of someone who'd actually been in a biker gang, sparked an idea —what if she could impress the big magazine with an exposé on a real gang? Even if the special issue rumor wasn't true, she could certainly get some notice with a true-life biker gang article.

Her heart sank when she found the address she was looking for. It was one of the worst on the block.

She'd been surprised when William Jackson, the supposed ex-gang member, suggested she meet him on New Year's Day. Most people liked to reserve today for recovering from the previous night's festivities. She would've liked that, too, but she was never one to turn down an opportunity, regardless of how strange it was. If he was up for a conversation, then so was she, even if her head and stomach disagreed.

She pulled up to the curb and let out a big sigh. There was so much junk in the yard that she could barely see a pathway to the front door.

Reluctantly, she gathered her things and got out of the car, sure to lock it behind her. It wasn't the best or newest car, but it was all she had. Shouldering her purse and her bravado, she walked as confidently as she could to the porch and rang the bell. There was no sound. It must be broken. A dog barked in the distance. She knocked on the weathered front door and turned her back to it as she surveyed the obstacle course of trash she'd just made her way through. A beat-up old car was in the driveway. The rest of the yard was full of everything from an old kitchen sink to stacks of tires. Her eyes slowly scanned the yard, taking inventory of bicycle parts, an oven door, several toilet seat lids, and an orange beanbag chair. It reminded her of a sad and deflated pumpkin.

"You must be the reporter," she heard a male voice say from behind her. She swung around and was at a loss for words. This couldn't be William Jackson, the old gang member. She was staring at a very tall, very handsome young man with bright blue eyes, full lips, and shoulder length curly black hair. She couldn't gauge his age, either late teens or early twenties. He had the kind of classic good looks that belonged on the front of the magazine she was trying to impress. He was wearing jeans and a faded denim shirt with the sleeves rolled up to his elbows. The tops of his forearms and what she could see of his upper chest were heavily tattooed. He appeared slender but solidly built. He needed a shave and a haircut.

She liked what she saw.

"Mr. Jackson?" She was immediately aware of her disheveled appearance. After climbing out of John Doe's bed that morning, she'd only had a few minutes to clean herself up in his bathroom before coming straight to the interview.

"No. You want my uncle." He stepped aside and waved her inside the house, silently shutting the door behind her.

She was surprised the inside wasn't as horrible as the outside. It smelled like cigarettes and bacon, and even though it was filled with outdated and worn furnishings, it was tidy.

She immediately zeroed in on a man sitting on the couch. He was wearing sweatpants and a T-shirt that said, "drop dead." He had clear tubes draped over each ear, and they were obviously feeding him some much-needed oxygen. She started to walk toward him to extend her hand when she stopped. He was smoking a cigarette. That seemed awfully dangerous.

"This is Uncle Will. Don't let the oxygen tank and cigarettes scare you. If he hasn't blown us up by now, he probably won't."

Leslie gave Mr. Cute Nephew a half smile. He took this opportunity to extend his own hand.

"I'm Nick Rosman." He saw the question in Leslie's eyes as she extended her own hand. "Uncle Will isn't my real uncle. My mom used to date his younger brother. I grew up calling them both "uncle." Paul still lives here with him, but he's currently doing his third stint in rehab. Prescription drugs and alcohol. I'm just here to help out till he comes home."

As was his general practice, he'd decided it was best to tell her some things up front and avoid the chitchat and questions that would inevitably follow. He wasn't one to make small talk. He'd noticed the interest in her eyes at the front door and known immediately this was one piece of snatch he wouldn't be chasing. And if it was chasing him, it certainly wouldn't catch him. He could spot trash a mile away.

"So your mom dates Mr. Jackson's brother, Paul?"

"Dated," Nick emphasized as he waved her toward a chair. "They broke up years ago. But like I said, I grew up around them. I still do what I can to help."

After Leslie seated herself and pulled her notepad and pencil out of her bag, Nick offered her something to drink. She politely declined, and after introducing herself and quickly thanking William Jackson for agreeing to talk to her, the interview began. Nick parked himself on the arm of another chair and only half listened as his adopted uncle shared stories of his younger years in the motorcycle gang that had been headquartered in a rundown old motel off State Road 84.

Nick had been hearing these stories since he was a kid. Uncle Will considered this bygone era to be his glory days and would occasionally brag to the boy that he was the one whose testimony helped put Jason "Grizz" Talbot on Florida's Death Row. Nick had heard it all. Or at least thought he had. His ears perked up when he heard his uncle reply to the reporter's last comment.

"That name. Jason Talbot. That's kind of familiar." Leslie's brows drew together in concentration. "An excavating company found the remains of a woman last year who was linked to him or something. I can't exactly remember. It made its way around the reporters' gossip circuit, but it seemed nobody wanted to touch it. I don't know if they were afraid to or it just wasn't newsworthy. I can't even remember her name."

"That would've been Moe," Jackson said casually as he took a short drag on his cigarette.

"You knew the woman they found?" Leslie sat up straight.

"Knew her in the most intimate sense. If you know what I mean." William Jackson winked at her, a glint in his eyes.

Leslie leaned closer. Now this was getting interesting.

"This gang, this 'club' you're talking about. You're telling me it was run by a guy who's now on death row? Jason Talbot went to prison for having this motorcycle gang?"

"He went to prison for a lot of things." Jackson gave her a serious look. "He was the most evil son-of-a-bitch I've ever come across. I watched him snap a woman's neck like it was nothing and toss her in the swamp. It was my testimony on the stand that helped put him on death row. He's still there. Why don't you try and get an interview with him? You want a real biker story, that's who you wanna talk to. Or better yet, you should probably talk to his wife. You know, he kidnapped her when she was a teenager. Forced her to marry him. At least she used to be his wife. Ended up marrying one of the other gang members before Grizz was even sentenced. I think they still live right here in South Florida somewhere."

Leslie couldn't believe what she was hearing. She was chomping at the bit to get this interview over with so she could get home and fire up her computer to see what she could find on Jason Talbot. She didn't remember hearing anything about him being a biker when she heard about Moe's remains being found. Then again, she'd never asked or tried to dig deeper. This changed everything.

She ended the interview as quickly and politely as she could. She asked Mr. Jackson if she could come back if she needed to ask him some more questions. She was certain she wouldn't have to. She knew she'd be able to find everything she needed on the Internet.

———

LESS THAN A WEEK LATER, SHE FOUND HERSELF SITTING IN THE SAME CHAIR across from William Jackson as he sucked on a half-smoked cigarette. Nick was perched in the same spot as before. This time he was shirtless, but Leslie barely noticed. She was infuriated, disappointed, and maybe even a little desperate.

"Nothing." She scowled. "I can't find a damn thing on anybody or anything that had to do with this Jason Talbot. I've scoured the Internet for old news reports, and I can't find anything about a girl kidnapped in the seventies. Actually, that's not true," she admitted. "There were several missing girls, most thought to be runaways, but none I've been able to link to a biker gang kidnapping. I've typed the name 'Grizz' into every search engine there is, and all I get are pictures of grizzly bears and off-brand hunting supplies. I've typed in his real name and I get online phone books for every Jason Talbot in the country. Obviously, none of them are him. I've even tried the gang's name, and some scary-looking cult websites come up. I've tried the courts. No record of a trial. If it's there, it's been hidden or sealed. It's almost as if this man doesn't really exist."

She narrowed her eyes then and gave William Jackson a suspicious look, waiting for him to say something. When he didn't, she added, "I mean, he's obviously real. I found the prison where he's at, so I know a Jason Talbot is on death row. I was able to talk to someone there, but they told me he was sentenced to death because of a carjacking gone bad. Yes, he obviously murdered some guy whose car he stole, but the man I talked to at the prison also told me he had no biker gang affiliation they'd ever heard of." She crossed her arms. "So right now, I'm guessing you've had a lot of time to sit on your couch, and I'm thinking your need for oxygen has given you hallucinations, Mr. Jackson. You were never part of this big, bad motorcycle gang, were you? It's all in your head. Jason Talbot exists. But his gang never did."

Nick was surprised at the reporter's anger and accusations. She must have been living under a rock to never have heard of Jason "Grizz" Talbot. Nick knew he existed for sure because he knew Grizz's old gang was still out there. They no longer wore the jackets, and they didn't let themselves be known like they used to, but they were still underground and an extremely well organized group of criminals.

And if Nick had to guess right, Talbot was still calling the shots from prison. Come on—how simple would it be to have some nobody office-worker on the bottom of the prison hierarchy lie about his history? Too easy.

Nick knew that not only Grizz's gang but rival gangs existed because he'd been trying his damnedest to get in with them. There weren't many of them left, but they were out there. He wasn't surprised his uncle had bragged about helping to put Grizz in prison. A smart person would've been scared of Talbot's retaliation, but not Uncle Will. When Nick had asked him about it after Leslie's first visit, his uncle had told him, "He don't want vengeance on me. His attorney told me to tell the truth about him. He said Grizz wanted it that way. Whatever his reason was, he was looking to go to prison. I was just following an order by telling them what I saw that night."

Nick had hinted to his uncle about wanting to get in with the right people, but Will wouldn't have it. He knew Uncle Will probably only had to make some calls and Nick would be given a chance to prove himself through whatever initiation ritual they required. But his adopted uncle didn't want that for Nick. Nick was bright and could make a living the legal way.

Little did William Jackson know that Nick had no intention of earning his way as a respectable American citizen. He would prove himself. He didn't know how, but he would get someone to notice him.

Nick's thoughts were interrupted when his uncle started laughing. Uncle Will threw his head back, sat up to slap his knee.

"Couldn't find anything on Grizz, huh? Doesn't surprise me one damn bit. He was always a clever bastard, owned more than half this city. Prob'ly still does. You have any old newspaper or police contacts? You ask anybody about him?"

Leslie stiffened and raised her chin.

"Of course. I've asked a few people I know. They all say the same thing. The name sounds familiar but they don't remember why. It was a long time ago. What? Fifteen years at least?"

"And you believe them?" Uncle Will snorted. "Like I said, it don't surprise me one bit that you can't get anybody to talk. They're still afraid of him. Were you raised here, Miss Cowan? In South Florida?"

"No. I've been here two years. I was raised up north. Why?"

"Because you go up to any stranger on the street, ask them if they lived here in the seventies or eighties, and say the name 'Grizz.' They'll remember. They may not wanna talk about it, but they'll remember."

She rolled her eyes. "Is there anything else, Mr. Jackson? Anything else you can tell me before I decide whether or not it's worth my time to follow your idiotic suggestion that I interview strangers off the street?"

"Yeah, there's something else. Why don't you go talk to the woman he used to be married to? Oh, wait, that's right. You can't because you don't know her name. You're not even sure she exists."

Jackson sat up to reach for his cigarette, which was smoldering in an ashtray on the coffee table. Leslie stared at him without saying anything as he brought the cigarette to his lips and inhaled. He blew the smoke out slowly, then leaned back.

"The new husband used to be called Grunt. He worked at some fancy architectural firm but quit after the trial. The trial you can't seem to find. You must be one helluva reporter." He sneered. "I hear Grunt has his own company now. Dillon and Something, somewhere in Fort Lauderdale."

This caught Nick's attention. Dillon? He knew Keith "Blue" Dillon wasn't an architect. They must be related. Interesting.

Jackson watched as Leslie stiffened at the insult and wrote something in her notebook.

"And because I'm feeling mighty generous I'll even throw you a bone," he said. "Rumor had it that when Grizz's wife married Dillon, she was pregnant with Grizz's baby. Heard it was a girl. She'd be about what, fourteen or fifteen by now? If you can't find Dillon, maybe you'll find something through hospital records. Who knows."

Leslie stood to leave, but not before she asked one more question.

"Why, Mr. Jackson? Why did you say you'd talk to me? Why are you sharing all this? If this guy really is as evil as you say he is, why risk telling me if there's a chance he'll send somebody after you?"

He looked at her seriously. "I've got nothing better to do. And besides, I know you're too smart to let anybody know you actually talked to me. Aren't you, Miss Cowan?"

The way he said the last sentence sent a chill up Leslie's spine. Had she been too casual with this man? She'd interviewed worse criminals than him. How dangerous could a shriveled-up old man attached to an oxygen tank be?

But what if it was true and he had belonged to a biker gang? Just because she couldn't find anything didn't mean they didn't exist, and if she was going to be honest with herself, she was even more intrigued now that she'd found out all of this could really be true and someone had gone to extreme measures to make sure it was erased. This could be one heck of a story if she could just get some facts to substantiate even a few of the tales William Jackson had told her the last time she was here.

The one thing she hadn't told Jackson was that she wasn't being exactly truthful about talking to newspaper or police contacts. She didn't really have any. Leslie had pissed off all the wrong people when she'd first started out in Fort Lauderdale. She'd always been the type to not care. As far as she was concerned, even bad publicity was some publicity. Yes, she was making a name for herself, but not in a good way.

She'd find out more about this Grizz person and she would write her article, have it published. And they could all kiss her ass.

She nodded at the man and headed for the front door. She was closing the door behind her when she heard William Jackson's voice call out:

"Don't let the oxygen tank fool you, Miss Cowan. Call me idiotic again, and I'll strangle the life out of that pretty neck of yours. After all, I've got nothing better to do."

14

Mimi, 2000, Fort Lauderdale (Five Months Before Grizz's Execution)

"Yes, sir, that's a dozen white roses, and yes, I can guarantee they'll be delivered on Friday afternoon to your wife's work."

Mimi was typing the man's information into the computer and balancing the telephone tightly between her cheek and shoulder. She paused as the man said something else. She repeated the delivery address and message that was to be written on the card, took his credit card information, and patiently explained for a second time that the delivery was guaranteed for the date and time he requested. She ignored his comment that the price for the roses was ridiculous considering they would be dead and in the garbage in a week. Then they hung up.

"If you're worried about them dying, buy her something that won't die," she grumbled to herself.

"Somebody giving you a hard time?" a male voice asked.

Mimi whipped around and came face-to-chest with a customer who'd slipped into the flower shop unnoticed. She quickly looked away, embarrassed she'd been heard. Without looking up, she said to the counter, "I think some people aren't happy unless they're complaining."

"I hope he wasn't too nasty. If he was, you'll have to ask your boyfriend to beat him up or something."

She raised her eyes at the comment and found herself looking into the face of the cutest guy who'd ever walked through the doors of the flower shop. She'd been working there since right before Valentine's Day, and she'd never waited on somebody this young or this handsome.

His good looks and wide, bright smile caught her off-guard, and she didn't know what to say. He must've realized he made her uncomfortable, because he quickly added, "I'm sorry. Didn't mean anything by it. I mean, I'm sure you have a boyfriend, and what he does or doesn't do isn't any of my business. I'm just saying I wouldn't let anybody talk to my girlfriend like that. Not that you're my girlfriend! I mean, of course you're not my girlfriend. I don't even know your name. Not that knowing your name would mean you're my girlfriend. I don't know what I'm even saying. I'm shutting up now."

Mimi just smiled at him. She realized he was even more nervous than she was. She couldn't take her eyes off the deep dimple in his left cheek. The cheek that was turning bright red along with the rest of his face.

She extended her hand over the counter.

"I'm Mimi."

He breathed a visible sigh of relief and accepted her outreached hand.

"Elliott. I'm Elliott. It's nice to meet you, Mimi."

After a brief and uncomfortable pause, Mimi asked, "What can I help you with?"

"Oh, yeah, flowers. I need some flowers for my grandmother's eightieth birthday. I want something special, but not too much money."

He looked away, embarrassed.

Mimi almost sighed out loud. Oh, my gosh. How cute was this guy, and he's buying flowers for his grandmother? She had to stifle a nervous giggle.

To prevent herself from turning into a full-fledged idiot, she kicked into professional mode. It took about thirty minutes for him to finally decide on a spring arrangement in his price range. Mimi was grateful nobody had come into the shop. She couldn't be certain, but she was pretty sure he'd been flirting with her and actually dragging out the time it had taken to select such a simple arrangement. Her employer, Maggie, was out making deliveries, and Mimi was in the shop by herself. She was only fifteen, but she'd proven herself to be a trustworthy and competent employee. Maggie was relieved and grateful Mimi could manage the shop alone when Maggie had to make deliveries. They'd recently lost two full-time employees.

Elliott almost seemed reluctant to leave after paying for his flowers and watching Mimi carefully wrap them.

"It was nice meeting you," he said as she handed him his bouquet. He walked slowly to the door.

"Nice meeting you, too," Mimi called out after him, an annoyed look on her face as the telephone interrupted their goodbye. She wondered if she would ever see him again.

It's just as well. She stifled a remorseful sigh. This was probably the first and last time she'd ever lay eyes on Elliott.

"Maggie's Floral Designs, this is Mimi, how can I help you?"

Listening to the caller, her demeanor immediately changed. Gone was the girl who was still a little high from flirting with a cute boy. She stood up straight, and in her best business voice replied to the woman on the other end of the phone.

"I got your message, Leslie. I'll be there."

She hung up unceremoniously and walked to the window to see if she could catch a glimpse of Elliott driving or walking away. She was too late. He was already gone.

Mimi spent the rest of the afternoon keeping busy and reflecting on the first time she'd met Leslie. It was right after New Year's. Mimi had been walking around the mall asking some of the smaller shops for job applications. She'd taken a break to sit down on a bench and sort through the paperwork she'd collected when Leslie sat down beside her and struck up a casual conversation. Mimi hadn't wanted to appear rude by completely ignoring the woman, so she only half-engaged in the conversation. Her friend Lindsay would be meeting up with her in less than twenty minutes to give her a ride home. Lindsay had no interest in working, so she used the afternoon to shop while Mimi gathered applications.

"You don't even have to work," Lindsay had said when they'd first arrived at the mall. "Why do you need to get a job? Your parents are making you, aren't they?"

"Yes and no. I don't have to work, but my parents think it's a good idea, and I do, too."

Lindsay stopped in her tracks and stared at Mimi, mouth agape. "You want to? Are you serious, Mimi?"

Mimi kept on walking. "You act like work is a death sentence."

"It is a death sentence. You are nuts!" Lindsay quickened her pace to catch back up to Mimi. "I'm going to marry the richest guy that comes along. He doesn't even need to be good looking. I don't care. I'll have a cute boyfriend on the side if I need to, but I am not working. Besides, I can't think of anything I want to do that could earn the kind of money needed to keep me in designer shoes and purses. Nope, I'm not going to even try to get those things by earning them." She paused as something occurred to her. "On second thought, I'll earn them all right, but not with a regular job." She laughed at her own innuendo.

Mimi shook her head and smiled. She knew Lindsay wasn't teasing. And she was certain her friend would have no trouble at all finding a man willing to take care of her and finance her expensive tastes.

Lindsay was runway model beautiful. Tall and slender, with caramel colored skin and exotic almond shaped eyes, she was a natural beauty. But while she was a sweet girl, she had no ambition—or at least not the same kind of ambition as Mimi's. Mimi was going to be a journalist, and even though her parents thought it was their prompting that had motivated her to look for a job, she was more than happy to do it. She wanted to put herself out there, get some interaction with people outside of her comfort zones, which were school and church. Retail would be the perfect opportunity. She'd be exposed to all different kinds of characters, and she actually looked forward to it. She'd already applied for a work permit since she wouldn't be sixteen until next year, and had submitted applications to a local ice cream shop and florist, but she hadn't heard anything. Yet. When Lindsay had suggested a trip to the mall, Mimi decided to shop for a job instead.

Now on the bench with the random woman who wouldn't stop chitchatting, Mimi stifled a yawn.

"So, looks like you're applying for jobs. Is that what you're interested in? Retail?" the woman, Leslie, asked.

"Nope." Mimi scanned the shops, not looking at the woman. "Just looking to get some real-world experience. I'm going to be a journalist."

This was too good to be true, Leslie thought to herself.

"Why don't you try to get a job at a newspaper or something? That's what I did when I was starting out."

Mimi looked over then. "You're a journalist?"

"Yep. I work for a little magazine called Loving Lauderdale, and I freelance for other, bigger publications." Leslie nonchalantly mentioned the name of a huge magazine, before asking, "You've heard of them, right?"

"Uh, yeah, I've heard of them. Everybody's heard of them. You write for them?" Mimi's eyes widened with admiration.

"Working on a story for them right now. It's a rough story, though." Leslie shook her head. "I had to take a break from writing and just do something different. That's why I'm here. Taking a break to do some people-watching. It helps me relax. So why aren't you trying to get a job with a newspaper or something?"

"I tried. They flat-out told me they weren't hiring, and if they were, it would be college-age applicants with a little more experience than me," Mimi said, the disappointment in her tone unmistakable.

"What? You're not in college? I took you for someone much older," Leslie lied. She knew Mimi's age.

"No," Mimi smiled. "I'm still in high school. I thought a job in retail would at least give me some experience dealing with the public."

"Oh, so you're smart and ambitious. You'll be a great journalist." Leslie looked at her watch, feigning mild disinterest and trying to provide a subtle hint that this conversation would soon be over. It didn't go unnoticed. She had the girl's attention.

"So what's the rough story you're working on?" Mimi asked. "What's so awful that you needed to take a break from writing?"

"Oh, I'm not sure I can tell you. It's pretty serious, and I'd have to be able to trust you, and I don't even know you. I mean, we just met."

Mimi sat up straight and looked at Leslie with wide eyes. "You can trust me. I won't tell a soul. Nobody. Not my friends. Not my parents. Especially not my parents."

"You don't like your parents?"

"I like my parents. I love my parents. I'm just not sure about them. I'm not sure I really know them. I don't feel like they've been truthful with me about some things."

Leslie wasn't sure what she was dealing with here. Mimi didn't seem like a rebellious teen, but from her body language and the comment about her parents, who Leslie had already learned were Tommy and Ginny Dillon, she seemed to have some kind of trust issue. This could help Leslie or hurt her. Tread lightly.

"I don't know anything about your parents, but with most parents I know who aren't truthful, it's usually because they're trying to protect their children. Trying to prevent them from being hurt by something."

"Yeah, maybe you're right. Either way, I'm not going to tell them or anybody what your story is about. I'll probably never even see you again after today. Please tell me."

"Okay," Leslie said finally. "You want to be a journalist, so you'll understand the need for secrecy. I don't want anyone scooping my story." She gave Mimi a conspiratorial wink. She leaned in and whispered, "I'm investigating biker gangs. Apparently, there was a real bad one back in the sixties and seventies from right around this area. The publication I write for is dedicating an issue to celebrity bikers and asked me to write a story about real bikers." Leslie glanced around like she was making sure she wasn't overheard. "There's a biker guy sitting on death row right now who's supposed to be executed this summer. I've been told he's a pretty bad guy. I'm trying to get an interview with him before he dies."

Leslie smiled inwardly. She'd laid the foundation, and now all she had to do was suggest that Mimi might like to cut her journalistic teeth helping with research. She didn't think the fifteen-year-old could offer any real help, but Leslie would use the time with her to learn everything she could about the Dillons. Of course, she'd tell Mimi they'd have to work together in secret.

But before Leslie could say a word, she saw Mimi's body language change, watched the girl transform before her eyes. Gone was the admiring and naïve interest. Leslie's heart skipped a beat and her confidence started to wane as she tried to figure out what had caused the sudden change in Mimi.

Mimi stood up and glared down at Leslie. "You are some journalist. Wow. Almost had me, too. You never told me your name."

Leslie stood, too, and pretended ignorance. She quickly reminded herself that she'd stared down hardened criminals. She could certainly handle a teenage girl with an attitude. Her confidence restored, she extended her hand. "I don't know what you mean. I'm Leslie Cowan."

Mimi ignored the outstretched hand. "I'm Mimi Dillon, but I suspect you already know that. And if you wanted me to help you get an interview with my biological father, who I refer to as the evil sperm donor, you could've just asked me."

15

Ginny, 2000, Fort Lauderdale (After Grizz's Execution)

I don't remember how long I sat in the tub that night, crying my eyes out. I wavered between anger, self-pity, and copious amounts of guilt. I let the tears flow along with the water that filled the tub until my eyes ran dry.

I do remember opening the tub plug to let some of the cold water drain away, along with the false bravado I'd shown Carter and myself that morning and whatever love I may have had left for Grizz. I added hot water until the tub reached a comfortable temperature, and began to think about the man who slept just outside the bathroom door.

My tears for Grizz felt like I was betraying Tommy. Guilt seeped in like an unwanted breath of roadkill. But then I had to remind myself I had done nothing wrong. I had fallen in love with two men who'd been engaged in their own secret battle for my heart—never once considering what they were doing to mine.

I instantly thought of the few unmarried friends I had, and how they were always lamenting their unhappy lives as single women. I recalled how many times I'd comforted them with encouraging words like, "You just haven't found the right one," and, "He's right around the corner and he'll be worth the wait." I meant those words when I said them, but I had to wonder now—what was worse? Being alone or having your heart truly ripped in half by two real loves? Why couldn't he really be dead? Then I immediately felt bad for the thought.

I didn't want Grizz dead. What I wanted was my heart to be dead to him.

"How many times will I have to mourn you?" I whispered.

By the time I finally climbed out of the tub that night, my skin might have been shriveled, but my determination to move past all the lies and deceit and live my life for me was stronger than ever. I was feeling strong as I ripped the bandana from my hair and threw it in the bathroom wastebasket. After getting dressed, I carried the small garbage can to the kitchen and emptied it into the trash compactor.

I was finished.

I woke the next morning to sun streaming through the bedroom windows and the enticing scent of coffee. It floated up the stairs, and the assault on my nostrils gave me an instant onslaught of energy as well as the confidence to confront something that I'd been putting off. I threw off the covers and bounded down the stairs noticing that both kids' bedroom doors were still closed. They'd both gotten home late after spending the evening with friends and would no doubt be sleeping in.

Tommy was sitting at the kitchen table reading the Saturday newspaper. He smiled at me, the memory of last night's lovemaking still lingering in his eyes. His smile started to fade, and he peered at me over the top of the paper.

"What is it, Gin? What's wrong?"

I strode to the coffee pot and grabbed the mug he'd laid out for me. "Absolutely nothing is wrong, Tommy. Nothing at all. Do you want a refill?" I made my way toward him, pot in hand.

"No, I'm good. You look different. What's up?" he asked me, newspaper forgotten.

"How do you mean? What looks different?" I took the seat beside him.

"I don't know. You look like you want to jump into a boxing ring with somebody. What's going on?"

I smiled at him. He knew me so well.

"You're right. I'm feeling determined. But I'm not looking for a fight. What I am is ready to handle something I've been putting off." I gave him a look that dared him to challenge me. But he didn't.

He sat up straighter in the hard kitchen chair. Why were kitchen chairs always hard and uninviting? I always thought of the kitchen as the heart of the family. We rarely ate in the formal dining room. The chairs surrounding that table were plush and comfortable, yet we hadn't used them since we'd returned home from our belated honeymoon several weeks ago. I'll swap out these ridiculously hard chairs for the comfortable ones in the dining room—formality be darned.

"I thought cleaning out Carter's garage was something big you wanted to tackle. You just handled that yesterday. What is it you think you need to do now?"

I took a sip of my coffee and leaned toward him, giving him a serious look.

"I've respected your time with Mimi. I've been waiting for you to tell me something - anything about your time together. You haven't told me a thing, and obviously, she hasn't either. I've been biting my tongue and trying to give you the time I think you two need. I mean, we are going to drop a bomb on her about you not being her biological father. And I think we both know she'll want to know who he is. So I want you to tell me what you've talked about with her."

"Do we need to talk about this now?" Tommy whispered. "The kids are upstairs."

"They were both up late, and they sleep like the dead." I folded my arms. I wanted to hash this out. It had gone unresolved long enough.

Tommy shifted uncomfortably in the already uncomfortable chair. I knew I'd struck a nerve, but I was ready to have this conversation. Ready to discuss Grizz with Mimi. Finding out he was alive only made my resolve to put this behind me stronger. The sooner we came clean with Mimi, the quicker we would eventually get to the point of healing and completeness.

"Tell me, Tommy. If you don't, I'll just ask her."

I leaned back in my chair and cradled my mug with both hands. I took another sip, inhaling the fragrant steam, and stared at him over the rim. The hot mist spiraled upward and gave me an almost hazy view of his face as I stared through it. I calmly waited for him to say something.

He sighed heavily and looked away. Folding up the newspaper, he slapped it hard on the table and looked back at me. His face was drawn with a look that could only be described as masked anger.

"She knows, Gin. She already knows I'm not her biological father. She knows Grizz is her father."

"What?" I struggled to keep my voice low as I sat straight up and set my mug on the table with a loud thud, not caring that the coffee spilled over the sides. "We were going to tell her together! That's what Perry told us. And even though I haven't agreed with everything he's suggested, I do agree with that. What do you mean she already knows? How is that even possible?"

My mind swirled with thoughts of how Mimi could've discovered this. Of course, there were people who knew—Carter, Christy, Sarah Jo, Casey. But I was certain none of them would ever discuss this with Mimi, and if she had gone to them, they would've immediately come to me.

Tommy set his jaw. "She got into my office safe a few years ago. She was looking for our marriage certificate to make us some kind of special plaque, and apparently she came across the original birth certificate. I guess you never got rid of it."

I swallowed hard and remembered why that birth certificate had listed Grizz as her father. I'd dreamt he'd been there for her birth. The dream had been so realistic that I'd spent days in a warm haze of the memory. I remembered writing Jason William Talbot on the documents the hospital had me fill out. It wasn't until he refused to see her that I had her birth certificate changed to reflect Thomas James Dillon as her father. I remembered showing up several times at the jail where Grizz was awaiting his trial, cradling Mimi in my arms.

"What do you mean, I can't see him?" I'd cried to the deputy at the desk, clutching a newborn Mimi to my chest. "I know you let other inmates have visits with their children!"

The leftover pain from my C-section didn't come close to the crushing loss in my heart.

"He said not to come back unless you're alone." The man's expression was unfriendly.

I did go back alone. I showed up with a picture of her, and I could've sworn he had tears in his eyes as he just stared at her sweet, round face.

"She looks like you," he'd said. "She has your eyes."

He handed the photo back to me and said, "Don't come back here, Kit. Ever."

I bristled at the pain that memory dredged up. I never saw him again before his trial, but I did make a couple of trips to the maximum-security prison in northern Florida where he was sentenced to wait out his execution. After about a year, he told me to stop visiting him. I mourned him even harder then. I'd tried to tell myself he was no longer the man I'd fallen in love with. He'd even changed his appearance by then. His long blond locks had been shaved off, and a full beard replaced the smooth chin I was used to. He wasn't the same Grizz.

Now, sitting in my sunny kitchen, I shook off the memory and gazed at Tommy in disbelief.

"She's known all along? She knew that he was her father last year when they found Moe's remains and we sat her down to tell her a little about our past?" I looked down at my lap, my voice cracking. "She's known and never once told us or asked us anything?"

I swept a hand through my long hair, forced myself to breathe. "Why didn't you tell me?"

"She wanted to tell you, Gin. We've been talking about ways for her to bring it up. She begged me to let her be the one. What was I supposed to do? Tell her no and then come running to you and sever any trust she may have started to feel?"

He sat back, and the reality of what he'd said sunk in.

"Another thing you had to keep from me?" My voice rose.

"Dammit, Ginny, look at it from my viewpoint." He lowered his voice and chanced a glance toward the living room and the staircase landing. "The daughter I've raised—the child I've loved as my own since the day she was born, was spilling her heart. How hurt she'd been by us keeping the truth from her. Then finding out who her biological father was. And he wasn't just 'some guy.' He was some guy on fucking death row, Ginny."

I bristled at Tommy's language and looked away as the truth washed over me.

"Look, Gin. Grizz has been dead for months, and Mimi just told me two weeks ago, okay? I haven't told you for two weeks. It's not like you weren't dealing with other things. You were preparing your-self to get rid of the cars and bikes and all of his shit. She wanted to tell you. I had to give her that. Can you please, please just give me a break here?"

I looked at him, saw the desperation in his expression. I could understand where he was coming from. I thought about my attempts at trying to get close to my daughter and the rejection I'd felt. He was making progress with Mimi. To betray her confidence would certainly unravel that. I had to be the mature one here. I had to swallow my anger and pride and let this play out in a way that would be best for Mimi.

At least now I knew why she'd pulled away from us all those years ago.

Tommy's voice brought me out of my thoughts. "She also told me about Leslie."

"What about Leslie?" I asked, my voice skeptical.

"Leslie approached Mimi before she came to you. She used Mimi to not only help her get the interview with you but the one with Grizz, too. He mentioned it to me before his execution. I wanted to ask Mimi about it before I told you. And with everything that's been going on since he died, it just never seemed like the right time."

I jumped up from the table, my quick action startling Tommy. He sat back and looked at me, unsure of what I would do next. And he should be because I was furious.

With my hands balled into tight fists, I screamed at the top of my lungs, "Miiiimmmmiiiii!! Get. Down. Here. Now."

Tommy jumped up too, almost knocking over the chair he sat on.

"What are you doing, Ginny? Stop screaming and let's talk about this," he stage whispered so Mimi wouldn't hear him.

My breathing was heavy, and I was thrumming with fury. I was too angry to care that I wasn't behaving maturely, and as far as ruining what little trust Tommy had been building with Mimi? Well, let's just say I think everyone has a breaking point. I'd just reached mine, and I wasn't going to apologize for it.

I heard the unmistakable thump of someone coming down the stairs. I was surprised when a sleepy Mimi rounded the corner. I guess the tone in my voice or the rarity of this type of outburst had aroused her curiosity. She looked at me, then Tommy, then back to me.

With my arms crossed over my chest, I addressed them both.

"I'm getting a shower. You, Mimi, have twenty minutes to eat some breakfast and get some clothes on." I looked hard at Tommy. "You can get both of my guns out of the safe. I'm taking Mimi to the shooting range. Time to have a little heart-to-heart with my daughter."

I looked back at Mimi and saw the surprise on her face. She was staring at me as if seeing me for the first time. My mild exterior had been peeled away. She was seeing a different mother than the one she was used to. Witnessing the strength beneath the softness. If she had gotten into the safe and found her birth certificate, then she'd seen those guns and probably thought they were Tommy's. She'd been wrong.

I started to walk out of the kitchen but turned around and faced them both. Giving Tommy a level look, I said, "Secrets have almost ruined my life. I won't let them ruin our children's, Tommy."

I then addressed my daughter. "Your biological father made sure I learned how to protect myself. Those are my guns, and I'm sure you saw them when you got into the safe a few years ago. Think you can handle some truths?"

She looked at Tommy, then back at me. With a defiant tilt to her chin that I recognized as my own, she said, "Yeah, I can handle the truth." She paused then and seemed to rethink her answer. Her confidence restored, her posture changed. "I already know everything, anyway."

I cocked my head, gave her a serious look. "You don't know anything, sweetheart. You don't know a darn thing."

I could hear Tommy's voice follow me up the stairs.

"Gin, Perry said we should do this when we're all together. You need to calm down. We'll talk about this in his office."

I'd felt we'd made some progress with Perry, but I was ready to be done. I didn't want someone telling me the right or wrong way to handle my life. We'd started out with good intentions, but if I let myself think about it, I really didn't care for Perry. There was something smug and condescending about his personality. Yeah, I wouldn't be seeing Perry again.

"I'm finished with Perry, Tommy. He's stretching this out. The more times we visit his office, the bigger his piggy bank gets."

"He told us we need to wait, Ginny!" Tommy yelled.

"And I'm telling you I'm tired of being told what I can and can't do. And besides, it's too late. The cat is out of the bag." I didn't give him a chance to reply as I quickly added, "And Perry can kiss my ass."

As I flounced up the stairs, giving Jason a pat on his head as he made his way down, I could hear Mimi ask Tommy, "Did Mom just cuss?"

16

Carter, 1981, Fort Lauderdale

C arter stood at her kitchen counter and sliced an apple, popping a piece into her mouth to enjoy as she worked.

"We'll go for a walk as soon as everybody gets their treats," she said to her Australian shepherd, Cooper, who stood next to her with his leash dangling from his mouth.

A knock at her door interrupted her work. She stiffened and with the paring knife still in hand and Cooper at her heels, cautiously approached the front door. She didn't get many unexpected visitors.

She took a quick look through the peephole and gasped. Him. He'd been looking down, but she recognized the haircut and general shape of his head.

He knocked louder this time, causing her to jump.

"I know you're home, Carter. I see your car. Please open up. I'm only here to apologize."

Yeah, right.

"Look, please, just tell your friend to stay away from me, okay?" There was desperation in his voice that she'd never heard. "I'm only here to tell you I'm sorry about what I did to scare you with the raccoon. I didn't kill it. It was already dead on the side of the road when I found it. I only put it in your car to shake you up."

She bit her lip.

"Look, can you please open up so I don't have to yell? I can't do anything to hurt you with a broken arm. I don't want trouble. I just want you to call off your attack dog."

She looked through the peephole again and this time saw he was holding up his right arm. It had a cast on it. It could be a fake cast. Would he go to all this trouble to get inside her apartment? Before she could ponder further, he lowered his arm, and it was then she noticed his left eye was swollen, and the side of his face was sporting some bright blue bruises.

What was going on?

She undid the chain and slid the deadbolt open. She opened the door and noticed the look of relief on his face.

"Thank you. Can I come in?" A pause. "Please?"

She stood aside and motioned with her hand that still held the knife.

"I can promise you that you won't be needing that. Okay?" he said as he walked into the apartment and sat uninvited on the couch.

He looked up at her. He looked so different than the confident and cocky jock she'd gone on exactly one date with. She'd enjoyed herself on that date and had been looking forward to going out again. The only problem was she'd been busy—and he took that as flat-out rejection. Which it wasn't.

She'd tried telling him her schedule was full, had even tried to say she could meet up for quick lunches until they could actually plan another date night. But he'd rapidly jumped into full-fledged stalker mode. When she let herself think about it, it was almost as if he enjoyed tormenting her. The dead raccoon was the straw that broke the camel's back. She'd told Kit, who convinced her to go to the police and file for a restraining order.

And that was exactly what she'd planned on doing, right after taking her dog for a walk this morning.

She remembered thinking before how good-looking he was. Interesting how someone's personality can affect how they look. She was seeing him through new eyes now, and she had to admit—he was downright ugly. And the fresh bruises and swollen eye had nothing to do with it.

Now, watching him visibly shake while sitting on her couch, she saw something new in his expression. Something she'd not seen before.

Fear.

"Please," he said in a trembling voice. "Please tell him I came here and apologized. Tell him I'm never coming near you again. Tell him I'm not some sociopath who gets off on killing animals. Just tell him. Tell him you'll never lay eyes on me again. Please tell him all of that. Okay?"

He gave her a pleading look. Carter was truly baffled. She sat down on the chair across from him and absently petted Cooper, who sat at her feet. Her brows furrowed.

"Who? Who am I supposed to tell this to?"

She saw a quick flash of anger in his face, but he reeled it in quickly and drove it back.

"Don't play dumb, Carter. Your friend. That fucking gigantic monster with the crazy long hair and scary-ass tattoos. The one that rides a motorcycle?"

She blinked without saying anything. She only knew one person who fit that description, and she'd only met him once. Kit's husband. Grizz.

She'd been invited to Kit's house in Shady Ranches while her husband was away on business. He'd returned early, and Carter almost crapped herself when he'd let himself in the back door.

Grizz was nothing like she'd expected. She always associated "being away on business" with someone who wore a suit and tie and carried a briefcase. They'd just stared at each other for what seemed like an eternity but was only a few seconds when Kit, who'd been putting a load of clothes in the dryer, came back into the room and launched herself into his arms. She looked so small compared to the giant man that Carter slowly gave the once-over, taking in the long hair, five o'clock shadow, and tattoos that covered his massive body.

But it was the look of love and gentleness he gave his wife that shocked Carter far more than his appearance. He'd missed her, and he was totally smitten. It was too obvious to miss.

Carter shook off the memory as she listened to her repentant stalker.

"You're going to try and tell me you don't know who I'm talking about? Honestly, I get it. You have to play dumb, don't you? He probably doesn't want me to go to the police."

Carter raised a brow.

He rushed on, watching her face. "Okay, so he's not the kind of guy to care what I'd do, which is nothing. I wouldn't do anything.

Don't tell him about the police comment, Okay? I—I was just kidding."

Carter couldn't help herself. She smiled. Then she gave him a serious look.

"I'll tell him you apologized. I'll tell him you won't bother me again. I'll tell him you don't kill small animals. At least, I don't think you do. You could be lying. You seemed to enjoy tormenting me."

"It was roadkill, Carter. I swear the raccoon was roadkill that I found." He stood up then, raised his broken arm. "He did this slowly. Not quick. Slowly, so I could feel it. He wanted me to hurt for scaring you." He gulped. "I can promise you I never want to see him again in my life. And don't take this as an insult, but you're not worth it. Nobody would be worth it."

He didn't wait for her to answer, just walked to the front door and opened it. He stopped to look back at her.

"Okay?"

She nodded her agreement, and he was gone.

Three days later, Carter sat at the gas station and watched Kit's husband, Grizz, lean back against his car while he pumped gas. She swallowed thickly, put her car in park, and approached him.

Without making eye contact, she heard him say, "I was wondering when you were going to make yourself known. You've been following me."

"Uhhh...I didn't realize you noticed. It just never seemed like a good time to talk to you," she stammered.

He smiled at her then. Her heart actually gave a jolt from the attention he gave her in that one smile. She didn't remember thinking he was good-looking that first and only time she'd met him. Her only recollection had been big. But his smile was disarming.

"I know you followed me to my bars and out to the motel, at least until you thought better of it and turned around. That was smart. Turning around. I'm thinking that you don't want Kit to know what I did. You could've asked to see me or made an excuse to see her in the hopes of running into me, but you didn't." He nodded as he spoke. "I appreciate that."

"You do?" The surprise in her voice evident.

"Yeah, I do. I try to protect her as much as I can. She doesn't need to know I broke that shitbag's arm."

"Why? Why did you do it?" She couldn't help but ask.

He retrieved the nozzle from his gas tank, placed it back on the pump, and started to put the gas cap back on. Without looking at her, he told her.

"Because Kit was afraid for you. She cares about you, and he was scaring and upsetting you. That was scaring and upsetting her. And nobody upsets my wife if I can help it."

Carter smiled shyly. "Still, no matter why you did it, I appreciate it, and I owe you."

"You don't owe me." He leaned back on his car, crossing his arms over his chest. The look on his face was serious and totally focused.

The sound of traffic and the smell of gasoline were nothing compared to his captivating stare. His green eyes bored into hers. No wonder Kit fell in love with this guy. There was something about him that was powerful and extremely attractive. *I am not going to crush on my new friend's husband. Not happening, Carter.*

She swallowed hard and gave him a genuine smile.

"But I feel like I do. So if there's anything I can do for you, and I can't imagine what that could even be, but if there's anything, let me know."

He didn't answer her. He just nodded. She nodded back and turned to walk back to her car.

She was getting ready to open the door and get in when she yelled back over her shoulder, "Just remind me never to do anything to upset your wife!"

She giggled and looked his way to see if she could gauge his reaction, but he'd already climbed back into his black Corvette. *Gee, if he heard me, I hope he knows I'm only kidding. I don't ever want to get on the wrong side of him.*

She thought about what he'd done to her stalker and shuddered as she got into her car.

17

Mimi, 2000, Fort Lauderdale (Before Grizz's Execution)

"That's him. That's him!" Maggie whispered, gently poking Mimi with her elbow.

Mimi looked up and saw Elliott approaching. She could feel her pulse quicken. He broke into a wide grin when they made eye contact.

"That's the guy who always asks about you," Maggie said quietly, looking down as she pretended to arrange flowers. "He's been in here at least three times and always misses you."

Mimi didn't say anything. She just smiled as Elliott approached.

"I'll be in the back. Can you help this customer, Mimi?" Maggie asked in a voice that was too loud and obvious. Mimi could feel the embarrassment creeping up her neck and face in the form of a healthy red blush as Maggie headed for the back room.

"I've been in a few times," Elliott shyly told Mimi.

"I'm sorry I missed you." She meant it. She'd spent countless hours daydreaming about the young man who'd waltzed in and out of her life last month. She'd prayed she'd see him again, and God had heard her.

She took in his physique. He was wearing blue jeans, a T-shirt, and a light threadbare jacket. His hair was a little longer than she remembered. As if sensing her scrutiny, he ran his hand through it and stammered.

"So, umm, when I was here last time I kind of mentioned you having a boyfriend, but I realized I never actually found out if it was true. I'm just here to see, ah—if you don't, um—if maybe you'd like to do something sometime? Maybe let me take you out somewhere?"

He bit his lip and looked away quickly before looking back at her.

"You mean, like hang out?" She caught a whiff of his cologne and her heart flip-flopped. She absently started fiddling with a flower.

"No, I don't want to hang out with you, Mimi. I want to take you out. On a date. That is, if you don't have a boyfriend." He started to turn red.

"I don't have a boyfriend, and I'd like very much to go out with you, Elliott." She started twirling her hair and bit the edge of her lip.

"Great!" He gave her a wide smile and rolled back on his heels, hands shoved tightly into his jeans pockets. "I guess I'll need your phone number, and maybe you can tell me where you live so I can pick you up? Maybe tomorrow night? If you're available?"

He looked at her hopefully.

She didn't want Elliott coming to her house to meet her parents. They hadn't talked enough to exchange ages, but she was certain he didn't know how young she was, and she was pretty sure he was at least eighteen, if not older. She would have to play this carefully.

She gave him a genuinely disappointed look.

"I can't tomorrow night. Unfortunately, I'm busy for the next few nights."

"Oh," was all he said. He looked away, and Mimi could tell he was grappling with whether or not she wanted to go out with him.

She inhaled a huge dose of air and prayed for a confidence she wasn't quite feeling. The overpowering smell of flowers brought an unexpected calmness to her. With more boldness than she felt, she decided to take the plunge.

"But, I get off in a couple of hours. If you want to come back then, we could go out tonight. That is, if you want to. If you already have other plans and can't, I completely understand."

He grinned. "No, I don't have any plans. Tonight is great! Do you want to go out for dinner?"

"Sure, as long as it's not fancy. I won't be going home to change. You'll have to come back here for me, and what you see is what you get," she couldn't help but laugh at her own joke.

Elliott, who'd been staring into Mimi's eyes, allowed himself to slowly scan his way down her body, making sure not to linger on her chest. She was wearing a lacy white top that wasn't too tight, dark jeans she'd rolled up mid-calf, and white sneakers with no socks. He noticed a silver chain on her left ankle. He gulped.

"Nothing fancy. And even if it was fancy, I think you look perfect." He caught her blushing again and quickly asked, "What time should I come back here for you?"

"I'll be out front at five o'clock."

"Okay then, I'll see you at five." He gave a final smile and wave and headed out the door.

Mimi was still staring at the door when Maggie came out from the back.

"So? Tell me!" Her boss elbowed her.

"There's nothing to tell," Mimi answered, giving Maggie a small smile. "Yet."

At Maggie's questioning look, she added, "He's picking me up when I get off, and he's going to drive me home so he can meet my parents. I figured it's the best way to start."

"Good girl!" Maggie said. "I've got a few deliveries and won't be coming back, so you can just lock up. I'm so excited for you. I don't think you're back in until next Tuesday, and I'll want details!"

"I'll tell you everything then."

Less than ten minutes later, Mimi had arranged all the details. First, she'd called Lindsay to let her know she needed an alibi.

"I'm going to tell my mom she doesn't need to pick me up after work. I'll tell her you asked me to go to the mall because you need a new dress for your dad's work thing and we'll grab something at the food court."

She could practically hear Lindsay rolling her eyes.

"Yeah, that's kind of true. The whole family has to go to his stupid banquet every year. It's not important enough to warrant a new dress, but it sounds convincing enough."

"So can you find an excuse to be driving your mom's van around six-ish so it's not in the driveway? My dad gets home from work every night around six," Mimi said. "I don't know if he'd notice when he drives by your house."

"Won't be an issue," Lindsay said. "It's been in the shop for two days. I think she's going to have to get something new. I hope whatever it is it's going to be better than an ugly minivan." Then as an afterthought, "How are you going to get home? Are you going to have this guy drop you off at your house?"

"No. I was thinking he could drop me off at your house, and you could walk home with me. Maybe we could say that the trip to the mall was unsuccessful, and we were going to comb through my closet to see if I had anything you could wear. I think that would really be convincing. What do you think?"

"I think I'm in!"

Mimi then made the necessary call to her mother. It wasn't unusual for Mimi to get a ride home from work with her friend Lindsay. And they usually involved pit stops, so this wasn't out of the ordinary. Her deceitfulness, however, was. She hoped there was nothing in her voice that betrayed her true motive. She'd never realized how exhausting deception could be. She wondered how her parents had pulled it off for so many years.

The rest of the afternoon passed slowly as Mimi tried to concentrate on work. So many thoughts about her upcoming date were doing battle in her brain. The lie to her mother. Involving Lindsay in the story. How would Elliott react when she told him her age? Would she even tell him? Would he care?

Her mind was so full of thoughts she could barely pay attention to what she'd been doing. She was certain that Maggie would have some rearranging to do. Mimi's feeble attempts at arranging some of the heartier bouquets were a disaster.

At five o'clock sharp, Mimi was standing in front of the flower shop when she spotted an older model tan pickup truck coming down the road. She watched as Elliott parked right in front of the shop and got out. He'd changed into black trousers and a long-sleeved casual blue shirt.

He opened the passenger door. "Your chariot awaits, my lady."

But he must've had second thoughts about what he'd said, because as soon as the words were out of his mouth he looked uncomfortable, like he'd just exposed his inner nerdiness.

Mimi tried not to giggle as she approached and climbed in. This was her first real date alone with a guy. She'd had casual boyfriends before, but they were always school-age friends, and dating was limited to boy-girl parties that were closely chaperoned or school and church events. This was the first time she'd actually been picked up by a guy who drove his own truck.

As she settled herself in the seat, she realized she was probably way behind other girls her age when it came to boys. She knew

Lindsay had lost her virginity last year to the school's football captain, though she'd vowed to never do it again.

"It hurt, and he was a slobbering pig," Lindsay had announced to her friends. "Never again. I'm never having sex again."

Mimi shook off the thought as she tried not to let her nervousness show. He climbed into the driver's side of the truck and gave her a smile that caused her heart to have palpitations.

"Do you like Italian?" he asked.

"I love Italian." It was the truth. The Olive Garden was her favorite restaurant. It couldn't rival her mother's cooking, but she still loved it there.

"Does Marcella's sound good?"

Even better. "It sounds perfect, Elliott."

They made small talk during the drive. She asked him a lot of questions, mostly because she wanted to steer the conversation away from herself, but also because she was truly interested.

She found out the vintage truck they were riding in had belonged to his grandfather. It was in pristine condition, and she could tell Elliott took pride in caring for it. He was a senior in high school and would be graduating soon. His parents had divorced when he was very young. His father had moved away to Michigan, and Elliott had hardly known him. To his surprise, his parents had found each other again thanks to the Internet, and after a whirlwind reconnection, remarried after almost fifteen years apart. His mother moved to Michigan, and Elliott stayed in Florida with his grandmother.

"Did you miss your father? Did you miss having a man around while you were growing up?"

"I don't know if I can answer that. I mean, there were other men around. My mom dated. They all seemed like nice guys. I had male teachers along the way. I don't know if I missed the man so much as I missed the idea of a father. Am I making any sense?"

"Yeah, I think I know what you mean." Mimi looked at her lap. She thought about her own painful feelings concerning the man who was her biological father. The murderer who sat on death row. The man who was scheduled to die this summer. Such a sharp contrast to the respectable architect she'd known as Daddy. She dismissed the thoughts with a shake of her head. "So you're graduating soon. I guess you're eighteen, then?"

"Not yet. My birthday is right after graduation. Almost there, but not yet. How about you? How old are—"

"So what are your plans after graduation?"

He downshifted and slowly glided into a parking spot at the restaurant.

Mimi glanced around the parking lot and wondered why he'd parked so far away when there were so many open spots closer to the restaurant. He answered her unspoken question.

"Dings. Trying to avoid the jerks who don't care if they slam their car doors into somebody else's car. I've taken care of this truck, and I'm not going to let some careless door-slinger mess it up."

Turning off the engine, he looked over at her and answered her other question.

"I'll keep working and go to college."

They found themselves having so much to say over dinner that they kept interrupting each other. There were no awkward silences or uncomfortable lulls. As a matter of fact, it was just the opposite. Mimi was relieved he never pressed her about her age. They talked about school, friends, dreams, hobbies, even church. But he never asked what grade she was in. She was relieved.

While they were waiting for dessert, Elliott fidgeted uncomfortably.

"It's getting hot in here. Are you hot?"

"No, I'm not warm at all. Why don't you roll up your sleeves?" She'd wondered why he was wearing long sleeves. It wasn't hot, but it was warm out, though she imagined he'd been trying to dress up for her.

He looked away nervously. "I don't want to give you the wrong impression."

"What do you mean?" She leaned forward.

"I, uh, have a lot of tattoos." He blushed. "Not all of them are very nice ones. I went through a bad spell. The wrong types of friends. What I put my poor grandmother through." His blush deepened, and he shook his head.

Mimi smiled. "Most guys would be trying to impress a girl with all of their ink, and here you're afraid to show me yours. I actually think that's kind of admirable."

He looked at her as if he was embarrassed. "There's more."

"I'm listening."

"I don't usually drive my grandpa's truck. It's too nice to take out and drive to school and work." He looked down. "I normally drive a motorcycle."

She laughed out loud. "Stop looking so nervous, Elliott. My father has some incredible tattoos, and he drives the baddest Harley around."

She caught the surprise on Elliott's face. Then his expression turned to concern.

"Don't worry, though," she quickly added. "My dad's a nice guy. He's an architect and my mother is a housewife who does accounting part-time. Tattoos and a motorcycle don't always mean bad."

At least I don't think they do. She remembered the things she'd learned about her parents' past—things she was still learning from Leslie's interviews with her mother.

He looked relieved and rolled up his right sleeve, held his right arm out to show her.

"This was an early graduation gift to myself. It's my newest." He turned his forearm over so she could see it. Mimi's eyes widened in admiration.

"Oh, Elliott, it has to be the most beautiful tattoo I've ever seen. The details are amazing." Her fingers gently caressed his forearm.

In a quiet voice, he asked, "It doesn't turn you off? I mean, you don't think you're dating some kind of religious freak, do you?"

Mimi stared at the tattoo. It was a cross and had a beautiful vine of flowers intertwined around it. They were detailed and colorful. She peered closer and saw a tiny white dove amongst them. A crown of thorns hung at the top. Drops of bright red blood dripped from it and was spattered on some of the flowers.

"Are you serious? Turned off? No, I'm not turned off. The edges are a little pink. Does it still hurt?"

"No. It's tender 'cause I'm still having my guy fill in the detail, but it doesn't hurt."

He smiled at her but she couldn't hold his gaze. She looked away.

Something was wrong. "What is it?" His eyes looked sad. "Too much for you? I've just unloaded so much on you and you're probably confused. Is that it? The tattoos, the bad friends, the motorcycle, and now you know I'm a Christian. I've just unloaded a total ball of confusion, didn't I? TMI?"

She shifted in her seat, and the squeak of the vinyl made an embarrassing sound, bringing her out of her thoughts.

"That was not what it sounded like," she said smiling.

He just smiled back. "What's wrong then, Mimi? What is it?"

She let out a resigned breath. "I like you, Elliott, and I'm not sure if this is going to matter to you or not. I guess I think it matters, otherwise I would've told you up front."

"Told me what?" He shifted, too, and the seat made the same sound. They ignored it.

"You're going to be eighteen soon. I—I just turned fifteen."

Before he could respond, the waitress showed up with their desserts. After asking if there was anything else they needed, she left them alone.

Mimi chanced a glance at Elliott. He was looking at her.

"Whoa. Yeah. I see what you mean. You just turned fifteen, which means you were fourteen not so very long ago." He leaned back against the booth and stared at his cheesecake.

Mimi watched him. Her own dessert no longer held any appeal.

Then he sat up. "You know what? I don't care. You are fifteen. I am seventeen. That doesn't sound so bad. I think the best thing for us to do, for me to do, is meet your parents. Ask them if I can formally take you out. I know there will be limitations, but honestly, Mimi, I like you enough to chance their refusal."

"What if they do refuse? I mean, I like you, too, Elliott. I don't want to think about how I'll feel if they don't let us see each other."

"Then let's not think about it for now. Let's enjoy tonight, and we'll talk about when we think it would be a good time for me to meet them. I don't like sneaking around, but I'm guessing that's what you did to arrange tonight. Am I right?"

"Yes. They think I'm with a friend, and before you think bad of me, I've never lied or snuck around behind their back before." At least not with a boy. She didn't want to think about her secret meetings with Leslie as sneaking around. Besides, it was her parents' fault. If they'd been truthful with her, she would've been truthful with them.

"I don't think bad of you at all."

She gave him a little smile. "Listen, if you don't mind seeing me once in a while, just so we can see if we like each other enough to pursue this, see if it'll be worth it, can we keep it to ourselves just for now? I'm dealing with some really heavy personal things right now, and so are my parents. It might not be good timing to throw into their lives a soon-to-be-eighteen-year-old that their just-turned fifteen-year-old daughter would like to date. Like I said, I'm not one for sneaking around, but I'd like to do it that way for a little bit. Is that okay?"

She couldn't tell him she'd been talking to a reporter on the sly while trying simultaneously to convince her mother to give an interview about the evil sperm donor. It was too much pressure to try to introduce a potential boyfriend into the mix. No. She'd like to keep Elliott all to herself. At least until after the execution. That would be coming up soon enough.

His brow creased. "I don't know, Mimi. If things do work out with us, I'll feel funny meeting your parents knowing I've been seeing you behind their back."

She stiffened. "My parents are in no way perfect, Elliott," she said, her voice cool. "And as much as I appreciate your concern and respect for their feelings, let's just say I'm in a place right now in my relationship with them where I'm not certain they deserve it."

Her change in attitude stunned him, but he didn't say anything. So she had a feisty side, he mused. That wasn't so bad.

"As long as it's before I turn eighteen, though," he said finally. "I'm pretty sure if I see you after I'm eighteen, I could get into legal trouble."

She softened. He was a nice guy, and she could understand his concern.

"It may not matter anyway." She looked down at her lap. "We may find out we don't get along so well after all."

He reached over then, tucked her hair behind her ear. He grabbed her chin and turned her face toward his.

"I can guarantee that will not be the case for me, Mimi. I've felt more comfortable with you this last hour than I've ever felt with any girl. And it's not like there have been a lot of them. I've had a few girlfriends, but they were always about shopping and gossip. I can tell you're not like that at all."

She gave him a smile, and he leaned over, gently kissed her cheek. He signaled to the waitress for their check.

"Now tell me. When can I see you again?" he asked.

18

Ginny, 2000, Fort Lauderdale (After Grizz's Execution)

I'd never felt so invigorated and optimistic after that first trip to the shooting range with Mimi, and the long walk at a local park that followed it.

Tommy had retrieved my guns from the safe like I'd asked him. As I stood in front of the desk in his office and loaded up my range bag with everything we'd need, I could feel his eyes boring into me.

"I'm sorry for telling her what you told me," I said without looking at him.

He didn't reply. I stopped what I was doing and looked at him. He didn't say anything, just stared at me. He looked hurt and unsure of himself.

"No." My jaw tightened, and I thrust a pair of shooting glasses into the bag. "I take that back. I'm not sorry. I'm tired of being sorry, Tommy. I'm not apologizing for anything anymore."

"It's okay, Gin," he said softly. "I'm just worried she won't trust me anymore."

"Well, don't worry about it. I'm going to have a nice long talk with our daughter today. I'm going to start at the beginning, and we either move forward from here, or we don't. I'm tired of tiptoeing around my past. I'm tired of tiptoeing around Grizz. Yeah, I said it. The name that's always been the elephant in the room. Not even *the* room—*every* room. The name that's been lurking around every corner threatening to ruin our happily ever after. I'm so over this, Tommy."

He smiled at me then, and his expression instantly changed. I thought I knew what he was going to say.

"Does she know the other thing? About you being his son?" I whispered.

The ticking of the grandfather clock sounded louder than it usually did, its steady heartbeat filling the space between us.

"We hadn't gotten that far, Gin. Leslie could've told her, but I doubt it. Mimi told me they've had no contact since about three weeks before Grizz died. I'm guessing that's about the time Grizz beat the shit out of Leslie at the prison. Mimi even admitted she tried to find out from Leslie when the article would be coming out, but the woman has flat-out ignored her."

I nodded. Good. Leslie took whatever threat Grizz had issued seriously. She was smart to retreat.

I hoisted my bag onto my shoulder and gave Tommy a level look.

"We're still telling her. You know that, right? I won't even try to go there today with her, but we will tell her. It's something we should do together."

I watched as Tommy ran his hand through his hair. He let out a resigned sigh.

"I can't say I'm looking forward to that, but yeah, fine. We'll tell her, Gin. We'll tell her together."

I could see the worry and doubt in his expression and my heart ached for him. I walked toward him, kissed him lightly on the lips. The stubble on his chin grazed my own, and I realized my earlier anger had dissolved and was transforming into something else. I was feeling hopeful. Hopeful of a future without secrets. A future where the barrier Mimi had erected, through no fault of hers, was broken down.

I couldn't blame her for pulling back from us after finding out about Grizz. I should've known our past would catch up with us, and if I hadn't tried to avoid it, I wouldn't be struggling right now to make things whole again. I wouldn't have lost three years with my daughter.

As I let myself ponder these things, I could feel something else creeping into my consciousness. It was a feeling I'd not had too much experience with, so I wasn't sure if it was real or a defense mechanism against my deep-rooted pain of Grizz's rejection. I could feel an unsettling darkness seeping in. If I didn't deal with it, it would most certainly rear its ugly head. I thought about the man responsible for all of this, and I congratulated myself for throwing away that bandana.

It's a good thing you're not around anymore, Grizz. It's a good thing you chose to reject me and live the rest of your life away from me.

Tommy must have noticed a change in my expression because he looked down at me, his hands resting on my shoulders.

"What is it, Gin? What are you thinking?"

I stared at a spot on the wall over his left shoulder and, without looking him in the eyes, I answered him in a voice void of emotion.

"I was thinking that if Grizz wasn't already dead, I'd think about shooting him myself."

Without waiting for Tommy to reply, I spun and headed toward the front door, shouting, "Mimi, let's go! I'll be in the car."

As we approached the first stop sign in our neighborhood, and before allowing any awkward silences to come between us, I dove in headfirst with Mimi.

"Let's start with Leslie. I know you talked to her, and I'm sure she shared some of the things I told her with you. I also know the article won't be coming out." I glanced at Mimi, who looked slightly surprised. "Tell me how you and Leslie found each other."

Mimi plunged right in, starting with her first encounter with Leslie at a mall. She was only partway through when my cell phone interrupted us. Mimi looked at it.

"It's Dad."

I asked her to put the phone on speaker.

"Hey. You're on speaker," I told Tommy.

"Listen, I just wanted to let you know my day changed up a little. I was going to take Jason to practice and stay with him, but Sarah Jo called and wants me to meet her for lunch," he said.

"Is something wrong with her?" Concern prickled at the edge of my thoughts. I was still focused on my conversation with Mimi.

"No, I don't think anything's wrong. I think she may just want to talk about her move and some of Stan's options."

This was understandable, but I may have been feeling slightly hurt. I'd reached out to Jo more than once since Grizz's execution, and she was always busy. I was probably being overly sensitive. Besides, Tommy had done extensive traveling outside the U.S. over the years, and Jo may have just wanted his opinion about some of the places he'd visited. Tommy and Jo had been best friends long before I came on the scene—and besides, I was doing something much more important.

"And remember to tell her I still don't want her to move and that I'm giving you a direct order to talk her out of it." I laughed. "And tell her I love her."

"Yeah, I'll tell her. I don't know how long I'll be, so Denise said she'd bring Jason home with her if I'm not back in time to get him."

I said a mental prayer of thanks. Denise had been a Godsend when it came to helping out with Jason, especially during our brief separation.

"Got it. We'll all meet back at home later. I don't know how long Mimi and I will be, either, so we'll see you when we see you."

"Okay, honey. I love you. I love you both."

"I love you too, babe," I said, then gave Mimi an imploring look. She knew what I wanted and complied without hesitation.

"I love you, too, Dad."

Good. This told us both Mimi wasn't upset that Tommy had spilled the beans. I could almost hear the relief in his answer.

"I love you too, Dreamy Mimi."

We hung up, and the silence fell between us heavily like wet cement. I wouldn't let it cover us.

"He hasn't called you that in a while." I gave her a sidelong glance as I navigated the busy streets. Dreamy Mimi was a nickname Tommy had given her when she was younger. She was only about five or six when Tommy was trying to get her attention. When he'd asked if she'd been daydreaming again, she'd innocently replied, "No, Daddy. I dream about night things, too. Not just about day things." He'd started calling her Dreamy Mimi then, and it'd stuck until she was about twelve. It was then that she'd told her father she was too old to be called Dreamy Mimi. It reminded me of when I first started insisting that people call me Ginny instead of Gwinny.

"I told him not to. You know, after I found out about...about..."

"About him not being your biological father?" My voice might have had an edge to it I hadn't intended.

"I guess I didn't know if he meant it. If he wanted to be my father, or if it was a job he just got stuck with," she said quietly. "Dreamy Mimi sounded like more of a taunt, Mom. I can't explain it."

"I understand." And I did.

I filled her in on some things she wouldn't know about, or have no way of remembering, like the time I'd eavesdropped as Tommy told her a made up story about the Princess Mimi. I told her about the time he'd threatened the father of a little girl who'd mercilessly been bullying Mimi at school. Mimi had been about eight years old and came home crying one day because the new girl, Marigold, had been picking on her. Of course, I'd gone to the teacher and spoken with the girl's mother, yet the bullying had continued in the privacy of the girl's restroom and out-of-the-way corners in the library or playground.

When I'd told Tommy it was getting harder and harder to get Mimi to go to school, he paid a visit to Marigold's father and told the man, "Every time my little girl comes home from school crying because of your daughter, I'm going to come see you and punch you in the face. It's that simple. My daughter hurts, you're going to hurt."

Tommy told me how the guy scoffed at him. "Kids are kids. They need to work it out themselves."

"I'm not making empty threats," Tommy had told the man. "You've been warned. I suggest you get your daughter under control. If my Mimi comes home crying, you'll be crying."

The man had just laughed as Tommy walked away. Sure enough, Mimi came home with evidence on the inside of her upper arm where Marigold had pinched her, hard enough for us to see bruises.

"I remember that!" Mimi sat up straight in the car and looked over at me, the seatbelt tight against her chest. "I remember trying to stay away from Marigold after that, but I didn't have to. She left me alone, and I think they moved anyway. What did Dad do?"

"You really want to know?"

She nodded.

"He went to the man's work, asked to speak to him outside, and punched him right in the face. Just like he said he would."

Mimi's eyes were wide as saucers. "He did that? He did that for me?"

"Mimi, your father does not condone violence. I can tell you the truth when I say I've only seen him lose his temper a few times. I didn't see him punch Marigold's father, but I know it happened. And I also know that punch was nothing compared to what he'd be willing to do for you. He would lay down his life for you, Mimi. You are his daughter as far as he is concerned. You always have been, honey."

I'd just pulled into the shooting range, found a spot, and shifted the car into park. I looked over at my daughter then and noticed the change in her posture. It was relaxed and welcoming. Almost as if a burden had been lifted. I smiled at her, and she smiled back.

"I guess we won't be able to talk much while we're shooting the guns?" she asked.

"Probably not. It'll be loud."

She nodded. "Mom, when we're done, can we go somewhere else and keep talking?"

"Of course we can, Mimi," I said, my heart feeling lighter.

"Good. Cause you said in the kitchen, I didn't know anything. You know Leslie told me some of the stories?"

I plastered on a phony smile at the mention of the reporter's name.

"You tell me everything Leslie told you, and I'll do my best to fill in the missing pieces."

"Good," she said with a wide grin. Then her brown eyes got serious. "I want you to tell me everything you can about the evil sperm donor."

19

Tommy, 2000, Fort Lauderdale (After Grizz's Execution)

Tommy reflected on the last couple of weeks as he made his way to the little diner in the heart of an old but beautifully restored downtown Davie.

He thought about the progress he'd made in getting to know his daughter again, and how concerned he'd been as to whether or not Ginny's outburst would cause that to crumble. It hadn't. Mimi had told him she loved him. It was a start. A good start. He hadn't heard her say those words in years. His heart felt lighter in spite of this last-minute lunch with Sarah Jo.

Jo. He frowned as he idled at a red light, the memory of who he was meeting aggravating him.

He leaned his elbow on the steering wheel and pinched his nose between his fingers. The beep of an impatient motorist behind him brought him back from his thoughts. Jo had been pestering him for weeks to meet for a talk. He was certain she wanted to convince him he was wrong about her, that he had no right to tell her what she should be doing with her life.

He knew how this would go down. She would start off with small talk, then work her way into how difficult it was trying to arrange such a monumental move out of the country. It would be followed with whining and trying to convince him of her love for him and Ginny.

And it would probably end in her being angry at his refusal to budge. He just hoped she wouldn't make a scene. He sighed as he pulled into the diner parking lot and spotted her car.

Inside, Sarah Jo drummed her fingers against the table.

"Can I get you something while you wait, ma'am?" the waitress asked. "Ma'am?"

"No," Sarah Jo snapped at the waitress. "I already told you. I'll order when my friend gets here."

She barely glanced at the waitress who crept away, embarrassed by Sarah Jo's rudeness.

Jo rolled her eyes as she sat up straighter to look out the window. She nervously clutched her mother's pendant. It was a large Marcasite pendant with a ruby in the center. Sarah Jo never took it off. When she was younger, she'd wear it tucked inside her blouse and was always comforted by the cold metallic feel of it resting between her breasts. As she got older, she got in the habit of wearing it out. It was now more suited to her age and went well with her business attire.

He'd better not stand me up again. She rubbed the precious keepsake between her fingers. She was starting to get upset thinking about what she would do if he didn't show when she noticed his car pull in.

She sat back in the booth triumphantly. He was here and willing to talk. It was a beginning.

She watched Tommy walk to the restaurant's front door. She could hear him as he made his way up behind her and casually plop himself in the seat in front of her.

"I don't have a lot of time." His voice sounded tired. "What do you want, Jo?"

"Wow, haven't seen you in months and not even a 'hello' or 'how've you been?' Nothing?" Before Tommy could answer, her lips pursed in mock outrage. "What does somebody need to do to get a waitress around here? I've been waiting for you for over twenty minutes. You think somebody would've asked me if they could at least get me a drink."

"I'm not hungry or thirsty. What did you want to see me for?"

"So that's how it's going to be? Just business?"

"Did you honestly think it could be more?"

Without answering, she looked up at the girl who'd returned to their table.

"Two coffees, please. And would you be a doll and bring me extra cream?" she asked, giving the girl the sweetest smile she could muster. "And no need for menus. We're just having coffee. Thank you, love."

Tommy didn't notice the waitress's confused expression as she left to get their drinks.

Sarah Jo hunched over the table between them.

"Look, I know you've seen the effort I've been making. Stan has been on three interviews since our talk. I've avoided Ginny at every opportunity, and that hasn't been easy. She calls me a lot. Although I have to admit, it's been dying off a bit. She knows I'm busy with making arrangements for the move. I just think now that you've seen I can be in the same city as her and not be in your lives, you need to reconsider your threat." She emphasized the word with air quotes.

"Why would I do that? Why would you even think I'd change my mind?"

The waitress set down their coffees. Tommy politely thanked her and stared at Jo.

"Why? I'll tell you why, Tommy. Because it's not easy packing up my life and moving to the other side of the world. Show some compassion, how 'bout it?"

She loaded her coffee with cream and sugar as she glared at him.

"Compassion? Like you showed when you set up Ginny's rape all those years ago?" Sarah Jo cringed, but he pressed on. "Compassion, like when Chicky tried to get close to Fess? How about the compassion you showed Moe? That kind of compassion, Jo? Is that what you mean?"

His voice was tight with anger.

"Why are you still harping on something that happened over twenty years ago? Why can't you let this obsession with getting me out of town go? Why can't you get past this?"

He sat back. Cocking his head to one side, he seriously considered his answer.

"It's the only way I can get justice for Gin without her knowing it. But I'll know it. I'll know that you'll be miserable living outside your little safety zone. The perfect little cocoon of a life that you've built by crushing others."

She started to say something, but he held up a hand.

"Yeah, Jo, I know now. I can look back at our friendship over these years, and I can see how you've twisted certain stories, always making yourself the victim. I know how you throw your husband's status around to get what you want at work. How you walk on people to make yourself look better. How you let others take the fall when you've fucked up. Ginny and I have heard these stories and even sympathized with you about some things." He narrowed his eyes. "But we were wrong, weren't we? You've always been conniving, but we never let ourselves see it because you were our friend. Of course, we were always going to side with you. I'm going to guess Stan knows, too, but he's too whipped by you to ever call you out on anything."

Just like that day at her house, when he'd confronted her about what he'd read in Moe's journal, he knew he'd riled her. He'd hit a sore spot, and it was showing on her face. He watched as she sat back and reached for her mother's pendant, fingering it frantically.

"So you think you have me all figured out?" Her eyes flashed. "Good for you, Tommy. But there's something you need to know. I am not moving my family out of the country, out of this state or even out of this city. You will not tell Ginny about my part in her rape. Do you understand? Do you realize what I'm telling you?"

He laughed at her. "You have no choice, Jo. Not only will I tell Gin what you did, but I'll tell someone else, too. I bet that journalist who was so sure she could get the scoop on Grizz's execution would love to hear this story. I can imagine the headline in her little magazine." He raised his hand for emphasis as if highlighting each word. "Prominent and Respected Surgeon's Wife Played Major Role in Rape and Attempted Murder of Her Best Friend."

He gave her a smirk before taking another sip of coffee. Of course, the threat to talk to Leslie was empty. He was just playing with Jo's emotions. He would never do anything to purposely bring attention back into their lives. But Sarah Jo didn't know that.

Sarah Jo rolled her eyes. "You're an asshole." She smiled smugly. "And if we're telling stories, then I'll tell her one, too." She paused dramatically, careful not to break his stare, and idly tapped her thumb on the rim of her coffee cup.

"What story would that be, Jo?"

"Oh, you know the story," she cooed. "The one when Ginny was pregnant way back in, what was it, 1980? When she was living at that dump with Grizz?"

"Yeah, what about it?"

"Surely you remember, don't you?" she asked mockingly. "She was having that awful morning sickness, and you were so worried about her. You were stupid back then, too, Tommy. Only you would pine over a woman who was pregnant with another man's child."

She could tell by his expression she'd hit a nerve. Time to go in for the kill. She should have told him this when he'd first threatened her. It would've saved her a lot of frustration.

"I gave you those herbal powders to give her so they would make the morning sickness go away. Remember how I told you I didn't want credit for it? How I wanted her to think the powders were from you because you were such a good friend to her?"

"Yeah, what about them? They didn't even work. Didn't matter anyway. She lost that baby shortly afterward."

He paused and inhaled sharply as the realization of what he was saying caught him by surprise.

"Jo, you didn't. Tell me you didn't."

"Of course, I did, you idiot. I didn't want her having that baby. She told me Grizz was going to retire from the gang when the baby came. I couldn't let him have a happily ever after!"

Tommy felt like he'd taken a punch to the gut. He remembered everything so clearly—Sarah Jo calling him from her college in northern Florida. Talking about her environmentally conscious, vegetarian, herb-making roommate. How that roommate had concocted the perfect mixture to ease Ginny's morning sickness. Tommy had specifically asked for the ingredients and looked them up in his encyclopedias, even consulted one of his teachers at school. Jo was right. A combination of these herbs was supposed to help with morning sickness and posed no threat to the mother or baby. He'd told her to mail him the roommate's remedy and, most importantly, he remembered Sarah Jo's insistence that he say it was his idea.

"You love her, Grunt. Let her think this is from you. When she's feeling better, it's you she'll thank." Sarah Jo had laughed, then added, "I swear, if you tell her those little packets are from me, I'll deny it. I want you to get the credit."

As the reality of what he'd done sank in, he felt an enormous blackness enveloping him. He'd given Ginny herbs that were supposed to help with morning sickness, but in truth, had caused her miscarriage. What had he done?

Jo was right. Ginny would remember Tommy giving her the herbs to put in her tea. He'd never mentioned they came from Sarah Jo. Actually, he'd mentioned it to one person, but that person was dead.

"What have you done, Jo?" He rested his elbows on the table, lowered his face to his hands. The sound of his heartbeat pulsed in his ears, muffling the sounds in the diner. He had an instant and intense headache. He rubbed his temples hard.

He also had an immediate and heightened sense of smell. The combination of baking bread, some kind of meat roasting, and the bleach-soaked dishrag that must've been used to wipe their table caused his stomach to churn.

With his elbows still resting on the table and his fingers digging into his temples, he raised his eyes to Sarah Jo and asked in a whisper, "What did you do?"

She gave him a victorious grin and grabbed her purse as she quickly stood up. She looked down at him with mock pity.

"I didn't do anything, Tommy. You did."

She spun around on her heel and triumphantly headed for the door, telling their waitress on the way out, "This place sucks, and so do you."

20

Grizz, 1990, Prison, North Florida

G rizz stood over the sink in his cell and watched the blood trickle down the drain. The metallic smell was even more obvious as he realized some of Bobby Ringer's blood had also settled itself in his beard.

A quick glance in the mirror—an item that definitely shouldn't have been in a death row inmate's cell—told him he was right. He grabbed the bar of soap and scrubbed away the last evidence of what he'd done. Not that it mattered. He wouldn't be interrogated. The guard who'd looked the other way after unlocking Ringer's cell would be taking his family on a very nice vacation with the money that would show up in his bank account. Money that, if questioned, would look like a reimbursement from his mortgage company for a major miscalculation in his escrow fund. That is, if anybody even bothered to look. That same guard would make sure Grizz's bloody clothes would be tossed in the prison's furnace.

After hearing Kit gave birth to a son, Grunt's son, Grizz needed to find an outlet for his fury. He decided on the prison's most famous and despised serial killer, Bobby Ringer. Unfortunately, to Grizz's disappointment, Ringer didn't put up a fight. He went down too quickly, not giving Grizz the time he needed to burn off his anger.

Grizz looked down at his blood-free hands and realized he hadn't even bruised his knuckles. Fucking milquetoast.

He lay down on his bed and laced his fingers behind his head. He glanced at the ceiling and thought about her. Kit. He thought about being in the delivery room for the birth of their daughter. Even though it was a beautiful memory, a good memory, it made his chest feel heavy, and his soul feel empty.

Another memory found its way into his thoughts. This one not so good.

He stiffened when he remembered the look in Kit's eyes when he'd refused to see Mimi when Kit had brought their newborn to the jail. He'd had no choice. They watched him closely back then. He wanted Kit and Mimi as far away from him as possible. He'd caved a few times, letting Kit see him first in jail and then prison. But after Grunt's visit, telling him how much she was suffering and him knowing he was being selfish and putting her in potential danger, he'd finally told her to stay away. To have her life with Grunt. That it was okay if she loved Grunt.

His jaw clenched at the pain that memory invoked.

He'd had a face to face with Grunt when her pregnancy had gotten back to him. The pregnancy was painful to hear about, but he was able to tuck it away. But then, hearing she'd actually given birth to Grunt's child sent him over the edge and faded any hope, even false hope, that they'd be together again.

And how could he even let himself hope when, as far as she was concerned, he was being put to death? Hell. Maybe he was going to be put to death. Maybe they didn't care if what he had on them went public. They'd been fucking with him for five years now.

The worst part was they knew she'd moved on with her life. They knew it was probably torturing him, and they were reveling in it. They were enjoying his pain.

Or maybe they weren't. Maybe they didn't give a shit. Maybe what he'd found all those years ago was no longer important. He wouldn't know because they ignored every attempt he'd made to set up a meeting. Motherfuckers.

He swiped his hand over his face and tugged on his beard. He would now need to get a message to Carter to make sure the guard was compensated appropriately. He smiled as he thought about how well the communication system he'd set up with Carter through her inmate/canine rehabilitation program was working. He remembered summoning Carter almost five years ago to the county jail while he was awaiting trial.

"You said to let you know if you could ever do anything for me," he'd said to her. They were sitting in the same room Kit had been shown into weeks earlier, when he'd suggested a middle name if their baby was a girl. Ruth, his little sister's name.

Carter had looked at him wide-eyed and tried to put on a brave front, but Grizz could tell she was nervous. A dank and mildew-laced room in the county jail with an alleged murderer was obviously outside of her comfort zone. He tried to put her mind at ease.

"First, thank you for staying with her. I know she won't let Grunt live there, and it's not good for her to be alone. Especially with a baby on the way."

She visibly relaxed and gave him a smile. She tucked some of her chin-length brown hair behind an ear and told him, "You're welcome, and it's easy being there. I love Kit more than I could love a sister, and it's working out for me, too. I've been taking home some of the animals from the shelter and, well—"

She caught herself. She had no way of knowing if he approved of her using their land to foster abandoned pets.

"I know what you've been doing with the animals, and it's okay," he quietly told her. "As a matter of fact, that's what I want to talk to you about today. If anybody asks, though, we're talking about Kit and how you're there to make her life easier. Got it?"

Carter nodded her understanding. They continued their discussion in hushed tones. He'd just finished telling her what he wanted her to do when there was a quick knock on the door, and the guard came in.

"Five minutes, Talbot." He shut the door without waiting for Grizz's reply.

It was then that Grizz asked Carter for another favor.

"I need to tell you about the blue bandana hanging on my bike in the garage."

Carter listened to what he told her, nodding before the guard returned to escort Grizz back to his cell.

Now, Grizz sighed as he continued to stare at his ceiling. He was relieved Kit hadn't worn the blue bandana. He was also disappointed. She didn't need him. It was to be expected, and it wasn't like he could've personally come to her rescue. He could've arranged it, but he couldn't be the one to physically execute it.

Execute. What an appropriate word.

Lying on his bed now, he crossed his legs and thought about how flawlessly the dog ministry was working. It wasn't his only means of communicating with the outside world, but it was a major one. He knew the warden and guards looked the other way as the inmates took on the responsibility of cleaning up after the dogs. Grizz made sure they put on a show of whisking the dog's shit to a private place to bag it up for the incinerator. Everyone looked the other way as they surmised the inmates sorted through the fecal matter for tiny rubber balloons filled with contraband.

Grizz chuckled to himself. There were no rubber balloons. Yes, Grizz had drugs brought into the prison, but not through the dogs like the prison brass thought. It was a decoy for what he was really doing. Sending coded messages through tiny compartments sewn into the dog's collars.

Each dog had a collar that represented their stage of training. A blue collar represented a brand new dog that had been brought to the prison and sometimes carried a message from Carter. Yellow meant they were halfway through their training. Red meant they were close to graduating from the program, and black meant they were ready to leave the prison and be placed with someone that had special needs.

It was arranged so every dog with a black collar had to go back to Carter's organization in Fort Lauderdale. The black collars were removed, and they were given new ones. The collars were then sent to Carter for recycling.

Carter checked the collars for any messages and discreetly and anonymously had the cryptic notes sent to the intended recipients. Sometimes the recipients were inmates in different facilities throughout the State of Florida. He didn't use the system very often, but it was in place for some of Grizz's more important business. If anyone suspected Kit's friend was helping him move drugs or communicate through the various prison systems, they looked the other way or just didn't care.

Some dogs would be graduating soon, Grizz thought, and he needed Carter to get a message to Bill to make sure the guard who gave him access to Ringer's cell was compensated. Bill would handle it electronically. Grizz smiled as he thought how that would be one message that wouldn't need to be delivered anonymously. He had no way of knowing his casual suggestion to Bill—William Petty—to seek out Carter for a job would turn into love. Just like Bill had told Grizz back then, he'd managed to get released early.

Grizz had known Bill had a soft spot for animals, and he'd suggested maybe he could work with Carter on the very real and legitimate side of her rescue organizations. Apparently, their mutual love for animals turned into a real romance. They'd quickly married and were now living in Grizz's house at Shady Ranches.

He did have one request, though. He didn't want Kit to have any knowledge Bill had known Grizz from prison. That seemed like one part of Bill's past he was only too willing not to share, and the three agreed to keep it to themselves.

As Bill and Carter's marriage flourished, Bill continued to stay somewhat involved with her animal charities, but Grizz knew he'd found legitimate employment within his field of expertise—computers. Not the programming or software side of computers. He'd continued to keep his hacking skills to himself. No, Bill thrived in computer hardware sales. Apparently, he could sell garlic to a vampire, and his sales commissions were impressive. Nobody ever suspected he was a freaking genius when it came to infiltrating computer systems.

Thinking about Bill and Carter and the home he'd shared with Kit caused his mind to drift even more. He thought about happier times. He thought about that house. How it was not just a house, but a home. The only real home he'd ever known. Of course, anywhere with Kit would be a real home. He remembered how he'd made good on his declaration to her when it was being built that he would make love to her in every room of that house.

The memory was so real he could smell her hair and feel her warm, sweet breath on his neck. He let the memory swallow him whole as his hand reached inside his pants and roughly pulled out his cock.

He let his mind drift to a time when they'd just finished making love and were lying side by side, Kit nestled in his arms. They were talking about whether or not they'd just made a baby.

"I feel like I'm pregnant," she'd said, and the expectation in her voice was heartwarming.

He'd chuckled and pulled her closer to kiss the top of her head.

"Kitten, I barely just pulled my dick out of you. How could you feel like you're knocked up?"

She leaned up on her elbow to look at him. "Why does every sentence in your vocabulary have to be so crude?"

He raised an eyebrow and gave her a serious look.

"You're right, sweetheart. You've asked me to watch my mouth before. How about this? Kitten, I barely just withdrew my penis from inside of you. How could you feel like I've impregnated you so soon?" Before she could comment, he added, "Or would you prefer 'throbbing member' or maybe 'rod of love' instead of penis?"

She'd started laughing then. "I get it. For some reason, crude does sound more natural coming from you."

"And just to show you I don't mean to be crude when our first son is born, we'll name him Richard and call him Dick. That way you'll never associate that word with my throbbing member."

"You are such a butthead, Grizz. I'm not calling our first son, Dick, especially when your intention is the opposite. I'll never call our son that name without thinking of your penis." She looked heavenward. "Which was probably your intention all along, right? For me to always be thinking about your rod of love?"

He remembered thinking how much he loved her innocence. How she responded in his arms with the passion of a woman that rivaled his own desires, but her teasing and use of names like butthead endeared her to him even more. He'd only ever known hard women before falling in love with Kit. Women who'd liked trying to shock him with their filthy language and boldness in the bedroom. Their willingness to do anything. He'd thought he liked it, too. He'd been wrong.

She reached for a pillow that had been tossed aside and swung it at his head, but he blocked it and grabbed her wrist, pulling her up on top of him. He gently grabbed the back of her head with his free hand and pulled her face down to his.

The kiss started slow and became more heated as she felt his hardness beneath her. She pulled away and looked down at him.

"Again? Already?"

"Yes, again, Kit. You want to make that baby don't you?" he teased.

He took the break in their kiss as an opportunity to sit up straight pulling her with him. With his back against the headboard, he tenderly lowered her onto his hardness.

Now, on his prison cot, he closed his eyes, letting the memory of her tight warmness envelop him. He remembered breathing deeply to catch the scent of her that floated up between them. The heady mixture that was uniquely Kit's always caused him to get hard. Then, when he'd actually experienced it, and now, just remembering it.

She'd started to slowly glide up and down on him. Her pace was quickening, and he moved his hand to where he could gently massage her with his thumb, knowing the exact rhythm that would bring her to orgasm. He realized he was going to come quickly, too, but he didn't want to. Not yet. He wanted to savor her just a bit longer.

"Stop, Kit. Slow down, baby."

She stopped and looked at him.

Taking her face in his hands, he brought his mouth down to hers. "I want to kiss on you for a few minutes. I can't do that if you're bouncing up and down."

He remembered kissing her then, slowly making his way down her neck, stopping to ask her to kneel up so he could take one of her full, beautiful breasts into his mouth. He mourned the loss of her warm tightness as she raised herself off of him, but quickly reveled in the taste and feel of her nipple as it hardened beneath his tongue. He remembered.

A loud knock on his cell door jolted him from the memory. He barely had time to shove his dick back into his pants when the door swung open.

The guard stood there with a shit-eating grin on his face. He'd obviously peeked through the slot and knew what he'd interrupted. The murderous look Grizz gave him caused his smile to fade, and his discomfort became obvious.

"Errr ... someone here to see you. Maybe she can help you finish what you started?" He gulped and tugged at his collar. It suddenly felt tight around his neck.

The guard stepped aside, and a woman that Grizz didn't know breezed inside the cell like she owned the place.

"Lighten up, Grizz. I told him to make sure we weren't interrupting anything."

She glanced at the tented area of Grizz's pants and raised an eyebrow. Cocking her hip to one side and hooking her well-manicured fingers through the loop in her jeans, she said in a voice that Grizz recognized immediately.

"Looks like I got here just in time, honey."

21

Mimi, 2000, Fort Lauderdale (Two Days After Grizz's Execution)

M imi clung tightly to Elliott's back as they sped through the streets of South Florida.

The motorcycle vibrated between her thighs as she rested her chin on his shoulder. The wind so strong against her face, blocking out the scent she'd come to associate with him. She loved how Elliott smelled, and her emotions were so conflicted at what had happened two days ago that she wanted more than her chin resting on his shoulder. She wanted to feel his arms around her. To bury her face in his chest. She wanted to feel safe. She wanted to feel loved.

She wanted to feel special.

"I promised Edith we'd have a late breakfast with her. Hope that's okay with you," he said loudly as they idled at a red light.

Mimi gave him a thumbs-up, and twenty minutes later they were sitting across from Elliott's grandmother at the tiny table in her cozy kitchen. Elliott had introduced Mimi to his grandmother not long after their first date at Marcella's earlier that year. She'd yet to introduce Elliott to her parents. She still wasn't ready.

"My friends are picking me up soon," his grandmother told them. "We're going to see "Death of a Salesman" at the community theater. I'm sure there are plenty of tickets left. Would you two like to come?"

Elliott smiled at his grandmother. "I know you're worried about leaving us alone in the house—"

"Young unmarried couples were never left unchaperoned in my day," she told him in her gravelly voice. Elliott had told Mimi his grandmother had been a smoker up until she'd had a lung removed five years ago. Her voice always sounded like she needed to clear her throat.

"We won't be here long after you leave. We'll clean up the kitchen as a thank you for making this great breakfast." Elliott looked at Mimi, who gave a quick nod. "Then I'm just going to take Mimi for a nice long motorcycle ride. Maybe up by the beach."

Edith looked at her grandson with an expression Mimi couldn't read. She patted his cheek a little too roughly as she stood to excuse herself. She would need to brush her teeth and freshen her lipstick before her friends arrived.

"Just don't do anything that would make me ashamed of you, Elliott."

Her voice almost had a pleading sound, and Mimi could see the worry on her lined face.

Elliott stood then and gently took her by the elbow. "Those days are gone, Grandma. I've straightened up my life, and you know that. I've proven it to you."

"I guess you're right. I thank the good Lord every day that you stopped your shenanigans before you got into any trouble with the law. You're blessed, boy. I hope you know that. You don't have any record, and the Lord's seen fit to give you a new start. Use it wisely."

"I am, Grandma. I'm trying to prove to you and God and my new girlfriend," he paused and winked at Mimi, "that I can do something with my life."

He gently guided her out of the kitchen. Mimi could hear him continuing to give his grandmother gentle reassurances that he wouldn't be going back to his old habits.

Mimi smiled to herself and started to clear the breakfast dishes. She remembered her first date with Elliott and how he had shown her the beautiful cross tattoo on the underside of his forearm. She remembered how she took his arm in both of her hands that day and slowly turned it over, noticing some of the tattoos on the other side. She'd stiffened when she saw a heart with the name Edith in the center of it. She shook her head now as she loaded the dishwasher. She'd had an instant jolt of jealousy after seeing that name and knew she blushed when Elliott had quickly explained, "Edith is my grandmother." She thought she remembered him blushing, too.

She had just closed the dishwasher when she felt arms surround her from behind and a soft kiss on the side of her neck.

"You should've waited for me to help," he whispered in her ear.

She turned her face sideways so his mouth was now against her cheek.

"You can wipe the table," she answered, her voice coming out like a squeak.

They pulled apart when they heard a horn honk, and Elliott went to find his grandmother. After a quick hug goodbye and an insistence that Mimi come back to see her, Edith let her grandson escort her to the waiting car of her elderly friends.

Back inside the house, Elliott took Mimi by the hand and led her to the sofa. He sat down and pulled her onto his lap.

"Do you want to talk about it?" he asked gently.

She chanced a look at his face, and her eyes filled up with tears.

"It's done. It's over with. I only saw my dad for a few minutes before you picked me up. I haven't seen my mom yet, so I don't know how she's going to act."

"How did your dad act?"

"When I got home this morning I found him in the den by himself. Just staring at the wall. When I tried to get his attention he barely heard me." She got quiet then and looked at Elliott's chin. "I lied again. Told him Lindsay and I were invited to spend the day at Courtney's. I have until late tonight, so we can do anything you wanna do."

She swallowed hard and chanced a glance into his eyes. What she saw scared and excited her.

Elliott stared for a second without answering.

"I know what I want to do, Mimi," he said without breaking away from her glance. "Geez, I'm a guy. Do I need to spell out what I want to do? What I've always wanted to do? But I'm not going to. I'm not going there with you. Not yet anyway."

"But, I—"

"No. You heard Edith. You heard her talk about making the right choices. She's right, you know. It's a miracle I didn't get arrested for all the shit I've pulled. I'm lucky my friends got caught, but I didn't. Lucky they didn't point the finger at me. I know it's a shitty way to think, but it's true. They have records now, not me. I can't blow this."

"How is being with me going to blow it?" But she was secretly relieved. She wasn't sure how she felt about the physical awakening her body had been experiencing. She was raised in the church and knew premarital sex was wrong.

"You know how. Our ages. When I turned eighteen, you became officially off limits to me." He sighed and in one quick motion hefted her off his lap and placed her next to him on the couch. He adjusted his pants. "I shouldn't have pulled you down on my lap like that."

"What are you waiting for? My parents' blessing? Because there is a pretty good chance that won't happen."

"And it will definitely never happen if I don't meet them." His voice turned hard. "How can I ask for their blessing if they don't even know about me?"

She started to say something, but he put up his hand to stop her.

"You told me you were going through some heavy shit, and you needed time, and I understand that. Man, all that crap you told me about your real father and the reporter approaching you and all that. Yeah, I get it, Mimi. I really do. I even understand why you've had a serious hard-on for your parents all these years. They should've told you." He saw her chin start to quiver and reached out to steady it with his hand.

Tilting her face up to his he continued, "I'm sorry, Mimi. Maybe this isn't the right time to bring up meeting your parents. I just really care about you. I want to be able to meet your dad for the first time, shake his hand, and look him in the eye knowing I didn't do anything to disrespect him. I feel bad enough sneaking around behind their backs, and I'm even lying to Edith. She's asked me more than once if your parents approve of me." He looked away, shaking his head. Then something occurred to him. "Are you crying because he's dead? You got tears in your eyes when you told me he was dead."

"Oh, Elliott, I don't know what's wrong." She swiped her fingers beneath her eyes. "Maybe I feel bad about it in some way. I mean, a guy is dead. Or maybe I feel guilty for helping Leslie behind my parents' backs. I don't know why I'm crying." She sniffled. "We get so little time together, and I don't want to spend it blubbering all over Edith's couch."

She smiled at him then and sat up a little straighter.

"Can we go for that long ride on your bike now?"

He took her hand and gently kissed it.

"Yes. And I'm limiting my kisses to your hand, because if I start kissing you the way I want to, I'll never stop. It's probably not a good idea to be here alone, you know. Unchaperoned."

They both laughed out loud at his use of Edith's antiquated term.

Late that night, Elliott laid on his bed and listened to Judas Priest's "You've Got Another Thing Comin'" blaring through his earphones. He thought about his day with Mimi and how when they weren't on the motorcycle, she had opened up more about her biological father and some of the more recent tidbits she'd learned about him from Leslie.

The journalist had been filling Mimi in on some of the stories she'd been pulling out of Mimi's mother. Apparently, Leslie hadn't told Mimi anything since her accident a few weeks ago, but Elliott hadn't known about that. Today was the first day he'd spent with Mimi in almost a month.

He shook his head as some of those sordid tales sunk in. He'd definitely heard the name Grizz before and tried not to let Mimi see the recognition on his face when she'd first started confiding in him. Her real father was one bad motherfucker. Good thing he was dead.

A combination of his dark thoughts and the loud music were starting to make him antsy. He wanted to scream, shout, put his fist through a wall, raise hell. He wanted to do anything but lie in his bed and do nothing.

He reached for a cell phone on his nightstand and quickly sent a text, smiling at the reply that came back almost immediately.

He then sent another text. This time to Mimi.

Did you talk to them? Can I meet them this week?

Mimi's reply was almost immediate.

No. My mom moved out today.

"Fuck!" he shouted out loud as he threw his phone across the room.

He sat up quickly and pulled his boots on. He left his room and grabbed his helmet off the chair by the front door.

He wouldn't worry about his motorcycle waking up Edith. She slept like the fucking dead.

22

Ginny, 2000, Fort Lauderdale (After Grizz's Execution)

That first time I took Mimi to the shooting range hadn't been perfect, but it was a start. I shuddered when I learned how much Leslie had been sharing with Mimi. Things I'd shared with the reporter only as a way to help provide a truthful foundation for my real experience. They were never going to be in the article, and they certainly shouldn't have been told to my fifteen-year-old daughter. I'd been so stupid.

I surmised from my conversations with Mimi that Leslie had stopped talking to her around the time Grizz beat her up at the prison. This told me Tommy was right. Mimi didn't know Grizz was Tommy's father. We would have plenty of time to get to that.

One thing came as a welcome surprise after that first day together. Mimi started making an effort to spend time with me. It wasn't easy, because I still had to manage my time equally between running our household, church, work, and volunteering. Tommy and the kids were my first priority, and I didn't want the new attention I was getting from Mimi to take away from my two best guys, so I told Tommy after that first week that I was giving my clients notice they needed to find somebody else to do their bookkeeping. It might've seemed like I was jumping the gun, but I was so excited to have Mimi back in my life on a deeper level that I would've done anything to hold onto it.

Tommy had been standing in front of our dresser adjusting his tie. He couldn't get it right. I'd noticed he'd been acting differently since the day I'd taken Mimi to the shooting range, the day he'd met Jo for lunch. I figured it was a combination of worrying about the big reveal we'd be making to Mimi, or maybe he was just sad about Sarah Jo's move. A lot had happened these past months. Grizz's execution, our separation and reconciliation, his childhood friend's announcement that she'd be moving out of the country. I was even concerned that maybe he was still upset at my outburst in the kitchen the morning he told me that Mimi knew about Grizz being her biological father.

Maybe it was all just too much.

I walked up behind him and tiptoed to peek over his shoulder. I could see his reflection in the mirror over our dresser. He was frowning as he undid and redid his tie for the third time. Something was definitely on his mind because Tommy could put on a necktie with his eyes closed.

I guided him around to face me and slowly undid the third mess he'd made.

"What's bothering you?" I looped the tie gently. "You haven't been yourself since that day I talked to Mimi. I figured it can't be her because I've noticed a positive change in her attitude with us. I know it's only been a week, but she seems different somehow. Don't you think so?" I glanced up to meet his eyes and quickly looked back at his necktie. I could feel his eyes on me as I worked.

"Things with her have been better than I thought. She still has some attitude, but—"

"She's a teenager."

He smiled and nodded. "She's a teenager. Which is what I was going to say if you'd let me finish my sentence."

I pulled snugly on the tie and, satisfied with my job, sat down on our bed and looked up at him.

"I think this week with her has been fabulous since we've been trying to set right a secret that she's been keeping inside for almost three years. She seems almost relieved, Tommy. Like she's just been holding her breath and finally let it out."

"I know that feeling. It's how I felt at Grizz's execution."

I wanted to look away from him then but wouldn't let myself. I had to bite the inside of my cheek so I didn't scoff out loud at the thought of the execution that never happened.

"You still don't seem right, though," I said. "Is it because of what we still need to tell her?"

"Yeah, it's that, Gin. But it's other things, too. Like Leslie using our daughter, and then telling her some of the more serious things that you shared with her in the interview." He shook his head. "I still don't know why you ever agreed to give Leslie that stupid interview. You had to know Mimi would've been able to read it. That everybody would be able to read it."

Intense and immediate anger flared. I jumped up from the bed then and stood inches from his face. My fists were tightly clenched at my sides.

He stepped back. I wasn't sure if my anger was because what he was saying was true, or because I was furious with myself for being so gullible. I'd wanted to please Mimi so much that when she told me that she'd eavesdropped on Tommy and me discussing it, I'd let down the carefully constructed walls that had been in place for years. I'd allowed Leslie into that sacred place because I'd felt it would be a connection back to my daughter. Little had I known that Mimi hadn't eavesdropped on my conversation with Tommy. She'd been goaded into persuading me by Leslie.

"You know why I did it! And you also know I went into it never intending to tell Leslie some of the things I ended up telling her. We agreed on anonymity and that certain things would be left out." I paused for effect. "Like the billy-club incident."

I felt a small stab of guilt as I watched Tommy cringe.

"I don't know why I told her more than I should have," I added in a calmer tone. I could feel my anger slowly deflating. I looked at Tommy apologetically. "I guess it was kind of therapeutic. Talking about it."

He nodded slightly, an indication that my unspoken apology had been accepted and that he understood why I'd agreed to give Leslie the interview. We'd had a conversation after my first day at the shooting range with Mimi. I'd told him that evening about my anger toward Leslie and how I'd planned to have a serious discussion with her. Possibly I could even file a complaint with the state press association over her unethical tactics.

Tommy had convinced me to let it go, saying that Leslie was out of our lives now, and while using our daughter was wrong, we didn't need to dredge it up. Enough was enough.

"I'm sorry for bringing it up, Gin," he said now. "I'm the one who told you to let it go, and then I go and bring it up. I guess I'm just feeling—damn, I don't know what I'm feeling. I know you're spending a lot of time with Mimi. I know she's asking you details, and I'm guessing you're not holding a lot back."

He gave me a questioning look. I shrugged.

"She's handling it pretty darn well. I told you I wouldn't tell her the other thing until we could do it together. It's not time yet, and I promise you I won't do it without you," I said. And I meant it.

"It's not that." He took my hand and seated us both on the edge of the bed. "You're going to think I'm being ridiculous, Gin. And I am being ridiculous. I've always been her father. I guess I'm afraid that when she hears how much you loved Grizz, she'll look at me differently. I don't know." He swiped his hand through his hair. "I can't explain it. I'm afraid she won't look at me like she used to. I was her hero up until a few years ago. I was the only man who would lasso the moon for her mother. I wonder if she sees me differently now that she knows I've not always been the only man in her mother's life. That there was somebody before me. And then we're going to add into the mix that she and I have the same father? I don't know if I can do it, Gin. I just don't know."

I saw the pain and emotional devastation on his face. He was at war with his feelings, and here I was so excited to have a connection with Mimi when Tommy's only connection could be shattered when we told her the truth. Did I believe she would be able to handle knowing Tommy was her half-brother? I had to seriously rethink this.

I swallowed hard and turned to him, and took both his hands in mine.

"Tommy, maybe we don't have to tell her. Hearing you say it like that does make me wonder if it'll do more harm than good. Can we agree that we'll wait? We have our Thanksgiving cruise coming up and then Christmas. Let's get to know our daughter again, okay? You had some alone time with her, and now I'm starting to have time with her. How about we start having some together time with her? Would that make you feel any better?"

"I don't know, Ginny. I don't know if I want to see the look on her face when she asks you something about Grizz and you tell her honestly, like we agreed you should. I don't think I can bear to see her as she mourns the father she'll never know. I don't think I can handle it."

This surprised me, and I sat back to look at him.

"What?" He gave me a funny look. "Why are you looking at me like that?"

"You already know I've been answering her questions all week, right?" He nodded, so I continued. "I was thinking it would be a good idea for the three of us to talk about Grizz. I need your help with something."

He raised an inquisitive eyebrow. "What do you need my help with?"

I sighed and answered Tommy honestly.

"I need you to help me convince Mimi not to hate the man that she will only refer to as the evil sperm donor."

23

Tommy, 2000, Fort Lauderdale (After Grizz's Execution)

"So how was last night?" Tommy asked Alec as he walked inside his partner's office. He shut the door behind him and took the chair in front of Alec's desk.

Alec leaned back, his chair giving a small squeak. Ginny's college friend, Casey, was in town for a while, and Ginny had thought the two should meet. The four of them met for dinner the previous night. After, Alec took Casey out for drinks and dancing, and Tommy took Ginny home.

"Well?" Tommy grinned. "You have to tell me something. I'm sure Ginny is grilling Casey, and she'll want to know if you said anything to me. And if I go home and tell my wife you didn't say anything, I'll have to hear it that I should've asked you. So I'm asking you. Did you have a good time?"

Alec smiled awkwardly. "Yeah, I had a good time, Tom. Casey is beautiful and smart, and I really enjoyed her company."

"Really enjoyed her company, huh? Sounds like dullsville."

Alec's smile faded. "I just don't think I'm ready, man. I thought I was, otherwise, I wouldn't have agreed to go. And I'm flattered that Ginny tried to set me up with somebody so gorgeous and successful. I really am. I know Casey has dated NBA players and NASCAR drivers and even some hotshot tech CEO. Honestly, Tom, I think she's looking to settle down. And I just can't go there right now. The separation is still too fresh."

What Alec didn't add, couldn't add, was how the date had ended. He'd walked Casey to her door and bent down to give her a kiss on the cheek. She'd smiled up at him to thank him for a lovely evening, but the words had caught in her throat, and her face grew serious.

"So how do you intend to handle it?" she asked as they'd stood at her front door.

The full moon cast a soft glow over them. They could hear the gentle murmuring of an elderly couple as they took a midnight walk with their dog on the sidewalk in front of Casey's rented townhouse.

"Handle what?"

Her reply caught him off guard. "Handle the fact that you're either already in love with or falling in love with Ginny."

Casey's words had shocked him. She'd invited him in for coffee and politely explained how he probably hadn't realized it, but he'd spent most of their date talking about how lucky Tommy was and what a good mother Ginny was and did Tommy know what he had.

Alec swallowed now, fumbling for the right words to say to Tommy. Casey was right. Alec had slowly been falling for Ginny.

And he realized with a jolt that it had happened long before Paulina had left him. It was all those times they'd spent together with the kids. There were even a few instances when both Paulina and Tommy hadn't been able to make it to some family function, and he'd been alone with Gin and the children. It had never bordered on inappropriate, but his feelings had been there all along, and he couldn't deny them. He remembered the recent lunch date with Ginny and how he'd gone home that night and jerked off in the shower while fantasizing about her. The thought of slowly undressing her and what he'd find under that sexy outfit she'd been wearing that day almost undid him.

But he also knew he wouldn't allow himself to act on it. He respected Tommy too much. He wouldn't do to a friend what had been done to him. It was different, but not really.

He'd made up his mind last night after the conversation with Casey and was at the boys' school first thing this morning to make sure it wouldn't be a problem.

Tommy nodded in understanding. "At least you're honest about not being ready, man. I appreciate that. Casey's not just an easy lay. From what Gin's told me, she's gone into those relationships looking for more than a good time, but it's never worked out for her. You could've led her on and made her think there could've been something more. I'm glad you didn't. Is she expecting to hear from you again?"

"I don't think so. The chemistry just wasn't there. I'm pretty sure we're both on the same page."

"So are the boys getting excited about the cruise?" Tommy asked as he stood. He knew Ginny would be disappointed to hear Alec and Casey hadn't ignited any sparks.

"Yeah, ummm, listen. I need to talk to you about that. Sit back down." He gestured toward the seat Tommy just vacated.

"Sounds serious. What's up?"

"The kids and I are going to pass on the cruise. I appreciate that you and Ginny invited us to be part of your Thanksgiving holiday, but I think we need to save it for another time. I—I need some time away, Tom. I'm thinking of taking the boys for a couple of months and heading up to my grandparents' old cabin in Kentucky. It's in the mountains, away from everything and everyone. No phones, no cell reception, no cable or satellite TV. It'll be good for the kids and me."

"Paulina?"

"Are you asking if I'm leaving because of Paulina, or are you asking if she knows?" Before Tommy could reply, Alec said, "I'm not leaving because of her, and she doesn't know yet, though I can assure you she won't care. I've already talked to the boys' teachers and can get advanced assignments. They won't be penalized and can pick up where they left off when we get back. It's just been a lot, and I guess having time with a beautiful woman last night and not feeling anything is telling me something. I need to regroup and get my life together. Make a plan for my boys and me. Honestly, Tom, I'm not sure if my future is in South Florida."

Tommy hadn't expected this, but he understood. He'd been sincere when he'd suggested to Ginny not too long ago that they sell everything and start fresh somewhere.

"You covered for me when I was going through my shit. I can certainly handle things here for you."

"There won't be much to handle. I've got most of my clients wrapped up. I haven't been taking on anything new, so you'll only have to deal with your clients. And of course, you'll have Phil and Brody." Phil and Brody were junior architects and would easily pick up any slack if needed.

Tommy didn't say anything, and Alec wasn't sure what he was thinking. Then something occurred to Alec, and he quickly added, "Unless you need me here. I've not asked how things are with you and Ginny. I figured the family cruise was a good thing. Am I right?"

Tommy scratched his chin and let out an audible sigh. He let both hands land with a thud on the chair armrest.

"Yeah, the cruise is a good thing. Things are good with Ginny. Better than they've been in a while. I don't know. I just still feel like crap about some things."

Sarah Jo's threat had weighed heavily on him, and when Ginny had recognized something was bothering him, he'd done the lousiest thing he could've done. He'd brought up her interview with Leslie. He'd done it to steer the conversation away from what was really bothering him. Sarah Jo.

This surprised Alec. Even when Tommy and Ginny were separated, he never saw his friend act anything other than upbeat, positive, and always professional. Then again, he'd been going through his own nightmare with Paulina and may not have noticed.

"If you wanna talk, man, feel free to unload. I won't judge. I'll just listen."

Tommy cast a wary eye at his friend. Alec had been a good partner and a good friend. Tommy hated to admit it, but he'd had Axel do an extensive background check on Alec before Tommy accepted him into the firm, eventually promoting him to a full partner. He found they fell into an easy and comfortable relationship and mixed just enough business with pleasure to have a trusting and amicable friendship.

But it had never gone so far that Tommy shared any of his and Ginny's background. He'd trusted Alec with his business. Could he trust him with some personal revelations, as well? It would be nice to get some things off his chest. Not all things. He would never tell Alec about Grizz or the motel. But he could share, without giving any details, the burden he'd been carrying about Sarah Jo.

"Yeah, man. I could use an ear. Maybe even some advice."

Alec looked at his watch and pressed the intercom on his phone. When his assistant responded, he told her, "Please reschedule my one o'clock with Mr. Sanders." He nodded at Tommy.

Tommy took a deep breath. "Have you ever met or heard me or Ginny talk about Sarah Jo before?"

"Yeah. I know her. Husband's a surgeon? I've seen her a couple of times at your get-togethers. I don't think I ever said anything to her other than 'please pass the potato salad.' One of Ginny's friends, right?"

Tommy swallowed thickly and tugged at his collar. Was the room getting hot or was he just getting riled at the mention of her name?

He didn't go into any of the sordid details, purposely leaving Ginny's miscarriage and rape out of the story, but he did tell Alec he'd recently discovered Sarah Jo hadn't exactly been the friend that Ginny and he always thought she was. He never mentioned the threats or what Sarah Jo was capable of, pretending he only needed advice on how much one should share with their spouse when it would only hurt them.

"You said that all of the shit happened years ago, when you were younger? Do you think she's grown past it, or does she still pull crap?" Alec asked.

"I don't think she's done anything bad in years, but I don't have a way to know that for sure." Tommy let out a sigh. "I just don't think I can stand to be in the same room with her knowing what she was capable of."

Alec shrugged. "If it wasn't life or death stuff, I'd say she outgrew it, but the decision to stay friends or not should be left up to your wife. I would tell her."

Tommy had no intention of telling Ginny about Sarah Jo's deceitfulness. He just needed to talk, and spilling some frustrations to Alec had helped. He was certain Alec would've been appalled to hear the brutal truth of what Sarah Jo was capable of—and their threats to each other.

He thanked Alec and quickly changed the subject to a recent client who'd threatened to fire them and take her business to a rival firm.

Alec leaned back in his chair and placed his hands behind his head. He stared at the ceiling without saying anything for a minute. This particular client had been stringing them along for months. He thought they should cut their losses and say goodbye. She'd been a thorn in their side and they could take the financial hit. But the thought of her trying to blackmail them into more work at no expense to her snooty self didn't sit well with Alec.

"Call her bluff, Tom. Call her fucking bluff."

TOMMY TURNED UP THE RADIO IN HIS CAR AS HE SAT IN BUMPER-TO-bumper traffic on I-95. "If I'd Been The One" by 38 Special reminded him of a smaller, simpler South Florida.

He was getting tired of the traffic, the crowds, and seeing all the places that used to be home to palm trees replaced with concrete. He was serious when he'd told Ginny a few months ago that they should sell everything and start over fresh somewhere. Maybe she would still consider it.

Mimi would be bringing home a boy tonight. A boy she'd secretly been seeing behind their backs for months before Grizz's execution.

He couldn't blame his daughter for the secrecy, and he was grateful that she'd confided about the guy to Gin. He'd almost gone through the roof when Ginny told him the boy, Elliott, had turned eighteen this year. But, when Ginny explained that Elliott had wanted to meet them and it was Mimi who'd avoided it, he calmed down a bit.

"We have to give him a chance, Tommy. He's trying to do right by her. Can you imagine how nervous he must be?"

So they would be meeting Elliott for the first time tonight, and Ginny had told him Mimi didn't know who she was more worried about: her father intimidating Elliott or ten-year-old Jason embarrassing her to death. Tommy knew he wouldn't do anything to make his daughter or Elliott feel uncomfortable, but he sure as heck couldn't vouch for what Jason might do. She was probably right. Jason would embarrass her.

For Tommy's part, he would be nice. Polite but firm. If—and it was a big if—he approved of this young man, there would be strict rules until his daughter turned eighteen. He'd let Ginny and Grizz down once by not being on top of Mimi's activities. It wouldn't happen again.

TOMMY WAS GETTING READY FOR WORK THE NEXT MORNING AS HE LET himself think about the night before. The dinner had passed without incident. That is, if you could forget about Jason's awkwardly timed questions about whether or not Mimi and Elliott made out, Tommy would say it was downright successful.

He had to admit he didn't like the ink and he didn't like the bike, but he had to give the kid credit for not trying to hide it. Elliott was up front about not always being on his best behavior. He talked about his grandmother, Edith. He talked about school and work, and these were all things that could easily be verified. And they would be, as soon as Tommy had a few minutes to talk to Axel. He wasn't going to feel guilty or apologize for asking Axel to do a background check on Elliott.

He found himself hoping Elliott was being truthful. He didn't want to find out the boy had been dishonest about anything. Tommy thought Elliott looked like he could've been older than eighteen, but he knew Axel would find out for sure.

He'd just finished combing his hair and spraying on some cologne. He wouldn't let himself think about how he'd handle it if something did come to light that he didn't care for. It was troublesome enough for him and Ginny to deal with Mimi falling for a boy three years older than her.

He bounded down the stairs and could hear his family's light-hearted banter at the breakfast table. The smell of freshly brewed coffee and something cooking caused his stomach to rumble.

He walked into the kitchen and headed straight for the coffee pot, planting a kiss on Ginny's cheek as she stood at the stove and flipped pancakes. He chanced a peek at Mimi's face. She was smiling at something Jason had said to her. He paused for a second before the reality of what he was seeing sunk in. He hadn't seen this look on Mimi's face in a while. She was happy. She was teasing with her brother.

He sent up a silent prayer. *God, please let this boy be who he says he is.*

"Maybe Mom has another pink one you can use," Mimi teased her brother. "Maybe you can even take it on the cruise with us next week."

"No!" Jason yelled at his sister. "Pink is for girls! Mom, you have a blue one, don't you?"

Tommy had his back to the table as he poured his coffee. He started to turn but stopped when he heard Ginny's reply.

"I'm sure I have a spare toothbrush that isn't pink, Jason. Dr. McDonough always gives us freebies when we get our cleanings."

Tommy carried his mug to the table and sat down, asking casually, "What's all this about pink and blue toothbrushes?"

Mimi looked at her father and said, "Jason dropped his toothbrush in the toilet last night. Again. Last time he did it, Mom had to give him the only spare one she had, and it was pink. He got so mad at her that he threw it away after he used it."

"I did not throw it away!" Jason stated emphatically. "I didn't,

Mom, I swear. It was gone when I got home from school." He picked up his orange juice and shot a glare at his sister, whining, "I don't know why you had to bring something up from over a year ago, Mimi."

Ginny loaded pancakes on the plate in the middle of the table and cast an amused eye at her son.

"I don't know where it went," Ginny told Jason, "but I remember getting you a new one that same day, and I never did find the pink one I gave you." She smiled at Tommy and her smile faded as she noticed his expression.

"Tommy? Are you okay, babe? You look like you've seen a ghost."

He caught himself and smiled. "Coffee went down funny. Feel like I have some heartburn coming on. I just need to eat."

"As you can see, there's plenty," she said. "Mimi, you'll miss your bus, and I don't have time to drive you. Jason, keep eating or you'll miss yours, too. You still need to brush your teeth."

"But, Mom..." Jason started to whine.

"I have a spare toothbrush, and I'm pretty sure it's blue. Now eat!"

Tommy wasn't sure how to ask without it sounding too awkward, so he blurted out the first thing that came to mind.

"So I guess Mom needs to save the pink ones for Mimi, right? Like Jason said, pink is for girls." He looked at his plate as he cut his pancakes.

"That's what I think, too, Dad, but Mimi always calls first dibs on the colors when we go to the dentist and we get our new toothbrushes."

Mimi had already stood and pushed her chair in with her hip.

"Pink? Are you serious, Dad? I haven't had a pink anything since I was ten years old." She turned to her mother. "I like using the dining room chairs in here, Mom. They're easier on the butt."

She walked over to the bench by the back door and picked up her backpack and teasingly addressed her little brother.

"And what do you care anyway, Jason? I always pick green because I know you like blue. I cannot believe we're even having this conversation."

She rolled her eyes and walked out of the kitchen, but not before Ginny caught a hint of a smile. Her Mimi was back.

24

Grizz, 1990, Prison, North Florida

"Are you going to just stare at me, or are you going to stand up and at least give me a hug?"

By now, Grizz had sat up on his bed and just stared at the extremely thin brunette.

"Didn't recognize you, Chicky. You don't look like yourself." He stood, and after a long hug, he stepped back and held her at arm's length, giving her a once-over. "You've changed your look since the trial."

With a half smirk plastered on her face she looked him up and down. "So did you."

He instantly ran his hand over his shaved head and grabbed at his beard.

"I was going to suggest you let me trim up that rat's nest you have hanging from your chin, but I guess you probably don't get to play with scissors in here."

She paused then and looked around the cell. There was the standard toilet and sink, but that was all that was standard. The sink had a mirror over it, and she noticed razors on a small shelf. The bed was not prison issue. It was a twin-sized bed, but the mattress was thick. An overstuffed chair sat in the corner with a reading light behind it. A small shelf held a microwave. A microwave? And she wasn't sure, but she could've sworn she smelled blood.

"Looks like you have everything you could need in here. Why am I not shocked?" She shook her head as she smiled and looked down. She was standing on a braided rug. "I'm surprised you don't have the fancy chess set Kit bought you all those years ago. I guess she still has it."

"It's in an office I have use of."

"Of course, it is." She laughed.

He gave her a wide smile then. "Have a game going on with one of the guards. I win, I get even more privileges. He wins, I make sure he gets something for it."

"Looks like you've been winning a lot," she said as she took another glance around the cell. "And besides, since when do you have to win a chess game to get what you want?"

"I don't. But the games keep it interesting."

He motioned her to the only chair and sat on the end of the bed to face her. The cell was small, and their knees almost touched.

"Tell me what you've been up to? How has life been treating you since the trial?"

Chicky then told him in great detail about the last few years. How she'd tried to make a go of it with Fess, but it hadn't worked out. She'd found herself heading a little north and settling in a small town in South Carolina. She'd met an older man who owned his own bar.

"My topless days were over, but I'd picked up just enough on how to make a bar successful." She paused then and motioned to her chest, giggled. "Without the titties. Anyway, Ed's an old geezer, but he's my old geezer, and I love him. We just got married. I have to give him credit, you know, marrying me without really knowing how much time I have left."

The realization of what she was telling him slowly dawned, and she answered his unspoken question.

"Cancer. It's still early, and the doctors have told me I can fight it with treatment, but not to get too hopeful. Lost all my hair and decided I'd give life a shot as a brunette. What do you think?" She motioned to her brown hair, which Grizz suddenly realized was a wig.

Grizz wasn't one to get emotional, but something about seeing Chicky not looking like herself caused a lump to form in his throat. That, along with hearing Kit had given birth to a son that should've been his, combined to jolt him. He stood quickly and turned his back to her. His voice came out raspy when he finally answered her question.

"Beautiful. You've always been beautiful, Chicky."

"I wish all that emotion I can hear in your voice was for me, but I know it's not." Her voice was quiet.

He turned back quickly to her then, and she stood and took both of his hands in her own.

"I heard," she said. "I still keep in touch with some people, you know? I heard yesterday that she was in labor, and I took the first flight down to see you. I'm sorry I hadn't done it before, but something in my gut told me you might need a friend."

He didn't know what to say so he didn't say anything. With her hands still clasping his own tightly, he sat back down on his bed and closed his eyes. Chicky took her seat and waited until he made eye contact with her.

"I ain't never seen a man that loves a woman the way you love her. Ever. Why didn't you just take life without parole, Grizz? She would've accepted that, you know. She would've brought that baby girl here to see her daddy, and don't tell me with all of your clout that you couldn't have had as many conjugal visits as you wanted. She could've still been yours."

He could never tell Chicky the real reason he didn't accept life without parole. He was counting on the death penalty as a bargaining chip. But it wasn't working.

"This isn't the kind of life I want for her or my daughter," he told her gruffly, pulling his hands away.

He stood and walked to the sink. He turned it on and started to splash cold water on his face.

"And I know what you were doing before I walked in here," she said. "I know you have a prostitution ring and can have access to as many women as you want. That's probably why the guard let me in here. But something tells me you don't. You're still in love with her. You're still loyal to her."

He ignored her last comment and reached for a towel.

"And you pushed for the death penalty because you're too fucking prideful to rot in a prison cell for the rest of your life. You always were an egotistical ass, Grizz."

He was drying his face when he stopped and turned around to look at her.

"Yeah, I guess I am," he answered with a grin.

She didn't know if he was answering the charge that he was still in love with and loyal to Kit or acknowledging that he was an ass. Either way, Chicky's comment had sliced through the tension, and they both laughed as they realized that she would've never spoken to him like that in years past. But it was okay now, and she was right—about all of it. Chicky was his friend. And he needed a friend.

"I bet she's a great mother," Grizz said quietly.

"Oh, honey, I'm sure she is the best mother. If you can take one thing off your worry plate, if you even have a worry plate, I'm sure it can be any doubt about Kit's love and devotion as a momma."

He nodded and smiled. Neither would say what they both were thinking. That Grunt would be an excellent father, as well. Grunt had run as far away as he could from that life, ensuring his education at a young age. If Grizz had done anything right in his life, it was rescuing his son from the misery he'd been living in with Candy's sister, Karen. If he wasn't so fucked up in the head over Kit and Grunt having a baby together, he might even have let himself be proud of his son.

Sensing the conversation might go somewhere neither one of them wanted, she added, "You remember how sick she was that first time she got pregnant? Poor thing couldn't keep water down and wouldn't let you take her to the doctor for medicine. That alone told me how dedicated she was." Chicky smiled warmly at him.

He returned her smile. "Yeah, she was so fucking sick with that baby. But you're right, she wouldn't even go to the doctor. Said she wasn't going to put drugs in her body because it might hurt the baby."

"She wouldn't even use the herbs Grunt gave her," Chicky said. "And they were all natural. She just needed to add them to her tea and they were supposed to help."

"I don't remember Grunt giving her any herbs."

"She probably never told you about them because she never took them. Grunt told me he'd gotten them from Sarah Jo. Her college roommate had made a little concoction that was supposed to help Kit keep some food in her stomach. Anyway, it didn't matter. I caught Kit throwing them away, and she begged me not to tell Grunt. She didn't want to hurt his feelings."

"Yeah, that sounds like Kit." The memories of the Kit he'd been so in love with, was still in love with, warmed his heart, and he realized he was grateful Chicky had come to see him. Maybe she would be able to visit him in the future. Or maybe not.

"Chicky, are you getting the right kind of medical help? You have everything you need?"

"We have good insurance, Grizz. I can't think of anything they won't pay for. I've been told about some experimental drugs that are being used in trials, but those are out of the country. That would definitely be something not in our budget. But I'm okay. I'm confident I'm getting the best care I can."

"If you had the money, would you go for the trials?"

"Of course, I would. I've been told I'm going to die from this cancer, and the chemo and radiation can only help for so long. It's inevitable. So yeah, I'd go for the trials. What's the worst that could happen? It's gonna kill me?" She laughed then and waved her hand in the air in typical Chicky fashion. "We all gotta die some time." She flinched at her words. "I'm sorry, Grizz. I didn't mean that like it sounded."

"It's fine, Chicky. I didn't take it that way. Before you leave today, write down all your banking information for me. Okay?"

She cocked her head and smiled, giving him a nod. He then made another request that surprised her.

"And if you ever have some free time and aren't feeling too bad, do you think you can keep coming to see me? You know, just to talk?"

Before she could answer him, he quickly added, "I'll pay all your travel expenses, of course."

"Awww, Grizz, honey. I'd be glad to come back and see you. Now, will you do something for me?"

He nodded slightly.

"Tell me why this prison cell of yours smells like blood."

25

Tommy, 2000, Fort Lauderdale (After Grizz's Execution)

Tommy sat in the office of Axel's auto repair shop and watched through the big glass window as the mechanics worked on high-end cars and motorcycles.

Axel had a thriving and legitimate business and, from the looks of it, an extremely successful one. Tommy had called Axel to ask for a favor the day after Mimi brought Elliott home for dinner.

Just then, the door opened from behind him, and Axel came in. Tommy stood and went to shake his hand, but Axel pulled him in for a hug.

"Grunt—errr, Tommy! Man, you look fantastic. How have you and Gin been?"

"We've been good, Axel. The usual. Work, kids. Life in general."

Axel nodded as they both took a seat. "I was wondering how things have been since, you know, this summer?"

Tommy knew Axel was referring to Grizz's execution.

"It's all good, Axel. We're good. I'm glad it's over," Tommy said honestly. Of course, he wouldn't tell him about the problems he and Ginny had after the execution, not to mention the ongoing drama with Sarah Jo.

Axel didn't know what to say so he didn't say anything. He'd known Grizz since they were children, and in spite of Grizz's ruthlessness, Axel actually missed his friend.

"Hey, before I forget," Axel said, breaking the spell, "I got a quick and lucrative deal on the cars and bikes." He reached into a drawer, pulled out a check, and handed it to Tommy. "I had it made out to Ginny. Can you give her this check?"

"That was fast." Tommy pocketed the check. "Thanks for handling it, man. I wouldn't have a clue what those cars and bikes were worth, but I bet you got a pretty penny for the seventy-five Harley."

"I didn't sell a seventy-five," Axel said as he picked up another envelope and started to pull its contents out.

"So it's still there? You didn't sell Grizz's favorite bike?"

"I don't know what you mean, Tom. Ginny told me to sell the bikes and cars in the garage. My guys picked up a Trans Am, a Corvette, and two Harleys, an eighty-one and an eighty-five." Axel handed him the contents of the envelope. "And here—the other thing. I didn't have a lot of time because you wanted this back so quickly."

"Yeah. We leave for our cruise tomorrow, and I would've gone nuts wondering if there's anything I needed to know about this kid. And I really appreciate you doing this. I know it's not your thing anymore."

Axel raised an eyebrow. "The Ax Man still has the right connections."

Tommy smiled. Just then someone outside in the shop caught Tommy's eye. Axel noticed and followed the direction of Tommy's gaze.

"Looks like the spitting image of his father, doesn't he?" Axel said.

"Damn, yeah. If I didn't know better, I'd think I was looking at Anthony Bear. That's not Slade, is it?"

"No, Slade favors his mother, but Christian looks exactly like Anthony at that age except for his eyes," Axel said. "He's just as mean, too. I would know. I knew Anthony as a kid." Axel shrugged. "I've given Christian a job. He's been in and out of trouble. His parents even let him do a stint in juvie hoping it would straighten his ass out, but it didn't help. Anthony tried putting him on one of his landscaping crews, but the kid has no interest in lawns, so Anthony asked me for a favor and I said I'd do what I could. I have to give the kid credit. He knows his way around an engine, and it's keeping him busy. Hopefully, it'll keep him out of trouble. Seems to be working."

Tommy hadn't seen Anthony and Christy's family in years. He was never comfortable around them because Anthony had been Grizz's friend. But Ginny had formed a friendship with Christy and wasn't giving that up because Grizz went to prison. Tommy knew the women had gotten together with the children many times over the past years. Since Anthony and Christy had moved over here from the west coast of Florida, Ginny and Christy frequently met for lunch, and he knew Christy had been invited on an occasional girl's night out, but he was pretty certain the kids hadn't crossed paths in some time.

Good thing. He couldn't imagine Mimi bringing home a Christian Bear. It had been a while, but he thought he remembered Ginny telling him how Christy had told her Christian used to have a small crush on Mimi. Tommy dismissed the recollection and was reminded as to why he was there to see Axel.

"So, this kid, Elliott. What did you find out?"

"According to what you're holding, he checks out." Axel swiveled in his chair and picked up a soda can from his desk. He took a big swig and watched as Tommy read the report.

"So he really did just turn eighteen this past summer," Tommy said more to himself than Axel. "I thought he looked older."

"I agree. But he is who he says he is. He graduated high school in June and lives with his maternal grandmother, Edith Wainright. He's named after his grandfather, Elliott Wainright, but as far as I can tell, his grandmother is the only one who calls him Elliott. He's mostly known to his friends by his middle name. He was raised by a single mother who remarried the kid's father. When she left to be with him, Elliott moved in with his grandmother to finish school. The mom is a bank teller, and the dad works in a car factory in Michigan."

"Why would he introduce himself to Mimi as Elliott if his friends call him something different?"

"I don't know. You told me the kid admitted to coming close to being in trouble. Maybe he wants a fresh start with Mimi. I can't tell you for certain, but if you're worried about aliases and gang affiliations, I couldn't find any. Like I said, I can dig more, but you haven't given me a lot of time."

Tommy read over the papers as Axel talked.

"I didn't have the time to put the kind of detail on him I normally would. I can confirm some of the shit he's already told you. He is taking classes at the community college and works at the hardware store. I had him followed twice. One time he took his grandmother to church, then out to lunch. The next time he met with some friends in the parking lot of a fast food restaurant. Looked like they were just hanging. No drugs that my guy could see, but they were all having a beer. They weren't crazy drunk, and they weren't causing trouble. Just to be sure, my guy got a couple of license plates. I ran them, and looks like he's still friends with the kids that were trouble, but he didn't leave with them or anything. He just went home. That's as far as I got. I can do some more digging if you want."

"What kind of trouble were his friends in?"

"Punk shit. Some vandalism, petty theft, joyriding."

"Are they his age and are they staying straight, like him?"

"They're all younger than him. Two are still in high school, and one should be, but he dropped out. Nothing on the record for any of them since January, almost a year ago. I don't know. Maybe he's their leader, and he's setting a good example, and they're following suit. I still think they're punks, but maybe we could ask Christian. He's been around the streets, and he hears shit. Let's run these names by him, see if he recognizes anyone."

Before Tommy could stop Axel from dragging Christian into his business, Axel stood and opened the office door. He jumped back with a start causing Tommy to look up.

"Fuck, Christian, you scared the shit out of me. I was just coming to get you," Axel said.

"I was just coming to tell you Mrs. Fuckface wants to talk to you," Christian said.

Axel rolled his eyes and stepped aside, motioning for Christian to come into the office. He shut the door behind him.

"You can't refer to one of our regulars as Mrs. Fuckface. As a matter of fact, you can't be calling any of our client's names, Christian. Are you trying to get fired?"

Christian rolled his eyes.

"And I told you to keep your hair in a ponytail or something. You should know how dangerous it is to have your hair around the engines."

Tommy cleared his throat, and Axel remembered the reason he'd wanted to talk to Christian.

"Listen, Christian, I know it's a big city, but I also know that for someone your age, you've been around," Axel said.

"Yeah, so what?"

"I'm going to say four names. I just want to know if you know them or know anything about them. Okay?"

"Why?"

151

"It's none of your fucking business why."

He then proceeded to say the four names, slowly. First, middle, and last names. One guy even had a nickname Axel made sure to mention.

Christian shook his head. "Never heard of any of 'em. Anything else?"

"No. That's it. Thanks. And tell Mrs. Fu...Mrs. Marquart I'll be out in a minute."

Christian looked at Tommy then. "How's Mimi? Haven't seen her in a long time."

Tommy was caught off-guard. He hadn't seen Christian in years and was a little surprised the boy remembered and recognized him.

"Mimi's doing really good," Tommy said. "You know girls. She's got herself a serious boyfriend and thinks he's 'the one.'"

Christian nodded and, without saying anything, left the office and shut the door behind him.

Tommy looked at Axel and shrugged. "What? I remember Gin telling me he had a crush on Mimi when they were kids. You think I'm opening the door for him to show up one day? No fucking way."

Axel started laughing then and stood. "It was nice to see you again, Tommy. Let me know if I can do anything else for you."

They said their goodbyes, and Tommy followed Axel out as Axel went to look for the upset customer.

Tommy was relieved. Elliott had been truthful. Tommy would be taking his family on their cruise tomorrow, and he wouldn't have the burden of not knowing if Elliott was who he said he was. Of course, now Tommy would have to handle the thought of Mimi dating an eighteen-year-old, but at least now Tommy knew who he was dealing with. A kid who'd almost found himself on the wrong side of the law but came to his senses just in time.

Christian watched out of the corner of his eye as Mimi's father left Axel's office. He'd noticed him walk in earlier, and he'd purposely pissed off Mrs. Marquart so she'd insist on speaking with Axel. He'd wanted an excuse to ask about Mimi.

He hadn't spoken to Mimi in years, but he still had deep and unresolved feelings for her. He couldn't understand why. They were so young the last time he'd seen her, and he'd been with plenty of girls since then. But there was always one face that kept coming back to haunt him. Mimi's.

He never sought her out or suggested to his mother that they do something as a family. As a matter of fact, he was so disturbed by his fascination with her that he ran as far away from it as he could.

Then, at the beginning of this year, he'd seen her from afar. She was at the mall and had been sitting on a bench talking to a woman. He'd stopped in his tracks and ducked into a store. He watched her from the store window as he remembered how they'd played as children and when they'd gotten a little older, just old enough to be aware that they were the opposite sex, how those play dates had turned a little awkward and shy. Then, the family get-togethers just stopped, but he never stopped thinking about her.

He was getting ready to walk into Axel's office and interrupt whatever they were talking about when he heard Mimi's name. Most of the conversation was muffled, but he was sure he heard them mention Mimi. He stopped to see if he could hear more. He then heard his own name and had his hand on the knob to turn it when Axel swung the door open.

He'd gone inside and listened as Axel recited the four names. He'd politely inquired about Mimi. He'd noticed the concern in her father's eyes, and he'd feigned indifference as he walked out.

But he wasn't feeling indifference now. He was pissed. He was angry. He wanted to beat on something or someone.

He wouldn't let his temper get the best of him. He would have to play along to figure out what the fuck was going on. He wanted to know which of the guys Axel named was dating Mimi.

And more specifically, he wanted to know why that piece of shit gang-wannabe Nick Rosman was calling himself Elliott.

26

Ginny, 2000, Fort Lauderdale (After Grizz's Execution)

The Thanksgiving cruise couldn't have been more perfect. There was some disappointment for Jason because Alec and his boys had backed out, but he quickly made friends and enjoyed himself immensely. Between the nonstop activity and all the food, my normally rambunctious and energetic son collapsed into his small bed every night and fell into a quick and heavy sleep. As a matter of fact, we all did.

The days were full, and as much as I'd wanted to make love with Tommy in the privacy of our cabin, we both found ourselves worn out by the day's activities, and we succumbed to sleep as quickly as our children did. That was okay. *We have the rest of our lives to make love,* I'd told myself.

"I really wish Casey and Alec had connected," I'd told Tommy as I slipped into my bathing suit.

"Alec told me they just didn't have chemistry, and maybe it was a little too soon to be dating. I think what happened with Paulina may have screwed with him more than he's willing to admit." Tommy had already pulled on his bathing suit and was slathering his arms with sunscreen.

"I know. She told me the same thing." I grabbed the lotion out of

Tommy's hand and indicated for him to turn around. I squirted some on his back.

"Ahhh, Ginny, it's cold. Warm it up in your hands first!"

A pounding at our door interrupted us, and I went to answer it as Tommy put on a tank top.

"We're ready! Are you guys ready?" Jason asked with his toothy grin. Mimi stood behind her brother and smiled.

Now, I was lying on the isolated beach with Mimi, leaning back on my elbows and watching as Jason and Tommy snorkeled. We'd taken a small boat to the island and walked quite a distance until we'd found a spot we could call our own.

"I can't believe Dad would think I'd stop loving him when I found out," Mimi said.

Tommy and I had more than one conversation with Mimi since that day in my bedroom when Tommy told me he was concerned about Mimi having feelings for Grizz. I'd told him the truth that day when I'd said I needed him to help me convince her not to hate Grizz. I hadn't realized how powerful the word hate was until I saw it in my own daughter's eyes. Saw it as we talked about the man who'd given her life.

I had been wrestling with what I thought was my hatred of Grizz since I'd learned he was still alive. I'd come to realize, through my discussions with Mimi, that it wasn't hate I was feeling. It was hurt and confusion. I was totally baffled by his rejection of me.

But I also couldn't deny my love for him. I had been totally and completely in love with Grizz, and I'd realized it was important to me that the child who'd been conceived in that love knew it. She had to know how much she was wanted and loved by both of us.

It wasn't easy to convince her. She held onto her dislike of him like an iron fist welded to a steel pole. The fact that I was being truthful about him and our past didn't help. Grizz had done some horrible things. But I made sure she knew how he treated me. How it was his idea for Tommy to marry me so I wouldn't be alone. That Grizz was the one who'd insisted Tommy raise the child he couldn't because he knew Tommy loved me and would love my child as his own.

"I guess it's important to me to know you really love Dad," Mimi said to me as she motioned toward the man out snorkeling in the crystal clear waters. "I don't like the thought that he was stuck with us because Grizz commanded it."

It had taken some convincing, but I finally was able to persuade her to stop referring to him as the evil sperm donor. I also cautioned her on how it wouldn't be a good idea to use his name in public. I didn't have any specific concern, just that the name Grizz might still be recognized in South Florida.

"I can promise you that your father and I are completely and totally in love, Mimi. I told you the truth when I said I wasn't totally on board with marrying him at first. I was numb and still very much in love with Grizz, but I did fall in love with your father. I'm still in love with him."

"Tell me another good story about Grizz. Tell me something you never told anybody."

"Your dad knows this story," I said as I proceeded to tell her about my moonlight dates with Grizz and, in particular, the one at the zoo. I told her about the stuffed gorilla I'd thrown away and the diamond earrings I'd be giving her.

"He sounded like he was romantic," she said, making a face. "A murderer with a romantic side. Sounds like it would make a great book."

I shot her a glance and could see she was teasing me. I laughed and nodded. It was a start.

I thought the conversation was over when she said something that surprised me.

"I know you don't want me to hate him, Mom. I guess I don't. I mean, how can I hate someone I never knew? Never will know. I almost wish I'd told you and Dad I knew when I found out. I'd tried to hint at it that time you sat me down when they found that lady's bones. You and Dad told me a little bit about your past, and I told you it was the coolest thing I'd ever heard. I guess that was my way of hoping you'd tell me more."

She looked at me with expectant eyes.

"I'm sorry your father and I didn't take the hint. It just didn't seem like the right time, Mimi," I answered honestly.

She nodded. "Now that I'm talking to you about it and not getting horrible secondhand stories from Leslie, it's made me more curious. Is it wrong of me to regret that I never got to meet him?"

How could I even begin to answer this question? We'd kept her away from the truth because of all the awful things Grizz had done. I was now lying on the beach trying to convince my daughter she shouldn't hate the man who was her biological father, and now that she was telling me she wished she could've met him, I was back paddling in my thoughts.

I answered her with the truth. "I don't know, Mimi. I honestly don't know if meeting him would've been good for either of you."

Even though I was wearing sunglasses, I put my hand to my brow to gauge her reaction. The sun was brilliant, and I wanted to see the expression on her face.

She sat up a little and leaned on one elbow, facing me. A gentle breeze carried her scent past me. I could smell coconut sunscreen and something fruity. I sat up, too, cross-legged.

"I looked him up once, you know?"

"No, I didn't know that."

"There's not a lot about him, Mom. There wasn't even anything on the news or in the newspapers when he died. I find that a little hard to believe, don't you?"

The question caught me off-guard as I realized she was right. There had been no major announcements about Grizz's execution. I remembered Jason's friend, Corbin, had told him Tommy and I went away that weekend to see some guy get fried. Tommy and I had skirted around that with Jason. We knew Moe's remains being found in 1999 had gotten a little press, and apparently some nosy longtime locals, including Corbin's parents, had exercised their memory banks and put some pieces together. I'd recently sought out Corbin's mother after his comment to Jason about Grizz's execution, and politely asked her to keep her thoughts to herself. Surprisingly, she apologized. I'd wondered if she'd remembered just enough about Grizz to frighten her.

"No. I don't find it hard to believe, Mimi. People die on death row all the time. How many have you heard about?"

"None. But he sounded like a big deal. I guess I thought it might've gotten some notice."

"I can see why you would think that." I made little swirls in the sand with my fingers. She had a point. "Maybe there's another reason. He was a powerful man. Even from behind bars. I guess he paid people off. He was quite wealthy, you know. You should probably know you're quite wealthy."

"I already know I own Aunt Carter and Uncle Bill's house," she told me sheepishly. "I saw the deed in your safe."

I sighed. "You own more than their house." Why did I just say that? How smart was it to let a fifteen-year-old know how rich she was? I was mentally kicking myself for bringing up Grizz's wealth, but Mimi passed right over the subject.

"I think it's why Leslie came to me, Mom." She faced me, tanned legs curled beneath her.

"What is why Leslie came to you?"

"The fact that there wasn't anything about him anywhere. She couldn't get any background on him, and I knew she was right because I tried and I only found one article."

"What do you mean?" This was curious.

"There is very little information on him. Very little. I found a mug shot once on the Internet. When I went back to look it up again, it was gone. I even tried the old microfiche machines at the libraries, and they not only didn't have anything on him, but entire years were missing. I guess they didn't keep up with them as well as they should have."

"You said you found one article. Where did you find it?" She had my attention now.

"When my class went to Disney World in Orlando, we had to spend one day doing something educational, so I suggested we go to their county library. I found an article about him on their microfiche from 1985. It was just one article, and it had a picture of him. I told Leslie about it, and she had them copy it and send it to her."

"What did you read?" *Did I want to know?*

"Just that he'd been arrested for kidnapping but would face other charges. Your name wasn't mentioned or anything, Mom. It must've been when he was first arrested. There was even a picture of him that didn't look anything like the mug shot. He looked kind of like a hippie."

I smiled and looked down. If there was one thing Grizz was not, it was a hippie. She had probably seen an earlier picture of him with his long hair.

I looked up and started to say something when I noticed a single tear running down her cheek. Her bottom lip was quivering.

"Mimi?"

"I'm so sorry, Mom." She reached for me. I pulled her toward me as she scooted closer. "I'm so sorry for tricking you both into that interview with Leslie."

I patted her back and tried to reassure her. "It's okay, Mimi. It's really okay."

"No, it's not! Don't pretend like what I did was okay."

She pulled back from me and wiped her eyes, hiccupping.

"Everything you've been telling me these past weeks was about how much he loved you and how much he tried to protect you. I ruined it. I know Leslie's article never got printed, but you and him and Dad were willing to risk exposure because of me. It's true, Mom. I used his love for you to make him think I was you on the phone, and I guilted him into giving Leslie that interview."

"Mimi—"

"And I made you think I wanted to bond with you over you coming clean about your past by talking to Leslie. I'd known the truth about some of it. I'd read that article in Orlando. I'd looked up his mug shot that time. Plus, based on what you and Dad told me when that lady's skeleton was found last year, I knew you had a past you were ashamed of, and I wanted to hurt you for not telling me who my real father was. For keeping secrets."

She started sobbing heavily, and I began rocking her back and forth, trying to soothe her.

"Mimi, I'm a grown woman. I knew what I was doing when I gave Leslie those interviews. Maybe subconsciously I wanted to get it all out. I can't be sure. I do know I wasn't worried about being exposed. That article was going to be truthful about certain events, but ambiguous on facts like names, dates, cities. And it was for a major publication. Not a little hometown story that people might've remembered. It could've been about any prisoner on death row in any state during any given year. It wasn't tied directly to Grizz."

"But people could've started digging, Mom. If someone did their homework, they could link it back to you. That's what I was hoping would happen. Somebody would come knocking on your door and show the world you weren't perfect. I wanted to hurt you and Dad for keeping a secret from me. I'm—I'm so sorry."

"I guess you're right, sweetie. Somebody could've figured it out"—like Corbin's parents—"and shown up. But they haven't." I took her face in my hands. "Let us just be grateful the article didn't get printed and we don't have to worry about that now. Besides, you told me yourself how hard it was to find details about him. Right?"

Mimi nodded and said, "There's more."

I tilted my head.

"I told Elliott some of it. I just needed to confide in somebody. He knows my biological father died on death row this summer. But he won't tell, Mom. I know he'd never tell."

"Well, if he's as special as you say he is, and I think he might be," I winked at her, "then I'm sure he'd be willing to keep this secret for you."

"Oh, he would, Mom. He's so good to me and wonderful and kind and understanding."

She was bouncing now, and I realized her burden had just become lighter. So had mine.

We reapplied our sunscreen and lay back down. The sound of Tommy and Jason splashing in the distance brought a contentment that matched the warm breeze as it danced along my skin. I could hear seagulls and was enjoying the sounds and smells of our little hideaway when I sensed movement to my left.

I peeked at Mimi and noticed she was back up on her elbow, facing me. I started to ask her if there was something else she wanted to talk about, but she beat me to it.

"So, Mom." She grinned. "How old were you when you first had sex, and what was it like?"

27

Mimi, 2000, Fort Lauderdale (After Grizz's Execution)

"Why do I think I missed you more than you missed me?" Elliott asked Mimi, smiling over at her as they made their way toward Ft. Lauderdale beach.

"Are you serious?" Mimi squeezed his arm. "The cruise was really nice and we stayed busy, but sometimes it just dragged. Seven days felt like seven years! I couldn't wait to get home and see you, and it felt so good to have you come to my house to pick me up. My dad freaked over this truck." She smoothed her hand over the old but pristine seat, then scooted closer to Elliott. He pulled her close, planting a kiss on her temple.

"I wanted to take you someplace nice for dinner, and I didn't want to do it on my bike. You sure you don't mind if we pop in to check on Edith first?"

"Of course not. I love your grandmother. But aren't we heading in the wrong direction?" Mimi glanced out the window as they made their way east on Commercial Boulevard.

"Edith has a timeshare she uses every year between Thanksgiving and Christmas. It's her little getaway with her friends. They sit on the beach all day and play shuffleboard or cards or whatever it is grandmothers do." He laughed. "I promise we won't stay long. She forgot some of her medicine. We'll just do a quick drop-off and leave, okay?"

"Sure! So you're staying at your house all by yourself?"

Elliott eyed her knowingly and gulped. "Yeah, I'm there all by myself."

"Are we going there after dinner?" She forced herself to keep her tone light, to look straight ahead at the road.

He shot her a glance. "Only if you want to, Mimi. You know I want to be with you, but I wouldn't ever want to force you into doing something you don't want to do. I'll never do something you're not ready for."

"I talked to my mom about it," she said shyly.

"You what?"

"I talked to my mom. I asked her how old she was her first time, and I asked her what it was like."

"Was it with your real dad? The one who died?"

"Believe it or not, no. It was with Dad. The dad you met. The one she's married to now. But I don't want to go into it. It's messed up."

He exhaled sharply. "Ugh, why did you have to ask her about sex? Every time I take you out she's going to be thinking we're doing it. Shit, she may even be thinking that tonight!" His tone was laced with worry.

"She's not thinking that. I promise you. I told her I wasn't ready and promised I would go to her before anything happens."

"And that was it? She believed you?"

"Of course she believed me. Besides, it's true. We've only kissed, Elliott. I'm not sure I'm ready to go any further. I told you before that it was important to me to wait until I'm married."

Elliott had to tamp down his anger. Why the hell was she asking if they'd be going back to Edith's vacant house later if she wasn't willing? Little cock tease. She'd be changing her mind. Of that he was certain.

ACROSS TOWN, CHRISTIAN BEAR SAT ON THE END OF HIS FRIEND'S BED AND watched him do pushups on the bedroom floor. When Dustin was finished, he got up and walked over to his dresser, picked up a beer, and took a long swallow. He swiped his arm across his mouth and turned to Christian.

"Heard you've been hanging out with those losers from Sandpiper High."

"Yeah," was all Christian said before taking a swig of his own beer.

"Why? They're a bunch of punks. You've downgraded, bro."

"They entertain me," Christian said. "I'm bored and they amuse me."

"And Rosman isn't freaking out? He likes being their fearless leader even if he has graduated. Seems like he'd feel threatened by having a badass like you around, Chris."

"I ain't seen Nick yet, and when I do, I could care less what he thinks."

Christian couldn't tell Dustin the real reason he'd insinuated himself into their group. He'd been trying to find out for the last week what their connection was to Mimi. When the big mouth of the pathetic trio told him Nick, whose full name was Elliott Nicholas Rosman, was planning something huge to get the notice of some local biker clubs, Christian knew it must've had something to do with Mimi. It was just too much of a coincidence that Nick and Mimi were dating—and that Mimi's real father had died in prison this past summer.

Christian knew about Grizz. His father, Anthony, was always forthcoming about his past. A past that included Mimi's real father.

Of course, both of Anthony's sons knew to keep whatever tales their father shared to themselves.

Christian had displayed just enough disinterest with Rosman's three friends that it made them want to tell him more. Christian had a reputation for being a bad boy, and asshats like these three were always trying to get his attention to make themselves look more important than they actually were. Christian had casually told them he wanted in if they could deliver. Their immature egos fell for the little bit of interest he'd shown, and they'd been practically doing backflips to impress him since.

Christian's phone vibrated, and he reached into his back pocket.

Tonight at 8. Blue Moon condos on beach. #907

After reading the text message, Christian snapped his phone shut and told Dustin, "Later, man."

He ran out the front door and jumped on his motorcycle. He didn't have much time if he was going to make it by eight. Less than a minute later, he was back in his friend's room.

"My bike won't start so I need your car keys." He held out his hand. "C'mon, give 'em to me."

"Can't you fix your bike?"

"Yeah, but I don't have time. Give me your fuckin' keys, Dustin."

"I don't know if my parents' insurance will cover you. I'm not letting you take my car. I'll drive you home so you can get your truck."

"It's an emergency!" Christian yelled. "And I drive better than you do! Give me your keys!"

Dustin reluctantly turned over his keys, and Christian raced out.

"You better have it back here tonight, Chris," he yelled after his friend. "I fucking mean it!"

LESS THAN TEN MINUTES LATER, CHRISTIAN BEAR FOUND HIMSELF IN THE back of a police cruiser with his hands cuffed behind his back. He'd been pulled over for speeding. The cop probably would've let him call his parents or the friend whose car he borrowed, but Christian's attitude sealed his fate. He was too much like his father.

"Shut up about your phone call," the cop yelled over his shoulder as he drove. "You can make your call from the station."

Slade Bear had just washed his hands and was coming out of the men's room at a sports bar when his cell phone rang. It was his younger brother, Christian.

"What's up, Chri—"

"Slade! You need to listen to me. I don't know where you are or what you're doing, but you have to do something right now for me. It's important, man. I wouldn't ask if it wasn't."

Slade held the phone tight against his right ear and used his left hand to cover his other ear. The bar was loud. He walked back toward the restroom. Christian wasn't one to ask for favors. Something was up.

"Yeah. Sure, Chris. I can help you out. What's up?"

"You know that big-ass condo on Commercial and the beach, the Blue Moon?"

"No."

"Yes, you do!" Christian yelled. "It's the one where Mom dragged us all the way from the other coast to somebody's kid's Bar Mitzvah when we were younger. Remember the big ballroom with the glitter that was still in our hair a week later?"

"Oh yeah, I remem—"

"Shut up, Slade. Just listen. You have to go there, and you have to go there now. Go to condo nine-oh-seven. Some guys I've made friends with will be there. Something is going down with Mimi. I'm afraid something bad might happen, but I don't know what. You have to go there and make sure she's okay. You hear me?"

"Mimi who?"

"How many fucking Mimis do we know, Slade?"

"Mimi Dillon?" Slade walked out of the restroom, pulled a twenty from his wallet, and handed it to his waitress. He left the bar and headed out to the parking lot, listening as his brother filled him in. *What the hell is Christian getting me into?*

FIFTEEN MINUTES LATER, SLADE STOOD IN FRONT OF DOOR 907 AND knocked. It swung open, and a kid with acne that he didn't recognize said, "Didn't know if you were going to come..."

He stopped and stared at Slade.

"Who are you?" He gave Slade the once-over.

"My brother Chris said I should meet him here. Said something was going down and I'd want in." He tried to look past the boy and into the room, then narrowed his eyes. "You're just a bunch of kids. There isn't anything happening here tonight, is there? I can't believe you tricked my little brother. He'll beat the shit out of you when I tell him."

The boy's eyes got wide then, and he stepped back. "No! C'mon in and have a beer. We weren't pulling nothing over on Chris. This is big, dude. C'mon in. We'll tell you."

Slade walked in and slowly perused the room. Two teenagers were lounging on a couch, their feet on an expensive coffee table. The smell of cheap weed filled the room. He looked over to the guy that let him in.

"Which one of you lives here?"

"None of us," the boy answered, nodding toward a kid with bleached blond dreadlocks. "Isaac's dad is the head maintenance guy for the whole building. The couple that owns this condo and the douchebag fag that owns nine-oh-eight are part-timers. Only use their condos in the summer. We have both places to ourselves."

Slade walked to the two boys lounging on the couch.

"Where's Rosman?" he asked no one in particular.

"He's next door in nine-oh-eight, and he should have blood on his dick by now. She's a virgin. Can you believe he's with a fucking virgin?" This from the boy who answered the door.

"Yeah, and we get to see everything. He's filming it. This is gonna be so righteous, dude." Isaac took a deep pull on his joint. As he exhaled, he said, "He's been planning this for so fucking long. Even got some freaky religious tattoo to impress her."

The boy who'd let Slade in the door started to give him a high five when Slade grabbed his arm and twisted it behind his back. With the boy on the floor and Slade's knee pressing into his shoulder blades, he looked at Isaac. "Give me the key to next door."

Isaac and the other boy both jumped up from the couch and started to approach Slade but stopped. Their friend was screaming from the floor.

"He's breaking my arm. He's breaking my fucking arm!"

"I'll break all of your arms if you don't give me that key," Slade said in a calm voice laced with menace.

He could tell they were weighing their options. It was three to one, and one of them was already down. He'd break this little shit's arm and then crack the two numbskulls' heads together. He knew it would be a piece of cake, and he saw by their expressions they knew it, too.

"I don't have the key to nine-oh-eight. I gave it to Nick," Isaac said, his voice suddenly whiny.

"Then you better pray your dad has a master on that ring." Slade nodded at the small ring of keys laying on the coffee table. "If not, I'll use your fucking head to bust that door down."

IN THE CONDOMINIUM NEXT DOOR, MIMI SAT ON THE COUCH AND SIPPED the iced tea Elliott had offered her. He'd gone into the bedroom to put Edith's medication on the dresser. When they'd first arrived, they'd found a handwritten note that said, "Sorry I'm missing you. Went to an eight o'clock movie with my friends."

"Guess it's good you had a spare key," Mimi called out to the other room.

She'd been worried when Edith didn't answer the door. She'd seen the television commercial where the elderly lady had fallen and couldn't get up. She shuddered to think that Elliott's sweet grandma was inside the condo and unable to get up or call for help.

Elliott came out of the bedroom with a big smile on his face.

"True. I'd have been kind of pissed if I drove all the way out here and couldn't leave her pills." He took the seat next to her and said, "Drink up. You love Edith's homemade iced tea."

Mimi took another small sip. "I was thinking more along the lines that she could've been hurt or something."

She put her glass back on the coffee table.

Elliott put his arm around her and pulled her close.

"Edith won't be home for hours. We could order takeout and eat it on the balcony. Have you seen the view?"

"If that's what you want to do, that's okay with me, I guess," Mimi said, suddenly feeling a bit shy.

He stood up then and reached for her hand.

"C'mon, let me show you the view."

Mimi stood and started to walk in the direction of the sliding doors, but Elliott pulled her toward the bedroom.

"I'll have to show you from the bedroom balcony. The living room sliders have been sticking, and Edith told me maintenance hasn't been up yet to fix them. I don't want to get them open and then not be able to close them. You know what I mean?"

Before Mimi could respond, he added, "You better drink more tea. Edith will be hurt if she thinks you passed up her famous iced tea."

An odd feeling caused Mimi to look up at Elliott. Something was off. This wasn't the Elliott she knew. There was something different about him. He seemed somewhat anxious.

For what, she didn't know. She'd noticed his jaw tightened when they were in the truck talking about sex, when she'd reminded him she wanted to wait until she was married. She thought she imagined it, but now her senses were suddenly on alert.

She was reminded of a conversation she'd once had with her mother. Ginny had told her the story of when she used to babysit for a little boy who'd been abused. The signs were there and her intuition had been right, but she'd ignored them at first because those kinds of things didn't happen in those kinds of families.

Her mother had been wrong.

"You know what, Elliott? I think maybe I would rather go out to dinner. I don't feel right hanging in Edith's vacation condo without her being here." She tried to lighten the mood by reminding him of a funny moment they'd shared months earlier. "You know, 'unchaperoned.'"

The last word came out in a squeak. Her lungs suddenly felt heavy and she thought she might have to fight for breath.

She noticed the same tightening of his jaw, but it was quickly gone as he plastered on a smile. A smile she realized wasn't sincere.

Mimi felt a bead of sweat as it tickled its way down her neck. The room was suddenly very hot.

"Okay," he said with exaggerated enthusiasm. "But not until you finish your iced tea."

There it was again. The iced tea. She'd already taken a few sips. Did she feel any different? Yes, she thought maybe she did. Her body felt relaxed, which was in sharp contrast to what her mind was feeling.

"I'm not really thirsty," was all she could muster.

She started to feel lightheaded and sat back down.

"What's wrong, Mimi? Are you okay?"

His fake sincerity was so obvious it was making her nauseated.

"Just a little lightheaded. Probably because I haven't eaten all day. I'll be fine as soon as we get to the restaurant."

He pulled her roughly to her feet and caught her around the waist as she swayed. "C'mon. Why don't you lie down on Edith's bed for a few minutes?"

"Take me home, Elliott,"

"Not until you rest," he said sternly as he half walked, half dragged her toward the bedroom.

"No, Elliott! I don't want to lie down. I want to go home." It sounded slightly slurred even to her own ears.

"You are not going to ruin this for me, Mimi. I've waited for almost a fucking year for this. I even insisted on meeting your parents." He glared at her. "And you're nothing but a prick-tease. Always looking at me like you want me to do you and then saying the opposite." His voice turned hard. "You're going to come in the bedroom and I'm going to make love to you, and you're going to like it. Got it? You understand?"

He smirked to himself. Make love to her? Shit. He was going to ball her brains out.

"Ruin what?" she cried. "I think you put something in the iced tea. You want me to pass out."

"I only gave you something to help you relax. I don't want you to pass out. I want you to be awake. I want you to like it, and I promise you will, Mimi. I promise." His voice was calmer now. "I'll go down on you first. If you just let yourself relax, you'll like it, I swear. I'll make sure you come, and you'll be begging me to fuck you, okay? It'll be good. Now come on!"

Just then the front door of the condo flew open and a guy walked in, slamming the door behind him.

"Take your hands off her, Nick."

"Who the fuck are you?" Elliott asked, his arms still clutched tightly around Mimi's waist.

"I'm the guy who's here to break your fucking face."

28

Mimi, 2000, Fort Lauderdale (After Grizz's Execution)

S lade watched as Mimi sipped the coffee and made a face.

"Drink it, Mimi. It should help," he told her in a soothing voice.

He watched her take a sip of the coffee and slowly swallow it. Then, with a trembling hand, she placed it in the cup holder, pulled the blanket they'd swiped from the condo tightly around her shoulders, and started to cry.

"So stupid. So stupid. So embarrassed," was all she said as she rocked back and forth.

They were sitting in an isolated parking spot behind the fast food joint Slade had brought her to. He'd bought two coffees in the drive-thru and parked behind the restaurant. He tried to console her.

"It's okay, Mimi. You're okay. I got there in time. Nothing happened. Nothing will happen." His voice was quiet.

"If you hadn't gotten there when you did, I don't know how far Elliott would've gone and I, I, I..."

"But I did get there, Mimi, and nothing happened."

He then went on to explain what Christian had told him to say. That he knew Elliott as Nick Rosman and had heard through some friends what Nick had planned on doing to try to get the notice of some biker gangs.

"I knew they were talking about Grizz, Mimi, and that's how I made the connection to you. I guess I'm a little shocked that you know about Grizz. I didn't think you knew he was your real father."

She took a shuddery breath. "I found out by accident. It's a long story, but I know who he is. It's just unbelievable that you knew these guys, too."

"Yeah, I hadn't realized who they were talking about until it was almost too late," he lied.

He wouldn't tell her his brother, Christian, was the one who'd purposely buddied up to these idiots. He wanted to save her the embarrassment of thinking someone else knew what Rosman had planned to do.

"I just can't believe they were going to film me having sex with Elliott—err, Nick." She shivered and pulled the blanket tighter around her shoulders.

She looked up then at Slade and, with the biggest, most expressive eyes he'd ever seen, and with complete adoration in her voice, said, "You saved me, Slade. You saved me."

"What do you mean, you messed his face up? Why didn't you put him in the fucking hospital, Slade?" Christian's face was red.

"Because I'm not you," Slade yelled back.

It had been a long night and Slade was tired. After quietly dropping Mimi off at her home, he returned to the apartment he shared with three roommates and had gone to bed. He'd had trouble falling asleep, though. He hadn't seen Mimi in years and had been startled by what he saw. The sweet little brown-haired girl with the big eyes had turned into a real beauty. He had to remind himself she was only fifteen. That fucking Rosman should've been shot for what he'd planned on doing to her.

Slade had known his parents would bail Christian out of jail, and he'd been right. He just didn't think it would happen so quickly—or that Chris would show up at his apartment so early in the morning.

"You knew what that motherfucker was planning on doing. He shouldn't have walked out of that condo, Slade." Christian leaned against the kitchen counter, arms crossed.

Slade poured himself some coffee and sat at the small kitchen table.

"You're screwed in the head. You know that? If I'd done something that had caused the police or an ambulance to have to come to that condo, they would've tracked down those three goons, and it would all have been traced back to Mimi and me. You want the police knocking on her door waking up her parents to find out why the guy she was dating was put in the hospital by one of Anthony Bear's kids? It's a good thing you gave that cop some lip, Christian. If he hadn't hauled your ass to jail, you'd have brought down a load of shit on everybody. You and your damn temper!"

Slade looked up at his brother then and recognized an expression that had always made him uncomfortable.

"Don't even think about it, Chris." He held up a warning hand. "Let it go. Besides, if word gets around to certain people of what he even attempted to do, he's dead. Grizz still has loyal followers. Even from the grave that guy has clout, and Rosman must be an imbecile to think he would be impressing anybody with his stunt. Yeah, maybe some rival gangs from back in the day would've been amused, but with Grizz dead and gone, none of his old enemies really give a shit."

Slade took a sip of coffee and let out a long breath. He stared at his brother who was still standing there, arms crossed and a furious expression on his face. After a few minutes, Slade's expression softened.

"I don't get this thing with you and Mimi. Why are you so riled up over this? I thought you crushed on her when we were kids, but we haven't seen them in years. You still like her that much?"

Christian didn't say anything. He walked to the refrigerator and took out a beer. He turned around and looked at Slade as he took a sip, ignoring the look of disapproval from his older brother.

"How did you handle her parents?"

"I didn't have to," Slade said tiredly. "We came up with a story for her to tell her mom and dad, and I dropped her a few houses down from her own." He caught his brother's look. "I made sure she got in her house before I drove off, okay? I didn't want my car to be seen in front of their house. Her parents don't need to be asking why I was bringing her home. They'll think Nick dropped her off."

Christian just nodded.

Slade felt compelled to add, "If you think you like her, why don't you do something about it? Maybe you could run into her somewhere or even go by her house. Say you were in the neighborhood and wanted to say hi. You know Aunt Ginny would welcome you with open arms."

"I saw her father at Axel's place. He looked at me like I was a piece of trash. Couldn't tell me quick enough how she was in love with some guy. He doesn't want me around. He thinks she can do better than me. He's probably right."

"That's bullshit. If it weren't for you, Mimi would've been raped tonight. And if the wrong people found out about it, Rosman would've died for it. Still might. You took the initiative to find out what was going on. You may be a hothead, bro, but you are one bad motherfucker who'd make sure nobody'd ever go near their daughter. Quit selling yourself short, Christian. You want a chance with Mimi? A real chance? Start working on your grades and get rid of some of your friends. I don't know if it'll help you get a foot in the door with the Dillons, but at least you'd make Mom and Dad a lot happier."

Christian guzzled the last of his beer and set the bottle on the counter. Ignoring his brother's advice, he headed for the door, calling out over his shoulder as he went.

"I owe you one, Slade."

29

Ginny, 2001, Fort Lauderdale

The weeks after our Thanksgiving cruise flew by in a frenzy of activity. Between Christmas, the start of a new year, and our busy family schedule, it seemed every day on the calendar had something penciled in. There were also some things during that time that weren't on the calendar. One that stuck out was that Mimi and Elliott had ended their relationship.

I'd waited up that night for her first date with him after we returned from our cruise. She quietly let herself in the front door and was heading up the stairs when I called her back down. When I saw she'd been crying, I knew something was wrong.

She let me hold her as she sobbed for almost five minutes that finally ended in a fit of hiccups. I made some tea while she washed her face. We sat in the den, and she told me how Elliott had taken her to a nice restaurant for dinner and they'd run into one of his ex-girlfriends, who'd made a scene.

"It was just so humiliating, Mom. She was older than him and obviously still loved him. She asked if he'd resorted to picking up little girls from the playground at elementary schools."

I listened as Mimi told me how Elliott's ex-girlfriend must have been drinking. She was making such a scene that they were all asked to leave by the restaurant manager.

"I just saw him in a different light, I guess. He wasn't defending himself to her. I felt like he was embarrassed by me. I don't think that I'll ever look at him the same way." She looked down at her mug as tears rolled down her cheeks, "I think he cares more about what others think than he does about me."

"So did you break up?" I was conflicted. Part of me was secretly hoping I wouldn't have to worry about my daughter dating an eighteen-year-old, yet also feeling a real ache in my heart for her pain. It had been a long time ago, but even I remembered the sting of Matthew Rockman telling me he'd no longer need me to tutor him.

"I guess it was mutual," she said. "Mom?"

"Yes, Mimi?"

"Would it be okay if we don't talk about it anymore? I mean, Elliott and I already agreed to take each other's numbers out of our phones. We've already decided it's not going to work. He said something about maybe trying to see me again when I'm older, but let's face it. He was just being nice. That's not going to happen and I'm pretty sure I don't want it to."

She blew out a breath and looked at me pleadingly.

I watched Mimi closely for weeks after that conversation, and even though I could tell she was hurting, she put on a brave face and dove back into her regular activities. School, work, and friends fell back into their usual place, and she even asked to go with me the next time I met Christy Bear for lunch. I was relieved to see she was resilient and had resolved to move on. And I knew Tommy certainly breathed a sigh of relief when I told him about the breakup.

The discussions with Mimi about Grizz had slowly faded away. Her guilt about Leslie had been absolved, and her curiosity about Grizz had waned. Life was getting back to normal. The kids had been back in school for weeks, and we were almost nearing the end of January. Since I had given up my bookkeeping clients, I had more time on my hands than usual.

Lately, I'd had Sister Mary Katherine on my mind. I'd recently dreamed about the nun who I'd been so close to when I was a child. The same nun who'd pushed authorities to find me. Was my subconscious speaking to me in dreams that maybe I had some unfinished business with her?

"How do you even know where to find her, Ginny?" Tommy asked me early one morning in our bedroom. He'd been sitting on our bed putting on his shoes for work.

"I asked about her when we renewed our wedding vows. I should've tried to find her years ago, Tommy. I feel like she's one of those unresolved things in my life."

"So, she's still alive?"

"Yes, she's in a nursing home for retired nuns in Illinois. I'd like to visit her. To tell her I'm alive. I don't even know if she'll remember me, Tommy, but she's been on my mind since last summer, and I've been putting it off. And with everything that's happened since then, you can't blame me for putting it off. But still—I want to see her before it's too late. Maybe that's why I dreamed about her. She has to be ancient by now, wouldn't you think?"

"I don't know, Gin. I didn't know her, so I don't know how old she'd be by now. If it's something you feel strongly about, then definitely do it."

"Do you want to go with me? I thought I'd take a Friday afternoon flight. Stay two nights and come home on a Sunday."

"I don't think so. Now that Alec is back from his sabbatical in the mountains, we're taking on more clients, and I'll be working some weekends. You go, and I can stay home with the kids. Then we won't have to arrange for them to stay with friends or ask Carter to come here."

"I don't know if I want to go alone. Without you."

"I think it would be good for you, Gin." He stood and walked toward me, gently tilting my chin up to him. "It sounds like you should have time alone with her. If you don't want to go alone, I'll go with you. But I'm just thinking this is something you might like to do by yourself."

THE NEXT WEEK, I FOUND MYSELF STANDING IN THE COZY FAMILY ROOM AT the Sisters of Mercy Retirement Home in Illinois. It was an old convent that had been condemned as uninhabitable and was slated for demolition years ago when it had caught the eye of a wealthy donor who'd had it restored. I stood next to a roaring brick fireplace and stared at the ceiling and surrounding walls, captivated by the architecture.

A young novitiate had been sent to collect Sister Mary Katherine and bring her to me. I assumed that meant she was most likely in a wheelchair. I secretly wondered if maybe this had been a mistake. She probably wouldn't even remember me. It was now 2001. I'd been abducted in 1975. That was more than twenty-five years ago. What was I thinking?

"It smells like roses, but not a flower or air freshener in sight," a young woman had commented to me. We made small talk as we waited. She was waiting for her aunt, another retired nun. I'd started to tell her I agreed when I heard a voice I recognized instantly.

"Guinevere Love Lemon. It's about time you came to see me!"

Sister Mary Katherine bounded toward me with an energy that belied her age. Then, clasping my arm tightly, she began to walk me through the warm and inviting halls of the beautiful building. It didn't feel like a retirement home. It reminded me of an elegant mansion with a lot of bedrooms. She'd explained on the way to her room that she was now almost ninety, and even though she was officially retired, she didn't have a tired bone in her body.

In her room, she listened without interrupting as I told her everything that had transpired since that fateful day in May 1975. Her blue eyes were bright, and I expected to see some curiosity in them, but it wasn't there.

"I knew you were okay," she told me confidently.

"How?"

She held her hand over her heart. "Can't tell you how. I just knew. After a while, I felt peace about it, and from what you've told me, sounds like I should've been worrying about you, but I wasn't. Something deep inside told me you were fine. I prayed that God would tell me one day it was true. And today is that day. Praise the good Lord, Guinevere."

We hugged, and then she looked at the watch on her bony wrist.

"Do you want to come with me on my rounds?"

"Your rounds?"

"I need to fetch Sister Agnes. She's blind and handicapped. I need to get her back to her room and settled in. Would you like to come with me?"

"I would love to, Sister Mary Katherine."

I stood in Sister Agnes's room and watched as Sister Mary Katherine lovingly readied the blind nun for her afternoon nap. For a woman nearing ninety, she moved with the agility of a cat. I smiled to myself as I took in the beautiful and tasteful furniture and the window that looked out on a snowy scene that could have come right out of a Thomas Kincaid painting.

Then I noticed something I found odd. Almost every available space of furniture was covered in framed pictures. I walked to one low dresser and bent over to get a better look. Sister Agnes was blind. Why would she have so many pictures in her room? She couldn't see them.

As if reading my thoughts, Sister Mary Katherine said, "They're her unanswered prayers."

I turned to look at the holy sister. "Unanswered prayers?"

"When she was younger, Bevin was a photographer," Sister Mary Katherine told me. "Bevin was her name before she became a nun."

I looked back at the pictures and noticed they were all black and whites. I picked one up.

"Sister Agnes, this one is of a man changing a car tire. He's smiling at you, like he stopped what he was doing so you could snap his picture."

"New Orleans, 1950. I was maybe only twenty-five or twenty-six then and had just discovered my love of photography," said the nun from the bed. Sister Agnes had thinning white hair and a heavily lined face. Her unseeing dark eyes exuded warmth and compassion. "That was Mr. Payroux. He later lost his wife and two children in a house fire. That picture was taken in happier times. If you look closely, you can see his wife sitting on their porch in the background. I went back to visit years after I took that picture and was told by the neighbors that, after his family's deaths, he'd spiraled into a dark world of depression and drinking. One day, he up and disappeared. Nobody knew what had happened to him."

"This was so many years ago, Sister. He must have died by now. Is this still an unanswered prayer of yours?"

"I pray for every person in every one of those pictures that the Lord will see fit to put on my heart what became of them. Sometimes He answers me in a dream. Sometimes, someone like Sister Mary Katherine will help me do some investigating, get me my answers. I have a whole drawer full of answered prayers over there."

I watched as her unseeing eyes followed the direction of where she was now pointing. My eyes followed, too, and saw a tall dresser that stood in the corner.

"Oh, yes, we have a whole drawer full of answered prayers," Sister Mary Katherine told me proudly.

I smiled and went back to perusing the unanswered prayer frames. One caught my eye. There was something beautiful yet sad about it. Maybe it was the dog. It was a Rottweiler and brought me immediately back to memories of Lucifer and Damien. I picked it up and studied it closer.

"Which one are you looking at?" Sister Agnes asked.

"It's a little girl and her dog. They're sitting in tall grass, and she's smiling, but it's not reaching her eyes."

"Florida. A town smaller than a speck called Macon's Grove. 1956. That would be Ruthie and Razor."

30

Tommy, 2001, Fort Lauderdale

T ommy sat behind his desk at Dillon & Davis Architects. He was still a little high from what he'd learned that morning. He wanted to call Ginny but knew she'd be right in the middle of her visit with Sister Mary Katherine, and he didn't want to interrupt her. Her plane would be getting in tomorrow afternoon, and he decided he'd pick her up from the airport and take her straight to a pricey hotel on Fort Lauderdale beach.

Not for sex, although he wouldn't say no to that. He wanted to celebrate his news, and he wanted to do it in style. He'd already arranged for Carter to spend tomorrow afternoon and Sunday night at their home and get the kids up and off to school Monday morning so he and Ginny could have a night away.

He looked up from his desk and saw her approaching. Her confident walk sickened him. She still thought she'd won.

He couldn't hate her more.

"Working on Saturday? What are Gin and the kids up to?" Sarah Jo took the seat in front of Tommy's desk and crossed her legs after she laid her purse on his desk. She slowly perused his office, finally met his eyes, and yawned.

"Gin is visiting an old friend, Mimi is working, and Jason has games all day." His voice was cold.

Sarah Jo studied the fingernails on her right hand. "So what do you want? I wouldn't be here if I wasn't shopping close by. You're not calling the shots, remember?"

She was surprised to see he was smiling.

"When are you moving?" he asked.

"I'm not moving, and you know that. We discussed this at that shithole diner a couple of months ago. Or did you forget?" Condescension dripped from every word she spoke.

"No. I didn't forget. What I can't remember is why you think you don't have to leave."

"You know why. I told you—"

"Yeah, I remember. The threat to tell Ginny about the morning sickness remedy. I've thought about it and decided it's okay if you tell her. She won't believe you." He was following Alec's advice from before Thanksgiving. Advice Alec had offered about a spiteful client who'd surprisingly become useful in Tommy's secret feud with Sarah Jo—call her bluff, Tom. Call her fucking bluff.

Sarah Jo snorted. "What makes you so sure she won't believe me?"

"Because it's your word against mine, and when I show her Moe's journal, the one I told you about, she'll read for herself in Moe's words how it was you who set up her rape. Who's she going to believe then, Jo?"

He leaned back in his chair and idly tapped his pen on his knee. He was going out on a limb here. He'd thrown Moe's journal in the garbage months ago, but he never told Jo that. He had one more hunch, and if he was right, he'd be able to see it on her face. It was worth a try.

"And when she finds out it was you, I mean Wendy, who tracked down Matthew Rockman and fed him all that information over the phone about Grizz and his gang and who he should talk to..."

He paused and let the relevance of what he was saying sink in. He was certain by the expression on her face that his intuition was right.

He leaned forward, and stared at her. "You told me you had friends at Ginny's high school back in 1975. You would've heard the rumors about the school's star running back being tutored by the missing girl. Then, as time passed, you noticed him making headlines with his legal career. You were always worried about Fess getting in trouble, so you kept up with everything. It explains why Fess and I weren't on their radar immediately. You would never have implicated your father." His jaw tightened. "And I have to say, I do believe you thought you were helping me out by not implicating me, too. But you would've known about Froggy's love for Willow—and his festering hatred for Grizz for casting her out. You would've known Blue's marriage was falling apart. You told Rockman to talk to Jan. He'd probably moved on and forgotten about Ginny, but you stirred it all up again when you saw him in the news winning all his cases."

She shifted uncomfortably in her chair.

"So I suppose Matthew told you this. That he heard from a Wendy, too? I don't see how you can be talking to a man you're supposed to be testifying against."

"No, Jo. Your face just did. But I'm sure if I ask him if he'd ever been contacted by someone named Wendy, he'd confirm it."

She stood up. "Fuck you, Tommy!"

She picked up her purse and stomped out of his office. She made her way through the empty and dark lobby, slamming the front door behind her.

Tommy stood up then, too, but he didn't smile. He didn't feel victorious. He felt tired. He was glad it was Saturday, and there was nobody in the other offices to witness what just happened.

He also made a decision. One he knew Ginny would agree with. He was supposed to testify in Matthew Rockman's murder trial. Tommy couldn't implicate Grizz and Blue in Jan's murder, but he was smart enough to figure out a way to answer the questions in a manner that would plant reasonable doubt in the minds of the jurors. He might piss off the prosecution, but he was willing to take that chance.

Rockman may have been guilty of being a manipulative, conniving son-of-a-bitch, but he wasn't a murderer.

31

Ginny, 2001, Illinois

I stood frozen and stared at the framed picture in my hand. I could feel a pulsing in my ears as my heart raced. I was aware of every vein in my body. It was almost as if I could feel the blood coursing its way through every artery.

This couldn't be. It was too much of a coincidence. I remembered how Grizz had asked me to give Mimi the middle name of Ruth. After Tommy told me about the early part of Grizz's real childhood, I'd suspected maybe Ruth was the name of his little sister, though I couldn't confirm it. I also had no proof he was raised in Florida.

But I did know he had a real love for Rottweilers and that he'd owned a bar named Razors. My head was spinning with possibilities.

"What's the matter, child? You look like you've seen a ghost," Sister Mary Katherine said as she watched me.

She guided me by the elbow to a comfortable chair. I sat without taking my eyes off the picture.

"Sister Agnes, where exactly in Florida is Macon's Grove?" My voice cracked.

"Oh, it was so small it's probably been swallowed up by some bigger city by now. It's right smack dab in the middle of Florida. Nothing but orange groves as far as the eye could see," she said.

By now my hand was shaking, and Sister Mary Katherine grabbed the picture from me before I dropped it.

"Guinevere?"

I swallowed thickly and took a deep breath. "I'd like to come back after Sister Agnes's nap and ask her some more questions about this picture. That is, if you think it's okay and if she'll remember."

"I can hear you, you know?" came the small voice from the bed. "And I may be blind and infirm, but I can tell you the license plate number of my first car. All of a sudden, I'm not so tired after all." I could feel her blind eyes swivel toward me. "What do you want to know about Ruthie and Razor?"

I looked at Sister Mary Katherine. She nodded for me to continue.

"Everything. Please, sister. Tell me everything you remember about them and why you still have this picture."

Sister Agnes cleared her throat. "It didn't start with Ruthie and Razor. It started with another child. A baby boy." My heart thudded. She sat up straighter in her bed. "It was 1947, and I was just twenty-two. I'd lost my husband in the war and was aimlessly wandering from relative to relative in the hopes of finding myself. I was so lost then. I was visiting an elderly aunt who lived near Macon's Grove. She didn't really live near it since it was in the middle of nowhere, but she lived close enough that she was sought by a man whose wife was in labor. My aunt had a decent reputation as a midwife, and she was closer than a hospital, so when he showed up at her door, she grabbed her supplies and took me with her."

She paused and asked Sister Mary Katherine for a drink of water. After she sipped her water, she continued.

"It was sad. So sad. This little house in the middle of some orange groves. The poor woman was almost delirious with pain by the time we got there. I will never understand why the man just didn't drive her to a hospital. Anyway, she gave birth to a beautiful baby boy. He was a big one, too. Came out screaming at the top of his lungs. My aunt handed him off to me to get him cleaned up. I brought him into the kitchen to wipe him down. I can still see his round little face."

I gulped and wondered if she could've been describing Grizz as a newborn. My head became thick with the sound of my blood pulsing. I watched as Sister Agnes's expression turned wistful.

"When I brought him back to his mother, I could hear my aunt telling her husband she was concerned. The woman was bleeding more than normal, and my aunt thought she should be taken to a hospital. The man left to drive to the closest neighbor and call an ambulance. I guess we thought an ambulance would've brought medical help quicker than if we tried to load her up in a car and drive her ourselves. My aunt would later tell me it didn't matter. Her blood loss was so quick and so heavy it was doubtful she could've been saved."

The holy sister took a big breath. "While the husband was gone, the mother regained consciousness and asked for her baby. We placed him in her arms and watched as she kissed his little head and spoke to him in a low voice. She looked up at my aunt then and in her very weakened state told us she wanted someone to know the truth about her baby."

I sat up straighter in my chair. Sister Agnes's voice was like a drug. I couldn't hear the next word fast enough. I was taking in every syllable, every inflection in her voice, every detail. My heart was thumping so loudly I was certain the holy sisters could hear it beating in my chest.

"She told us she was raised in a little tiny town in the foothills of the Blue Ridge Mountains. She'd been in love with the same boy since first grade. They'd made plans to be married when he was called away in the final draft for World War II. The same war I lost my husband in. She found herself pregnant and alone." Sister Agnes sighed. "She lived with an elderly uncle, a nasty old man who would've kicked her out without a second thought. She'd written to her fiancé, and never received a reply. Neither she nor his family could find anything out about his whereabouts and before too long, her pregnancy would be noticeable."

"In those days, 'nice girls' didn't have unmarried relations. At least, they weren't supposed to. She was ashamed and embarrassed. In hindsight, she wished she'd have risked the shame and stayed there. Wished she'd confessed to his parents she was carrying their son's baby. When the man who'd later become her husband passed through her town as part of a logging crew and showed some interest, she jumped. Even after she explained her situation, he didn't care. I could understand that. She was a real beauty. She left with him and never went back."

I couldn't believe what I was hearing. I knew Grizz's real mother had died in childbirth and that the man who'd raised him wasn't his biological father. Could this be Grizz's mother Sister Agnes was telling me about? Was I hearing about Grizz's birth?

185

"How did the picture of Ruthie and Razor, which would've been taken years after this baby's birth, come to be?" I was almost bouncing in my chair.

"I'll get to that, child," Sister Agnes said softly. "After she told us this story, she kissed her baby and, with her last breath, told us to tell her husband what she wanted him to be named. Although, she asked us not to tell him why. She wanted his first name to be her mother's maiden name. It would be the only connection to her home and family that she could leave her baby boy. She died while holding him in her arms. I cried myself to sleep that night.

"I stayed with my aunt a little while longer after that and found myself driving out to the lonely farmhouse on occasion to check on that baby boy. When I finally decided what my calling was, I left my aunt, but asked her to keep checking on the family. She did for a while. I remember getting a letter from her telling me the baby had grown into a robust toddler with the brightest green eyes she'd ever seen. Brighter than the greenest grass on a spring morning."

Grizz. I gasped then, and Sister Mary Katherine looked at me, eyes filled with concern. I respectfully shook my head.

"I'm sorry, Sister Agnes. Please finish."

"My aunt also said she had a bad feeling, that maybe the child was a bit neglected, but she hoped things would get better when he finally remarried. My aunt died, and I never went back to that farmhouse." She paused. "That is, until 1956."

"I'd joined the Catholic Church by then and taken my vows and had been living in different states. When I found myself back in Florida, I made it a point to visit that little house in Macon's Grove. That's when I came upon Ruthie and Razor playing in the front yard. I remember Razor growled at me as I approached, but little Ruthie shushed him. I asked if her mother was home, and she said she was in the back yard. I asked who she lived there with, and she told me she had a daddy and a brother. I'd wondered if her brother was the baby I'd delivered all those years ago. I asked his name, but Ruthie just called him Brother. She was a beautiful child, but there was something sad and distant in her eyes. It was only when I asked more about her brother that her little face lit up.

"Anyway, I always carried my camera, and I started taking pictures of them playing in the grass. Then her mother, who wasn't a very nice woman, came barreling around the side of the house and told me to mind my own business. I tried to explain that I'd been to this house years earlier, and I was just checking to see how the family was doing. That woman told me in words that a nun and a child should never have to hear what I could do with myself. And what business did I have taking pictures of her child? I apologized and said that if she told me her address, I would be sure to send her a picture after I had my film developed. Which I did. It was a picture similar to the one you're holding. I mailed it off to her as soon as I had it developed."

She sighed then. I could tell the story was wearing her out, but I wanted her to finish. As if sensing my desperation, she continued in a voice laced with sadness.

"To make a long story short, I was sent to India right after that. Many, many years later I came back to the states and found myself in Macon's Grove once again. I found the house, but all traces of the family were long gone. I asked around town, and people said the family packed up and left town without telling a soul." She shook her head. "Ruthie and Razor have been on my unanswered prayers table ever since. I guess I think of them as the only connection to the baby I once held. He didn't have green eyes when I held him right after he was born, but I've been haunted by them nonetheless. I guess I was living off a memory that belonged to my aunt. That baby boy, that little girl, and her dog, they've all left an imprint on my soul that won't go away. They are most definitely one of my unanswered prayers."

A few silent minutes passed as what she'd told me sank in. I was waiting for the elderly nun to continue when I heard soft snores and realized she'd fallen asleep. I turned to Sister Mary Katherine.

"Sister, can I come back after she wakes up?"

"Of course, Guinevere. May I ask why?" she asked as we walked arm-in-arm to the door of Sister Agnes's room.

I stopped and looked into her lined and intelligent face.

"Because I'm not sure, but I think you might be able to add Ruthie and Razor's picture to Sister Agnes's answered prayers drawer."

32

Tommy, 2001, Fort Lauderdale

Tommy and Ginny walked hand-in-hand down Fort Lauderdale beach. It was winter in South Florida, but the hot afternoon sun warmed them as the gentle ocean breeze caressed their skin.

It was the weekend after Ginny was supposed to return home from her visit to Illinois. She'd called Tommy the previous Saturday night and told him she wanted to make another stop on her way back and wouldn't be returning on Sunday like she'd originally planned. She'd then filled him in on everything she'd learned from Sister Agnes.

Tommy was disappointed, but he knew it was something she felt compelled to do, and he wouldn't interfere. He rescheduled their special night on the beach. He'd been excited to tell her his news, but the reason for her change in travel plans had put a damper on his enthusiasm.

Now, he clenched her hand tightly in his and blurted out, "Grizz isn't my father, Ginny."

She froze. "What?"

"You heard me right, Gin. He's not my father."

"How could you possibly know this, Tommy? I mean, how can you know for sure?"

Her voice sounded cautious but hopeful.

Tommy explained how he'd had his DNA compared to Mimi's

back in 1999. Or rather, what he thought was Mimi's DNA. How he'd taken a pink toothbrush to his friend Dale. A toothbrush he'd mistakenly thought belonged to Mimi.

"So that pink toothbrush you took to your friend back in 1999 was Jason's? And Dale confirmed the DNA was a match to yours?"

Tommy smiled. "Yes. And it was a match to mine, because it was Jason's, but I didn't know that. Then I heard the kids talking about their toothbrushes right before the cruise. I grabbed the fork Mimi used that morning for breakfast and took it back to him. I would've known sooner, but my friend was in a serious car accident. Then with Christmas and New Year's right after that, he couldn't get to it. Anyway, he got back to me last week." He squeezed Ginny's hand. "He checked and double-checked, Gin—Mimi and I are not biological relatives. I know you were faithful to Grizz. Mimi is definitely his daughter. But I'm not his son. I'm not Mimi's half-brother. I guess it's a good thing we never got around to telling her."

She squealed then and jumped on him, wrapping her legs tightly around his waist. The momentum caught him off guard, and they tumbled to the sand. He looked down at her and gently caressed her chin with his thumb. He brought his mouth to hers and softly kissed her. When he pulled away, she had a serious expression in her eyes.

"Your real father. Do you think you'll ever want to find your real father, Tommy? I mean, you've told me your mother's history. Would it even be possible for you to know who your real father might be?"

He took a deep breath. "I'm pretty sure I know who he is, Ginny."

She blinked. "How? How could you know?"

He sat up then and placed his elbows on his knees as he faced the ocean. He could feel her sit up next to him, and she gently laid her head on his shoulder.

"The Internet is a pretty amazing thing, you know? Search engines and social media. If it had been around in the seventies, you'd have probably been found the same day Monster took you."

She didn't answer, just rubbed his back lightly as she continued to listen.

"When Dale told me my DNA didn't match Mimi's, I decided to do some digging and started searching for Candy's mother, my grandmother. I probably should've done it years ago. It was easier than you might think. I found her, Ginny. She hasn't gone very far. Lives in a little trailer park just north of West Palm Beach. I took a drive up there this past week, and I didn't even have to introduce myself. She knew me. Recognized me. Or rather, she recognized someone else."

"Who?" Ginny lifted her head off Tommy's shoulder and stared at him. He could feel her eyes boring into him.

"It's not pretty. It's not a good story. Are you sure you want to know?"

"Yes, Tommy. I want to know." Her answer was so quiet he almost didn't hear her over the sounds of the crashing waves on the beach.

"I need to tell you some background first, Gin. I need to tell you the rest of Grizz's story. What he told me when I saw him before he died. You already know about his childhood and his little sister. You know he killed his family after his little sister died."

She nodded.

"There's more."

He then proceeded to tell her the rest of Grizz's story—about *them*, and the layers upon layers of deception—leaving nothing out.

She sat back and looked at him, eyes wide with disbelief. It explained everything. Now she knew why Grizz had rejected her. Why he'd insisted on her marriage to Tommy.

Before she could say anything, he returned his gaze to the ocean and continued.

"You're an intelligent woman, Gin. He could've trusted you with the truth, but believe it or not, I understand why he didn't. It's some pretty heavy shit. It's the reason we read books and watch movies. To escape into a world that's not real. Unfortunately, a lot of what we see and read is all too real, and Grizz's story, no matter how strange it might sound, is the truth. At least he believed it was the truth."

He paused and carefully weighed the significance of his next words. "But now that he's dead, it's a non-issue. It was probably a non-issue for them long before he was executed. They never wanted to hurt you. They just wanted to hurt him for blackmailing them for so many years."

He looked at her then and waited for her to say something. Anything.

He knew what he needed to hear. This would be the defining moment in their marriage. It all boiled down to the next words that would be coming out of her mouth. He was holding his breath.

Would she say them?

She swallowed thickly and looked into her husband's eyes. She knew she was being tested. He needed her to validate her real feelings for him, and the only way she could do it was with the truth. And she was certain he knew—or at least had guessed.

"Thank God. Thank God you know, Tommy. I never wanted to tell you because it was pointless as far as I was concerned." After all the talk of lies and secrets she'd convinced herself that what Tommy didn't know was best for him. She had been a hypocrite.

The words tumbled out before she could stop them.

"He's not dead."

His sigh of relief was audible. He grabbed her and pulled her into his arms, stroking her hair and whispering in her ear.

"Thank you. Thank you for telling me the truth, Gin."

They sat on the beach, wrapped in each other's arms, feeling safe and secure in the comfort of their love.

After a minute, she pulled away and tilted her head slightly as she looked at him.

"How did you know?"

"I suspected it when Axel paid me for the cars and bikes. I figured out Grizz's favorite bike wasn't in the garage. I thought about the story he told me when I visited him in prison before his supposed execution. I thought that if anyone could pull a stunt like that and get away with it, it would be Grizz."

He asked her how she'd found out and how long she'd known. She told him about the day she went to clean out Carter's garage and had planned on returning the blue bandana to Grizz's bike before she sold it.

"A story like the one I just told you is something you read in fictional suspense novels." He looked at her questioningly. "You don't seem surprised by it."

"I guess it's because I'm not surprised by it. Think about it, Tommy. Think about some of the Bible studies we've done or what we see in the news every day. I'm not shocked to learn there are unseen forces, and real people, out there running things behind the scenes. Or at least trying to run things. If Grizz was able to pull off a fake execution, why would the existence of this group surprise me?"

"And it doesn't scare you? What's happening behind the scenes?"

She looked at him seriously and gave a small smile.

"I know where my faith is, Tommy."

He nodded and smiled. His Ginny. So steadfast and strong in her faith. He loved her to the core of his being.

But he also knew he needed to bring up one more thing. He'd

thought long and hard about this after she postponed her trip home. He didn't want to do it, but he knew he had to. It was going against everything he fought for, but it was also the only way he could see a future with her without the shadow of Grizz lurking in their lives.

It was the only way to find peace.

"So what did you do with the bandana?" The hope in his eyes pierced her heart.

She smiled at him and told him the truth.

"I threw it in the garbage that same night, Tommy. It's gone."

She knew he believed her. His grin was so wide she thought his face would crack. He stood then and pulled her up to him.

Taking his face in her hands, he told her, "I want you to promise me something."

"Of course! Anything, Tommy."

"When we're finished with our little getaway, we need to stop at the store on our way home."

"A shopping trip? You know how much I hate to shop, Tommy, but a promise is a promise," she teased. "What are we buying?"

She snuggled into his chest, arms tightly wrapped around him. She could feel his chin resting on her head.

And gasped at his next words.

"We need to buy another blue bandana. I want you to wear it."

33

Ginny, 2001, Fort Lauderdale

I couldn't believe what I was hearing. I pulled away from Tommy and looked at him. My brows knitted in concentration as I tried to make sense of his last sentence.

"You want me to what?"

He didn't answer me right away as a small family made their way past us and continued happily down the beach. I placed my hands on my hips and waited for his reply.

"I want you to signal Grizz. I want you to wear it."

"Have you lost your mind?" I glared at him. "After everything you just told me? You want me to see him?"

My eyes narrowed as another thought occurred to me.

"Is this a trick, Tommy? Are you using me to lure him out? So someone can actually kill him?"

Without giving him time to answer, I started marching back toward our hotel. I could feel him close at my heels. He grabbed me by the elbow, swung me around to face him.

"Absolutely not, Gin. That's not why."

His expression was so sincere, I was caught by surprise. I waited for him to continue. He looked up at the sky and shook his head slightly.

"I can't do it anymore, Ginny. I don't want to do it anymore, honey. You need to have Grizz come to you so you can figure out your heart."

"I know my heart!" I shouted it so loud some birds scattered. He wouldn't look at me. "I know my heart, Tommy. It's here, with you." I couldn't believe he was asking me to wear the bandana. Was Tommy purposely sabotaging the progress we'd made? And if so, why? My heart ached at the possibility and my sense of disappointment was acute.

He looked at me then, and I saw something in his eyes that saddened me.

"No, it's not Gin. Not all of it. I can't compete with Grizz. I don't want to spend the rest of my life looking over my shoulder, wondering if he'll show up again. I'm glad he left a way for you to contact him if you needed to. I just can't live like this anymore. I'm refusing to live like this anymore."

"I'm not stupid, Tommy. I know you just tested me back there, and I know I passed. Why are you doing this? Our future is finally here, right now. All the years you waited to be with me. The last fifteen years of our marriage, a good marriage, and it comes down to this?"

"If he's alive, you need to make a choice." The resolve in his voice was firm.

"I have made a choice, Tommy. I'm with you. I'm not going anywhere. Did you not hear me? The bandana is in a landfill."

"But you did go somewhere, Gin. After you talked to the nuns, you stopped on your way home. You stopped where Grizz's real parents were born. You're still searching. For what? Why?"

I swiped my hand through my hair as his accusation and question sunk in.

"I stopped there for you and Mimi. Grizz's roots are Mimi's roots, Tommy. And up until ten minutes ago, I was still under the impression that you were his son. They would've been your roots, too."

"And after everything we've been through, you're ready to connect Mimi back to Grizz's family? Don't you realize, Ginny, that it's not going away? It'll never go away. You need to see Grizz and confront your feelings once and for all. I don't like it. And you're right. It's going against everything that I've fought for, but all of a sudden, I'm tired. Ginny. I'm really tired."

I just stared at him. I wasn't sure how to react.

I was angry because I felt like he'd tricked me, but at the same time, I knew he was being sincere. And worse yet, I knew he was justified.

My shoulders slumped, then something else struck me.

"So I guess you don't believe the story he told you. I mean, if he comes to me, then I guess there isn't any threat to his life. My life. That's all nonsense?"

"I didn't say that. I believe the threat was real. But not anymore. If he's still alive, it's because they don't give a shit, Gin. If I believed there was still a plausible threat from them, no matter how small, I wouldn't be telling you to put on that bandana. I wouldn't have told you any of this. Besides, he won't be able to just roll up and knock on our door. He still needs to live off the grid. He wouldn't risk being seen or recognized by someone who may remember him."

I crossed my arms. "So if I decide I want to be with Grizz, how does that work? I ride away into the sunset, leaving you and my children?" I stomped my foot in the sand. "It sounds ludicrous, and it's not even a decision to be made, Tommy. I am your wife. Your wife."

I poked him in the chest. He didn't flinch.

"Seeing Grizz isn't going to make me change my mind," I added.

He softly grabbed both of my shoulders and what he said sent a chill up my spine. I knew it was painful for him, but I also knew he was serious.

"If it ever comes to that, I promise you we'll figure out a way to make it work. I don't know how. Don't ask me details, because believe me, it's not something I let myself think about."

I roughly shoved him away and spun around to head back to our hotel.

Instead of making love in our romantic hotel room that overlooked the ocean, we spent the rest of our night talking. We canceled our dinner reservations and opted to have room service. The hotel served a quality meal, but it might as well have been cardboard.

We put the bandana conversation on the backburner as Tommy told me more details about his meeting with his grandmother. Apparently, she'd mistaken him for someone else. Her mind, clouded by years of alcohol, thought she was being visited by someone from her past.

"Apparently, I'm the spitting image of David Enman," Tommy told me. "Or rather, what David would've looked like if he'd lived longer."

I shook my head, not recognizing the name.

"He was Donald Enman's brother," Tommy said. "Donald Enman

was Red, the guy I told you about that Grizz met at the motel. Red was Candy's godfather—and, I suspect, my father."

"Why do you suspect that? Maybe your father is David, Red's brother. That's who she thought you were."

Tommy explained how his grandmother knew both Donald and David Enman, and that David had died years before Candy got pregnant.

"Candy's mother, my grandmother, grew up with the Enman brothers. Red was responsible for introducing her to Candy's father, Tom, the man I was named after. She knew Donald and David Enman long before Tom even came into the picture." He stared at the wall over my shoulder and sighed.

"It makes sense now, Gin. What Grizz told me. How Red was obsessed with getting Candy off the street. How he had her practically held captive in Grizz's little apartment above the garages. I remember Grizz specifically telling me Red stayed there with her when Grizz and Anthony couldn't. I think he was raping her, Ginny. I think it had probably been happening long before her teens. I think that's why she turned to prostitution and drugs. To get away from him. I get creeped out when I think about how Grizz must've come up with her nickname."

"Tell me. How did he come up with Candy?" My stomach roiled.

"Grizz told me Red kept a bag of candy behind his bar because my mother, then Stacy Ann, loved candy. Makes the hair on my neck stand up thinking about predators and how they use sweets to bait kids. I wonder if he'd been doing the same thing to my Aunt Karen. Might explain why she was so miserable, too."

"Oh, Tommy. Grizz knew what Red was doing to your mother?"

"No. I don't think he knew at all, Gin. I really think Grizz thought I was his kid. He would never have known Red's brother, so he wouldn't have seen the similarities or made the connection like my grandmother did. Of course, I can't prove any of it. I suppose I could find out where Red or his brother, my biological father, are buried and have one of them exhumed; see if there's any usable DNA, but no. I have my proof. I think I'm done."

All of a sudden, I'd felt the weight of the world that had rested on my husband's shoulders and knew why he felt so tired. I did my best to console him.

I spent the rest of our mini vacation trying to talk him out of the ridiculous plan to summon Grizz. He was still insistent. But we also didn't stop on the way home to buy a bandana. I was relieved.

A WEEK PASSED, AND WE FELL BACK INTO OUR ROUTINE WITH OUR LIFE AND our children. I secretly hoped I'd dreamed the whole bandana nonsense. It hadn't been mentioned since that day at the beach, and I was certain Tommy's suggestion had only been brought on by the emotions of finding out about his real father.

Of course, I'd told him that night at the hotel that he was grabbing at straws based on an old woman's memories. He'd quietly reached for his wallet and pulled out a picture. My jaw dropped as I saw the truth. I was staring at a picture of an eighteen-year-old David Enman, and it could've been Tommy.

But by now, I thought everything was back to normal. I'd tucked what I'd found out about Grizz and his family into a corner of my mind, telling myself that if I ever decided to share it with Mimi, I wouldn't do it now and definitely wouldn't do it without Tommy.

I was in the laundry room folding clothes. Jason had a basketball game coming up, and all his uniforms were dirty. I heard Tommy come in through the garage, I could hear his briefcase as it made its familiar thunk on the bench. I was smiling to myself when he came up behind me and kissed my neck.

"Dinner smells good."

"It's your favorite," I said, leaning back into him.

"I'm going upstairs to change my clothes. I'll be back down in a few."

I turned to face him and stared into his eyes. My smile faded as I saw an expression that made me uneasy.

Without breaking from my gaze, he felt around for my hand and tucked something into it, slowly closing my fingers around it. He turned around and headed out of the laundry room. I could hear him walking up the stairs toward our bedroom.

I looked down and saw what he'd placed in my hand.

A blue bandana.

34

"I think you are being ridiculous, but you know what? If it's so important to you, if it's what I need to do to prove I'm over him, then I'll do it. But let me make it clear, Tommy. I'm not doing this for me. I know my heart. I'm doing it for you."

Ginny had done as promised and put her hair in a high ponytail, wrapping the blue bandana around it, and wore it that way throughout Jason's basketball game.

Tommy noticed Carter's discreet trip to the ladies' room.

It was done. No going back now.

To a casual observer, Tommy and Ginny appeared to be the epitome of happiness. Only Tommy sensed the undercurrent of her attitude. She was upset with him, and he couldn't blame her.

Ginny had said very little to him since the game that afternoon. He'd trudged up the stairs that night alone and after waiting up for her until after midnight, finally decided to turn the light off and try to get some sleep. She'd told him she was going to watch TV in the den and would be up shortly. She was either still upset or had fallen asleep.

He was awakened by his cell phone buzzing on his nightstand. He looked at the clock. 6:45 a.m. He picked up his phone, and not recognizing the number, answered it. It could've been one of the kids from the shelter where he volunteered.

"Yeah?" he mumbled.

He looked to his left and realized Ginny had never come to bed.

"It's Blue. I need to talk to you. I've heard something on the street. Don't know how much truth there is to it, but I want you to know what I heard."

"What is this about?" Tommy was fully awake now.

"It's something I heard about your daughter. About Mimi."

"Tell me." Tommy sat straight up. "What is it? Is she in danger?"

"No. She's not in danger. At least not anymore. It's been a few months, but I need to know if you want anything done about it. I don't want to go into it on the phone, and I'm trying to stay away from this type of shit, but I think this is important. Can you meet me?"

"Yeah. I'll meet you. I was going into the office today for a few hours, but I'll meet you first."

Tommy was already out of bed and heading for the shower.

"Do me a favor. Don't bring Ginny. I don't think this is something she'll want to know."

Then it's a damn good thing she wasn't laying next to me. Tommy hung up. How would he have explained an early morning call from Blue? Blue should've known better.

Less than twenty minutes later, Tommy headed downstairs. He found Ginny asleep in the den. The TV was still on.

"Gin. Gin, wake up." He gently shook her.

She groaned and opened her eyes.

"Uh, I guess I fell asleep. I meant to come up. I—"

"I can see that. You're still in your clothes," he told her.

"You look like you're ready to go somewhere." Her brows knitted together. It was Saturday, wasn't it?

"I forgot to tell you I have to meet with Phil and Brody. I need to go over some plans they're working on for a new client who's coming in on Monday. Do you want to meet me for lunch somewhere? Bring the kids with you? Jason doesn't have any games today. Maybe we can take them to a movie matinee afterward. That is, if you think you can find something everybody wants to see."

He was surprisingly calm and his emotions were steady.

"Yeah," she said in a groggy voice, sitting up. "Yeah, that sounds good. Even if we can't agree on a movie, they have to eat."

She rubbed at her eyes and stifled a yawn. "I smell coffee."

He kissed her forehead. "I just turned the pot on for you. It's still brewing. I'll grab some on my way to work. Call me about noon. We'll make a plan."

At 7:30 a.m. on a Saturday morning, the streets of South Florida were already alive and busy. His meeting with Blue wouldn't take him too far off his regular route to work. He pulled into a convenience store that also had gas pumps.

He left the nozzle running as he headed inside to grab a coffee to-go. He'd said good morning to the clerk behind the counter and headed toward the rear where he saw a coffee station. The clerk glanced up from the newspaper he was reading and grunted. Tommy was the only one inside the store and had just made his coffee when he realized there was something sticky on the handle of the carafe he used to pour the cream. Dammit. He left his cup on the coffee station and headed for the restroom to use the sink.

The moment he exited the men's room, he felt the tension in the air. The atmosphere had changed. He felt uneasy. Quietly, he made his way through the aisles. He could see his car at the gas pumps. He didn't see any other cars in front of the store.

"Keep your hands above the counter! Just give me the money. Put it in here."

A robbery. Tommy could hear the criminal's hand hit the counter hard as he slammed down what must've been a bag.

"If you try and reach for anything below the counter, I'll put a bullet in your head. Got that?"

Tommy ducked low as he surveyed the store. He reached for his cell phone and remembered he'd left it in the console of his car. Fuck. He raised his head slightly to see above the shelves. The thug was now waving the gun around. The nervous clerk was doing as he was told, but Tommy could tell he was shaking. Should he intervene? Should he stay put?

He glanced out the front window then. Another car had pulled up, and an elderly man was leaning against his car as his tank was being filled. He more than likely paid with a credit card and wouldn't be walking into the store. Good.

"You purposely dropped it, motherfucker!"

"No. No, I didn't drop it on purpose." The clerk's voice was desperate. "You're scaring me waving that thing around. It could go off."

"Yeah, well, it's going to go off now."

In two swift movements, the thief shot the clerk in the face and jumped over the counter to retrieve the bag of dropped money.

Time seemed to stand still. As if in slow motion, Tommy saw the man climb back over the counter. He had a plastic grocery bag, and Tommy could see through the thin sack that there was money in it. Tommy hadn't realized it, but he'd been slowly inching closer down the aisle toward the cash register. He could make one quick lunge from behind and knock the thief to the ground. Or he could let him leave and not take any risk.

Tommy and the man spotted her at the same time. A young woman approaching the door. The criminal started to raise his gun. He was going to shoot her when she came inside.

Tommy didn't have to make a decision. It had been made for him.

He started to leap at the man from behind, but something must have caught the guy's attention because he turned just in time to avoid Tommy's grasp. The gun went off, and Tommy felt a quick stab of pain in his stomach.

They were wrestling for the gun now. A split second seemed to play out over the course of an eternity.

Seconds slowed down and stretched out as they wrestled for the gun, time grinding to an abrupt halt. His mind was cluttered with thoughts trying to grapple for his attention, yet they all came to him in a proper and succinct order.

How odd that he hadn't heard from Blue in ages and yet, on the morning they were supposed to meet, Tommy had come upon a robbery. Was this a setup? Was he the actual target?

He could answer it as quickly as he thought it. No. He had randomly selected this store. If he'd stayed in the restroom longer, the perpetrator might've been gone before he came out. The criminal hadn't been looking for Tommy, he'd been heading for the exit.

He looked into the face of the man and stared into dull blue eyes that hadn't seen sleep in days. Eyes that were looking for their next fix. There was fear mixed with anger and hopelessness in those eyes. He was probably not even twenty. Had he killed before? Did he have a family? Did his parents know what their son was doing?

Even with all of these things racing through his mind, Tommy managed to glance at the door. He saw the girl come in. He saw the recognition and fear of what was happening on her face, watched as she turned around and ran, arms flailing frantically as she headed toward another motorist who'd just pulled up.

He looked back into the eyes of the man who'd gambled his entire life away with one bad decision.

Tommy felt the gun loosen from the man's grip, but not before it went off a second time. As he fell to the ground, another bullet lodged in his chest.

The gun now tightly in his own grip, Tommy's last conscious thoughts were of her.

"Ginny. Ginny. Please forgive me," he whispered.

And then his world went black.

GINNY STARED AT HER REFLECTION IN THE BATHROOM VANITY.

After Tommy had woken her up, she'd made her way to the kitchen and poured herself a cup of coffee. She took her mug back into the den and sat down.

Sipping her coffee, she'd quietly reflected on the last two weeks. The visit with Sister Mary Katherine and Sister Agnes. The detour on her way home that brought her to the place where she thought she might find some of Grizz's relatives. Could the elderly nun's memories and Ginny's suspicions be confirmed?

She'd been surprised by what she'd found there. A tight-knit community of people who had roots going back before the Civil War. She was quickly directed to the local historian, and he was more than happy to spend the morning with her sharing local legends, myths, and memories. He was also able to share some facts. He knew exactly who Ginny was asking about. As a matter of fact, he had a surprise for Ginny.

Ginny was shaken out of her thoughts when Spooky jumped up on her lap, almost causing her to spill her coffee.

"You little stinker. Where did you come from?" Ginny asked the cat as she laid her mug on the end table and started to stroke her soft fur. She smiled to herself as she thought about how Jason had insisted on being allowed to name her. They all threw suggestions at him, but he was insistent on Spooky.

"It just fits her," Jason had told them back then. "She's like a mystery gift since you don't know who the present was from. And she's black. It's all kind of... spooky."

Tommy and Ginny had known who the gift was from. Tommy had assured her then that it was Grizz's way of saying from the grave that he was happy for them. And she now knew, after talking to Tommy on the beach last weekend, that it was somebody else's way of letting them know their home was no longer under surveillance. She and Tommy knew that "somebody" was Carter's husband, Bill.

She shook her head at the thought of everything she'd learned. Tommy had told her he was tired. She could understand why. She was tired, too. But she was still also more than a little miffed about his insistence that she see Grizz again. How would she feel when she saw him? She almost hadn't recognized the Grizz she'd seen at the execution. She wondered if he'd shaved his head or if he was naturally going bald. And that beard! She never remembered him wearing one that long.

"Oh, Spooky!" she cried. The kitty had tired of her company, and in her haste to jump off Ginny's lap, had kicked the cup as Ginny was picking it back up off the end table.

Ginny now stared at herself in the bathroom mirror, dabbing spilled coffee off her shirt. No harm done. There hadn't been much left in her cup to clean up, anyway.

She'd passed Jason coming down the stairs as she was going up, told him Tommy wanted to meet later for lunch and a movie, and he should plan on talking to his sister after she woke up.

"You look like crap, Gin," she said to herself. A long hot shower will feel good.

She lifted both hands to remove the bandana and take out her ponytail when she was interrupted by a loud banging on the bathroom door.

Jason.

"Mom. Mom! You need to come downstairs, now! Some cops are here, and they want to talk to you."

35

Ginny, 2001, Fort Lauderdale

"Mrs. Dillon. Mrs. Dillon, I know this is a shock, and I know you've been severely traumatized, but please try and concentrate. Please answer my last question."

"I need to see him. They need to let me see my husband!" I couldn't breathe. "My children. Oh, my goodness, my children. Where are they? They need me!"

I was at the hospital sitting in a small office with two detectives. How I got there was a bit of a blur. I remembered them showing up at the house and asking to speak to me without Jason present. I remembered his curious and frightened look as I led them into Tommy's office and shut the French doors behind us.

I recalled hearing what they told me, that Tommy had been involved in a shooting and was in critical condition at the hospital. I remembered telling Jason to wake up his sister. Surprisingly, Mimi had the foresight to reach for my purse and phone as we followed the men out the door and into the back of the police cruiser. I remembered clinging tightly to Jason and Mimi as I explained to them the little I knew. I remembered hearing Mimi using my phone to call Carter, Christy, and Sarah Jo, and she asked each of them to meet us at the hospital. She told me Christy and Carter were on their way and that she'd left a message for Jo.

"Your children are fine. They're with your friends. You can't see your husband. Not yet, he's in surgery. Please—answer the question, ma'am."

"I'm sorry. I can't remember what you asked me," I said honestly before blowing my nose.

"You said your husband was on his way to work. Can you think of any reason why he would've strayed from his normal route?" the older of the two detectives asked.

I stopped blowing, my fingers still pressing the tissue tightly to my nose. *Tommy was at a gas station that wasn't on his way to work?* I had an instant and roaring headache.

"No," I whispered. "I don't know why he would've been there. You told me you thought it was random. That there were witnesses that said it was a robbery. They saw the guy running off."

"We do think it's random, but after finding out your husband is supposed to testify this year in a trial, we have to ask. We have to check every possibility. We need to make sure it wasn't a setup. That's why we're asking you if you know of any reason he would've strayed from his normal route."

I shook my head slowly. "No. I can't think of any reason. I saw him this morning before he left. He mentioned stopping for coffee on his way to work, but he never said where. We were going to meet later for lunch. There was nothing out of the ordinary."

My body stiffened as I realized there absolutely was something out of the ordinary. Yesterday, I'd worn the bandana to signal Grizz. And this morning Tommy had gotten shot.

But I wouldn't let my thoughts travel that path.

"Are we done? Please, I want to see my children. I need to be with them."

"Of course. We need to be able to stay in contact with you," the younger, more reserved detective answered. "We need to know the best way to contact you."

"That won't be a problem. I'm not leaving this hospital," I told him as I made my way past them and to the waiting room set up for families of trauma victims.

THE NEXT COUPLE OF HOURS DRAGGED. A DOCTOR CALLED ME ASIDE AND attempted to explain that Tommy was still in surgery due to the severity of his wounds. It was still too much to retain, and the only thing I can remember from that conversation was, "Two bullet wounds. One in the abdomen and one in his chest, and he'll be in surgery awhile."

It wasn't until Sarah Jo had shown up and ushered me into Stan's office that I was finally able to understand some of it. Apparently, she and Stan had been out of the country and were visiting some friends while on a layover in Atlanta on the return trip. They'd boarded a flight after getting Mimi's message and were back in Fort Lauderdale in less than two hours.

"You're the chief of surgery, Stan," I said to him through blurred vision. "Shouldn't you be doing his surgery or in there to make sure it's done right?"

"Ginny, I did go in, and he has our best team in there. I would've stayed and taken over if I thought otherwise. It's going smoothly. It's extremely difficult because it's basically two separate surgeries to remove two separate bullets." Stan's voice was calm and even. Reassuring.

He was sitting behind his desk. Jo and I sat in wing chairs facing him. She reached for my hand. I noticed her absently grab for where her mother's pendant normally would've been dangling. It wasn't there. Right after Jo had showed up in the waiting room, Carter was walking toward us to say something when she tripped. As she was falling, she grabbed for Jo and accidentally ripped the necklace from Jo's neck. She apologized profusely and promised Jo she'd send Bill off to have it fixed and returned to her within hours. I saw the concern in Jo's eyes—she was never without that necklace—but I calmly reassured her that Carter and Bill could be trusted with her mother's pendant.

"But it's been hours." I clutched Jo's hand. "It just doesn't seem like it should be taking this long!"

"Don't think like that, Ginny," Sarah Jo said, her voice calm and steady. "It doesn't mean something is going wrong with the surgery. It means they're being thorough. Like Stan said, it's two separate surgeries, and the seriousness of each can affect the other."

"Exactly," Stan said. "Each wound has its own separate and serious complications and needs to be treated as such."

I took a deep breath and sat up straight.

"What complications? Tell me."

Just then there was a knock at the door. Two men came in. They were Tommy's surgeons, and they told me he came through the surgery fine, and he was in recovery, but as Stan explained, his wounds were critical. Now the only thing we could do was wait. I looked up at them and waited for them to continue.

"As you know, he suffered two bullet wounds," said the doctor with the silver goatee, whose name I'd already forgotten. "The one that struck his lung caused air to escape, and the lung collapsed. We put a chest tube in to remove the air and blood in his chest cavity. His lung expanded, and the bleeding has apparently stopped."

I let out the breath I'd been holding.

The second surgeon cleared his throat. "The second bullet, the one in his abdomen, damaged his spleen and his liver, which caused a severe amount of blood loss. We removed the spleen and part of the liver. The blood loss was tremendous. We had to give him thirteen units of blood." His eyes were gentle. "Because of his shock and the massiveness of the transfusion required, his blood won't clot, and we're trying to correct this by giving him various clotting elements."

I started to shake. Jo gripped my hand tighter.

"We anticipate eventually being able to control this failure to clot, but his kidneys and brain have gone through a protracted period of time without being adequately supplied with blood. And there has been damage to the tissue to those two organs, as well as others. Whether those organs will recover, we don't know. Only time will tell."

I went back to the waiting room in a daze and found my children. I took them both into the small hospital chapel and explained everything I could.

I was holding them tightly and sobbing when I felt arms wrap me from behind and a familiar voice said, "I'd have been here sooner, Ginny. I had the boys out on the boat." It was Alec.

I can't remember details after that. Who came. Who went. Who offered to help with Mimi and Jason. Who offered to keep us fed and our clothes clean. Who would notify their schools and our church. Like a well-oiled machine, the acquaintances we'd made over the years, who came from vastly different walks of life, all melded together to make sure my children and I were cared for.

I was in too much shock to realize I'd never really let myself get close to people who weren't inside my tiny circle, yet the support they showed me and my children was beyond heartwarming and appreciated, even though I wasn't in a good enough place emotionally to express that gratitude. I was in a fog.

That first day, the three of us were led into the ICU and allowed to stand at his bedside for just a few minutes. I'd been warned that the trauma of seeing his father might be too much, but the ICU nurses gave into my begging after seeing how badly Jason was taking the news.

They'd been right. The tubes, machines, and wires were too much for him. Jason broke down when he saw his father and started crying. I clung to him and wanted to console him but couldn't bring myself to leave Tommy's side. What if this moment was the last one?

One of Tommy's nurses, Jonell, recognized the need in my eyes, and she gently pried Jason away from me and guided him out to our trusted friends in the waiting room. Mimi took my hand and quietly sobbed, never taking her eyes off Tommy's face.

I don't know how much time passed. Someone, I think it was Christy, brought me a change of clothes and toiletries. I was allowed to shower and sleep at the hospital. I wasn't sure if that was a privilege given to all family members of trauma patients, or if I was given special treatment due to Stan's status. I made sure my children knew I loved them and wanted to be with them, but I couldn't leave their father's side. They both understood and chose to stay at our house with Carter instead of being sent to stay with different families.

Now my children were back, and we stood huddled in the small ICU room watching Tommy. After the shock of seeing his father that first time, Jason approached Jonell all by himself and said he was ready to see his father again. She looked at me with a questioning glance and I nodded. We all linked hands, talking to him and looking for any sign that he'd heard us. An eyelash flutter, a change on any of the various monitors. We were desperate to know if he would wake up.

"Does he know I'm here? Do you think he can hear me?" I asked Tommy's second nurse. Her name was Jennie, and she was changing his IV bags. The kids had returned to the waiting room. "It's been more than two days."

She smiled kindly at me. "It's possible. He's still under sedation, but they changed his medication. It should allow him to have some awareness soon without dulling his pain medication. He should be able to open his eyes or squeeze your hand soon."

Her eyes scanned me with concern. "Have you eaten? I know you don't have an appetite, but you have to eat something, even if you force it down. You need to be strong for him—and them." She nodded her head toward the path the kids had followed out.

"I'm not hungry."

"My grandma made the best banana bread this side of the Mississippi, and she left me the recipe. You know what that means?"

I shook my head.

"It means that now I make the best banana bread this side of the Mississippi. Now, I brought a piece in for Jonell, but she's always saying I ruin her diet, so how about I go swipe that piece I brought her and bring it to you?"

I smiled and nodded, gratitude washing over me. She finished what she was doing, then I watched her walk toward the telemetry station and say something to Jonell, who looked up, smiled at me, and gave me the thumbs-up.

I turned my attention back to Tommy. Taking one of his hands in both of mine, I softly caressed the top of his, doing my best to avoid the IVs.

"Tommy, your nurse Jennie, one of the nurses who's caring for you, she said you might be able to hear me now. I hope you can. I hope you can hear me tell you how much I love you."

He wasn't responding, but that didn't keep me from talking.

"So many people are praying for you. I've been praying, too. I know we're supposed to pray for God's will, but I can't help myself. I'm praying for my will. And my will wants you back, Tommy."

I leaned over and whispered in his ear. "I tried to tell you that day on the beach. There was never a choice to make. I'm never leaving you, Tommy, so please don't leave me. Please wake up."

I was almost positive I felt him gently squeeze my hand. My heart thudded and my soul was filled with hope.

He was coming back to me.

36

Grizz, 2001, Somewhere Between Louisiana And South Florida

H e'd been sitting in the small diner in Louisiana when he saw on a national news station that Tommy had been shot. The fact that it made national news hadn't surprised him much. After all, Tommy had been linked to the arrest of Matthew Rockman, the prominent attorney who'd been arrested for murdering a woman he'd put in the Witness Protection Program fifteen years earlier. That story had made the national news so it wasn't hard to believe that Tommy's shooting had been picked up as well. What did surprise him was that he'd received no word from Carter. That is until he discovered that his pager had been turned off and once turned on, it displayed the words his gut ached to see. SHE NEEDS YOU.

So, immediately after seeing the news report and receiving the page from Carter, Grizz had laid a fifty on the lunch counter and headed for his bike—but not before asking Edna for directions to the nearest highway. He realized he'd found himself at The Green Bean diner by accident and wasn't sure of the fastest route back to Florida.

It was now dark, and he knew he needed to stop somewhere and get some rest. He'd been on the road for hours, and the immediate adrenalin rush that had come upon him had long since waned. He was exhausted.

After checking into the next chain hotel he came upon, he took a long hot shower. On the bed, he flipped through some TV channels, ate a premade chicken salad sandwich that he'd bought at the convenience store next to the hotel, and washed it down with a beer. Nothing was on the news about Tommy's shooting, so he turned off the television and resigned himself to sleep.

But sleep wouldn't come.

He was plagued by too many unknowns. What if this was a trap? He'd have to be extremely careful. And, exactly what did he think he was going to do when he got to Fort Lauderdale? Ride up to Ginny's house or the hospital on his bike and walk in the front door? That certainly wasn't a logical option. Normally, he'd signal Carter and have her set up a way to see Kit. But the longer he thought about it, the more impossible it seemed that this could be arranged. He'd already received another page from Carter letting him know Ginny wasn't in any danger, so he didn't have the sense of urgency he normally would have. But she needed him. That was all he needed to know for now.

Maybe he could watch Ginny from a distance and look for an opening. No. She would not only be surrounded by friends, but by law enforcement, as well. He chanced being spotted by someone who might recognize him. He knew he'd have to wait.

In the meantime, he'd want to find out everything he could about Tommy's shooting, and the only way he'd be able to do that was to trust someone other than Carter and Bill with the truth concerning his execution. Or rather, lack of one.

Blue was his first thought, but due to his personal relationship with a certain female detective, it was too damn risky. Even if they were no longer together, it wouldn't be a smart move. No. He needed somebody who still had connections to the biker world, but lived under law enforcement's radar. A hardworking family man who'd supposedly made a clean start on South Florida's east coast more than a year ago. Someone Grizz would trust with his life and this secret.

Anthony Bear.

His mind made up, he finally drifted into a deep and dreamless sleep. He was awakened several hours later by a loud banging on his hotel room door. Housekeeping. He told them to come back in an hour.

Less than fifteen minutes later, he was on his bike. First, he had to ride a few hours out of his way to a garage that he'd rented. He would retrieve the car he'd left there, along with more clothes, personal items, cash, and a burner phone he could use to contact Anthony. After setting up a way to see Bear, he'd toss the phone.

He looked at the credit cards that had been set up with his new identity and knew he'd never use them. He was putting them in his wallet when he pulled out his license and realized he no longer looked like the man in the picture. His hair had grown in over the past several months, and he'd trimmed his beard significantly. Anthony would be able to get a new picture for his new identity.

His new identity. Another fucking name to have to answer to. Dammit. But at least they gave him that. James Kirkland screamed "boring alias" as much as it screamed average American Joe. It would do. Besides, they'd held up their end of the bargain. He was told Jason "Grizz" Talbot's DNA and fingerprints had been replaced in the system by counterfeits. He was getting a clean slate, and if James Kirkland's DNA and fingerprints were run, the searches would come up empty unless James Kirkland did something to get himself in trouble.

Point being, if he found himself in hot water with the law, there would be nothing to connect him back to a dead Jason Talbot. It wouldn't be an issue. He planned on staying clean.

He was now a widowed father of two non-existent children who'd made a living as a heavy equipment operator until he suffered a back injury on the job. Shit, they even had the government sending disability checks to James Kirkland's bank account. You couldn't get any more vanilla than that. He'd tested his new identity early on when he purposely ran a red light somewhere in Georgia. The cop ran his bike's license plate and came back with a warning. He checked out. He was James Kirkland.

He turned up the car radio as he drove south and pondered whether he should do anything to get Blue out of town for a while. More than likely, Blue would be concerned about Tommy, Ginny, and their children and might even put a detail on them to make sure they were safe. Grizz still had no way of knowing if Tommy's shooting was random or planned. He heard them mention on the news that Tommy was supposed to testify in Rockman's trial, but Grizz was certain it wasn't a testimony that would make or break Matthew's case. Blue had made sure the evidence planted in Jan's murder pointed to Rockman.

He shook his head as he remembered another detail. When he'd questioned Tommy's loyalty at the end, he'd allowed some evidence to look like it could've pointed to Tommy. He was going to drop the ball on him if he thought he'd been deceitful, which he hadn't been. *Fuck me. Why couldn't I have just left it alone? What if Tommy was shot because of something to do with Rockman's trial? Shit.*

He allowed his mind to wander back to what, or rather who, he'd found in Louisiana. He had no doubt he'd met Kit's twin sister. He smiled when he thought about the note he could have Carter anonymously deliver to Blue: "Grizz's last order before his execution, specifically to be delivered to you several months after his death. He left something for you in a diner called The Green Bean. You will find this diner in Chinkaw, Louisiana, and you'll know the package and what to do with it when you see it."

Grizz laughed when he thought about Blue meeting Kit's twin sister, Jodi. But he also knew he'd never have the message sent. The last thing he needed to do was have Blue drag Jodi back to Fort Lauderdale to meet Ginny while he was trying to see her. No. He'd save this surprise for a future day and for now do everything he could to avoid Blue.

He was listening to Pink Floyd's "Run Like Hell" and enjoying the rumble and power of his 1972 Chevelle when he was hit with a wave of grief so profound it almost took his breath away.

He let up on the gas and turned down the radio. He'd never experienced anything like this before, and he didn't know how to react to it. He slowly took in his surroundings. He was on a stretch of highway that was desolate. He couldn't see any cars in front of him or behind him. Cows grazed lazily in green fields dotted with patches of dry, dead earth. He felt a weight so enormous, so thick, he wondered for a second if he was having a heart attack.

No. He wasn't feeling a physical chest pain. It was a pain of the soul. A pain of loss. He hadn't even felt this at his own execution.

Kit.

He pressed down on the accelerator.

37

Tommy, 2001, Fort Lauderdale

He could hear her. Her voice was breaking through his consciousness.

Where am I? Why couldn't he answer her? He thought he felt a gentle caress on his hand. It was so light it felt like a dusting of air. Her voice was doing battle with some other noise. It sounded like a hiss. And the beeps. What were those beeps?

He tried to let her know he could hear her. He was certain now she was holding his hand and softly stroking it. He wanted to reach for her, but his arm felt like it was encased in cement. Ginny, I can hear you! I can hear you telling me you love me. I love you, too. Why can't I say it? Why can't I reach for you?

The memory was instantaneous. The gas station. Coffee. A robbery. He'd been shot, and now he was in the hospital. He felt an incredible weight as the reality of what had happened to him started to sink in. His mind was starting to clear. Remembering the gunshots, he wondered how he could be semi-conscious and yet feel no pain. Must be the miracle of modern drugs.

Then he heard another voice. One that concerned him. Sarah Jo.

"Why don't you take a quick break and let me stay with him a minute, Gin?"

"Thanks, Jo, but I can't. I think he might be coming around. I swear he tried to squeeze my hand before." Tommy could hear the hope in Ginny's voice.

"Oh, Gin, that's wonderful news!" Jo said.

If Tommy didn't know Jo so well, he might've thought her response was sincere.

"I know you haven't left the room in hours. Why don't you at least go use the bathroom and grab a coffee. Stretch your legs. I promise I won't leave his side."

"Yeah, maybe you're right. Jennie promised me another piece of banana bread. I'll run to the restroom, then grab a coffee. Oh, you got your mother's necklace back! Carter told you Bill would get it fixed for you."

What Ginny was saying about Jo's necklace didn't make sense to Tommy. Even though he couldn't see her, he was certain Jo was clutching the pendant nervously. He'd watched her do it a thousand times.

"And Carter was right. I got it back after just a few hours. It's right as rain. Now, go. I'll stay and talk to him."

"I'll be right back. Do you want something?"

"I want you to take a break and know I won't leave his side until you come back, okay?"

Tommy couldn't hear Ginny's response so she must've nodded. He felt her lift his hand to her mouth and softly kiss the inside of his palm.

Don't leave me, Ginny. His mind was racing, yet a calmness and peace he hadn't expected settled over him. He felt his other hand being lifted and heard Sarah Jo's voice.

"Stan and I had just returned from Sydney and were visiting friends in Atlanta when Mimi called me. I was doing what you said, Tommy. Pushing Stan to interview in other countries. But, circumstances change, don't they?" There was a pause. She couldn't possibly have expected him to answer her. "Tommy, do you know how easy this would be for me? All I'd have to do is squeeze one of the tubes on your ventilator and stop the air flow."

He realized then that he wasn't breathing on his own. The hiss he'd woken to was a ventilator machine.

"Or I could slip a syringe out of my pocket and inject insulin right into your IV. I'd have my back to the nurses, and they wouldn't know what I was doing. You're already being given a certain amount of insulin, so if they ever did an autopsy, which I doubt they will because of the seriousness of your wounds, they'll never look for an insulin overdose. It would be so easy. Too easy."

Tommy knew he should've been panicking at what Jo was saying, but he wasn't. He felt a peaceful bliss come over him. He'd never felt anything like it. It certainly wasn't earthly. Jo was standing over his hospital bed threatening his life, and he knew with every fiber of his being she could get away with it. She was the director of nursing, and her husband was the chief of surgery. They were close personal friends. Nobody would suspect or even guess that she had caused his death.

He should've cared. He should've been frightened. But oddly, he wasn't.

He felt an unexplainable pull. A calling. He felt like he was being summoned. He suddenly became aware of a light and wanted to be near that light more than anything he'd ever wanted in his life. Even his lifelong quest for the woman he'd always been in love with didn't tug at him like the light did. The woman he loved. Ginny. His children. Mimi and Jason. He could see them now.

As he reflected back on the life he'd lived, he was given the gift of feeling every joyous moment he'd ever experienced with all of them. It was beautiful, and it almost pulled him back, but it didn't compare to the light. A light that was so brilliant it should've blinded him.

Ginny.

He couldn't leave. Wouldn't leave. They needed him. He needed them. He tried to turn away from the light then, and that's when he saw it. Just like the gift of instantaneous joy he'd felt seconds earlier, he saw a glimpse of a future for his family. He saw their grief about his death. And as much as it pained his heart, he knew it would be replaced with eventual acceptance and peace. He knew they would be cared for. He knew they would live happy and full lives. He knew he would always have a special place in their hearts.

And he knew in his own heart he needed to let them go. To let her go.

Ginny.

He'd forced something that wasn't meant to be. Did he think saving a pair of potholders or stamping her initials on a Bible would carry any weight in deciding their future? Did he really believe anything he did, calculated or otherwise, was because he was in charge of a fate that could be manipulated to his advantage? Should he have moved on after Grizz married her? Should he have gone on with his life and given another woman a chance?

He knew the answer was no. He'd spent the best fifteen years of his life married to Ginny. Being her husband and raising their children was a privilege, and he wouldn't have traded it for anything. He now believed with all of his heart that, for the short time he'd had her, she was his. Ginny loved wholly, honestly, and unconditionally, and he knew that if he woke up, she would spend the rest of her life with him. But he wasn't sure he wanted to wake up.

Ginny.

The shooting was random. What unseen force had pushed him to convince her to wear the bandana the day before? His mind wrestled with his motive. He even remembered questioning his own sanity when the idea came to him, but he couldn't let it go. Was it his final move in the chess game he'd started so long ago and later abandoned? Was he so prideful that he couldn't just accept Ginny's word that she wanted to be with him? He'd forced the last move to prove what? To have the satisfaction of looking Grizz in the eyes and seeing the pain that Ginny's rejection would inflict?

The euphoria that felt like liquid peace being poured into his soul gave him the miracle of seeing into his own heart. No, his insistence that she wear the bandana one more time wasn't his pride or a challenge to Grizz. It was something bigger.

Grizz. His nemesis for as long as he could remember. But all of a sudden, Tommy no longer saw him that way. It was as if a veil was being lifted, and instead of the heartless criminal, Tommy saw the man who'd come back, if Ginny allowed it, and care for and protect his family. The man that one day Mimi would accept and Jason would look up to. Tommy knew his earthly self would have been appalled by that thought. But his spirit knew differently. Was he seeing truth, or was he seeing what his subconscious wanted to see so he could step over into the light and not take guilt or fear with him? He then realized there would be no fear or guilt inside the light.

Ginny.

Every negative feeling he'd ever experienced was instantly gone. There was no jealousy, no despair, no depression, no grief, no fear. No hatred. Even his newfound disdain for Sarah Jo had evaporated. Extinguished itself. She was still standing by his bedside talking, but he was no longer hearing her. He caught a glimpse of the little girl he

BETH FLYNN

remembered from their childhood. He saw her sloppy pigtails and freckled nose and, more than anything, he saw her grief.

Then he felt something he hadn't expected. He felt the pain she'd endured at the loss of her mother. He felt the little girl who'd cried so long and so hard her eyes swelled completely shut. He could hear Fess's gentle voice as he held his only daughter. "You're my number one girl now, Sarah Jo. Now that Mom is in heaven, you're my best girl, and nobody will ever take your place." No matter how misguided, Tommy now understood why she'd done the things she had. And he forgave. How? How was he seeing and feeling these things?

Ginny.

The light was warm. It was beautiful and inviting, and he no longer wanted to resist, but he felt he needed to. Because of her. Because of his children.

Then he heard a voice.

"Tommy."

It was a voice he'd only heard over the course of a few weeks, and that was more than thirty years ago, but he recognized it as if it'd only been yesterday. A voice that had once been snippy and pushy and mean.

"When you're finished folding towels you need to clean Grizz's bathroom and write down anything he might be running low on," she'd snapped. Yes, he remembered that voice.

He looked to his left and smiled.

Moe.

She reached for his hand, and he gave it to her. He looked down then and saw the commotion. The people standing over him trying to bring him back to life. Even Sarah Jo looked like she was trying to help. He peered through the glass walls of his hospital room and saw two men holding Ginny back. He could hear her screams, see the coffee that had been splattered on the floor.

"He squeezed my hand! He heard me talking to him! He squeezed my hand!" she was screaming at the top of her lungs. Tears were streaming down her face. She was taking on two large orderlies and winning as she clawed her way back into his room.

He immediately felt her world, the one he was leaving behind, and sensed he was moving back down toward the hospital bed. Hovering above the cold reality and harshness of an earthly life. He gazed upon the sterile hospital room. The cold metallic sharpness that was in

218

complete opposition to everything he knew to be within the light that awaited him. His heart ached for the reality that Ginny would be facing without him. The grief she would experience with his passing. But with that knowledge came the peace that this wasn't the end for them. Something deep inside him stirred, and he knew Moe's next words to be true.

"She'll find you. They'll all find you, Tommy. They'll find us."

"How do you know?" He didn't actually speak the words, but he heard his own voice asking her.

"Because I found you," was her reply.

He looked at Moe and started to feel himself being tugged upward again, away from the hospital room and toward the light that was full of unconditional and all-encompassing love. Love. He thought he knew about love. He had been wrong.

"She'll be okay, Tommy. They'll all be okay."

It was then that he thanked God for the miraculous gift of tranquility and complete knowledge that what Moe said was true. It was then that he told Ginny one last time that he loved her and their children. It was then that he resigned himself with a peace beyond human understanding that it was his time.

Then, he reached into the depths of his soul and allowed himself to see a truth he'd always avoided. She was never meant to be just his and he realized, as Moe subtly nodded toward the light, that for the first time in his entire life, he was finally at a place of acceptance, peace, and pure love.

"He's waiting for you," Moe whispered.

Tommy remembered a Scripture then. Then the dust will return to the earth as it was, and the spirit will return to God who gave it.

He nodded and smiled at her. He was ready.

PART II

"Sometimes our lives have to be completely shaken up, changed, and rearranged to locate us to the place we're meant to be."

Unknown

38

Grizz, 2001, Fort Lauderdale

H e carried his groceries into the small efficiency apartment he'd
rented on the beach. He'd been back in Fort Lauderdale for two
days, and in that time he'd been unable to meet with Carter, but he'd
learned from the local news that Tommy had succumbed to his
wounds and died—at almost the same instant he'd had that overwhelming sense of grief while driving.

Had he been sensing Kit's pain? He wanted to believe he had that
type of connection with her. But he quickly reminded himself that
people that did the kinds of things he'd done didn't have those types
of experiences. It was probably heartburn from the chicken salad he'd
eaten.

Now there was nothing to do but sit and wait. He couldn't go to
Ginny, and he certainly couldn't have her brought to him. And he
didn't want to approach Anthony until after Tommy's funeral.

He was eager to talk to Anthony. He wanted to know what
Anthony might've heard on the street. Had it been a random act of
violence toward Tommy, or had it been connected in any way to something else?

He put away his groceries and made himself a sandwich. Sitting
down, he reached for the remote. He scanned the local news channels
and paused at one showing a sketch. It was a rendering of the alleged

perpetrator in the convenience store shooting. The newscaster explained that the convenience store didn't have surveillance cameras, so they had to rely on a few eyewitnesses. That sketch looked like every Joe Schmo between Miami and West Palm Beach.

If he could just get to Anthony, he could find out more. The street was always more reliable than any news station.

He washed his sandwich down with a soda and stared around the small efficiency. It was nicely furnished and clean. He stifled a yawn and realized he was bored stiff. The urge to ride summoned him. But he'd left his bike in that warehouse, and he wasn't going to buy one or steal one off the street for a joyride. Or, maybe he could borrow a bike for just a few hours. Damn. Staying out of trouble might be harder than he thought.

He crushed the empty soda can and tossed it at the garbage bin in the tiny kitchen. It missed and resounded with a loud ping on the tile. He got up to retrieve it and noticed the canvas bag he'd kept in one of his saddlebags on the motorcycle. He remembered hastily throwing it in the car when he'd emptied his bike.

It was the bag he'd stowed Moe's journal in. He'd never gotten around to reading it. He hadn't wanted to. A wave of nostalgia hit him, and he weighed his options.

Steal a bike for a couple of hours and chance getting caught, or open up that book and take a glimpse into Moe's life? He'd not let himself think about Moe too much. He knew it was because when he did think about Moe, it was only with regret. Regret was something he didn't like to face. Something he didn't like to admit he felt. People like him didn't feel regret. They accepted their choices and moved on.

Why wasn't he moving on?

"Okay, Moe," he said out loud. "What do you want to say to me?"

He was certain it was a big "fuck you, Grizz." But he'd avoided her long enough.

He took the journal out of his bag and sat back down on the couch. He had time to read a couple of pages.

THREE DAYS LATER, HE SAT IN A CAR AND WATCHED THROUGH DARK windows as cars pulled into the cemetery and people approached what would be Tommy's final resting place. Ginny was having him buried next to Delia and Vince. Grizz had "borrowed" a nondescript four-door sedan with heavily tinted windows to be able to attend the funeral. With the window slightly cracked, he could hear snippets of conversations as people made their way through the throng of cars starting to get backed up.

Others arrived on motorcycles, the loud pipes breaking the silence and symbolic of the stark contrast of the lifestyles of those who came to show their respect. He watched as the chairs that had been set out started to fill up. He couldn't miss the unmistakable outline of Anthony Bear. His head and shoulders rose above the rest. Christy sat on his left, and a handsome young man, who seemed to favor Christy, sat on his right. Didn't Bear have two boys? It was then that Grizz's focus was drawn to the right, and he had to squint to see if his eyes were playing tricks on him. A young man, whose resemblance to Anthony was uncanny, was leaned up against a tree some distance from the others. His arms were crossed as he balanced on one foot, the other perched behind him against the large trunk. This was definitely one of Anthony's boys, even though he wasn't as big as Anthony— yet. Grizz could tell by his posture that he exuded the same brooding countenance as his father.

He noticed a hearse and a black limousine, followed by a few cars, pulled up on a side access road. He recognized Carter and Bill, as well as Sarah Jo and her husband, whose name he couldn't remember and wasn't even sure if he'd ever known it. They walked toward the big, black vehicle and guided Ginny, Mimi, and Jason out of the car and to the folding chairs.

He hadn't realized he was holding his breath. Seeing her like this caught him off-guard. She walked stoically toward the designated area, clutching the arms of both her children, yet obviously carrying the burden of so much pain. At one point, she stopped and seemed to bring them closer to her. After a brief moment, she regained her composure and kept walking. Mimi and Jason. Mimi, an almost exact carbon copy of her mother at that age. Jason, the spitting image of a ten-year-old Tommy.

Grizz felt a lump forming in his throat and a hard wave of nausea. He felt as out-of-place as a football player in a ballet recital. An imposter. He was glimpsing a world he knew nothing about. One he tried to pretend existed for him and Ginny during their ten-year marriage, but one he hadn't experienced. Raising a family.

It was Tommy who'd been a real husband to her and a real father to the children. Tommy, who'd wiped butts and noses. Tommy, who'd gone to school recitals and met with teachers. Tommy, who'd purposely kept his family as far away as possible from anything criminal or illegal.

What had he done? He told Ginny he'd quit that lifestyle when they had a baby. He didn't get away from that life for her. He'd put a condition on it.

He was a prick.

He hadn't realized how far his thoughts had wandered when a voice carried on the soft breeze and found its way through the tiny opening of the car window. It was Sarah Jo. She was addressing the mourners. He listened with half an ear, his heart in his throat.

"Solomon told us in the Book of Ecclesiastes that there is a time for everything, and a season for every activity under the heavens. A time to be born and a time to die, a time to plant and a time to uproot, a time to kill and a time to heal, a time to tear down and a time to build, a time to weep and a time to laugh, a time to mourn and a time to dance, a time to scatter stones and a time to gather them, a time to embrace and a time to refrain from embracing, a time to search and a time to give up, a time to keep and a time to throw away, a time to tear and a time to mend, a time to be silent and a time to speak, a time to love and a time to hate, a time for war and a time for peace."

Sarah Jo then went on to share some stories about knowing Tommy as a child. Grizz stopped paying too much attention, instead gazing at Ginny, at her long hair and her beautiful face. He heard some mild chuckles as Sarah Jo recited a happy memory.

"And you know what I told him when he fell in that puddle? I told him he was getting his just desserts for squirting me down with the hose. It was tit for..." She paused as if she was overcome with emotion. She cleared her throat and started to tell another story.

Another round of quiet chuckles followed, but Grizz barely heard them. He stared out the windshield and was brought back from his thoughts when he sensed movement. The funeral was over. People were leaving.

He was parked behind two cars and knew he'd be expected to move his car when they pulled away. He couldn't help but notice when a handsome man, who hadn't been part of the group that showed up with Ginny, gently took her by the elbow and started walking her back toward the limo. There was something in the man's posture that raised an alarm. The man was followed by two boys who walked with Jason.

Grizz didn't know who the guy was, but he sensed a threat and instantly didn't like him.

He heard a soft beep from behind him, realized it was time to leave. After starting the car, he shifted into drive and pressed on the gas. Something was tickling his cheek. Had a bug flown in through the cracked window? He went to wipe his face and pulled his hand back. His fingers were wet. He glanced at his hand, his first instinct to see if it was blood.

He was surprised when he realized it wasn't blood at all.

It was tears.

39

Ginny, 2001, Fort Lauderdale

I thought I knew what grief was. I'd felt it many times in the past. I remember the crushing weight of Moe's suicide and the devastation of Grizz's arrest, incarceration, and what I believed to be his execution. I'd even experienced a profound sense of loss after learning I had a twin sister who'd died in infancy.

None of it compared to what I felt with Tommy's death. The pain was thick, heavy, and had found a home in the middle of my chest.

I wasn't grieving just for myself this time, but for my children, as well. The pain of knowing Tommy wouldn't be there for the milestones in Mimi and Jason's lives was almost more than I could bear.

I remembered clinging tightly to my children as we were escorted by our friends from the limousine to the graveside service. I grabbed them tighter when I felt Grizz's presence. I knew he was there and resolved myself to push him as far away from my thoughts as possible. I was angry about everything, and for whatever reason, I was channeling that anger at Grizz.

I'd had no time alone with Carter, but I was certain she'd signaled him and he was out there, waiting for me to come to him. I didn't know how or when it was going to be arranged, and quite frankly, I didn't care. It was a moot point anyway. As far as I was concerned, he could just go back to wherever it was he'd come from, and I made sure

Carter knew I meant it when she discreetly asked me at the hospital the day Tommy was shot if I thought I was in any danger.

The next two weeks were a blur as we buried our grief beneath the love and concern we'd received from all the people who'd reached out to provide comfort. I had no choice but to stay busy with the business and legal aspects of Tommy's death. I kept my children with me as much as possible and somewhat reluctantly let them spend time with friends. I knew it was good for them, and I was actually grateful and relieved when they returned to some activities that would help them forget, however briefly, that their father was gone.

Alec had taken Jason and his sons to a professional hockey game. Christy had taken Mimi to the mall. Christy and Anthony's little girl, Daisy, needed a new dress, and she thought Mimi would enjoy the shopping trip.

I now had the house to myself. The children were gone. The visits from friends had slowly trickled off. People went back to their normal lives and schedules.

But I couldn't see anything normal or routine in my future. It hurt too much to think about Tommy not being a part of it. The almost-silence weighed heavier than any noise I'd ever known. The ticking of the grandfather clock, the muffled sound of ice being dumped in the freezer bin, the quiet hum of the dryer. I felt a ridiculous sense of betrayal by the appliances in our home. How could they still function when I couldn't? Where were they getting their strength from? An electrical socket? I wish it were that simple for human beings. Plug yourself into the wall and just keep going.

It suddenly occurred to me I had nothing to do. The house was clean, and there was enough food in the refrigerator and freezer to feed us for a month. I would go to the one place where I knew I would find solace. My Bible.

I was getting ready to head upstairs to retrieve it from my night-stand when I was distracted by the sound of the mail truck. I walked to the front window and watched as it pulled up to our mailbox. I realized that I was eager to see if there were any cards or letters of sympathy. I found comfort in knowing someone had taken the time to write and mail a card with their condolences.

Slowly I walked back to the house, my head down as I sorted through the different envelopes. Seeing the electric bill mixed in with the other mail angered me. Doesn't anybody realize my husband is dead? Don't the people at the electric company know my life will never be the same? How dare they send me a bill in the middle of all this? How dare they expect me to carry on with my life as if everything is okay? It'll never be okay.

There was an official looking envelope from the State of Florida. My lips set into a thin line. Probably his death certificate.

I went inside, absently shutting the door behind me. I laid the mail on the table by the front door and opened up the envelope with the official state seal.

When I realized what I was looking at, I sank to the floor and wept uncontrollably. The ice-cold tile in our foyer felt good against my fevered skin.

It wasn't Tommy's death certificate. It was the official birth certificates he told me he'd have made for us the day I cleaned out Carter's garage. We'd always used the doctored ones we'd been given. These were the real deal. I was officially and legally Guinevere Lemon, and he was officially and legally Thomas Dillon.

Except now, it no longer mattered. Because he was gone.

The sobs finally subsided, but I couldn't bring myself to get up. I lay there for I don't know how long, thoughts of having to go through Tommy's personal things overwhelming me. How was I going to do this? I'd been faced with this task twice in the past. The first time was when Moe died, and the second time after Grizz was arrested. Both times I'd run from my obligation and let someone else handle it. I wouldn't do that this time.

I found the strength from an unbelievably wonderful and unexpected source: Mimi.

After Christy brought Mimi home that day, we sat in the den and talked about her father.

"Mom, can I ask you something?" she whispered.

"Of course, you can, honey," I sipped on the herbal tea I'd made the both of us.

"I don't know what's considered etiquette or proper. I mean, it hasn't been that long. But it must be hard for you going into your room every night. Seeing his things like he left them that morning."

She was right. I hadn't touched a thing. I refused to throw away the crumpled up Jolly Rancher wrappers he left all over the house. I couldn't even bring myself to pick up his toothbrush where he'd left it on the side of the sink and place it back in the holder where it belonged. I fell asleep every night clutching his pillow to my chest and inhaling his scent. I was petrified that I'd forget what he smelled like.

Terrified that I wouldn't remember his voice, the feeling of his caress, the softness of his lips on mine or the sense of oneness when we made love.

"Yes, it, it—" I said, a frog in my throat. "It's torture."

"Let me help you," she said. "Not one big project, but maybe a little bit at a time. Let me help you make decisions. Let me help you decide what's okay to let go and what you need to keep. Let me laugh with you, because we know you'll remember some funny times with him."

Before I could answer her, she said, "And let me cry with you, because I know that if my heart is breaking, yours must be shattered in a million tiny pieces."

I gulped back the tears that were threatening and nodded. My daughter was growing up.

IT WASN'T EASY, BUT I HAVE TO SAY THAT IF I DIDN'T HAVE MIMI, I DON'T know that I could've gotten through it. Mimi put herself in charge of organizing Tommy's things for donation. She came home one day from school carrying two cardboard boxes that she'd picked up somewhere along the way.

"The boy's shelter where Dad volunteered could really use toiletries, Mom. They don't even mind if they're slightly used."

A few days later she told me she'd found a nonprofit organization that helped rehabilitated drug addicts find jobs, and they needed decent clothes to wear for their interviews. Little by little, I inched my way toward healing as I told myself Tommy's things wouldn't be thrown away. They would serve the needs of someone less fortunate.

It still wasn't easy. I'd gone through his suits and pants pockets before letting Mimi take them, and I found some small items that tore my heart apart all over again. The hardest one was a small to-do list in the pocket of a blazer I hadn't seen Tommy wear in years. I remembered when he'd written it. We were out having dinner, and I'd excused myself to use the restroom. When I returned, he was writing a note to himself.

"What are you writing?" I asked as I sat down and picked up my napkin to put it back on my lap.

"I have to remember some things for work tomorrow," he'd said without looking up.

I now read what he wrote that night. His to-do list for the following day.

Have Eileen set up call with the Dakota people.

Look at Brody's file. Time for a raise?

Pull Scott specs for new client. Similar design to what they want.

Tell Ginny how beautiful she looked last night.

Mimi had told me that day in the den that she knew my heart must've been shattered into a million pieces. She was wrong.

Sitting on the bed, reading the handwritten note, remembering that he did tell me the next day how beautiful I looked that night at dinner, I was certain I would never find my way back from the grief. There was no heart still beating in my chest. I was empty. Void.

There was nothing left.

40

Ginny, 2001, Fort Lauderdale

Of course, I'd been wrong. The heart, I learned, was a resilient little muscle that wouldn't give up, even when I wanted to. Its steady beat was in total opposition to my emotional ups and downs, though more downs than ups in those weeks following Tommy's death.

I thanked the Lord every day for the gift of His presence and my children. In Him and in them, I found my strength to get up every morning.

Alec spent one afternoon with me as we went through Tommy's home office. He quietly excused himself as I sat on the leather couch and cried into the two homemade potholders Tommy had put back in his desk. Alec knew he was intruding on a personal moment, and he returned ten minutes later with two steaming mugs of coffee and a cold washcloth for me to wipe my face.

He sat next to me and shared stories from the office. Stories I'd never heard. We could hear the three boys playing in Jason's room above us. Alec did the same thing when it came time to clean out Tommy's personal things from Dillon & Davis Architects. He was a strong and steady friend, and I realized I'd started to rely on him not only for his friendship, but for Jason, as well. Alec and his boys were so good to Jason who, like me, would break down without warning.

I don't know how much time had passed when Carter showed up on my doorstep one day.

"Let's walk while it's still nice weather. I heard we're going to have an unusually hot spring," she told me, offering her arm.

I knew what this was about, and I wasn't ready to face it.

"No. I don't feel like walking," I said, my voice sour. "I know what you want. You want to tell me he's back, and he's been waiting for me. So I guess he's waited long enough, and he sent you over here with orders for me to meet him."

"Uh, no, that's not why I'm here at all, and before you say any more, remember—you're the one who summoned him. You wore the bandana."

"Well. I—I didn't mean to. I happened to be wearing a ponytail that night, and the bandana went with my jeans and top, and I forgot it was a way for you to signal him."

Carter looked at me sideways. "You are still the lousiest liar I know, Ginny."

I looked at the ground. "It doesn't matter now why I wore it. I told you that day at the hospital it was a false alarm, and the kids and I aren't in any danger. He can go away. And—and tell him he can absolve you from your duty. I won't be sending any more signals. Ever."

I thrust my chin in the air, and tried not to let it shake.

"If that's what you really want, then I'll get the message to him. But Gin, I'm here for one reason only. I'm here because I love you, and I know everybody has gone back to their lives. I really do just want to see if you want to take a walk with me. That's all. No ulterior motives."

She smiled at me. And after a few moments, I couldn't help but smile back. Of course, that was why she was here. This was Carter.

She came inside and waited for me to put on my sneakers. I ran up the stairs. But as I did, I realized I still wondered one thing: why Grizz had made no effort to try to see me.

It was so unlike him and, after all, I had worn the bandana.

41

Grizz, 2001, Fort Lauderdale

It was the hardest thing he'd done since telling her to marry Tommy all those years ago. Staying away from her was pure torture. Not knowing why she'd worn the bandana. Not knowing why she'd summoned him.

Carter couldn't offer an explanation. She could only confirm that Ginny wasn't in danger. He was relieved to know that, but still.

He had to let the weeks pass. Had to stay away. She was surrounded by too many people, too much activity. And who the fuck was that guy from the funeral?

Grizz had finally made himself known to Anthony Bear. After recovering from the shock of seeing his dead friend, and knowing better than to ask him the whys or hows of the situation, Anthony helped him settle back into society as James Kirkland. They both knew there were people out there living among society who were thought to be dead to the world, people who'd been murdered or died in accidents or disappeared and were presumed dead. Even people who'd been put to death. It wasn't as hard as one might think. People didn't recognize the dead among the living because they weren't looking for them. The only exception, of course, was Elvis. And everybody knew he was really dead. Wasn't he?

So that's what he and Anthony decided would be best. At least for now, Grizz would live in plain sight as James Kirkland. But, hiding in plain sight didn't mean he would put himself out there. Grizz rarely left his house, but he needed to keep himself busy. Since Anthony had moved over to this coast, he'd disassociated himself with his West coast gang and appeared to be running a legitimate landscaping business. It would be on one of these crews where Grizz would find employment. Since Anthony didn't employ anyone from his past, there would be no chance of Grizz running into one of his or Anthony's old club members. With his hair up beneath a baseball cap and dark sunglasses on most of the time, Grizz did his best to look like the guy next door. He'd even had some of his more memorable and identifiable tattoos changed while still in prison and in spite of the heat, even took to occasionally wearing long sleeve T-shirts in the hopes of drawing less attention to them.

He thought he'd hate it, being an average Joe, but he didn't. Anthony put him on a small crew of barely-English-speaking hard workers. No punks. No troublemakers. Just decent, hardworking men trying to earn an honest living. Their small crew was always assigned to work on homes on several acres and far away from the bustling and crowded neighborhoods. Grizz put on his sunscreen, ball cap, and sunglasses and rode the mower most of the day. Since discovering his love of reading in prison, he always wore earphones and would listen to audio books.

He avoided listening to his rock music. It got under his skin and would stir up old memories and make him anxious. For what, he wasn't sure. He was already restless enough. Waiting. For her.

"His name is Alec Davis," Anthony had told him one day. They were having lunch beneath the shade of a large tree. Anthony checked in daily with each of his crews, always making sure to show up on Grizz's jobsites around lunchtime where they would set themselves apart from the rest of the workers and talk.

"Tommy made him a partner years ago. Can't find anything on him, Grizz—err, James."

Anthony didn't have to call him James when they were alone, but he did it anyway to help retrain his mind so he didn't slip up in the future.

"He's legally separated and has sole custody of his kids. You saw them at the funeral. They're close to Jason's age. He has a decent amount of change in the bank, no debt, no vices that my guy could find."

Anthony noticed the muscles in Grizz's jaw tighten.

"Does he have a girlfriend?"

"No," Anthony said, and quickly added, "And there's no boyfriend, either. It's just him and his boys. Like I said, he's separated from his wife, but not divorced."

"Handsome, devoted father, no problems with money, drugs, or anything else. Why do you suppose he doesn't have a woman in his life?" Grizz's irritation was starting to show. "And has he seen Ginny since the funeral?"

"Several times," Anthony said. "Never alone, though. The kids are always with them. At least that's what's been reported back to me."

Grizz knew why Alec didn't have a girlfriend. He was interested in Ginny, and Grizz knew Anthony knew it, too, though Anthony would never voice it. He would put his friend's mind at ease.

"Don't worry, Bear," Grizz said. "I'm not going to do anything stupid." *At least not yet.* "Now. Tell me what the word on the street is about the guy who shot Tommy."

Anthony explained how the police hadn't found the man yet, but Anthony's guys had. Grizz was surprised Blue hadn't heard this and reported it back to his detective girlfriend. There should've been an arrest by now.

"Can't say. I know Blue's been trying to keep his nose clean. Your old crew's been floundering a bit. Looking for someone to be in charge. Blue told me you gave him your permission to walk away before your execution. Maybe he doesn't want to be involved. Last time I saw him, he told me something about Jan's murder. Something you should know."

Anthony explained the details of a conversation he'd had with Blue shortly after Jan's body was found.

"Really?" Grizz asked, the dismay in his voice evident.

"Yeah, really."

Grizz nodded. "Tell me about the guy who shot Tommy."

Grizz listened without interrupting as Anthony explained that, too.

"So it wasn't a hit? It was really a fucking random act of violence and Tommy was in the wrong place at the wrong time?"

"It wasn't planned. It was a junkie looking for a fix. I'm sure of it. What do you want me to do with him?"

He didn't have to ask Grizz this. He didn't have to seek out a specific order, but respect from days gone by took precedence. This was still Grizz's territory, whether he was alive to claim it or not.

"I can have it handled any way you want. Just say the word and it'll be done."

The old Grizz would've handled the man himself. The old Grizz wouldn't have shown mercy. The old Grizz would've consoled himself with the fact that what Ginny didn't know wouldn't hurt her.

He asked himself what Ginny would want.

"Make sure the police find him and let them deal with him," he told a stunned Anthony as he finished his sandwich in silence. *And if they don't get justice for Tommy and Ginny, I'll take care of it myself.*

Then he stood up and headed for the lawnmower.

Anthony watched Grizz walk toward his mower, climb on, and ride away. Anthony had made an executive decision not to tell his old friend something else he'd heard. Not on the street, but from one of his own sons.

He knew if Grizz was going to survive in society, he'd have to stay clean, and if Anthony told Grizz what he'd heard about what had been done to Mimi, it would only be a matter of time before things blew up and out of control. He needed to figure out a way to get Grizz out of South Florida and away from anything remotely connected to crime. Besides, the longer Grizz stayed around, whether hiding in plain sight or not, the odds would eventually be against him never being recognized.

Fuck. He hated complications. He looked at his watch, realized he was running late. He had to get home and shower so he could be at Daisy's school for a parent-teacher conference. If he missed another one, Christy would read him the riot act.

42

Ginny, 2001, Fort Lauderdale

The weeks slowly turned into months, and before long we fell into our ordinary family routine. Well, as ordinary as it could be. I didn't go back to work, but instead filled my days with attending every activity Mimi and Jason were involved in, as well as volunteering for different charitable organizations.

Alec suggested that if I was interested he would terminate the accountant they used at Dillon & Davis and I could immerse myself back in a job that I loved. Even though he meant well, I let him know I didn't want a perfectly capable accountant to lose a source of income because of me. Besides, I needed to distance myself from Tommy's work. It was too painful.

It was a Wednesday morning, and I stood now at the shooting range taking careful aim at the target. I fired off all twelve rounds, maintaining a two-inch grouping from a twenty-five-foot distance. I had to battle my inner demons that wanted to pretend I was aiming at Tommy's murderer. They'd finally arrested the man responsible. Tommy's murderer. The words just didn't ring true. It still didn't seem real, but I knew from the profound sense of grief I'd been living through with my children that it was all too real.

I ached for my husband, and I willed myself not to think about the man who'd stood behind me more than twenty years ago, his massive tattooed arms holding my hands steady, as I took my first shot.

Grizz.

I'd been to Carter's house a few times since Tommy's death. I always made sure I had one or both of the kids with me. Yes, it was nice that friends were stepping in and including them in family activities, but I made sure to spend as much time as possible with my children. I felt responsible for their healing and was noticing that I was healing, too. Helping at Carter's was good for all of us. I especially enjoyed the physical exhaustion that came with attending to her zoo.

She caught me eyeing the garage one day as I pumped water into the horse's trough. Jason had run into the house to use the bathroom. Mimi had to work that day and wasn't with us.

Without looking at me, Carter said matter-of-factly, "He's not there."

"I didn't think he was," I said a little too quickly.

But I wasn't being truthful. I'd wondered more than I cared to admit where Grizz had been living, though I tried not to think of Grizz, whether it was with anger or some other thing I wouldn't allow myself to identify. It felt like a disloyalty to Tommy.

Neither one of us said anything, and my curiosity finally got the best of me.

"But he was there, though. Right? When he first came back?" I tried to act casual but I could feel my pulse quickening. Was it my unresolved anger? Or something else?

"No, Ginny. He didn't stay here. I don't know where he stayed."

"Stayed? You mean, he's gone?"

She stopped what she was doing and stared hard at me.

"You told me to tell him to go away. I sent him your message and haven't heard from him since. I'm assuming he followed your wishes."

I was a bit shocked. This certainly didn't sound like the Grizz I'd known. He never did anything anybody told him.

I cocked my head. "Do you think he's really gone, Carter?"

"Do you care?"

I caught myself then, whirled, and made a beeline toward her barn.

"Of course, I don't care," I called back over my shoulder.

I made sure I had my back to her as I charged off. I didn't want her to read any doubt that may have been in my eyes. I didn't want her to be able to see what may have been buried deep in my heart, especially if I couldn't even see it or understand it myself.

TWO DAYS LATER, I SAT AMONGST THE THRONG OF OTHER PARENTS AND friends watching Mimi perform at her piano recital. I told her she didn't have to perform, but she was adamant that she wanted to do it for her father, and we both knew Tommy wouldn't have wanted her to miss it. He was the one who'd originally encouraged her to take piano lessons. I'd tried to teach her how to play guitar, but she never quite took to it. Tommy had noticed her infatuation with the piano at our church and had a piano delivered to our home for Mimi's eighth birthday.

After she finished and the applause came to a stop, she stood then and faced the audience.

"Mr. Dolan said I could play one more. This one is for my father. He loves this song, and he especially loves the end, the piano solo."

She then played the piano piece at the end of "Layla," by Derek and the Dominos. She played with a passion I'd never seen. The pounding of the keys resonated through the room, and before I knew it, it was over and the audience was standing, their applause becoming more and more frenzied before finally dying down. And I realized I'd been listening to it with warm and happy memories of Tommy. I wasn't sobbing and falling apart.

Jason turned to me and beamed.

"Mimi's right. That is one of Dad's favorite songs!"

I loved how neither Mimi or Jason said it *was* one of Tommy's favorite songs, or that it *used to be* one of Tommy's favorites. Instead, they spoke in the present tense. They said it because they didn't see their father as gone and out of our lives. They knew Tommy would always be with us.

I was finally healing. We were all healing.

Even before Tommy's death I'd noticed Mimi suggested more and more that we spend time as a family with the Bears. I figured out pretty early on that she was doing her best to hide the fact that she was crushing hard on Christy and Anthony's oldest son, eighteen-year-old Slade. The few times we did see them and Slade happened to join us, he seemed nice to Mimi, but I couldn't tell if his politeness translated to interest.

I asked Christy about it.

"Do you think there's something going on between Mimi and Slade?" I asked her one day over the phone.

"I'm not certain," she said. "I haven't heard anything from this end, but of course, he doesn't live at home anymore, so I probably wouldn't know. Have you asked her?"

"I have. Mimi said he was so nice to her at the hospital, and he always seems friendly the few times we've seen you guys, but she doesn't know if he's interested. I think she may be on the brink of a crush or something, Christy. I'm not sure how to handle it or if there's anything that even needs handling. Would Christian know?"

I realized then how ridiculous I sounded. I might as well have been sitting at the sixth-grade lunch table passing notes.

"If Christian knows anything about whether or not his brother has feelings for Mimi, I doubt he'd say. He's just like his father used to be," she said laughing. "He walks around with some kind of invisible chip on his shoulder hating everyone and everything. Makes me wonder if something like this can actually be in your genes."

Our conversation went from Mimi's possible crush to Christy's own concerns about Christian. I couldn't comment. I hadn't seen Christian since that day at the hospital, and that was only briefly in the waiting room. He'd not come to the few gatherings we'd had since then.

A week later I noticed a change in Mimi's attitude. I'd been right about her developing feelings toward Slade.

"And he turned you down?" I asked her.

We were in the kitchen making dinner together. Alec was bringing Jason back from a carnival, and I'd invited him and his boys to eat with us.

"Yeah, I guess you could say that." The disappointment was evident in her voice as she tossed a salad.

"Did he tell you he just didn't have time or wasn't interested?"

Mimi told me she'd texted Slade and asked if he had time if he could give her some driving lessons. She would be sixteen this year and would be able to get her license. I wasn't looking forward to Mimi driving. The thought of getting her a car seemed like a huge undertaking. Not from a financial perspective, but from a personal one. I always thought Tommy would be taking her out to test-drive vehicles, not me.

"He seemed surprised I didn't know how to drive. He asked me why I hadn't taken Driver's Ed. He felt bad when I told him I didn't take it because Dad always told me he would teach me, but then of course, with you moving out last year and all the problems we were having, it never happened."

She didn't say this with any intention of blame or trying to make me feel guilty. She was just stating facts.

"Then he suggested maybe Christian could teach me. Christian!"

I looked over at her then and realized she was right. That was definitely Slade's way of letting Mimi down. The words were out before I could stop them.

"What's wrong with asking Christian?"

She huffed out a breath. "I haven't seen Christian since that horrible day at the hospital, and goodness only knows how long it was before then. He just seems, I don't know, he seems mad at someone. He kept looking at me with those icy blue eyes of his. He didn't even say anything. Just sat there and stared."

I couldn't believe I was taking up for Christian, especially after what Christy had told me, but I couldn't seem to help myself.

"Maybe he just needs a friend. You know, you used to be close when you were little. You used to play wedding with him."

"Mom!" She rolled her eyes. "Could you please not bring that up? How embarrassing. I was, what, maybe five years old?"

I started to smile and was going to remind her of how close they'd been when she added, "I wonder if I did ask Christian, and he said yes, if it might make Slade even a little bit jealous."

I looked at her seriously. "I'm sure to your fifteen-year-old brain that sounds like a solid plan, but I will tell you now, Mimi, it's not a good idea. Please don't do that, honey. Don't use Christian. You wouldn't like it if somebody used you."

I thought I saw her flinch, and our conversation was interrupted when Jason came barreling in, Alec and his boys right behind him.

Alec held up some movies he'd rented and said as I laid a casserole on the table, "I picked up some flicks I thought the boys would enjoy. I was thinking if it wasn't too much of an imposition that maybe Mimi wouldn't mind staying here with the kids after we eat and letting me take you to a jazz club for a couple of hours. Just get you out of the house for some adult interaction, Ginny."

"Uh, thanks, but I don't like jazz," I said without looking up at him. I was suddenly very focused on my kitchen counter.

He laughed. "It doesn't have to be jazz. We can certainly find a club with another type of music."

"Um. I don't like clubs, and really, I have plenty of adult interaction."

The kids were too busy jabbering with each other to notice the exchange, but Mimi noticed.

"Ginny," he whispered. "I know what you're thinking. I'm not suggesting we go on a date. I'm suggesting you join me, as a friend, to listen to some music and maybe even enjoy a glass of wine. I know you have adult interaction, but it's always because you're volunteering somewhere. Doing something for someone else. I was thinking maybe you'd like some time to actually enjoy yourself."

He paused then, and I realized Alec was either always working or taking care of his children. I wasn't certain, but since he was the sole caregiver of his kids, I doubted he had much of a social life. Maybe he's the one who needs a friend.

No sooner had I thought it than he added, "I know I could use some adult companionship."

Before I could reply, Mimi chimed in, "Mom, go. I'll stay with the kids."

This was Alec. The same man who'd been Tommy's partner for years. The same man I'd come to rely on in recent months. The same man who never gave one hint of anything that didn't resemble friendship.

I nodded and sat down at the table to eat dinner. Yes, I would go.

43

Grizz, 2001, Fort Lauderdale

"She said that? She said those exact words?"

Carter looked down at the table. She was sitting in the rear booth of a fast food restaurant. Grizz sat with his back to the wall facing the patrons that came in. He'd never sit with his back to a crowd, in spite of the slight risk that he might be recognized.

She'd sent him a message some time ago that Ginny no longer needed him, but he'd stayed around. She hadn't told him in that message the other harsh words Ginny had said much later, words she told him now: That Grizz could relieve Carter of her duty to summon him. That Ginny would never send for him.

Carter was right in feeling he wouldn't leave without further explanation, but even though she knew he'd been hurt by the details she'd just relayed, she also knew she wouldn't lie.

"Yes." Carter chanced a glance at him. "But I don't think she means it. She's coming from a place of pain and anger. Look at what she's been through, not just since Tommy died, but knowing beforehand about your secret. Finding out you were his father. It's just too much. She needs more time." She took a quick sip of her soda and avoided eye contact with Grizz. Ginny had recently confided to her that Grizz was not Tommy's father. Should Ginny ever decide to see or talk with Grizz, it would be her story to share. Not Carter's.

This was the first time Grizz had actually met with Carter face-to-face since his return.

"I shouldn't have just smashed that bitch's face into the table. I should've fucking killed her!" The memory of the prison interview with Leslie was still fresh in Grizz's mind. It was her fault Ginny was having to deal with so much right now.

Carter quickly changed the subject.

"So how has it been for you? What are you doing with yourself, and where are you living?"

He explained in as few words as possible that he worked on a landscaping crew. He'd moved out of an efficiency apartment on the beach and was renting a furnished three-bedroom house in a little subdivision called Laurel Falls. He was surprised how much development there had been in South Florida since he went to prison.

"Every fucking house looks the same. So does every neighborhood. If there wasn't a sign in the front that said Laurel Falls, I wouldn't know where the hell I was."

Carter laughed. "I'm sure it's changed a lot since you've been here. A car dealership sits where your motel used to be."

"Yeah, I saw that. I can't believe how far west the development has spread. It's a concrete jungle."

"How are you doing with staying off the grid?" Carter knew the temptation to visit his old bars and biker hangouts must be difficult.

"Not as hard as I thought, but I still keep a hat on and wear sunglasses as a rule. Fucking crazy that I'm being forced to live by the same rules I placed on Kit all those years ago. Karma is biting me in my ass." He took a bite of his hamburger.

"At least you have an ass to bite. I don't know how you pulled this off, but you did."

He stared intently at Carter, slowly chewing his food.

"You're not asking me how I did it, right?"

"Wouldn't dream of asking," she said honestly, then smiled. "I'm sure it'll make a decent book one day."

"I still don't know why she sent for me after Tommy was shot." The bewilderment in his tone was obvious. "My first thought was that he'd been targeted, and she felt threatened in some way. Or maybe she thought the cops would never get the guy, and I might still have an ear to the ground. Shit, she could've just gone to Blue or Anthony for that. But I guess my gut wanted to believe she needed me because maybe she still loved me."

He said the last part over Carter's shoulder. He wouldn't look at her.

Carter gave him a funny look. "Grizz?"

He met her eyes. "Yeah?"

"Ginny was wearing the bandana the day *before* Tommy was shot. I paged you within minutes of seeing her. Are you telling me you didn't get it until after he'd been shot?"

Grizz sat up straight and focused on what Carter was telling him. She could see the wheels begin to turn.

"I'd accidentally turned my pager off. I got the page the day after it happened. I was actually sitting in a diner somewhere in Louisiana watching it on the national news when your message came through. I assumed it had been sent after the shooting." He frowned. "Do you know why she was wearing it the day before he was shot?"

"No. She told me she'd forgotten it was a way to signal you and she just happened to be wearing it that night. That it was a false alarm." She paused, then leaned over the table toward him. In almost a whisper, she added, "But I know she wasn't being honest."

HE SAT IN HIS CAR, FIGHTING THE TEMPTATION TO MARCH INTO THE CLUB and stake his claim on the only woman he'd ever loved. It was killing him.

He'd done everything within his power to stay away from her and keep a low profile as he'd slowly immersed himself back into society. It wasn't easy. The pull to go back to his old life was strong, especially since he didn't have her to anchor him. He had dark thoughts about reinventing himself underground, bringing his club back to its glory days, but he knew those thoughts were as misguided as they were ridiculous.

He hadn't tried to see her since the day of Tommy's funeral. The last couple of months had been agony for him. Knowing she was out there. Knowing she had needed him. Wondering why she hadn't asked Carter to arrange a meeting.

He figured the initial message that he was no longer needed was because of her grief, so he'd stayed, certain she would come around. He'd failed miserably at trying to accept she'd changed her mind after Tommy died.

But hearing from Carter that she'd been wearing the bandana the day *before* Tommy's shooting fueled his need to see her, to talk to her even further. To ask why.

For two days, he'd sat in a strip mall that faced the entrance to her neighborhood before seeing her. But when he finally did, it wasn't what he'd expected. He'd had to blink twice to see if she was really in the car with the man he'd seen at the funeral. She was smiling at something he'd said as the streetlight illuminated her face. His blood began to boil with fury.

Grizz had followed them to a club and felt the darkness start to invade. He hadn't felt anger like this since she'd given birth to Jason and he'd had to beat another prisoner to death. He knew there was only one thing he could do. He would have to drive away from the club before he did something stupid. He would have to find another outlet to quench his darkest fury. Because if he didn't, he knew beyond a shadow of a doubt that Alec Davis would become some lucky alligator's next meal.

He wouldn't be able to speak with her tonight. He'd have to patiently wait for the right time to approach her. He wanted to know why she'd worn the bandana and he didn't know how he would control himself until he got the answer. But one thing he did know for certain.

Whether she thought she needed him or not, he would never leave South Florida without his woman.

44

Ginny, 2001, Fort Lauderdale

Surprisingly, I enjoyed myself the night Alec took me to a club. He'd found the ideal venue with a band that played nothing but seventies music. The place had a retro-hippie feel to it, and I absolutely loved it. I even agreed to go again the following Saturday night.

Alec was a perfect gentleman, and I hadn't expected anything different. I remembered feeling a slight high from his compliment the day I'd gone to the office to surprise Tommy, but there was nothing in his actions during our night out that indicated he was interested in anything other than an evening without the kids. During the band's breaks, he filled me in on his time away from civilization. How he and the boys had bonded while living in Kentucky, away from the noise and busyness of city living.

"Being away from technology for those few months was the best decision I ever made," he said. "I felt closer to my boys, and I got them to open up about their feelings of abandonment by Paulina. It wasn't easy, but I had to explain some things to them."

A WEEK LATER, I WAS SLICING CARROTS AT THE KITCHEN COUNTER WHEN Jason came in and was digging through the refrigerator.

With his back to me, he blurted, "Caleb wants you to marry his dad."

I stopped slicing and turned to look at Jason, who was drinking milk from the carton. I was too stunned to reprimand him. Caleb was Alec's youngest. I just stared.

"He wondered if you were doing kissing things. That's what he called it." He rolled his eyes.

"If it ever comes up again, you can make sure he knows that I'm not doing kissing things with his father. We're just friends."

"I know. I told him that. I guess he thinks because he doesn't have a mother and I don't have a father, we would make a good family."

"He's young, and I can understand why he would think that, but I think you should continue to discourage him, honey. It's not going to happen."

"Good, Mom. I'm glad you said that. I don't want another father. Not even Alec."

He tossed the empty carton of milk in the garbage and, swiping his arm across his mouth, he left the kitchen.

"Good," I whispered to myself. "Because I don't want another husband."

I made sure Mimi would be home so I could sneak over to the church and work on my Sunday school lesson. Even though I'd prepared the actual lesson, I wanted to update the bulletin boards to coincide with the new unit I'd be introducing. I sat in one of the tiny chairs with my knees higher than the table.

Somehow, I was immediately reminded of being in the exact same position last year, when I'd made the right decision to go back to Tommy. I remembered the call I'd received from him, telling me Jan had been murdered. I shook off the sad memories and went back to cutting out letters from bright red construction paper.

I was wondering if I should cancel seeing Alec later that evening. Jason would be staying overnight with his friend, Max, and Mimi was going to be babysitting for Daisy, Anthony and Christy's little girl. I knew she genuinely loved little Daisy, but there had to be a part of her hoping she'd somehow run into Slade.

But now, after Jason's comment in the kitchen, I was seriously reconsidering my friendship with Alec. Not because I was having any feelings toward him or sensing he had feelings toward me, but because I was concerned about how our friendship might seem to the children. Our friend date the weekend before went smoothly, but I didn't want to give our kids the wrong impression. Maybe I'd talk to Alec about it tonight.

I was in my church classroom and standing on my tiptoes, trying to get a stubborn tack in the wall, when I sensed a shift in my surroundings. I couldn't place where the feeling was coming from; I just knew something had changed. I listened carefully. It wouldn't have been unusual for someone else to be in the building with me. I wasn't the only person with a key, nor was I the only teacher to work on my lessons the day before class. But what did seem unusual was that they hadn't made themselves known. I swallowed.

I'd used my key to come in the side entrance and up the back stair-case, but that didn't mean someone couldn't have come in through the church, which was kept unlocked on weekends, and found their way up through the front stairs.

I stepped to the small CD player on the windowsill and turned down the volume. With my back to the classroom door, I slowly scanned the side parking lot, leaning up and over to peek at the other parking lots. Mine was the only car.

I turned around and stopped myself from gasping.

My right hand flew to my heart.

Grizz.

He stood in the doorway of my classroom. Swallowing the lump in my throat, I willed myself to be calm, to not think, as I slowly scanned him, starting at his feet and finally coming to rest on his eyes.

Those eyes.

He looked like an older version of the Grizz I'd been married to. His hair had grown in and showed what I thought were slight streaks of gray, barely noticeable against his dark blond locks. The long beard I'd remembered from his execution was gone, replaced with a neatly trimmed one. He looked more muscular, if that was even possible. I also realized his arms sported different tattoos. I could recognize Grizz's ink in my sleep, knew every detail of every tattoo, and these were different. He'd had them worked on.

You'd think I'd have a million things to say to him. A million things to ask. But instead, I blurted out the first asinine thought that came to me.

"So. You're not naturally bald. I guess you'd been shaving your head all those years. Lucky for you it grew back." *Of all the things I could say, I picked that?* I forced myself to breathe, to act natural.

If I'd have been watching a movie, this would be the part where the heroine ran to the hero, threw herself into his arms, and gave thanks he was still alive. But not me. I was standing in front of a man who was supposed to be dead, discussing male pattern baldness.

Grizz raised a brow. A beat passed.

I could tell he was trying to suppress a smile when he replied, "I read somewhere that we inherit our tendency to be bald, or not, from our maternal grandfathers. I guess I had a grandpa with a decent head of hair."

I nodded like we had this conversation every day, like my heart wasn't beating straight out of my chest. I couldn't think of a reply, so I said nothing. I clenched my fists and stood straighter, waiting for him to say something else.

"When did you stop wearing your bangs, Kitten? You know how much I love them," he asked, his deep voice echoing off the walls of the tiny classroom.

"I stopped caring about what you love a long time ago," I lied. "Remember? I was following your orders."

He stood there and just nodded.

A full minute must have passed, and finally he muttered, "You must be wondering how this is possible—"

I wasn't prepared to have this conversation.

"I already know how this is possible. Tommy and I didn't keep secrets." Of course Tommy kept secrets, they both had, but I felt the need to go for the throat.

There was a barely perceptible tilt of his head as he waited for me to say something else.

I huffed out a breath. "Fine. So you're alive. I'm happy for you, Grizz. I hope you can carve out a nice life for yourself somewhere. Just do me a favor." I narrowed my eyes. "Make sure it's as far away from me and my children as possible."

My heart thudded as I scooped up my purse and keys. I had to get out of here. Now. Had to distance myself before I lost control of everything, even the places in my brain.

"I guess you didn't get Carter's message that you're no longer needed." My words came out in a high-pitched squeak. My body was betraying my actions. I looked at my hand holding my keys, saw it was starting to shake.

He stepped fully into the room now. "You're trembling, Kit. Are you afraid of me?"

I heaved my purse onto my shoulder. "I've never been afraid of you, and I don't go by Kit anymore. Please never call me that again. Oh, wait." I lifted my chin in a meager act of defiance. "That won't be a problem. Because we'll never be speaking again."

"Don't leave. Let me explain some things."

"Oh, twenty-five years later and now you want to explain some things'? You know what, Grizz? You could've done that in 1975, but you didn't. And now it doesn't matter. None of it." I stood up straight. "It's over. Done. You've accomplished whatever it was you set out to do. The almighty Grizz has somehow beaten the system."

He didn't address my sarcasm, but asked a question instead.

"Why did you wear the bandana?"

A ton of possible answers flashed through my mind. I could've made something up. Taunted him with some ridiculous story. But I decided the truth would hurt the most. And even though I knew it was wrong, right now I wanted him to hurt.

"It definitely wasn't my idea. Tommy asked me to wear it. After I told him you were still alive and left a way for me to signal you if I ever needed you, he asked me to wear it so I could make a decision. But I told him it wasn't necessary. I was with him, and seeing you wouldn't change that. But he insisted and so I wore it, and Carter sent the signal." I let out an ironic laugh. "And as you can see, it no longer matters."

He looked hard at me, the expression in his eyes unreadable.

I stared back. "I'll ask this only once, and if you ever loved me, you'll tell me the truth. I will absolve you of every lie and half-truth you've ever told me or allowed me to believe for twenty-five years. And keep in mind—I'm not the naïve teenager you married in 1975. I'll know if you're telling me the truth."

He never broke eye contact.

"The police caught Tommy's murderer, and they believe it was random. Did you or they have anything to do with his murder?"

"No." His voice was even.

I nodded slowly, believing and accepting his answer. I let out a long breath and started to walk past him. I stopped when my shoulder brushed his bicep, and I had to suppress a gasp. Static electricity had produced an actual shock. Or had I imagined it? I felt his gaze land on me, although I stared straight ahead at the open doorway.

His arm came up, and he softly caressed my cheek with his calloused knuckles. I froze, but his touch gave me a sensation I hadn't expected.

I shook him off and kept walking, calling out over my shoulder, "If you'll excuse me now, I don't want to be late for my nail appointment."

I knew he'd turned to watch me leave. I stopped in the doorway, and swung around to look at him.

"I have to get ready for my date tonight."

I raced to my car, doing my best to escape his presence while denying the hidden meaning behind the tears coursing down my cheeks.

45

Grizz, 2001, Fort Lauderdale

The urge to physically stop her from leaving the church was almost his undoing. He tried not to flinch when she said all those things. After all, he deserved them. But knowing she had a right to feel the way she did and actually hearing the words come out of her mouth were two different things.

She'd changed, and she was right. She was no longer the young girl he'd married. She was a woman who'd lost two husbands and was now raising two children on her own. Gone was the vulnerable teenager he'd forced himself on twenty-five years ago. She'd grown into a strong, self-assured, take-charge adult.

And perhaps because of it, he realized he was more drawn to her now than he'd ever been before.

His heart had been in his throat as he'd stood in the doorway of her classroom and watched her without her knowing it. Her youthful figure had been replaced by a fuller, curvier version that had known two full-term pregnancies and childbirth. Having children agreed with her. She was absolutely perfect.

One thing hadn't changed. Her big brown eyes. Not even the slight creases at the corners took away from the soulful gaze that had always held him captive. Somewhere deep inside, he'd hoped seeing her would displace all the feelings he'd been tormented by over the years.

255

Hoped she would be someone he'd always care about, but wouldn't have the same hold on him.

But one look told him he was still utterly, deeply, and completely in love with her. Even more so, now that she displayed a maturity and strength that spoke to the woman she had become.

His woman.

He didn't have a plan. Yet. But there was no way he'd walk away from her. He would fight for her, and there would be no losing. Because if he didn't win her back, he would just take what he wanted. He always had, and he was convinced he'd never be able to change that.

But he'd do it the right way. For now.

THE NEXT DAY HE NONCHALANTLY PUSHED HIS SMALL CART THROUGH THE aisles of the grocery store, catching sight of her in his peripheral vision. He knew she'd meant what she'd said the night before. That she was going on a date. He'd immediately called Anthony and was given access to a friend's privately owned gym. There was a back room used for illegal fighting, and Anthony was more than willing to go a couple of rounds with Grizz, let him take out some frustrations.

"Not the face," Anthony insisted. "I'm taking Christy out tonight. If I come home with a bloody face, she'll be pissed."

"Not a problem," Grizz said as he punched Anthony in the stomach.

He wished now that he'd given Anthony the same rule. Grizz was now sporting a bruised and swollen cheek. The pain at first was welcomed. Now he realized the bruises might give Kit—Ginny—the wrong impression.

Anthony's guy had reported back that she was a creature of habit on Sundays. Church, breakfast at the local pancake house with a few church friends, and then the grocery store. After all those years with him, he thought he'd taught her better.

Now, he just waited for her to come down his aisle and notice him. When she did, she stopped and stared.

"Hmph! I see some things never change," she muttered almost to herself after seeing his swollen face. "Are you following me?"

He shrugged. "Where are the kids?"

"Thank goodness they're not with me." Her eyes flashed. "Mimi babysat for the Bears last night and slept there, and Jason spent the night with a friend. Are you insane?"

"Not insane. Just hungry," he said casually, concentrating hard on the box of cereal he clutched.

She looked up and down the aisle. They were alone.

"I cannot believe you had the nerve to show up at my grocery store!" Her voice grew louder. "How dare you follow me!"

"I didn't follow you, it's not your grocery store, and I can shop wherever and whenever I want." He could feel her glare as he continued to stare at the cereal. "So how was your date last night?"

"That is none of your business!"

"I'm glad you're moving on, Ginny. You deserve to be happy." He almost choked on his words.

Based on her comments in the classroom she'd wanted him to believe she was genuinely happy for him, so maybe he'd just let her think he was genuinely happy for her. Which couldn't be farther from the truth. He'd never gone to high school, so he didn't know what kind of games kids played with each other, but he was pretty certain it went something like this. Who knows, maybe he'd enjoy this a little bit.

She stalked off, and he purposely didn't watch as she finished her shopping, paid, and left the store.

But the wind left his sails after he paid for his groceries and headed for his car.

Was this really how he wanted to play this? It had only been ten minutes, and he was already emotionally exhausted. It only verified in his mind how he'd become the person he was. He never had time for such nonsense, and he sure as shit didn't have time for it now. As far as taking what he wanted, how was he going to do that when there were children to be considered? Could he see himself being a father to Mimi and Jason?

If he let himself think about it, yes, he thought he could. There was a desire deep inside that kept calling to him, but he hadn't been able to pinpoint it. He'd always thought it had been Ginny, and yes, she was a major part of that, but he also realized while sitting at Tommy's funeral that there was something else he yearned for. Something he'd never experienced and wanted to try.

He wanted to be part of a family.

46

Mimi, 2001, Fort Lauderdale

S he didn't think it was possible to suffer so much humiliation in one lifetime. She sat in the front seat of Christian Bear's pickup truck and willed herself to be invisible. She never wanted to be as far away from South Florida than she did at this very moment. Her life had been feeling all-wrong anyway, and the recent incidents just cemented in her mind what she'd wanted all along.

To go away. To leave.

Of course, it had started to spiral downward at her own hand when she'd agreed to help Leslie. It had gotten worse when her parents separated, and even though she was happy they'd reconciled, her life had seriously tanked when Elliott—Nick, or whatever his real name was—had used her.

She didn't think it could get worse after that, but it had. Worse than she could've ever imagined. Oh, Dad.

She was still mourning her father's death. Yes, Tommy Dillon would always be her dad, not the guy who'd impregnated her mother. And though she felt she was mourning Tommy in a healthy way, she felt the silent pity from her friends. The unspoken words and whispers. She didn't know if she was imagining it or not, but something told her some of them knew her parents' history, and she felt their judgment—and admiration—without anyone actually saying something.

She knew some of their parents had figured out a long time ago her mother had been married to a man who'd been executed. She couldn't help but wonder if they'd figured out he was also her biological father. She no longer hated Grizz, the man she'd never know, but she hated what his legacy may have left in its wake.

She wanted out.

She'd hoped she would find comfort in someone. She knew she saw Slade Bear in a different light after the night he'd rescued her, and she hoped he'd seen her differently, too. She'd told herself he was so wrapped up in college he just wasn't getting the hint that she had feelings for him.

She'd been dead wrong. He did know about her feelings, and last night, he'd let her down as gently as possible. Her cheeks burned as she tried to block out the memories, but they came anyway.

He'd shown up the night before at his parents' house. He'd been stopping in to pick something up and was surprised when he came in the front door and saw her on the couch reading to his little sister, Daisy.

She tried to ask again for some driving lessons. He didn't answer, instead offering to help put Daisy to bed. Mimi had been thrilled. Slade wanted to be alone with her.

But after Daisy was tucked in, he'd told her in the kindest and nicest way possible: he wasn't interested. She was one of the sweetest and prettiest girls he knew, but…

There was more than one "but." Their families went back too far and it would be like dating a younger sister. He was in his first year in college and didn't want a serious girlfriend. He couldn't give her the time and attention she deserved.

She wanted to tell him he could stop after the first "but." She didn't want to hear any of it. She was going to be sixteen soon. And it was her fault she hadn't taken the first of several hints. For someone who considered herself to have a decent amount of intelligence, she was the absolute sorriest when it came to matters of the heart.

No, if Slade Bear had even the slightest interest in her, he would've shown it. He would've made it work. Her humiliation got even worse when she remembered the drugging predicament he'd saved her from. She was grateful he'd rescued her that night, but now she wished it had been anybody but him.

Even Christian would've been a better choice. Her mother had been right—they'd been friends when they were younger. If she had maintained that friendship, maybe he would've been the friend whose shoulder she would cry on.

And now, she was sitting in Christian's truck. More mortified than she'd ever been before. If there had been a cliff to jump off, she'd be over the edge by now.

Christy Bear had asked Christian that morning if he wouldn't mind taking Mimi home. He'd grunted a yes as they headed for his truck.

As they made the forty-five-minute drive to her house, she'd tried to break the uncomfortable silence by engaging him in casual conversation, and he seemed to lighten up. She watched his profile as they drove. He really was quite handsome. He favored his father, Anthony, who was a full-blooded Native American. Christian's intense blue eyes were the only thing he'd inherited from his mother, and they stood out in stark contrast to his dark tan skin and long black hair that almost reached his waist. He certainly hadn't inherited Christy's sweet disposition. Christian had a wildness that scared her, though she had to admit to herself she might've found him attractive if she hadn't been so swallowed up by Slade's rejection the night before.

She started to get an uncomfortable yet recognizable feeling then. *No! This isn't happening. Not now. Not in Christian's truck!* She squirmed slightly in the seat and realized with horror that, yes, it had happened. She had just felt her period come on in a rush, and it was now soaking through her shorts.

She wanted to die. How would she ever get out of the truck without him noticing? Worse yet, she was certain she was staining the seat beneath her.

He sensed she was upset, looked over at her. "You okay?" She thought she sensed genuine concern.

She hemmed and hawed, not sure how to tell him she had just gotten her period and she was sure it was now on his truck seat. She couldn't think of anything that would gross a guy out more than menstrual blood all over his nice leather. Especially a guy like Christian Bear.

He looked at her questioningly. She gritted her teeth. *What have I got to lose? I embarrassed myself with Slade last night, might as well just top it off and pray I never see another Bear for the rest of my life.*

"Christian, I don't know how to tell you this, but I'm pretty sure I just got my period." Her cheeks burned. "I'm just so sorry. I can feel that it's soaked through my panties and shorts, and I know it's on your seat. I just want to die. I'll pay for any damage."

His expression was indifferent. "No problem. Let's get you home. It'll wipe off. Don't sweat it, Mimi."

Christian had been trying to work up the nerve to ask her out, but her admission stopped his train of thought. All he could think about was putting her at ease. Besides, he was Christian Bear. Blood was the least of his hang-ups.

"You don't know how embarrassing this is," she said as she kept dialing a number and sending texts.

He shrugged. "It's normal girl shit, and I don't know a lot about normal girl shit, but I'm pretty sure this happens. Like I said, it'll clean up."

Mimi looked frantic now. "Uh, my mom's not home yet, and she's not answering my texts, and I don't have my key. She's either at the pancake house or grocery store. They're both on the way home. Can you run me by and we'll see if we can find her?"

He asked her which restaurant and which grocery store. When they came to a red light, he wordlessly reached in front of her and opened the glove box. He took out a hand towel and indicated for her to lift her butt up off the seat. He swiped at the leather.

"See? Came right off." He reached behind her into the backseat and pulled out a lightweight jacket. "You can wrap this around you. Tie it in the front. It'll cover your ass, and the sleeves are long enough to hang down in front of you."

Mimi accepted it wordlessly.

Ginny wasn't at the pancake house and still wasn't answering their home phone or replying to her texts. They pulled into the grocery store parking lot.

"She's here!" Mimi yelled when she spotted her mother's car in the lot. "Thank goodness—she's here."

"You want me to wait with you until she comes out?"

"That won't be necessary. You've done enough, and I don't know how long she'll be. She might've just started shopping. I'll just go in and find her."

"I don't mind, Mimi. Really. If you want to get your house key from her, I'll wait and drive you home."

Mimi had already started to get out of the truck and was reaching for her overnight bag that had been sitting on the floor in front of her.

She knew that, as kind as Christian had been, she was still embarrassed it had gone this far. Worst twelve hours ever. No. She'd find her mother, rush her through her shopping, and go home.

"You've done more than enough, Christian. I'll get your jacket back to you. Thank you."

She managed a smile.

He nodded a goodbye, and she slammed the truck door shut and went inside to look for her mother.

She made a quick pit stop in the ladies' room and changed into the used panties and shorts she'd worn to the Bears' the previous day. The grocery store restroom didn't have a machine that sold feminine hygiene products, so she loaded up her underwear with paper towels. They would do until she got home. Then she went to look for her mother.

But after walking up and down each aisle, she ran to the front of the store just in time to see her driving away. She must've been paying when I was walking in—I should've looked in the checkout lines first. Now what?

She went outside and sat on a bench. She would wait the five minutes it took for Ginny to get home, and she would call the house and ask her mother to come back.

She'd started to text Christian to thank him again for being so understanding when a movement to her left caught her eye. She saw a man she shouldn't recognize, but somehow did.

Maybe it was instinct. Maybe it was something spiritual. Maybe it was neither. Maybe she was wrong.

But her gut told her she wasn't.

She watched as he walked to a white Chevelle with a black stripe running down the middle of it. Super bad-looking dude in a super bad-looking car.

She didn't know how she knew it, but she did. She was looking at the evil sperm donor.

Grizz.

She was looking at her biological father.

47

Grizz, 2001, Fort Lauderdale

He had just loaded up his groceries and was getting ready to climb into his car when he heard her.

"It's you, isn't it?"

He stopped dead in his tracks as he watched his daughter walk up to the passenger side of his car and jiggle the door handle. The same daughter that had tricked him with a phone call to the prison pretending to be her mother. He didn't answer her but slowly scanned his surroundings.

"I'm alone. You are Grizz, aren't you?" she asked quietly. He barely heard her over the noise in the parking lot.

He still didn't answer.

"Did you have my father killed?" Her voice was calm, but he noticed the defiant tilt to her chin. He saw the same expression on her face he'd seen on her mother's more than twenty-five years ago. The night he'd had Ginny brought to the motel. And again not fifteen minutes ago in the cereal aisle.

He didn't answer her but got in the car, reached over to unlock her door and roll down her window.

"Get in," he said.

Her eyes widened. *So it is him.* She didn't know how it was possible, but she was right. She leaned down and looked at him through the passenger window.

"Why? So you can have me murdered, too? Then who's next? My little brother? Then you can kidnap my mom like you did all those years ago and disappear?"

As soon as the words were out of her mouth, she knew she shouldn't have said them. Leslie had shared with her some of the things he'd done. Her mother had confirmed part of it. But Ginny had also shared stories of their love, a love she believed to be a true one. Mimi knew Grizz would never hurt her mother. Could she trust her gut, which told her he hadn't had anything to do with Tommy's death and would never do anything to bring harm to her and Jason, as well? She was on the fence. But not for long. She'd just lived through the most painful few months in her life. *What do I have to lose?*

She climbed in and slammed the door behind her.

He didn't say anything. He didn't look at her. He just turned the key, and the loud engine roared to life. He pulled out onto the main road. Then, after driving for only a few minutes, he pulled over at the next shopping center. He parked under a shady tree far from the stores and turned off the engine. He looked over at her.

"Never. I mean fucking never are you to climb into a car with a strange man. Never!" His voice was a low, deep rumble.

It had taken less than three minutes to drive from one parking lot to the next, and she'd watched him the whole time. This was the last thing she expected him to say.

He held up a hand as she opened her mouth to speak. "And before you give me some teenage lip that I'm not your father and can't tell you what to do, you need to know I would be saying this to any girl who asked me for a ride. Got that?"

She didn't know what to expect, but it hadn't been a reprimand. Especially since he was right. He'd interrupted her right before she could tell him he wasn't her father. Darn it. Now what?

"You don't need to be afraid of me, and if you know some of the things I'm pretty sure you do know about me, I can understand why you might be. But I didn't have Tommy killed, and the last thing I'd ever do is cause harm or allow anyone near you, your mother, or your little brother."

He'd now turned to face her. He took off his sunglasses, and gave her a level look.

They say the eyes are the window to the soul. In the depths of his gaze, Mimi knew what he said was true. She blew out a long breath.

But how was it even possible she was having a conversation with a man who'd been executed last summer?

They talked for almost thirty minutes. Actually, she asked questions and he gave answers.

Finally, he said, "I need to get you home."

"You're going to take me home?" she blinked.

"Yeah. I'm going to take you home."

"I...I...I'm not sure that's such a good idea. Aren't you supposed to be dead? What if one of our neighbors recognizes you? And what were you even doing in a grocery store, right here in South Florida? I mean, shouldn't you be in hiding?"

He laughed. "It's called hiding in plain sight, and it's not too hard." His tone changed then, and he gave her a serious look. "It doesn't mean I want to be seen or recognized. I'm James Kirkland now. I might resemble Jason Talbot, but I'm not him, and I don't make a habit of being out."

"So if somebody does recognize you and tries to report it, what will you do? Will you kill them?" Her eyes were wide.

"I see your mother has been truthful about me." He didn't know whether he was sorry or relieved.

She nodded, and he recognized something in her expression. She was impressed.

He didn't like it.

"I'm not the same person I used to be," he said firmly.

"Will you go inside with me? Will you talk to Mom?"

She wasn't sure where she was going with this. She couldn't fathom her heart or her intentions, but she had come to several realizations in the last half-hour. First, she knew she had no reason to be afraid of him. Second, the wannabe journalist in her was intrigued. Three, she'd stumbled across something far more interesting than Slade Bear or her friend Lindsay's latest shopping trip.

And fourth, her inner spirit was telling her this man, her biological father, would be instrumental in making her mother happy again.

And for some reason, her mother's happiness had suddenly become very, very important to her.

48

Ginny, 2001, Fort Lauderdale

I was putting the groceries away when Denise dropped Jason back
at home. While I worked, I'd been pondering the events of the last
twenty-four hours.

Seeing Grizz at the church had been a shock, but I had to admit to
myself that I knew he'd show himself eventually. I hadn't believed
he'd leave after what I'd told Carter to relay to him. The fact that he'd
showed up at my grocery store earlier this morning had unnerved me
more than I cared to admit, and I found a bit of smug satisfaction in
knowing I'd been right that he wouldn't stay away.

I was also still a little stunned by Alec's admission last night. We'd
met for dinner prior to going to hear the same band we'd heard the
previous weekend, and I told him what Jason had said about Caleb
thinking we'd make a good family. I asked his opinion on how we
could still be friends but dissuade our children from the notion that
we might one day be a couple.

"Would that be so bad?" he'd shyly asked me.

I'd looked at Alec then. Really looked at him. And noticed something in his expression I hadn't seen, or hadn't allowed myself to see
before. Attraction.

Then of course came the awkwardness of trying to figure out how I
could stay friends with a man I wasn't interested in romantically. I

knew Alec would make any woman a wonderful partner, and even though I wasn't having those feelings for him now, I couldn't help but wonder if someday I might. Was I shooting myself in the foot? Would I be burning a bridge behind me?

I wouldn't answer his question. I skirted around it and let myself enjoy his company for the rest of the night. Thankfully, he made no attempt at anything intimate, not even hand holding.

At one point, I was a little surprised when Alec asked specifically about Sarah Jo. He wanted to know if we'd resumed what he perceived as a close friendship since she and Stan decided to stay in the States. I answered him honestly, told him Sarah Jo was there for me in the tragic weeks following Tommy's death, but like most people, she'd settled back into her busy life. I hadn't seen her that much if at all.

As I put a box of cereal on the shelf, I thought about Sarah Jo, about why we seemed to be drifting apart. Was it just the craziness of life, or something more?

My reverie was interrupted by an "I'm hungry" from Jason as he made his way into the kitchen.

"Not even a 'Hi, Mom, how are you'?" I asked as I placed a kiss on top of his head.

He gave me a wide smile and wrapped his arms around my waist. "Hi, Mom! How are you? I'm hungry."

"I just bought lunchmeat. Make yourself a sandwich," I told him.

"Awww, can you make it for me?"

"Sure," I said as I started to carry some canned goods into the pantry. "I was going to clean Spooky's litter box, which you were supposed to do before you went to Max's, but I'll make you a sandwich instead, and you can clean the box."

He followed me into the pantry and looked up at me with wide eyes.

"Sorry, Mom. I forgot."

"I know you did, Jason. I'm not upset with you. I've been forgetting a lot of things too lately, especially since we're all trying to get used to doing Dad's chores." I wasn't referring to Spooky's litter box but other household chores that had been Tommy's.

Twenty minutes later, the cat box was clean and Jason had finished his sandwich. I looked at the clock, and it occurred to me that Christy should've had Mimi home by now. I reached for my purse and realized my phone wasn't in it. When I thought about it, I hadn't had my phone with me all morning. I bet it was still charging on my nightstand.

I peeked in Tommy's office. Jason was sitting at the desk working on homework. It was his new favorite place to study.

I was heading upstairs to get my phone and see if Mimi had texted or called when the front door opened. I turned around and had to catch myself from gasping out loud.

Mimi came in the front door—followed by Grizz.

An intense anger hit me like a punch to the gut, followed by mild curiosity. I stood there, waiting for someone to say something. Anything.

"You don't keep your front door locked when you're home?" Grizz asked in his low, deep voice.

Typical Grizz.

Jason could see them through the French doors of Tommy's office, and he came out now, his curiosity aroused.

The four of us now stood in the foyer, just staring. Mimi broke the silence.

"I ran into an old friend of yours and Dad's at the Bears'. He offered to bring me home. He just heard about Dad and wanted to offer his condolences. You remember James Kirkland, don't you, Mom?"

Of course, she was lying, and the hundreds of things that wanted to come out of my mouth had to stay where they were because of Jason. The first, of course, was how had they run into each other? I certainly hadn't seen Mimi with him at the grocery store.

I looked at my son, who just stared at the mountain of a man who engulfed our entire foyer. His jaw was slightly agape as he slowly scanned Grizz from head to toe. Jason approached him and put his hand out, like his father had taught him.

"I'm Jason. You knew my dad?"

Grizz looked down and smiled at my son. A smile that had melted my heart in days gone by and was starting to have the same effect now. *Stop it, Ginny. This is a horrible and dangerous violation of your family. He has no right to be here.*

I don't remember the small snippets of conversation that were exchanged. There was a loud thrumming in my head, like a freight train was blasting through it. I do know Grizz said something that made Jason laugh. I hadn't invited him any further into the house, and I had no intention of doing so.

After a few minutes, I blurted out, "It's nice to see you again, James. Thank you for bringing Mimi home. I'll walk you to your car."

I gave Mimi a look that told her I'd be having a private conversation with her as soon as I made my way back into the house.

"Can he come back for dinner?" Jason asked. I could tell that he was captivated by Grizz.

"I'm sure he has plans for dinner." I looked at Grizz and saw understanding in his eyes.

"Maybe some other time, Jason," he said quietly.

Mimi jumped in before Jason could object. "C'mon, squirt, you still have to try and beat me at that new video game you just got."

If there was one other benefit besides the obvious that had made me happy since re-bonding with my daughter, it was how seamlessly and lovingly she'd inserted herself back into her little brother's life. He started to follow her as she headed for the den, but stopped to turn around and address Grizz.

"I hope you'll come back, Mr. Kirkland." Then, with half a wave, he chased his sister into the den.

I wordlessly followed Grizz to his car.

"You owe me an explanation," I said in a low voice as I stood with arms crossed and looked down into the driver's side of his car.

He reached into the ashtray and took out a business card. It was for Anthony's landscaping service. He grabbed a pen out of the console and wrote something on the back.

"I'm not calling you if that's what you think," I said, my fingernails digging into my upper arms.

Without looking up at me, he said, "Good, because I don't have a phone." He handed me the card. "That's my address on the back. You want an explanation, you come see me. I get home from work every night at six."

"You want me to come to you?"

"You can't have it all your way, Ginny. You obviously weren't happy to see me in your church classroom. You don't like that I shop at your grocery store. You don't want me in your home, and you already made it clear you wouldn't call me even if I did have a phone. If you don't get the explanation that you're looking for from Mimi, you know where to find me."

I tried to give him the stink eye, but he appeared oblivious to my efforts.

He started his car then, and shifted it into reverse.

"I won't bother you again, Ginny. I'll stay away. You have my word on that."

I stood there and watched him pull away, rolling my eyes at his last statement. Grizz would never stay away. He wouldn't know how to. He obviously wanted to immerse himself back in my life. And like the bully he'd always been, he would do it one way or another.

I was certain I would be seeing him again.

My neck prickled, and I turned, immediately aware of my surroundings again. Slowly I scanned my neighborhood. I wanted to be sure nobody had seen him. I needed to know he hadn't been spotted. But as I walked back to my house, I was struck with the sudden realization that I didn't need to worry about that. I was overthinking. Grizz was never stupid, and he wouldn't have let himself have any contact with Mimi, let alone drive her home, if there was even a hint of suspicion or danger.

Nobody cared about the dead biker who'd wreaked havoc on South Florida all those years ago. Apparently, nobody but me.

49

Grizz, 2001, Fort Lauderdale

G rizz headed back for his house in Laurel Falls. His mind was still spinning from the conversation he'd had with Mimi. She was sharp, and he felt like he'd been put through an official interrogation. If Mimi was this inquisitive, he could only imagine what his conversation with Ginny would be like. When he eventually got to have one with her.

He answered all of Mimi's questions honestly except for one—how he'd faked his death. He did, however, plant some truth in her mind: that anyone with enough power and the right amount of money can do anything they wanted.

"I know you are—or were—wealthy," she'd said, brow arched. Good. He was glad when she didn't pursue the subject further.

His daughter was smart and a bit sassy. She'd continued with other questions after that. He was a little taken aback when he thought he saw her lip quiver as she said in a low voice, "So I guess you never wanted me. You wanted Mom, but not me. You told her to make sure I never knew you. I guess that's because you didn't want to know me."

He could've explained to her then that it had never been his intention to stay away. He could've gone into a lengthy discussion about never believing his fake execution would take so many years.

Instead, he hefted his hip off the car seat and reached for his wallet.

He dug deep and pulled out three pictures that were worn and had been cropped to fit inside. He handed them to her.

Her hands shook as she looked at the pictures. They were of her when she was just a little girl.

"Mom sent these to you?" Something that may have resembled hope was in her voice.

"No," he said evenly. "She honored my request to keep you away. I had surveillance on you those first few years. I didn't want to miss anything. When it was obvious things were taking longer than I'd expected, I stopped the surveillance. It was too much for me and not fair to your parents. Or you."

She didn't say anything, and he thought her lip started to tremble harder.

"I'd like those back," he said, his deep voice bringing her back. "They're the only ones I still have."

She'd regained her composure and handed them back to him.

Now, his groceries put away, he'd made himself something to eat and was sitting on the couch staring at the blank TV screen.

"I won't bother you again, Ginny. I'll stay away. You have my word on that," he muttered to himself. His own words, spoken only hours ago, were laced with just a bit of sincerity, but he was really trying to call her bluff. He was certain he caught a moment of weakness in her glance when Jason introduced himself.

Had he read her right? Did she still have feelings for him? And if she did, to what end? Would she lead two lives? One of devoted and widowed mother of two children and another as mistress to a dead man? He knew how he would like to see things play out, but it would be a long shot, and he had no choice but to wait out the standoff he'd initiated.

Ginny was one of the most strong-willed and stubborn women he'd ever known, even when she was younger. She would only be stronger now.

He went to a second bedroom which he'd set up as an exercise room and lifted weights. When his muscles tired, he took a hot shower and did a load of laundry. He packed his lunch for the next day and headed back to the living room. He flipped through the TV channels and, not finding anything that interested him, tossed the remote aside.

Where had he put Moe's journal when he'd moved over here from the efficiency? He went into the bedroom and rummaged through his few belongings. There it was, stuffed back in the bag he'd shoved into one of the nightstand drawers.

He hadn't read too much the one and only time he'd picked it up. He was getting tired, and Monday morning would be here soon. Maybe he'd read just a little more.

Moe's Diary, 1975

Dear Elizabeth,

I can't believe he's still acting as if nothing happened between us. I know he told me that same night that it probably shouldn't have happened, that I shouldn't read anything into it, but I know it was more. I've never had a man make love to me. Men screw me. Even Fess tries to act like it's more special than just a lay, but I know what I am. I like Fess and care about him. But I don't love him.

It was different with Grunt. I know he was upset when he got back from the beach with Sarah Jo and figured out what Kit and Grizz were doing in Number Four. I saw him walk back to his room with his head down. I'd thought maybe I would show him some of my latest sketches. He seems to like them, and I like hearing I have talent. I took some of my drawings to his unit, and he acted nice, but I could tell his mind was on other things. He was thinking about her. I decided to leave and thought maybe I would just give him a hug. He held me longer than he ever had before, and when I looked up to see if he was okay, he kissed my forehead. Then he kissed my temple. Before I knew what was happening, he was kissing my neck. I closed my eyes and let myself enjoy it. He made his way down my body, and next thing I knew, we were undressed and in his bed.

If he didn't care and was just trying to get off, it would've been quick. But it wasn't. He really took his time with me, and it was so beautiful I almost cried a few times. I'd never had that feeling before. I know when a man gets his rocks off, but I never knew a woman could do that, too. Grunt made me feel things I never felt. Things I want to keep feeling, but he told me he was sorry that it happened and couldn't happen again. That he didn't want it to ruin our friendship, and that my friendship was very important to him.

I know he has feelings for her, but she doesn't love him. She doesn't care about him the way I do. It's not fair. It's just not fair.

So Moe had feelings for Tommy. Grizz wasn't surprised by this. Other than Fess and Ginny, Tommy was the only person who'd ever shown any kindness to Moe. And now knowing they'd had a night of passion only confirmed what he'd already learned in the back of that pool supply store in Tallahassee. Moe was the insider at the motel. Between her love for Tommy and her hatred of him, having Ginny gone would've served two purposes.

His jaw tightened as he finally came to the part where Moe had unwittingly helped set up Ginny's rape and almost murder. He believed what he was reading. That Moe hadn't intended for it to go that far, but that fucking bitch, Willow, posing as someone named Wendy, had tricked her. And Ginny had paid the price. At least he'd made sure Willow and her brainless boyfriend paid the ultimate price. He may have had some regrets about his criminal past, but he never had any regrets for something he'd done in retaliation for anything directed at Ginny. Willow's last words to Moe mocked him and clawed at his subconscious as he fell into a restless sleep that night. "It'll be tit for tat...it'll be tit for tat."

He had angry and violent dreams that night. Dreams of being helpless. Even though he hadn't witnessed it, he relived Ginny's torture and rape by a man in a black ski mask. He dreamed he was strapped to the gurney in the execution room, and he could see Ginny through the glass window. Except he wasn't seeing her calmly sitting with the rest of the spectators. He was seeing their bedroom in the motel. The man with the black ski mask had just finished raping and beating Ginny and she laid there, her face bloated and swollen. A trickle of blood flowed from her left nostril and ear. The man placed his ear to Ginny's chest to see if she had a heartbeat and, satisfied that he'd killed her, he slowly climbed off the bed.

Grizz watched in a helpless dream-state as the man stood and looked around the motel room, searching for something to steal. He noticed Gwinny jump up on the bed and gently approach Ginny. She started licking Ginny's face. Grizz watched the man grab Gwinny and kill her. He then tucked the black cat beneath the covers next to Ginny.

It was intended as a sadistic surprise for the person who'd eventually find Ginny's body.

Then he watched the man take off his ski mask. Even in the depths of so dark a dream, Grizz felt his heartbeat quicken. He wasn't looking at Ginny's rapist.

He was looking at her then-best friend. He was looking at Sarah Jo.

50

Ginny, 2001, Fort Lauderdale

I don't know how many times that week I picked up the business
card that Grizz had given me and just stared at it. I threw it in the
garbage at least three times, only to find myself digging it out and
wiping off strawberry and coffee stains along with a myriad of other
nastiness. I didn't have to keep it. I'd stared at it so many times that
I'd subconsciously memorized the address Grizz had written on the
back. I knew the subdivision. I didn't know anyone who lived there,
but I'd passed it enough when visiting clients who lived or worked in
that area. Of course, since I no longer had any clients, I had no reason
to be over that way.

After walking Grizz out to his car that day, I went back into the
house to talk to Mimi. We left Jason, who was absorbed in his video
game, and went into Tommy's office, shutting the door behind us.

Mimi explained everything. The disappointment of Slade's second
rejection. The uncomfortable ride home with Christian. Trying to find
me and ultimately running into Grizz at the grocery store.

"And you just knew it was him and walked right up to him?"

"He looked like an older version of that first picture I'd seen. You
know, the one with the long hair. Maybe I wanted it to be him, Mom. I
don't know. When he didn't deny who he was, I was more curious
than anything."

"But, Mimi, you climbed into a car with a stranger!"

"Yeah, I already got an earful from him for doing that," she said sheepishly.

That was something Grizz would've done. Reprimand the child he hadn't raised. As upset as I was, I felt a small smile trying to find its way to my lips, but I fought it.

Mimi explained that he'd been forthright and truthful. She'd even tested him by asking him things she already knew about. He didn't lie to her. Not once. Hmph.

"I hope you know I'm forbidding you to ever see him again. Never, Mimi. He is not welcome in our home or in our lives."

She looked at me. "I know, Mom. He told me you would be mad and not to try and get in touch with him or try to see him again. He wouldn't tell me where he was staying or anything. I could've tried to do a search on his name and license plate, but I'm not stupid. It's probably registered to a phony address."

My insides began to churn. "So he told you I'd be mad and not let you see him? He forbade you first?"

Mimi looked at me sideways with a curious expression on her face. "Mom, are you actually mad because he agreed with you, or are you mad because he told me first?"

I ran my hand through my hair and huffed out a breath. "I'm not mad. I'm just upset that he thinks he can show back up and get his hands into things he has no right to!"

My daughter just looked at me. I could tell she was trying to figure out what my feelings were for her biological father. I could only think that if she does figure them out, I hope she'll tell me what they are.

THE FOLLOWING WEEK DRAGGED. I HAD A LUNCH DATE WITH ALEC DOWN at a popular restaurant on the Intracoastal. We walked along the docks afterward. The sun was bright, and he grabbed my hand to steer me toward a little kiosk that sold visors. After buying me one, he casually retrieved my hand for the rest of the walk. It wasn't as hard or awkward as I thought it might be. It was very comfortable, and I convinced myself I liked the feathery kiss he placed on the side of my mouth after he escorted me to my car.

Now I was on my way home and letting myself wonder what it would've been like if he'd kissed me on the lips. Could I see myself kissing Alec back? Could I picture myself enjoying it? I raised my hand to the spot he kissed, letting my fingers mimic his mouth.

My ringing cell phone interrupted my daydream. Sarah Jo, calling to catch up and apologize for not being around the last several months.

"I'm sorry, Gin." Her voice was quiet. I hadn't seen her after the couple of weeks that followed the funeral. "I don't know what to say. It might sound awful, but I've been dealing with Tommy's loss, too, and, being around you was just too painful."

Relief washed over me. I think deep down I'd been wondering if it was something else. Something more.

"I understand completely, Jo. Please—don't feel bad." And I meant it.

I remembered that awful day at the hospital when I fell apart at Sarah Jo's arrival. I was certain I wouldn't be able to get through that awful time without her, but oddly enough, I had. Everybody grieved in their own way, and I understood her need to stay away. The truth was I had become accustomed to not seeing much of her, and if I was being honest with myself, I hadn't noticed her absence. I missed our friendship, but not as much as I probably should have. I couldn't explain why.

We made a plan to meet for lunch the following week. I hung up the phone and realized I'd lost track of the time and my route home. I had just pulled into the subdivision of Laurel Falls. Grizz's subdivision.

I slammed on the brakes, did a sharp U-turn in the middle of the road, and headed for home.

ANOTHER WEEK DRAGGED, AND WITH IT MY ANXIETY ONLY INCREASED. I just knew Grizz was going to show up again. I was able to find some relief in mentally preparing myself.

My lunch with Sarah Jo was pleasant, but something was off. I was certain it wasn't her. It was me and my preoccupation with Grizz's return.

Before I knew it, still another week had passed and there had been no sign of Grizz. He's staying away. He got the message. I tried to convince myself that this was a good thing.

But it didn't help that Jason had asked about his father's old friend, James Kirkland, more than once.

I'd seen Alec a couple more times in those weeks, and he didn't hold my hand or give me a goodbye kiss like he had at the docks. As a matter of fact, he went back to being the perfect friend and if I hadn't been so consumed by my angst over Grizz, I might've had my pride pricked or wondered if he was playing a game. He probably wondered the same about me.

I prayed for strength when I found my thoughts drifting to Grizz. I asked God to give me the strength to be able to forgive him for whatever anger and resentment I held onto. I needed the peace that only the Holy Spirit could give me.

I also found myself praying for the man I'd once been so in love with. I wanted him to find happiness. I wanted him to find God. And maybe, maybe buried deep down somewhere, I wanted him to find me and bring me back to the love I'd once felt. But it was just too late for that. At least that's what I told myself.

I hadn't let myself think about loving Grizz. It was easier to be mad, but it was also exhausting and so contrary to how I'd lived my life. Now I'd slip in and out of moods I wasn't used to experiencing. I'd always been so confident in my thoughts and in my actions. As I realized my anger about Grizz and our past had finally started to wane, I discovered it was replaced with a new anger. One I couldn't explain.

Grizz was following my orders. He was staying away from my church and my grocery store. He was staying away from my children and my home. He was staying away from me.

I convinced myself he was only keeping his distance to mess with my head. That it was all part of some big game he was playing to get me to go to him. Of course, this kind of behavior wasn't anything like the Grizz I'd known—the man who never asked permission but did and took what he wanted. The man who ran over people and squished them like insects. The man who'd wanted me enough to risk losing it all by having me abducted back in 1975.

No. This wasn't like Grizz at all.

It truly bothered me that I thought about him so much. I reasoned that I had to get him out of my head and out of my life once and for all. I also knew I couldn't go to him. I wouldn't give in to what I thought was a mental game.

Whether imagined or real, it consumed me. No, I decided. I wouldn't lose this one. I would never go to him.

Never.

51

Ginny, 2001, Fort Lauderdale

Two weeks later, I found myself standing at his front door mentally kicking myself in the butt for being so weak.

I'd purposely picked a day in the middle of the week and a time I knew he'd be at work. I just wanted to stand there. To see if I could pinpoint what I was feeling.

The emotional rollercoaster I'd been riding had been too much. I needed to resolve things in my head. I needed to see him. To confront my feelings. I couldn't even identify what they were, but they were there. My heart insisted this was the only way to move on from Grizz. And that's what I wanted, right?

I would come to learn my heart was even a worse liar than I was. I looked down at my feet and whispered, "You might've been right, Tommy."

The sound of a low-flying plane overhead and the continuous droning of insects did little to distract me as I tried to imagine how I'd feel if he were actually at home. Would I be happy to see him? Would I be angry, mad, accusatory? Would I puff myself up as I convinced myself I was feeling righteous anger? God spoke to me then. Not out loud. I never hear an actual voice, but I do know when my thoughts are from Him.

I knew then that I would come back to talk to Grizz. For in the moment I heard God, I'd felt instant shame about the way I'd treated him. I could convince myself all day long that I had a right to be rude, that he didn't deserve my forgiveness. But even Jesus asked God to forgive those who were persecuting and torturing him. "Forgive them, Father, for they know not what they do."

At that moment, I knew I would be able to have a calm and adult discussion with Grizz, not one laced with an unforgiving attitude and resentment. Yes, I could and would forgive Grizz. I would come back and talk to him.

A peace fell over me then, and I turned my face heavenward.

"Thank you for the gift of knowing Your peace, Father. Thank you for showing me this in Your time," I whispered.

Just then, the front door flew open and Grizz came barreling out, almost knocking me over. And just like that, my heart did a flip-flop.

"Kit...uh, Ginny!" He grabbed me roughly by my arms, his eyes wide with surprise. "I didn't see you. What are you doing here, honey?"

I started to snap back at him and ask him what he was doing here —he was supposed to be at work! I caught myself just in time.

"I—I didn't think you were here," I stammered, staring into his warm, green eyes. "I was just—just trying to see what I was feeling. Kind of practicing to maybe, uh, have a conversation with you."

He smiled. "I took today off. I have to go to the dentist. I have a tooth that's killing me. But I'll cancel the appointment."

"Thought you didn't have a phone." I looked up at him. I wasn't accusing, just curious.

"I didn't. Bear gave me one after the last time I saw you so we could communicate for work. Like this morning, I called and told him I had to go to the dentist."

I remembered how much Grizz had hated the dentist. He must be in some serious pain if he'd called a dentist. I didn't want him to miss his appointment. I surprised myself by making an offer.

"Let me go with you."

He looked a bit startled, and I could see him mentally calculating his options. Then he gave me a rueful smile.

"I'd rather invite you into my house, but it hurts bad enough that I'm going to take you up on your offer."

He locked the deadbolt on his front door and aimed his clicker at the small, detached garage. Before he pressed the button, I said, "I'll drive you."

Without giving him time to answer, I headed for my car and got in. He followed and awkwardly climbed into the passenger side of my SUV. He was so big that it was difficult for him to settle in. He slid the seat way back so he could ride comfortably.

After telling me where the dentist was located, the car became silent. I decided to fill it with idle chit-chat—questions about his job on the landscaping crew, his neighbors, how he was settling in. I was surprised he'd met some of his neighbors.

"I don't know the people on my left. Apparently, they only come down from up north in the winter. The couple across the street, can't think of their names, are too busy with four kids to be friendly, which is fine with me. The family on the right came up from Miami. The parents don't speak English. They have two kids. The boy is in high school, the daughter is in college. The daughter, Rosa, cleans my house once every two weeks, and occasionally picks up groceries for me. I think the family behind me just moved in from somewhere out west."

I cast him a sidelong glance, and he quickly added, "I'm not invited to family barbecues or anything like that. I just try not to be too much of a standoffish prick. I'm the nice widower from up north who goes to work every day and minds his own business."

"You're a widower?" I asked, my curiosity piqued.

He then told me about the alias that had been created for him. His new identity came with a family history and all kinds of official documentation.

"Aren't you tired of it, Grizz?" I blurted out, then wanted to eat my words.

But he knew exactly what I was talking about. The aliases and name changes were tiresome. He answered without looking at me.

"More tired than you know, Kitten." He scrubbed his hand down his face. "And before you give me shit for calling you Kitten, I know it's dangerous and you don't like it, but it's a habit."

"Jason wants me to invite you to the house for dinner." It had started to rain, and I flicked on the windshield wipers.

"No," he answered a little too quickly. "I shouldn't have come to your house with Mimi. I'm glad I did because I got to meet Jason. He seems like a great kid, Ginny. But it's just not a good idea."

"Tommy told me the story, and he told me you're free now. They don't care about you anymore."

"That's true or I wouldn't have made sure you knew I was still alive, but at the same time, I'm still trying to lay low. I know the population has multiplied by leaps and bounds since I went to prison, so blending into a bigger pot is easier therefore making the risk smaller. And my established identity should protect me."

The rain came down harder now, and I switched the wipers to maximum speed.

"But there's always that small chance that someone might recognize me. And maybe they'll tell themselves it's impossible because I'm supposed to be dead. But if someone thinks they recognize me and sees me with you—well, I just think it would cause them to think twice. I probably shouldn't have accepted your offer to come to the dentist with me, but I can't help it, Kit...Ginny."

I could feel his eyes on me. I wouldn't look over at him but stared straight ahead.

"You've always been my addiction." He didn't have to compete with the pounding rain. His voice was deep and clear and his next statement seared my soul.

"I can't see myself ever saying no to you. I love you, Ginny. I never stopped loving you for one single second. Ever."

Thwip, thwap, thwip, thwap. The windshield wipers were slamming back and forth, and their desperation to keep up with the pelting rain matched the rhythm of my heartbeat.

"How many people actually know?" I chanced a look at him. "Other than me, Mimi, Carter, Bill, and Anthony?"

"That's it. Anthony may have told Christy, but I'm not worried about that."

I nodded, then bit my lip.

"Grizz, why the bandana? Seems like such an old-fashioned way to handle things. I could've just said something to Carter. It would have been far easier."

"It was something I put in place back in 1985, after I was arrested. Didn't see any need to change things up. And because I'm familiar with what they're capable of, the last thing I wanted them to know was that you had a way to communicate with me. A face-to-face conversation, a phone call, even an email to Carter would've been too risky."

I could feel the intensity of his glance when he added, "It's one of the main reasons why I discouraged you from coming to see me."

I ignored the ache in my heart at his last admission, and asked him a little more then, delving into his relationship with Carter and Bill.

He answered everything casually and without hesitation. Finally, the curiosity I denied having got the best of me.

"How? How did you pull off a fake execution?" I blurted out. "I mean, I understand that this group is supposed to be powerful, but faking a death?"

"I almost didn't pull it off. I'm pretty sure I really did die on that table. I came around in the morgue where their doctors were working on me," he answered, his voice even.

I shuddered at the thought of waking up in a morgue. "But, couldn't they have still had you killed after you gave them their stuff back?" I gave him a sideways glance.

"Yes, they could have, Kit, and nobody would've been the wiser."

"But, they didn't, Grizz. Why didn't they?"

"Only two possibilities come to mind. They don't care anymore or someone has been watching out for me. I'll probably never know for sure."

I could tell by the tone of his voice that the subject was closed and I was secretly relieved.

Finally, we arrived at the dentist. The dentist's office was in a medical building that shared the same corner as a large shopping outlet. They were so common now in Florida. Developers had to make the best use of every space. You could pull into one complex and do your grocery shopping, eat, have a manicure, and see your chiropractor all in one visit. I lucked out and found a spot right up front.

"I think you should wait in the car, Ginny. Just to be safe. If you don't want to, I can get a cab home."

I agreed with him about not going in and told him I didn't mind waiting. He gave me a smile that made my toes tingle. My toes didn't tingle when Alec held my hand or kissed me. I passed the time by playing with my cell phone. I still wasn't used to all the things the kids told me I could do with it. I was trying to check my data usage and figure out how to pick ringtones when I looked up.

I'd noticed a small car kept circling the medical building. It had a handicapped sticker hanging from the rearview mirror. A quick glance told me all the handicapped spots were taken. I should pull out and let them have this spot. I waited until I saw them come around for the umpteenth time, and I started to back up slowly. I saw them stop and put on their blinker. I drove to the farthest spot and backed into a space so I would be facing the dentist when Grizz came out. I was glad the rain had stopped. The couple took forever to get out of their car and make their way up to the sidewalk.

I wasn't sure how much time passed when something caused me to look up from my phone. I knew he'd come out. I couldn't explain it, but somehow I felt Grizz. I think I always had.

I started the car and watched as he casually walked down the sidewalk. He crossed over to the next building and strode past a deli, hair salon, and sportswear store. He appeared to be looking for something. He wasn't looking out into the parking lot at the cars. He wasn't looking for me.

I finally caught up with him and lightly tapped my horn. Without missing a beat, he came toward my car and got in.

"Thought you left." He didn't sound mad or hurt, just stating a fact.

"I gave up my spot for a couple that needed it. How'd it go in there?"

"He fixed me up. I don't need to go back."

"What were you doing? You looked like you were looking for something or someone."

"I thought you left so I was going to call a cab. But I left the phone Anthony gave me at home."

"So what were you doing?"

"I was looking for a fucking phone booth!"

I gave him a half-smile. "Phone booths have become an endangered species."

"A lot of shit has changed since I've been gone," he said matter-of-factly.

"A lot of things have changed," I said. "But I can see your use of profanity isn't one of them."

"You don't survive in prison for fifteen years saying 'intercourse' and 'poop.'"

Just hearing him say the words intercourse and poop sounded comical. As much as I disliked the use of profanity, I couldn't help myself. I smiled at the thought of him using the alternatives.

He asked if I would come into the house after I dropped him off. But I shook my head. Not only was it probably not a good idea to let myself be alone with him, but I also wanted to be at the bus stop when Jason got off. I told Grizz Jason had been getting in fights in school, and one bully in particular rode his bus. Grizz seemed interested and asked me to elaborate.

"It has to do with Tommy," I said. "Everyone was so nice and understanding after Tommy died, but there's always that one person that sees someone's pain as a way to manipulate and make themselves feel better. In this case, it's a kid named Corbin. He's been awful to Jason recently. I don't know why or where it's coming from, but he's said some hurtful things."

"Like what?" Grizz frowned.

"The last thing that got Jason upset was that Tommy was stupid to have gotten himself killed. That if it was Corbin's father, he would've been smart enough to hide, and if he did try to stop the shooter, he wouldn't have been dumb enough to get shot."

"So what happened? Jason clocked him?"

"No! Tommy and I have taught Jason to turn the other cheek, to ignore bullies and only fight back if there's no other choice." I could sense Grizz rolling his eyes as I kept mine on the road in front of me. "It actually bothered Corbin that Jason wasn't reacting to the taunts, so he started getting physical. Of course, Jason fought back. He's sporting a black eye, but it's nothing compared to his bruised heart. To have to go through the loss of his father and be teased about it? It's been really hard for him."

I wasn't going to tell Grizz about the other emotional blow Jason had suffered. One that had come from Alec. It explained why Alec had gone back to being just a friend after that walk on the docks so many weeks ago.

Jason had been visiting Alec's boys. They'd been playing in the back yard when he went inside to use the bathroom. Apparently, Alec's estranged wife, Paulina, had stopped by, and Jason overhead a conversation he shouldn't have. I'd noticed a change in Jason's personality after he came home from that visit, and it took me days to get him to tell me what was wrong—he'd heard Alec and Paulina talking about getting back together. And Paulina had specifically asked Alec to ease off spending so much time with Jason and me.

I'd asked Alec to meet me for a quick dinner one night, and he explained.

"I feel like shit. I had no idea Jason heard us talking or I would've talked to you. I probably should've talked to you anyway." He swiped a hand through his hair. "I feel like I need to do it for my boys, Ginny. She wants to try again. She said the lesbian thing was a phase."

I took a sip of my drink and looked at him over the rim of my glass.

"Is something like that a phase?" I wasn't being sarcastic. I honestly didn't know, and apparently, neither did he.

"I don't know, but Paulina is different now. Sherry may have been good for her in some ways. She's more positive, energetic, less self-centered. She's becoming the mother the boys never had, and I can tell it's not an act. She's totally immersing herself in them. She asked me if she can move back home."

"Alec, I know that I have no rights here. I'm happy for you if this is what you want. But can I tell you as my friend to please be careful?"

I'd looked at him warmly, and he reached for my hand across the table.

"I would've liked more from you, Ginny. I can't deny that, and I won't try to. I think after our lunch down at the docks and that little kiss, I let myself believe there might've been a chance. But I didn't see it in your eyes. I'm right, aren't I?"

I'd looked away but didn't pull my hand from his.

"You have been such a good friend, Alec...."

"But?" A small smile played at his lips.

I took a breath. "I feel like we would be forcing it. Like, we need to be a couple because you don't have a wife and because I lost my husband and because your son wants us to be a family. And of course, I may not have wanted to let myself think it, but there is an attraction. I don't think I imagined that. But it's all too compact. Too neat. Almost too perfect. Does that make sense?"

"Yes." He nodded. "I see what you're saying."

I pulled my hand back and fiddled with the napkin on my lap. I stared at the untouched chicken Caesar salad on my plate, the inviting aroma not enough to make me want to take a bite. My stomach was churning.

"Can I ask you something and ask for your complete honesty?" he asked softly.

"Of course."

"Does this have anything to do with James?"

I blinked at him, totally taken off guard.

Alec gave an embarrassed smile. "Jason mentioned an old friend of Tommy's had visited the house. He said he only came by once, but Jason seemed a bit taken with him."

I let out a sigh of relief. I'd secretly wondered if Grizz had done something to make himself known to Alec. He hadn't.

"James told Jason some stories about Tommy when he was

younger," I said. "Of course, Jason would be fascinated by him. He wants me to invite him over so he can hear more. I'm sure that's what it is."

"Do you want to invite him over?" Alec asked.

I looked at him then as my mind swirled with a myriad of possible answers. In the end, I decided on the truth.

"I honestly don't know, Alec. I honestly don't know."

Now, sitting in Grizz's driveway, I looked over at him.

"Does Jason know how to defend himself?" Grizz asked. "Did Tommy teach him how to fight?"

"Of course, he taught him how to defend himself. But Jason wasn't raised in the same environment Tommy was." I gripped the steering wheel hard. "Tommy didn't have a lot of reason to practice with him."

"Can't say I blame him."

I was stunned by the admission and looked over at him. Without any prompting from me, Grizz said, "I guess Tommy was afraid he'd be making the kid into me. Probably scared to tap into that gene. Like I said, I can't blame him. He was probably worried the apple wouldn't fall far from the tree. I mean, it skipped a generation because Tommy didn't inherit my mean streak, but he was probably afraid my grandson might."

My mouth agape, I realized then that Grizz didn't know. Grizz really did believe Tommy was his son.

"We don't need to worry about Jason inheriting anything from you, Grizz," I told him quietly. I hadn't intended sarcasm, and I was hoping it hadn't come across that way.

"Why's that?" He had already gotten out of my car and shut the door. He was now bent over and leaning through the passenger window that I had rolled down.

"Because Tommy was not your son."

Before he had a chance to reply, I quickly added, "I'm really sorry." And I meant it. "I don't mean to toss this at you and then run off, but I need to get to the bus stop. I don't have time to go into it now." I shifted into reverse. "I promise to explain later."

He nodded and stepped back from the car, but not before I detected something in his eyes. I was almost positive it was disappointment.

52

Grizz, 2001, Fort Lauderdale

Two days later, Grizz was still reflecting on Ginny's revelation. He had truly believed he'd fathered Tommy. Was Ginny telling some lie to hurt him, pay him back for all he'd done to her? Had Tommy convinced Ginny of some wild untruth in a misguided effort to shield her—or keep her by his side? Or was it the truth?

He drove home from work, letting the thoughts run over him. He was learning how to be a patient man. He wanted to call her, ask for an explanation, but he knew he was being tested. Either by Ginny or by some higher being whose existence may or may not have been trying to seep into his conscience.

For months, his routine had been the same. He went to work every day and ate dinner alone in his house every night. He had no interest in television, so he either worked out in his weight room or spent the evening reading one of the many books he'd checked out from the local library.

He spent his weekends riding. He'd finally given in to the call of his bike and paid a visit to that warehouse and towed it back to South Florida. But, he never rode in Fort Lauderdale, where he now temporarily lived. He always made the long drive over Alligator Alley to the other side of the state. Even that was a risk, but with the one-year anniversary of his execution a few months back, he felt he'd passed a milestone. Earned it, somehow.

He rode just to ride. To feel the wind in his hair. He was grateful Florida had passed the no-helmet law. He'd never worn one and wouldn't have wanted to risk getting stopped. He always rode alone and avoided attention.

But not once did he ride where he didn't fantasize about having her on the back. Her arms wrapped tightly around his waist, her breasts pressing against his back. The anticipation building as he imagined making love to her when they arrived at their destination or returned home.

He grinned when he thought about the times they didn't even make it back home. He remembered how he'd reach behind him while they were riding and find the space between her legs that made her squirm. How his fingers built up a burning, a desire that caused her to insist he pull over at the most convenient and out-of-the-way spot so he could make love to her.

Would he ever know days like those again? Would he ever get another chance with her?

Now, as he pulled on to his street, his heart began to thud. He could see her SUV parked on the swale in front of his house. He'd been tired after spending all day in the sun, but seeing her car gave him an instant onset of energy.

He opened the garage door and drove in. He walked out to find her standing on the sidewalk that led to his front door, hands on her hips and staring pointedly at the motorcycle.

"You're not actually riding that around town, are you?"

"Why? You wanna go for a spin?" He couldn't help but smile.

"No, I don't want to go for a spin. Seems like the last place you should be is on top of a motorcycle."

"If you can think of another place I should be on top of, I'm open for suggestions."

Her face started to turn red, and he could see he'd flustered her. He quickly changed tactics; he didn't want to make her uncomfortable to the point where she'd want to leave.

"It's good to see you, sweetheart," he said as gently as possible. "Can you come in?"

She gifted him with a sincere smile. "Yeah, but I can't stay too long. I just wanted to give you an explanation after what I told you the other day."

This wasn't exactly true. She wanted to have a long talk with him, but wanted to see how things progressed first.

"You could've called me. Saved yourself the trouble of driving over," he said casually. He'd given her his cell phone number two days ago.

"I lost the number."

He chanced a glance at her. She was standing only a few feet away, looking at the sidewalk with her arms crossed and kicking the ground with her right foot.

She never could get away with lying. He smiled as he unlocked his front door, then stepped aside so she could walk in first. He followed and shut the door behind them, locking it and trying to ignore the instant erection after he caught a whiff of her. Like he'd already discovered, she still smelled the same.

He watched her as she stood in the middle of his living room and slowly took in her surroundings. The blinds were drawn, but natural light from the overhead skylights filled the space, giving it a warm and inviting aura.

"It's nice." He detected genuine admiration in her tone.

"It came furnished. You want something to drink?"

"Do you have anything diet?"

"Hell, no. And why do you need to be drinking anything diet?"

She ignored the question and tried not to stare at his butt as he walked past her and headed for the open kitchen area. She didn't know how it was possible, but he actually looked like he was in better shape now than before he went to prison. He was in his fifties now, and had been in prison for fifteen years. He wasn't supposed to look better. He was supposed to look old and beaten down.

He handed her a bottled water. Twisting off the cap of his own, he downed the entire thing in a succession of huge gulps, then watched as she took a delicate sip of hers and screwed the cap back in place.

"You here to tell me why you think Tommy isn't my son?"

"I'm here to tell you why I know he isn't your son."

"Can I have ten minutes to shower?"

"Yeah, sure."

He showered in record time and came out of the bathroom wearing only his jeans and still towel-drying his hair. He thought he smelled food and noticed her on the other side of the kitchen island with her back to him. She was standing at the stove.

"What smells so good?" he asked.

Without turning around, she said, "Figured you might not feel like cooking after working all day. I dug through your fridge and pulled out what I could use. Hope you don't mind chicken stir-fry."

The truth was, she needed to keep her hands and mind busy. She'd allowed one quick thought into her brain about Grizz being in that shower, naked. Yeah, she wouldn't go there.

"Don't mind at all," he said truthfully. "You'll stay and eat with me, won't you?"

She turned around to answer him and was instantly tongue-tied. Grizz stood before her shirtless. Both hands casually gripped a white towel that was draped around his neck. His long wet hair was tousled. She was staring at his chest when he interrupted her thoughts.

"Will you? Stay and eat with me?" he asked, a sweet yet determined look in his eyes.

She wondered about the last time he may have sat down to a home-cooked meal and had somebody to share it with. She could, she realized. The kids had plans for this evening, so she had time.

"Yes, I'll stay," she answered a little breathlessly as he returned to the bedroom to throw his towel in the hamper and put on a shirt.

As if fifteen years hadn't come between them, he sat silently and respectfully like he used to do when she said her meal blessing. And then she wasted no time telling him about Tommy's revelations concerning his and Mimi's DNA.

"After Tommy told me he was your son, I convinced myself I saw a resemblance, but now that I think about it, Tommy almost had your height, but not your width. His brown eyes took on a hazel sheen in certain light, but I guess that was it. I didn't want to believe he was your son, but because he actually did believe it, I guess I did, too."

Grizz stared at her, taking it all in. He nodded, but didn't say anything.

"I know all about his mother, Candy. I know what you told Tommy while you were in prison. How that guy Red made you and Anthony stay with her." Her voice held no accusations.

She then told him about Tommy's visit to his paternal grandmother's house.

"Red." Grizz tightened his jaw. "He really was a rotten piece of shit. Using me and Anthony to keep Candy prisoner under the guise that 'it was for her own good.' She must've been scared to death of him because she never once told me or Anthony what Red was doing to her."

They'd finished their meal and were sitting at the table. Grizz took a sip of his drink and set the glass back down.

"And you're sure Red was Tommy's father?" he asked.

Without answering him, she got up from the small kitchen table and walked to the living room to retrieve her purse. He followed her as she sat on a chair that faced the couch. Taking a seat on the sofa in front of her, he watched as she pulled an envelope from her bag.

"This is Red's brother, David Enman." She handed him a picture. "What do you think?"

"Son of a bitch," Grizz said under his breath. "Strange how Tommy doesn't look like Red, but like Red's brother instead. You said David Enman was dead years before Candy got pregnant, right?"

"Yes." She nodded. "And I've never understood something. Truthfully, there's a lot I haven't understood, but one thing after learning this is why you never really did anything to confirm paternity. You assumed you were Tommy's father based on the same blood type and based on the mistaken notion that you and Anthony were the only ones having sex with Candy during the time. Big assumption for someone like you. Why?"

"It was a different world. They didn't do paternity tests. I saw a picture of him when he was younger that I thought looked like me. We both have a rare blood type. His birthday lined up with when I'd been banging Candy. It was good enough back then." He didn't meet her eyes.

"Not good enough for someone like you though, Grizz," she said softly. "I think you wanted to believe it. You wanted him to be your son, didn't you?"

He snorted. "Why would I want something like that? Why would I want to bring a kid into that lifestyle? Don't be ridiculous, Kit."

She cocked her head. "Because, other than having Mavis look after me, maybe fathering a child as bright as Tommy was the only good thing you'd ever done. The only decent legacy you might've left in the world."

He didn't answer her, and she used the opportunity to segue into the next conversation she wanted to have with him. She didn't know what he was expecting from her. She didn't even know what she was expecting from him. The one thing she did know was that she wanted to hear some things from his own mouth. She wanted to hear the truths behind his past. She wasn't interested in his criminal involvement and shady dealings with the people he'd blackmailed, the ones responsible for his fake execution. She'd already asked him the one question that had aroused her curiosity concerning how he'd pulled it off. She didn't need or want to know more.

No, she wanted the truth from Grizz about his personal past. She was testing him now. And she didn't know why, but she desperately wanted him to pass the test.

"So, how old were you when you supposedly got Candy pregnant? She obviously believed you were fourteen because I heard her say it to you that night at the motel."

He looked hard at her. She could see by the expression on his face that he was carefully thinking. He was either calculating the math or trying to figure out whether he could or should lie to her.

"You know what, let's not start there," she said before he could answer. "Let's start with the basics. Your childhood. I don't know why it's important to me, but bear with me here, Grizz. Let's see if you can be honest with me. It's no longer necessary to hide things or protect me, right?"

"I don't like to talk about my childhood, Kit, so if you're going there, forget it."

She let the second slip of her nickname pass, but she wouldn't let the comment go.

"I know about your childhood. I know about your sister. Tommy told me everything."

He stared. She couldn't read his expression.

"But I don't know her name. Tell me her name, Grizz. Tell me your little sister's name."

"I don't see why it's importa—"

"Please just tell me, Grizz," she begged.

She had jumped up and now stood, looking down at him.

"Tell me one thing," she pleaded. "One truth from your past. Telling me her name isn't putting anyone in danger. She's been gone for years. You have no excuses to keep anything from me anymore."

Her voice echoed through the house. She watched him swallow. He was still sitting on the sofa, but on the edge of it now. His face was even with her waist. Without looking up, he whispered, "Ruth. Her name was Ruth Ann. I called her Ruthie."

Ginny's sigh was easy to hear. She slowly closed the gap and he reached for her, pulling her close and burying his face in her stomach. She let him hold her and found herself running her hands through his still damp hair. He wasn't crying, she realized, but just holding her, taking in her warmth. Taking in her light.

"So, Mimi's middle name that you suggested. It was in memory of Ruthie."

Gently, she took his face in her hand and turned it up to look at her. His eyes were filled with pain, but slowly changing into something else. Something heated.

"Yes, that's why I suggested it," he murmured. "I'm glad you now know why."

She swallowed thickly. She needed to disengage. She saw the need in his eyes, wondered if he saw the same need in hers. No. Not yet. Maybe not ever. The thought made her shoulders sag.

Back to business. She calmly removed herself from his embrace and sat back down in the chair.

"What's your real name?" she asked next, crossing her legs.

"Aww, honey, don't go there. It's not important."

"It's important to me."

She saw the familiar clench of his jaw when he was upset or agitated. He stood up and started to head for his bedroom. She didn't follow. He came back out with his hair pulled back in a ponytail. He was stalling.

"Why is my real name important to you?"

"Grizz, are you here in South Florida because you see a future with me? Not that I'm sure how that could be accomplished, but you know I'm not in danger. Tommy's shooting was random. You don't need to watch over me and my kids. I'm self-sufficient. I can raise my children alone. Why are you still here?"

He didn't answer but just stood in front of her, hands clenched into tight fists. She was making him mad. Good. Let him feel some anger. It was a feeling she disliked, but at least it was an emotion.

"I guess you're battling your old demons, aren't you? Nobody tells Grizz what to do or gives him an ultimatum? Well, I'm giving you one. If you want to stay remotely connected to my life, even if it's peripherally, I suggest you tell me the truth. You tell me your real name, or I will walk out of that door." She nodded toward the front door. "And I will never look back," she threatened, hoping he didn't recognize the lie behind her eyes.

Nothing. They stared. Neither one broke their gaze.

"Your decision," she said firmly.

Still nothing.

Minutes passed.

"Fine," she said, standing up quickly. She didn't want him to see her disappointment so she absently dug in her purse for her keys. Then he came to her, and grabbed her by both arms.

"No, Kit. It's not what you think." His voice carried a note of sincerity.

"Then what is it, Grizz?"

"I'll tell you my real name, but you probably won't believe me because it's similar to my new alias. I don't want you to think I'm making it up. You'll have no way to verify the truth, so I can only hope you'll believe me. I've not given you any reason to trust me with these things, but I can't stand the thought of you thinking I was lying about something that I'm actually being honest about."

She sat back down.

He looked at the floor. "The only people who ever called me by my real name were teachers and some kids from the school. The couple that raised me called me Boy, and Ruthie called me Brother. I saw my birth certificate only once before I destroyed it by sinking it in the family car in a canal. The last name was my stepfather's, so I don't know my real last name. You understand I'm going to tell you only what I know based on a memory that's more than forty years old?"

She nodded.

Without taking his eyes away from hers, he said, "My real first name is Jamison. It's similar to my alias James, so I don't want you thinking I'm trying to trick you or make it sound close on purpose. Some people called me Jamison. Some Jamie, Some James."

He waited for her reaction. He hadn't expected the wide smile.

"I believe you."

He blew out a long breath.

"So, you don't think I'm making it up to sound close to the new alias?"

"I know you're not making it up." She stood, walked toward him.

"How do you know that, honey?"

"Because I know your real name, Grizz. I probably know more than you do about your past."

"How? How could you know anything about me? I don't even know my real last name."

She clasped his hands. "Your mother's name was Frances Fowler. Her mother's maiden name was Jamison. And I know it's true because I've met your father."

53

Ginny, 2001, Fort Lauderdale

The expression on Grizz's face was one I'd never seen. He was dumbfounded. He was shocked. And more importantly, he looked hopeful.

I went to the kitchen and brewed some coffee as he sat on the couch and stared at the blank television screen. When it was done, I handed him the steaming mug of strong, black coffee, just like he liked. He sat there and listened as I told him about my visit with Sister Mary Katherine and Sister Agnes several months ago, right before Tommy's death.

"No." He shook his head, the coffee untouched. "Things like that, coincidences like that, don't just happen."

I took a sip of my coffee and sat it on the small glass coffee table. I had the strangest thought as I took Grizz's untouched mug from his big hands and sat it next to mine. This coffee table is too delicate to be in Grizz's home. I wonder if it will ever get shattered. Like hearts. Hearts get shattered.

I shook off the morbid thoughts. "Those were my exact words to Sister Mary Katherine. I just couldn't believe it. Sister smiled at me and told me she didn't believe in coincidences, either. She liked to call them 'Godincidences.'"

I reached for my purse and retrieved the envelope that contained David Enman's picture. I pulled out another one.

"Sister Agnes let me have this." I handed it to Grizz. "Is this Ruthie? Is this your little sister?"

He stared down at the picture, his face unreadable.

"Grizz?"

When he finally spoke, his voice was thick.

"I never thought I'd see her face again. I just can't believe it." A slow smile spread across his face. "And Razor. He was the best damn dog a man could ever ask for. Lucifer and Damien were smart dogs, but Razor had more brains than some people I know."

I told him about my visit to a sleepy little North Carolina town in the foothills of the Blue Ridge Mountains, and gave him every detail of the afternoon I spent with his father.

"Your father's name is Micah Hunter. Both of your parents' last names, Fowler and Hunter, can be traced back to families that settled there before the Civil War. Your roots run deep."

He listened without interrupting.

"He returned from the war and spent almost eight years tracking down every lead he could find on your mother's disappearance. The rumor had gotten around that she'd left with a man who'd been working for a logging crew just passing through. She had confided to a friend she was pregnant, and that only made your father more desperate to find her. He made it a point to talk to hundreds of men over the years. He visited logging camps all over the state. He even had a few false leads that he traced to Tennessee and Virginia, but he never found her. He said the despair finally took its toll, and he turned to alcohol. He almost drank himself to death and found himself inconsolable until he met a lady. He said Margaret Mae gave him a reason to clean up his act. With her help, he was able to replace the alcohol with something better."

Grizz looked over at me then. "With what? What did he replace it with?"

"He replaced it with God. Your father is a preacher."

"A preacher?"

"Yes, a preacher. And he's been widowed for years. He lost Margaret Mae to lung cancer. The poor thing never smoked a day in her life and died of lung cancer. They never had children, but your father has eight brothers and sisters. All but two are still alive. You have a ton of cousins."

Grizz didn't say anything but reached to his right to turn on a light. The sun was setting, and the living room was getting dark. He stared straight ahead, and I studied his profile. I almost reached out to tuck a piece of hair that had come loose behind his ear and caught myself. *What do you think you're doing, Ginny?*

"It's too bad I'll never get to meet them." His voice was low.

"Why not? Why can't you meet them?"

"Are you serious, Kit? And before you give me shit about calling you Kit," he paused and cast me a knowing glance, "or my cussing, you'll have to get over it. I promise never to call you Kit in public, but when we're alone, you're Kit. And I'll try and tone down the language, but that's easier said than done."

I shook off the explanation. I wanted to hear why he didn't think he'd get to meet his family.

"Why can't you meet your family?"

"After the things I've done, you think I'm going to drive up to the top of some mountain and be the welcomed son? He's a preacher, for fuck's sake, Kit. It's too late for people like me."

I took a deep breath, my heart thumping. "I tell you I visited a nun I hadn't seen in twenty-five years. She just happens to be caring for a nun who was there the day you were born. That nun remembers every single detail about your birth, and then I track down and find not only your original birth certificate in Florida, but the man who fathered you in North Carolina, and you think it's too late?" I barked out a laugh. "Grizz, it's just the opposite. It's all about God's timing. He's never early and He's most definitely never late. His timing is perfect, and it's time for you to meet your father and your family. He's wonderful, Grizz. I think you'll love him. I know he loves you. He didn't even know if his child survived. He didn't know if his child was a boy or a girl, but he never once stopped loving you."

Grizz shook his head.

"I could never meet him and tell him the things I've done, Kit. Never. You said he was a preacher. C'mon, honey. This isn't a good idea." He stood and walked his cold coffee to the kitchen. His back was to me as he robotically cleared our dinner dishes away.

I followed him and stood next to the island. He still had his back to me and was scraping food into the sink. Before he could switch the disposal on, I said, "You don't have to tell him the things you've done. I already told him."

He stopped what he was doing, and I saw his back stiffen. He slowly turned around and looked at me.

"I told him everything. I left no detail out. No detail. You know what I'm saying, right?"

He didn't answer.

"Your father wants to meet you, Grizz. He's been waiting. I've spoken with him a few times since Tommy died. He knew about my confusion where you were concerned and that there was a good chance I wouldn't ever speak to you or see you again. But he never once tried to coerce me. Even when he thought the only link to seeing his only child might've been severed if I never came around, he didn't push. He's a kind and gentle man. Even if you don't want to meet him, I'll make sure Mimi does. He's a man worth knowing. And like I said, he knows everything—and he still wants to meet you."

After a few moments, he said, "I'll think about it."

I knew when not to push. I smiled at him and bumped him aside as I took over at the sink. I could've loaded the dishwasher, but just like when I made dinner, I felt like I needed to keep my hands busy. I talked as I washed dishes. My hands welcomed the hot soapy water. He sat down at the table and watched me. I could feel his eyes boring into my back.

"What was prison like?" I asked casually. Not that it was a casual subject, but I tried to act nonchalant. I didn't think he'd answer.

"Shitty."

I couldn't help but smile. "I'm sure it was crummy, but what was it like? I mean you were on death row, so I assume you were confined to a cell maybe twenty-three hours a day, an hour for exercise?"

"That's what it should've been like, but I had privileges."

"I guess I should've seen that one coming. Was there like a hierarchy in the prison population?"

"Yeah. There were several different gangs and they filtered up and were separated by ethnicity. The Hispanics, the Asians, the blacks, the whites. They each had their own organizations within the prison, and they each had their own leaders. It didn't take me too long to establish myself over all of them."

I shot him a glance. "How did you do that? I can see why you might've been able to be in charge of the white guys, but the others?"

"I just did. I may have been a lot of things, but there was one thing I always made clear. I didn't care what color a man's skin was. If he got the job done, he was treated fairly. When everyone realized I would deal with them equally and could get them more privileges, they respected me. In some ways, I helped keep the peace between the different groups. It actually benefited me, too. A prisoner on death row wouldn't normally be able to eat with the general prison population. Letting me eat in the chow hall or lift weights in the yard whenever I wanted to, helped ease some tensions between the groups."

I cocked my hip to one side. "And the name Grizz didn't have anything to do with them appointing you as their head guy or whatever you call it?"

He laughed. "Yeah. It probably helped."

I turned away from him again and started to dry the dishes I'd just washed. And then I brought up another subject. One I'd dropped earlier.

"So how old are you?"

"You know how old I am. You told me you found my original birth certificate."

"Oh, right. So, let's see. You were born in 1947, which means you're fifty-three now, but you'll be turning fifty-four at the end of this year."

"Yeah. So what?"

I laid down the plate I'd been drying and turned around to face him again. Using my fingers to tick off the years I said, "And Tommy was born in 1959, which means you must've been...let's see...twelve years old when you had sex with Candy? And for some reason, she thought you were fourteen."

"I had assumed Pop's son's identity. The real Jason Talbot would have been fourteen."

"But you were only twelve years old."

"Yeah, but almost thirteen. So what?"

I snapped him with my dishtowel.

"Twelve?" I shouted. "Don't you think twelve is not only too young to be having sex, but to think you actually got her pregnant? You sure have a high opinion of your sperm!"

I should've known the revelation wouldn't have embarrassed him. He grinned and shrugged.

"She was a seventeen-year-old hooker. She made the first move. You think I didn't take advantage of that? Find me a twelve-year-old boy who hasn't discovered his dick and I'll show you a girl."

I shook my head in exasperation. "I just think it's horrible!"

"Just because you think it's horrible doesn't mean it isn't happening. That it doesn't happen all the time. Even I heard about that schoolteacher who seduced her sixth-grade student. I think she even got some time for it."

"Just stop talking, Grizz. I shouldn't have brought this up when I knew it would get under my skin. I don't even know if a twelve-year-old can get a woman pregnant. I still can't see how you thought Tommy could've been your son."

"Had a lot of time on my hands in prison. Did some reading. A boy has the ability to get a girl pregnant when he reaches puberty. Every kid is different. Youngest-known father on record is—"

"Stop. I don't want to hear it. This conversation is over." I held up a hand.

"You brought it up."

"Yeah, well I've lived three minutes long enough to regret bringing it up."

I looked at my watch and let out a sigh. I'd stayed long enough.

"I have to run. Pollyanna will be bringing Jason home in less than an hour. Mimi won't be home, so I want to make sure I'm there."

I started to gather my things when he asked, "Pollyanna?"

"She's his friend Max's older sister. She's a cheerleader for the high school football team, and Max and Jason wanted to go to the game. Their mother, Denise, has to leave right after the game and has an appointment in the opposite direction, so Pollyanna volunteered to drive Jason."

He didn't say anything, and when I looked at him, he was smiling.

"What?"

"Nothing," he said, trying to hide his grin.

"What? What's so funny?"

"Nothing. Just thinking—friend's older sister. Older sister in a cheerleading uniform."

"My son just turned eleven!" I could see by his expression he didn't know he'd gone too far.

"I didn't mean anything by it, Kit."

I walked over to him and punched him hard on the chest. It was so out-of-character for me, but it felt good. He didn't flinch, and it only made me madder. I pulled back to swing again. This time, he caught my fist with one hand. I tried to pull away, but he wouldn't let go.

"Let go," I told him.

"No. Not until you accept my apology."

I hmphed. I doubted any apology from Grizz could be sincere.

"Let go of my hand," I said in my most threatening tone.

"I'm sorry, and I mean it," he said without loosening his grip on my balled up hand. "I know you and Tommy raised him up right. I wouldn't want him to lose his childhood like I did, but don't assume he's naïve, either."

I wouldn't admit to him that Jason may have only been eleven, but he was in no way naïve about what happened between a man and a woman behind closed doors. I remembered Mimi making a comment last year when Tommy and I returned from our honeymoon about us "doing it," and Jason had innocently wanted to know what we were doing because he wanted to do it, too. Tommy later told me he took the time to have "the talk" with Jason and was surprised to learn Jason already knew about the birds and the bees, and he only commented because he'd thought there was something else he'd missed out on. No, Jason may have been a sweet and lovable child, but he wasn't naïve about sex.

"I was only teasing with you, honey," Grizz explained.

I saw sincerity in his eyes and relaxed as realization dawned that maybe he'd deliberately goaded me into the conversation. That he'd wanted to get me riled enough to punch him. To get some of my anger out. He slowly raised my hand to his mouth and gently kissed the inside of my wrist.

I pulled back like I'd been burned. And then, gathering up my things, I walked out of the house without saying goodbye or looking back.

I was upset. The only problem was I couldn't figure out if I was troubled by his deliberate crude teasing, the way that kiss made me feel or that he didn't come after me.

54

Grizz, 2001, Fort Lauderdale

I t had been four days since Ginny had been in his home. She'd not come back or tried to call. He let her have her space as he waited.

It was now Tuesday morning. Grizz came out of the convenience store, barely paying attention to his surroundings when he heard a loud voice coming from near his work truck. His landscaping crew had finished up an early morning job and decided to make a pit stop for some ice before heading to the next one. Grizz had run into the store to grab some Hershey's Kisses, his most recent and only vice. Well, his other vice. His first one was and always would be Ginny.

"You need to take your sorry, Spanish-speaking asses back across the water where you belong. First, you take our jobs, and now you're trying to turn Fort Lauderdale into Cuba? Isn't it bad enough you already took over Miami? You gotta come up here, too?"

Grizz slowed and surveyed the scene. He hadn't been spotted yet, and he listened as the crew foreman, Carlos, tried to explain in broken English that they didn't want any trouble and would be leaving as soon as the rest of his men came out of the store. Grizz liked Carlos. He was mild-mannered and worked hard for Anthony, ensuring that his crew did, too. He watched as the source of the accusations stepped closer to Carlos, his spit spraying as he continued his tirade.

"Sorry ain't good enough, amigo. You think sorry is good enough, Rick?"

Grizz noticed another man then, leaning up against a beat up truck, arms crossed and a toothpick sticking out of his mouth.

"Nah, Jesse," he drawled. "I think they need to do more than apologize for tarnishing the good old U.S. of A. by trying to replace the English language."

Grizz didn't know what Jesse and his ugly friend Rick had in mind, but he'd seen enough. He shoved his bag of Kisses into his back pocket and walked up behind the man who was in Carlos's face. The one named Jesse. He grabbed him roughly by the back of the neck and, squeezing, said in a low voice, "I think you owe my friend, Carlos, an apology."

Jesse's eyes widened and his posture straightened as the pressure on his neck hardened. He was being held so tightly he couldn't turn his head to see who had grabbed him, but he could see his friend, Rick, jump to attention and quickly get in the passenger side of their truck.

Grizz noticed the movement, too, and looked over at the man.

"Don't you think he owes Carlos an apology, Rick?" Grizz barked.

Rick's response was to nod and roll up the truck's window.

"Just having some fun. Didn't mean anything by it," Jesse choked out.

Carlos started telling Grizz he was okay and there was no harm done, that they should be leaving. The other men on the landscape crew had already loaded up. Three of them in the back seat of the truck and three more in the bed of the pickup. They stared in awestruck silence as the big quiet man, who'd joined their crew all those months ago, showed a side they hadn't seen.

"You still haven't apologized," Grizz told him.

"Sorry. Sorry, uh, Carlos. Sorry, man," Jesse said with a squeak.

Grizz shoved him toward his own truck and watched as he walked around the back of it. Jesse's dog, a white Pit Bull with brown markings, had been watching from the bed of the pickup. As Jesse passed him, Grizz heard him say, "You useless piece of shit-for-brains dog. Could've used some help back there, Rocky."

He punched the dog right in the side of the head.

Before Jesse reached the driver's door, Grizz had him by the back of the head, this time smashing his face hard into the side view mirror, breaking his nose. The crunch was loud, and Grizz heard the collective gasps from the landscape crew as they watched from their heightened perch in the bed of Carlos's work truck.

Jesse collapsed and began to cry as he cradled his broken and bloodied nose. Bullies are the worst crybabies ever, Grizz smirked. He headed to the back of Jesse's truck and yelled over his shoulder, "I'm taking your dog."

On the drive over to their next job, Carlos did his best to explain that he and his men had done nothing wrong. They had just been standing by the truck waiting for Grizz and two other men to come out of the store when Jesse and his friend Rick pulled up. Apparently, Jesse and Rick had been offended because the crew was talking in Spanish. It didn't happen a lot, but Carlos confided to Grizz that there was definitely some resentment and animosity, especially as South Florida's Hispanic community grew and expanded farther north from Miami.

Grizz knew Carlos and his guys hadn't done anything to incite the two men. They were bullies looking for a fight. Guess they picked the wrong people to taunt that day. Not to mention, there were only two of them and at least four of Carlos's crew who'd been standing there. They were counting on them not being legal immigrants and therefore submitting to the intimidation.

Grizz sat in the front passenger seat, his left hand absently stroking the back of Rocky's neck. The dog sat quietly between the two men.

"I'll have to tell Anthony today that I'll be quitting," he told Carlos. What he didn't mention was that going into the convenience store had been stupid. He should've stayed in the truck like he'd been doing and let one of the guys buy what he wanted. He was getting too comfortable and familiar and it was dangerous. He needed to reel himself back and stay alert.

Carlos looked over at him from the driver's seat, his eyes wide. "No. No, James. It's okay. We don't say anything to Mr. Anthony. He won't know." His English was broken and his accent was thick, but his voice was laced with sincerity.

Grizz didn't say anything. He knew he'd taken his retaliation too far. He hadn't intended to, but seeing Jesse abuse the dog crawled too far under his skin. He always was a sucker for a helpless animal. Should Jesse report the abuse and the stolen animal, it would bring the authorities to Anthony's door. The name of his landscaping company was advertised on the sides of the work truck. Stupid fool. He would let Anthony know before the end of the day.

They had arrived at the next job and were unloading their equipment when his cell phone buzzed. He wasn't used to getting calls. What if the incident had already been reported and Anthony had been contacted? Shit.

He squinted in the bright morning sun and immediately recognized the number. Not because he was used to seeing it, but because he'd memorized it in the event it was used to call him.

It was Ginny.

He walked away from the other men, Rocky at his heels.

"What's up, baby? You okay?"

"Oh, Grizz," she cried into the phone. He could tell she was upset.

He stopped and stiffened as she told him what had happened.

"I want to get my children," she cried. "I need to go to their schools and get them. I just want them near me."

He understood.

"Listen," he replied calmly. "I'll get a ride back to the yard and get my car. You get the kids and stop by the store. Get some sandwiches and drinks and bring them to my house. I would do it, but I don't know what they like. It'll be okay. I'll be waiting there for you, sweetheart."

"Okay," she whispered, her voice shaking.

"Baby, listen, can you do me a favor?" he asked before she hung up.

"Yeah. Sure," she replied.

"Will you bring your guitar?"

He closed the phone and stared down at Rocky. The dog looked up at him with soulful deep eyes.

"C'mon, boy. Time to meet your new family."

55

Ginny, 2001, Fort Lauderdale

M y hands shook as I drove my children first to the grocery store and then to Grizz's house in Laurel Falls. I had been doing some chores at home and listening to a morning TV program with half an ear when the program had been interrupted.

I don't know how long I stood there, staring at the screen as horror unfolded on live television. I cried for the victims in those airplanes and in those buildings. I cried for the families that didn't know if they'd be seeing their loved ones again. I cried for the country, my country, that I loved so dearly. This wasn't supposed to happen. Here. In the United States. But it had, and it would forever change the course of American history.

My first thought was for my children. I wanted to be near them. I didn't believe they were in any danger at their schools, but the need to be close to them was overpowering and definite.

My second thought was for Grizz. He made me feel safe. I wanted to be near Grizz. I racked my brain as I drove to their schools, trying to figure out if I knew anybody who might've been out of town and visiting where the attacks had taken place. I couldn't think of anyone then, but as the weeks passed, the tragic news of someone's loss would reach me, and I'd mourn for them. As it would turn out, I didn't know anybody that hadn't been affected to some degree by what happened that horrible Tuesday morning.

I talked with my children as we made our way to Grizz's house. I had told myself, and truly believed, that I would be keeping them away from him. Yet driving to his home with them somehow felt right. Was it because of the air of authority and protection he exuded? He'd always made me feel safe, and I wanted that for my children, as well. I felt they were especially vulnerable since they had lost their father earlier in the year.

I had been right. Jason was downright afraid. His voice was shaky as he peppered me with questions on the drive to Grizz's.

I saw his eyes widen when Grizz answered the door. I held my breath.

"James!" Jason cried.

He lunged for Grizz, wrapping his arms tightly around his waist. I watched Grizz hold him as he looked at me and then at Mimi, his eyes unsure as Jason clung tightly to him. My son had his face buried in Grizz's stomach. I blew out a long breath and nodded.

"Did you hear what happened, James? Did you hear about it?" Jason asked as Mimi and I walked in, closing the door behind us.

I started to get tears in my eyes as I watched Jason look up at Grizz, still clinging to him tightly. It was then that I remembered how loving my little boy always was, especially with Tommy. There had been lots of hugging and physical affection between father and son, and Jason had obviously missed that. The men in our lives—teachers, coaches, even Alec—who had stepped in to offer comfort had all eventually gone back to their lives. They were still kind and loving and continued to include Jason in their activities. But all talk and memories of Tommy, the stories Jason craved, the stories Jason still needed to hear had slowly faded away as people returned to their lives and routines.

This man from Tommy's past, James, would be a new source of comfort to my hurting child. I looked over at Mimi and could see she recognized it, too. I felt a warmness invade my heart. I swiped at the tears and was heading for the kitchen to get a napkin when I almost tripped over a dog.

Less than an hour later, I sat next to Mimi under the shade of a large tree and watched as Grizz showed Jason how to bait a hook and cast his line. I recognized the spot as one he'd taken me to more than fifteen years ago. I hadn't realized how far out we must have driven back in the eighties. Development had been spreading west but apparently still hadn't reached Grizz's favorite fishing spot. I quietly strummed my guitar as we talked.

"He likes him, Mom," Mimi said quietly. "He really likes him."

I knew she was referring to Jason's fascination with Grizz.

"I know he does."

We didn't say anything else for a few minutes. I watched Grizz lean over and say something to Jason as he nodded back my way. Jason handed Grizz his fishing pole and ran toward me, his face flushed.

"James thinks I might need more sunscreen," he told me breathlessly. It was hot, and the heat was taking its toll on my son.

I laid down my guitar and after lathering him up and sending him back to Grizz with two cold drinks, I turned to look at Mimi. She was sitting up, resting both elbows on her knees. She raised a bottle of water to her lips and took a sip.

"Do you?" I asked her. She looked over at me. "Like him?"

"I think I do, Mom. I can't tell you why. I certainly don't have a reasonable explanation as to why I like him. You seem happy right now. Happier than you've been since Dad died."

That was a revelation that startled me. Today had started out so awful, but as our day progressed, a calmness had settled over me. Grizz had been smart to take us away from the noise of the city. To a place where we wouldn't be continuously reminded of what had happened this morning.

Of course, we would have to face the harsh reality of today's events, but it was almost therapeutic being away for a few hours. It was nice being with him and my children. Together.

The realization that I was doing something Tommy would probably disapprove of caught me off-guard. Almost immediately, I jumped to my feet and started packing up our picnic lunch and shouting orders that it was time to go. Jason whined that it was still early and he didn't have homework.

I caught a questioning glance from Grizz, but he didn't try to dissuade me or change my mind. He quietly told Jason he would take him fishing another time.

"Thank you for the picnic, Gr...James," I said without looking at him. "We have a busy week coming up, though. Jason has back-to-back games, so probably not. There won't be time for another fishing trip."

"Aww, Mom," Jason started to say, but he recognized the look I gave him and didn't say anything else until something occurred to him.

"James, do you want to come watch me play? You wanna come to one of my games?"

"I'll see if I can make it, Jason."

I eyed Grizz and knew he was lying. He wouldn't be going to watch any of Jason's games and I knew why. He didn't want to be seen, and he didn't have the heart to tell my son he wouldn't be going and didn't want to disappoint him.

"You know what?" I asked, a reassuring sense of calm starting to come over me. "It's still early. We can stay longer. Go on, Jason. You haven't caught one yet."

I saw the small nod of approval from Mimi and avoided Grizz's glance as I sat back down, picked up my cell phone and started fiddling with it.

"No signal," Mimi said blandly.

"Yeah, I can see that now." I placed my phone back on the blanket between us. "I guess it's driving you a bit nuts, huh? Not being able to text your friends."

I leaned over and dug a container of fruit out of the cooler.

"Not really. Things have been different since school started."

"How's that?" I popped a chunk of pineapple in my mouth.

"I don't know, Mom. I can't explain it. With everything that's happened this past year—the Leslie thing, the disasters with Elliott and Slade, him." She nodded toward Grizz. "And of course, Dad dying. I guess the things that are important to my friends just don't seem so important to me anymore. Even more so after what happened today. I feel—different. I'm just not interested in the same things they are now."

It was totally understandable, and I told Mimi I thought maybe her feelings were what it meant to be on the brink of a different type of maturity. I also told her I was sorry her sudden leap into adulthood came with such a high cost, the biggest being the loss of Tommy, but she explained that she felt ready for it. She was ready for a change, but she wasn't sure exactly what it was.

"I hope you'll share it with me when you do decide, Mimi. I'm here for you. You know that, right, honey?"

She smiled at me, a bright big beautiful Mimi smile, and then lifted her water bottle as if making a toast.

"To the future, Mom."

"To the future, Mimi." I lifted my own drink as I pondered what our future could possibly hold.

WE FOUND OURSELVES BACK AT GRIZZ'S HOUSE WHERE WE GRILLED THE fish he and Jason had caught. After eating dinner and cleaning up, I told my children they needed to thank James for a nice day and say their goodbyes. Jason was disappointed but tired, so he didn't put up too much resistance. The afternoon heat of the Everglades had worn him down.

I felt a bit wilted myself and was suddenly concerned about my appearance. I self-consciously started tucking my hair behind my ear and touching my face when I felt a warm breath at my ear.

"You're beautiful."

I turned to see Grizz next to me, his green eyes reflecting the longing in my own, and I cast a quick glance at my children. They hadn't noticed. I was all of a sudden very anxious to get home to a hot shower.

After some more chit-chat in his doorway, I thought we'd said the last of our goodbyes when I heard Mimi ask, "So, James, do you think you can teach me how to drive?"

56

Grizz, 2001, Fort Lauderdale

G rizz had tried to tell Anthony he wouldn't be working for him anymore after what had happened at the convenience store, but Anthony was convinced the two guys wouldn't press charges. And he was right.

Anthony hadn't been contacted by the police about his wayward employee, and so Grizz continued to work for the landscaping company and noticed that his fellow workers tried to include him more in their conversations. He'd picked up enough Spanish in prison to communicate with them. He wasn't sure if that was a good thing or not.

Rocky was a bit of a challenge, but Grizz had always loved animals and found that he was a natural with them. He took pleasure in and was challenged by training the obviously abused animal. Rocky was turning out to be an excellent and well-behaved dog. He went to work with Grizz every single day and kept him company in the evenings and on the weekends.

Grizz had given Mimi a couple of driving lessons since that fateful day in September, and he enjoyed her company. She was a smart girl with a quick wit, and giving her driving lessons propelled him to distant memories of teaching her mother to drive so many years ago. He told her she was a fast learner. She told him that he was a good instructor. He couldn't be sure, but he felt like he may have been bonding with his daughter.

He hadn't meant to disappoint Jason by not openly attending his games, so he did the next best thing. He watched from afar and would explain to Jason that he'd been there but had been on his way somewhere and couldn't stay to say hello. It was the truth and so far, it had appeased the boy. He'd also seen something at a couple of the games that he didn't care for. Tommy's business partner, Alec Davis, had shown up as well, and he sat with Ginny. He couldn't be sure, but he was under the impression that their friendship had waned a bit. Maybe he'd been wrong. He would find out and make a plan to discreetly squelch whatever, if anything, had resurrected itself between them.

Thanksgiving was approaching, and Grizz checked with Ginny before deciding whether or not to accept Carter and Bill's invitation to come to dinner. She said she didn't have a problem with it, and so he'd told Carter he would be there. He knew he wouldn't even need to ask if anybody else was on the guest list. Carter knew better.

The young man who'd taken Tommy's life had pled guilty and was now serving a life sentence without the possibility of parole. He had optioned for the plea instead of risking the death penalty.

Matthew Rockman's trial had been postponed twice and was scheduled for this coming February, which would also be the one-year anniversary of Tommy's death.

"Tommy told me he'd changed his mind. He wasn't going to testify against Matthew, and I completely agreed with him," Ginny told him.

They'd just finished eating turkey at Carter and Bill's. Jason was playing a video game with Bill. Carter and Mimi were cleaning up. Carter had suggested that Grizz and Ginny go up to the guesthouse and retrieve the telescope that was stored up there. Maybe they could all watch the stars together later that night.

She sat on the bed in the little guesthouse, her hands folded together and clasped between her knees. She looked at Grizz accusingly.

"He'll get convicted with or without Tommy's testimony," Grizz stated confidently from the corner, where his telescope had been stored. "Not because of anything Blue did. Because Matthew is guilty. He did murder her."

Ginny stood and walked to him, her arms crossed.

"I know you must've had something to do with it. Admit it. You had her murdered and made it look like Matthew did it."

He'd bent down to fiddle with the telescope, but he stood and gave her his full attention.

"Yes and no. I did have Blue plan it, so yeah, I'm responsible. But it didn't happen that way."

She cocked her head and waited.

"It was all set to go down," he readily admitted. "Jan contacted Matthew with the intention of blackmailing him, and he agreed to meet her. After Matthew left the hotel room, someone was going there to handle her and plant evidence. Except when they got there, she was already dead. Don't know what she ended up saying to Rockman, but it must've put him over the edge, because he'd strangled her with the phone cord. It was not what we had planned, but it still provided truthful evidence against him."

He didn't say anything for a few more seconds, and before Ginny could comment, he turned back to the telescope and nonchalantly confessed, "I would've stopped it if I could. I would've called it off, but I couldn't." He'd purposely turned his back to her so she couldn't read the truth in his eyes. Not only would he not have stopped the hit on Jan, but if he hadn't been confined to a cell, he'd have killed her himself for helping Matthew Rockman.

Ginny didn't reply to his last admission because she wasn't sure she believed it.

"How do you know this? Who told you Matthew really did kill her?" she asked, her curiosity aroused.

"Anthony told me. He stays in touch with Blue." He paused and then turned to face her. "How much do you stay in touch with Blue?"

"Not at all. I can't even remember the last time I saw him before he came to the hospital when Tommy was shot. Mimi might remember him from the few times we saw him when she was younger, but Jason doesn't know him at all. Tommy and I really did stay away from everything gang-related, and eventually that included Blue." She looked at the ground. "I think it's for the best."

Grizz nodded his agreement. "It is for the best."

He didn't want them to have any reason to be in contact with Blue. He was glad she and Tommy had distanced themselves from that life.

She ran a hand through her hair and sighed.

"What is this? What are we doing?"

"Carrying the telescope downstairs to set it up."

"No, that's not what I mean."

"I know it's not what you mean, Kitten," he said, his deep voice quiet.

She shook her head slowly. "What good could possibly come from this? From us? I just can't see where or if it could be anything. Or even if we want it to be anything."

He took her gently by the hand and walked back toward the bed. She hesitated but let him lead her. After sitting down next to her, he softly said, "I know what I want to happen. I know that I'm still in love with you. I think about you constantly, Kit. I've never stopped thinking about you or loving you, and I've thought about this very question nonstop."

"And?"

"And, if I get to be in the same room with you, to hear your voice, to look into your eyes when you talk to me, just once in a while, then I'm willing to accept that." *But not forever,* he wanted to say, but the words didn't come.

There was distress in her admission. "It would be crumbs, and I can't see you living the rest of your life on crumbs."

Neither could he, so without meeting her eyes, he shrugged his shoulders.

"I've never seen you like this," she said honestly. "I've never seen you so patient. It's not how I remember you."

"Prison can change a man. Even me." His last words were more hopeful than honest. He didn't want her to see the doubt in his eyes, so he jumped up and went back to the telescope, his back to her. She followed him to see if she could help. Without knowing she was right behind him, he turned to ask her something and found himself smacking right into her.

His instinct to grab her was immediate. He stood there, looking down into her face, his hands gently clinging to both of her upper arms. She looked up at him, and their eyes met. He slowly moved his hands to her face, lightly caressing her left cheek with his thumb. Their eyes stayed locked. He looked at her lips, then back at her gaze. He saw the invitation, or at least what he thought was an invitation.

Invitation or not, he wanted his woman. He lowered his mouth to hers.

She held her breath and closed her eyes when she realized he was going to kiss her. She sighed when he gently nibbled her bottom lip. He stopped only to press his lips lightly against hers. He still held her face in his hands and found himself nibbling, kissing, nibbling, kissing. He had to restrain himself from parting her lips and plunging his tongue inside her mouth. The need to taste her sweetness was overwhelming.

He felt her hands reach up behind his neck, pull him closer. She parted her mouth first, the invitation now obvious.

He let his tongue explore the inside of her mouth and realized he didn't need to familiarize himself with her taste. The memory of every kiss they'd ever shared had been tattooed on his brain. His erection was immediate, intense and almost painful. He needed to reel it in before he threw her down on the bed. He had a plan and making love to her too soon wasn't part of it. He reluctantly broke the kiss and looked down at her.

"I don't want this to go too far, Kitten," he said in a low growl.

"I don't either," she said breathlessly, ignoring the ache she hadn't felt in a long time.

"I shouldn't have kissed you. It's too soon."

"Too soon?" she asked. Her voice held a dreamlike quality.

"I'm afraid you're still in mourning. It hasn't been a year yet," he said with a raspy voice as he reached down to adjust the front of his jeans.

She knew he was referring to Tommy's passing.

"I don't want to confuse you or make you do something you might regret later. I can wait until you're sure of what you're feeling."

The desire to do what he'd always done, which was take without permission, threatened to rear its ugly head. Could he be as patient as he needed to be? He'd had no choice but to learn patience while incarcerated for fifteen years. Waiting for his woman would be a test. And she was worth it.

He would try.

She was getting ready to answer him that she was a woman who knew exactly what she was feeling when Jason's voice floated up the guesthouse stairs.

"Did you find Aunt Carter's telescope?" Jason yelled from outside. "Do you need help?"

THE STARS WERE OUT IN FULL GLORY THAT NIGHT, AND THEY'D EACH taken turns looking through the telescope. Ginny watched as Jason excitedly told them he recognized some of the constellations. They were sitting on Carter and Bill's deck, roasting marshmallows in the fire pit and making s'mores. The porch light cast a warm glow over the happy stargazers as they ate their treats and talked about stars and the things they were thankful for.

"My Dad had some tattoos. But they weren't scary like some of yours, James."

The group fell silent and all eyes turned to Jason, who'd been standing next to Grizz as he adjusted the telescope.

"What is this one? I've never seen one like this," the boy said, pointing curiously at one on Grizz's neck.

"It's a prison tattoo," Grizz told Jason. He didn't look at Ginny for approval. It was going to come up eventually. No use pretending he could hide it.

Jason's eyes widened, and Ginny held her breath as she waited for what she knew would be Jason's next question.

"Were you in prison?" he asked, the fascination in his voice obvious.

Grizz turned away from the telescope and gave Jason his full attention. Not taking his eyes from Jason's, he said, "Yes, Jason. I was in prison."

"Wow. What did you do?"

"Let's just say I did things that were bad enough to send me to jail. One day, when you're older, if you still want to know, I'll tell you. But for today, let's just say it's not something I like to talk about. Is that okay with you?"

"Did you know the guy that died?" Jason asked. "Corbin said my parents knew some guy in prison who was getting killed. He owned a motorcycle gang."

Ginny had to put her hand to her mouth to stifle a gasp. Jason hadn't forgotten about Corbin's comment over a year ago.

"Yes, I knew him."

"Were you there when he died? Was he your friend? Did you like him?"

Grizz looked over Jason's head and met Ginny's eyes. Without breaking their gaze, he answered the child.

"I was there when he died. He wasn't my friend. And no, I didn't like him."

He looked down at the boy and said in a tone that brooked no further conversation on the subject, "And I'm glad he's dead."

Grizz turned back to the telescope. *And I'll do my best to keep him in the ground, but I can't promise it.* His heart sought the strength to do right by Kit and her children.

57

Ginny, 2001, Fort Lauderdale

After dropping Grizz off at his house, Jason peppered me with questions about how well and how long Tommy and I had known James, and was it before or after he went to prison. I told him most of the truth: We'd known him since we were teenagers, he went to prison after that, and neither one of us had seen or spoken with him for fifteen years. I also explained to my son that James had trusted him with a very important detail about his life, and it wouldn't be respectful or right for any of us to share this with other people.

"Maybe it's why he doesn't stay at your games, Jason," Mimi piped up. "Maybe he's embarrassed or ashamed and doesn't want people like Corbin saying things or judging him, which they would do if you told them."

Mimi understood what was hanging in the balance here, and I appreciated that she was able to talk to Jason on his level.

"Can I tell Alec?" Jason asked.

"Is it your story to tell, Jason, or is it James's story?"

Jason nodded sheepishly. He got it.

"And I have to tell you the truth, honey. James wants his privacy. If we want to stay friends with him, we need to respect that. We need to not get our feelings hurt if he doesn't accept invitations. He's a loner, and I think he likes it that way."

"Do you think he likes me, Mom?"

I looked in my rearview mirror and saw his hopeful eyes looking back at me.

"Yes, Jason. I think he likes you very much."

A WEEK LATER, GRIZZ ASKED ME WHEN I MIGHT HAVE AN EVENING FREE TO spend with him. I was hesitant at first, remembering the kiss we'd shared. But both kids would be occupied for most of the evening, so I found myself heading over to Laurel Falls.

I drove to his house with my windows down enjoying the cool breeze and the familiar fragrance of orange blossoms. The sun had almost completely set, and the air was cooler. He'd told me not to eat dinner, so I figured he was making something, getting takeout, or wanting to take me to an out-of-the-way restaurant.

I wondered if he remembered his invitation as I got out of my car and approached his front door. It was getting dark, and he had no outside lights on. The garage was closed so I didn't know if his car was there.

I knocked lightly and heard Rocky barking. I heard Grizz give a command and the barking ceased. He opened the door and with the movement came a whoosh of air that assaulted my nostrils. Him. His smell. His clean, sharp scent. Same cologne. Same deodorant he'd always worn. I didn't remember him smelling like this at Thanksgiving. My insides twisted.

He didn't say anything. He just stepped aside and gestured with his hand for me to come in.

I walked in and stopped suddenly as I took in what I was seeing and hearing. The sun had gone down, leaving only a warm glow on the western horizon, so light from his skylights was minimal, yet the living room, kitchen and dining area were glowing. I took in all the candles, the small table set for dinner, the enticing aroma of whatever had been in his oven.

I heard him shut the door behind me. This wasn't dinner. This was a set-up for seduction if I'd ever seen one. "Sharing the Night Together" by Dr. Hook was coming from a speaker.

How convenient.

Well, I would set him straight. Just like I let him know upfront more than twenty-five years ago my first night at the motel, I now blurted out, "I don't know how long I can stay. I'm on my period and have bad cramps."

It was a lie. As a matter of fact, I'd gone off the pill after Tommy's death, and my period was so sporadic I was certain I was premenopausal. But Grizz didn't have to know that. I felt him come up behind me and I turned to face him, my attitude evident.

"I'm sorry you don't feel good, honey. Do you want to come over another time or do you want me to get you something out of the medicine cabinet to help with your cramps?"

He looked sincere. I stiffened.

"You want me to come back when I'm not on my period?" I narrowed my eyes. "I'm sorry you went to so much trouble to try to get me into bed and it backfired."

I waved my hand toward the candles.

He raised an eyebrow. "You think I invited you over to get you into bed and because you have your period I don't want you here?"

"Isn't that why you invited me over? The candles, my kind of music playing in the background—why would I think otherwise?"

He chuckled. "Your music is playing because the house has a built-in sound system and I haven't figured out how to change the lame-ass station that it's set to. As a matter of fact, I don't even know how to turn the damn thing off."

I crossed my arms. "Fine. Whatever. And the candles?"

"The power's been out for two hours. I just lit them. Thought you would've noticed I didn't have any lights on when you pulled up. And like I said, the only reason the music is on is because the house has a small auxiliary backup for the alarm system and the sound system is somehow connected. The music came on by itself when the battery rebooted the alarm. Good thing the house has a gas oven or I'd have to take you out for dinner."

I just stared and could feel the heat rising up my face. What was I, sixteen again? I felt childish, stupid for the accusation and the period comment. He wasn't trying to seduce me. I needed to find a hole to crawl in, and I needed to find one fast.

"How about I take you out somewhere? It can't be fancy. It'll have to be somewhere quiet and out of the way."

I swallowed and looked away from him. "I thought...I thought..."

"I know what you thought, baby, and it's okay. I don't blame you. It does look like a set-up, but it's not. I meant what I said at Thanksgiving. I think it might still be too soon for you. I didn't want anything from you tonight except to enjoy a meal and your company."

I told him he didn't need to take me out to a restaurant. The lights came on midway through our meal. We cleaned up the kitchen together, blew out the candles, and settled ourselves on the couch. Rocky made himself comfortable between us. I looked at the man who I'd been so in love with for so long and wondered if I was falling for him again.

Then the bitterness I'd tried to swallow since Tommy's death finally reared its ugly head.

Before I could stop myself, I shouted, "I hate this. I just hate this!"

He looked over at me, bewilderment in his gaze. I stood up and crossed my arms over my chest. I paced back and forth as he just watched me and waited for an explanation.

"Since your execution..." I paused to give him a sarcastic glare, "my life has been turned upside down. So much turmoil and unnecessary drama because of that stupid interview. Thinking Tommy was your son almost ruined my marriage. You know that, don't you?"

He nodded, never taking his eyes from mine. I looked away and resumed pacing.

"Thank heavens, it turned out not to be true, so it was a good thing we never got around to talking to Mimi about it. But that's not the point. That's not what I'm trying to say here."

"What are you trying to say, Kit?"

"I'm trying to say I've never experienced a time in my life where I wasn't in control of my feelings." I stopped, took a shuddery breath. "I look back over the past year, and one minute I thought I hated you, the next minute I missed you, the next minute I resented you. I've been all over the map with my emotions, and it's so unlike me and not something I'm used to. Add the grief of Tommy's death on top of that and I—I... I just hate this feeling of not being sure about who I am and what I want."

He nodded, watching me.

"And—it's not about just me. I have my children to consider. On one hand, they seem to like and accept you. On another hand, if something did come of our relationship, I struggle with what Tommy would've wanted for our children, and I'm having a hard time convincing myself that it would include you." I eyed him warily.

"Understandable."

I swallowed. "I know without any doubt that you'd never bring any harm to me or my children. But I don't know if that's enough. There has to be more. I need for my children to love and respect you, but even more than that, I need you to love them, and Grizz, I don't know if you're capable of that. I watched your face when Jason hugged you the morning you took us fishing. I saw something in your eyes. Something I'd never seen. What was it?"

He looked away from me then and sighed. He absently stroked Rocky's fur as he stared past me. I didn't think he was going to answer me.

Finally, in a broken voice, he said, "Fear." He then looked me straight in the eyes. "You saw fear, Kit."

This was an admission that I never thought I'd hear Grizz make. Ever.

"Of?"

"Of giving your children the love I should've given Tommy. I really did believe he was my son, and I should've loved him like a son, but I couldn't. I wouldn't let myself. I had only loved one person before you came along. The pain of losing my baby sister was something I never wanted to experience again. I still don't. When we love, we become vulnerable. If I allow myself to love, I set myself up to not be in control. I did it with Ruthie, and I did it with you. I'm afraid to do it again, but it's too late, anyway."

"Too late? What's too late?" My heart started thumping as I realized he was going to tell me it was too late for us. That he'd changed his mind and life with me wouldn't be possible. Isn't that what I needed to hear so he could leave and we could move on?

I started to shake.

He stood and approached me, grabbing me and hugging me fiercely.

"I already love your children. I love my daughter. I love your son. I would give anything for a world where we could be a family, Kit. Anything."

I was moved and relieved by his admission. He let go of me and stepped back, looking down at me with a need in his eyes I recognized. I felt the tension and wasn't sure how I would react if he decided to kiss me. He sensed it too and asked, "Kiss?"

Before I could answer him, he'd reached into his front jeans pocket and held something out to me. "Hershey's Kiss?"

I knew he was trying to lighten the moment and I smiled at him. I looked at the coffee table and saw the tiny silver balls. I'd wondered more than once what they were, but had never asked. They were the remnants of his obviously new chocolate fetish. My heart tightened a little bit when I remembered how I would find empty Jolly Rancher wrappers all over the house and even in the washing machine. Tommy loved the hard candy and would stuff the cellophane wrappers in his pockets after opening them. I swallowed back my still lingering grief and accepted the Kiss.

That night as I drove home, I thought about Grizz's admission and the stab of panic I'd felt when I thought his comment meant it was too late for us.

Instead of driving directly home, I headed back toward our old neighborhood, Shady Ranches. I went way beyond where Carter and Bill lived and started driving some of the still-undeveloped roads. I wanted to think without the lights, traffic, and distractions of the city. I thought about all the phone conversations and emails I'd exchanged with Sister Mary Katherine since Tommy's death. One of our many conversations, the most recent one, came back to me.

"What is it exactly that you're afraid of, child?" she asked me as I clutched the phone to my ear.

"I don't know, Sister. I guess I'm afraid of what I might be starting to feel for him." *Or what I've always felt and don't want to accept.*

"And you're afraid of this why?"

"I guess it's several things. I'm thinking Tommy would disapprove because of the man Grizz was. Grizz spent almost his entire life doing the opposite of everything I've ever believed in, and the last fifteen years of his life have been in a maximum-security prison. Is that the kind of person I want to fall back in love with? To expose my children to?"

I heard a small chuckle from her end of the phone.

"I probably never mentioned that I frequented many prisons doing ministry in my day. In fact, one of the most wonderful days of my life was spent at the most notorious prison in our country."

"You did?" I was a little surprised. "Wonderful?"

"Yes, I did. They were the worst of the worst. So much hate there. So much loathing. So much pain. The outcasts of society. They were men who'd done terrible things and considered themselves unworthy of a life beyond those walls. But, worse yet, they considered themselves unworthy of forgiveness and love. I saw something that day. Do you know who I was there with?"

"No, Sister. I don't."

"I got to spend one glorious day visiting inmates with Mother Teresa. She was Sister Teresa back then."

I gulped.

"We were meeting murderers, rapists, human traffickers. Men who wore tattoos boasting of the number of people they'd killed. I remember one man in particular. He'd killed eleven people. When we approached him, I saw the defiance in his eyes. He had his emotional armor on because he was used to seeing the judgment, the hatred. And of course, he thought that as women of God, we would have every right to judge him. He wasn't going to be hurt by our rejection because he was prepared for it."

"What happened?" I was starting to get a little concerned about what she was going to tell me. I held my breath.

"I watched Mother Teresa approach him. I saw him stiffen, and then his entire demeanor changed when she took the crucifix from around her neck and lovingly placed it around his. She said three words to him." Sister paused for effect. "She said, 'I love you.' That was all. Three simple words that were heartfelt, sincere, and full of compassion. Three words that can change the world, if we'll let them."

I didn't know what to say, so I didn't say anything.

When she spoke again, Sister Mary Katherine's voice was full of joy.

"That man asked her why or how she could love him, and she went on to share the story of a loving, forgiving God. And do you know that man now runs one of the biggest prison ministries in the world? And he does it from a cell. That because of him, the prison where he has been incarcerated and will spend the rest of his natural life has seen a drastic reduction in inmate suicides and murders?"

"It's a beautiful story, Sister." I paused then and tried to grasp the deeper meaning of what she was trying to share with me. When she didn't reply, I added, "You told me when I visited that it's not by coincidence that everything comes full circle, back to the way it was meant to be. How do I know if loving Grizz is the way it's meant to be?"

"Ask Him and search your heart, Guinevere. And while you're looking for your answers, keep in mind that if only three simple words like 'I love you' can change a man's heart forever and give him hope in a hopeless place, imagine what a woman who loves the Lord and walks in His ways can do to a man who's only known darkness." She sighed, and I heard the unmistakable creak of a rocking chair. "I can't tell you it's okay for you to love and be with this man, Guinevere. You will have to find your own answers, but you're asking the wrong person, and I know you already know that."

I was quiet for a minute and realized with a sudden flash of insight that maybe my bitterness hadn't been toward Grizz. Maybe it had been toward God.

"I only ever asked God for one thing, Sister, and that was for Tommy not to die. That was the miracle I needed, and He didn't give it to me." I tried not to cry.

"Oh, my dear Guinevere. Just because He didn't give you what you asked for doesn't mean He didn't give you your miracle."

As I drove and remembered this conversation and the turmoil my heart was experiencing, I quickly pulled my car over to the side of the road. I was in the middle of nowhere. I could see lights far off in the distance, but no homes were nearby. Just shrubs and brush.

I put my car in park and jumped out, running in front of my head-lights and off to the side. I found a clear spot and knelt, tears streaming down my face.

"God," I said, looking up at the stars. "God, I've never asked for anything for myself except for once, and that was for Tommy not to die. I know You didn't cause it to happen, but I know You allowed it, and I don't know why. I don't know that I'll ever know why. My heart has never felt so heavy as I struggle with what Your will may be for my life. I've never felt so lost or uncertain. I need something, God. I need to know that You hear me. I need to know Tommy is with You now. I need to know that if I give Grizz a chance, it's the right thing. I just need something, anything. Please."

My sobs became heavy then, and my body shook. I kept my head tilted toward the stars praying for a sign. I didn't know what kind of sign I was looking for. I wasn't sure exactly how that worked, but if I'd seen a shooting star at that moment, I would've believed it to be from Him. But He didn't.

I don't know how long I knelt there, but eventually with my shoulders slumped I lowered myself into a crouch, defeated. I was just getting ready to wipe away my tears when something startled me. Quicker than a flash, I saw movement to my right and felt something as it ran up my right arm and perched on my shoulder.

Before I could react, I realized it was a kitten. And it was licking away my tears.

To a non-believer, I'm sure they would think I'd merely stumbled upon an abandoned kitten that was thirsty. I can accept that. But I also know that I didn't just accidentally decide to stop in the middle of nowhere to speak to God.

It was Divine intervention that brought me and that helpless kitten together that night under the stars. A cute and extremely thin little thing, it was all white except for a brown and black mask. When I brought it home that night, Mimi and Jason were tossing all kinds of names around—Bandit, Zorro, Swiper, Rascal.

"No," I told them firmly. After discovering it was a little girl, I said, "I'm calling her Hope."

58

Grizz, 2002, Fort Lauderdale

G rizz watched from the bench as the woman seated herself at a small table by the restaurant window and perused the menu as she waited for someone to join her. He held the newspaper up to block his face and would occasionally lower it so he could see just over the edge. He didn't know what he wanted to see, needed to see. He just knew he felt compelled to watch Sarah Jo.

He thought about all the things that had happened in his life since before Christmas and up until the anniversary of Tommy's murder. He remembered being unsure as to whether or not to accept an invitation to Ginny's for Christmas dinner. He'd made sure not to ever show up at her home uninvited like he'd done so many months before, when he'd driven Mimi home from the grocery store. It was probably for the best that he'd stayed away, yet he couldn't resist the invitation to spend Christmas with them. He knew Mimi and Jason were beginning to accept him.

He smiled when he thought about the confirmation he'd received that Christmas day.

"Hey, you two are standing under the mistletoe!" Jason grinned. "You know what that means."

It was Christmas night, and Grizz had been standing in their foyer getting ready to leave when Jason's words interrupted their goodbyes.

His emotions were scattered as he warred with wanting very much to kiss her, grateful that Jason wanted him to and wondering how to pull it off without it being too awkward. He was extremely mindful of the fact that this was their first Christmas without Tommy, and the last thing he wanted to do was appear disrespectful in Tommy's home.

"What are you waiting for?" Mimi had teased.

He took Ginny gently by the shoulders and softly kissed her forehead.

"Thank you for a delicious dinner," he'd told her. "And a wonderful day."

"Ah, that's no kiss," Jason said, laughing.

Setting memories of Christmas aside, he now watched as another woman made her way to the table and Sarah Jo stood to give her a hug. Her name was April. She had been married to a man named Stephen, and they had both been to his and Ginny's home in Shady Ranches many times back before Grizz's arrest in 1985. They were a nice couple, and he'd recently asked Ginny about them.

"I noticed Stephen was at Tommy's funeral, but he wasn't with April. He was with some redhead. What happened to April?"

"They divorced a few years back. Nothing bad. I guess they just grew apart." Ginny looked thoughtful. "April's settled down with someone new since then, but Stephen hasn't. She said he's having too much fun being single. Apparently, he enjoys chasing a certain body part around. It's a new woman every month."

"A certain body part?" He gave her an odd look. "You mean his dick? He's chasing his dick around?"

"Yes, that's what I mean, and that's what he's been doing. They've stayed friends, but I have to tell you, April is not only a natural beauty, but she's a genuinely sweet and caring person. He's been seeing women that seem a little...I don't know...edgier. Just so different from her. They seem to have a different look, too. It's odd."

"I have to agree. I remember the woman from the funeral." He paused before adding, "So how long has his dick been vision-impaired?"

Ginny gently scolded him and said Stephen's new girlfriends weren't unattractive, just different. In characteristic Grizz fashion, he disagreed with her and told her he thought the redhead was down-right ugly.

He now laid the newspaper aside and stood to leave. He had just ducked behind the side of a brick building when he decided to look over his shoulder. Sarah Jo just happened to glance up and quickly looked away. Her eyes returned to the spot where she was certain she'd just seen something that couldn't be.

It wasn't the first time since Christmas that her eyes had played tricks on her. She was certain she'd spotted him several times, but she knew it was impossible. What was wrong with her? Why was her brain screwing with her like this? Was it guilt over the falling out she'd had with Tommy? Guilt over the subtle way she'd drifted away from her tight friendship with Ginny?

Funny how that had been Tommy's goal and she'd resisted it, yet it's what was happening anyway. Whatever was behind the reason for her recent Grizz sightings, she needed to shake it off before it drove her crazy. After saying goodbye to April, she headed back to work.

Grizz drove back toward his side of town, lost in thoughts about why he'd begun spying on Sarah Jo in the first place. It wasn't until Christmas night when he'd gone home to Laurel Falls that something small and insignificant that Ginny had said at Christmas dinner triggered a memory. The memory had been nagging at him since reading Moe's journal. He knew there was something lurking in the back of his mind that kept poking at his subconscious, but he could never bring it to the surface, like when a song lyric or movie line keeps replaying itself in your head but you can't place the singer or the actor that said it. Then, one day, when you're doing something totally irrelevant, it lets itself be known.

That's what happened Christmas night. He was drifting off to sleep when he remembered who'd used the term "tit for tat." He hadn't even caught it when she gave the eulogy at Tommy's funeral, but when he did remember it, it came on him like a steel hammer to the head. He'd convinced himself all those years ago that it had been Willow who had used that phrase. He'd been wrong—and he knew Tommy must've been smart enough to have caught it when reading the journal.

He also knew Tommy had died in the very hospital where Sarah Jo and her husband worked. Did he really succumb to his injuries? Or was it something else?

He didn't have to think about whether or not Tommy's shooting was planned or random. Anthony Bear's sources were too reliable. It was not a setup by Sarah Jo or anyone else. But Tommy dying in Sarah Jo's hospital—he couldn't shake it.

And he wouldn't bring it up with Ginny. The few times he'd

mentioned Sarah Jo, Ginny talked fondly about her, though she confessed that they weren't as close as they used to be. He'd asked her if it was of her choosing or Sarah Jo's. She looked thoughtful when she said they'd started to grow apart after his execution in 2000. Right afterward, Jo's husband had started interviewing for jobs outside the country.

He couldn't help but wonder.

He didn't know why he felt compelled to watch Jo. It must've been an instinct left over from his old life. Would he allow himself to exact revenge on the woman? He honestly hoped not, but the call of that old life taunted him.

He was relieved when Ginny and the kids stoically made it through the one-year anniversary of Tommy's passing. He kept his distance, giving them the space he thought they needed. He felt like he'd held his breath for the week after that dreaded anniversary, but life continued. The one thing he couldn't continue to avoid and didn't know how to handle was Jason's constant invitations to public events.

He was now in his back yard throwing the ball for Rocky when the cell phone in his pocket buzzed.

"Hey, baby, I was just thinking about you," he said into his flip phone.

"Hey, yourself. What are you doing?" Ginny asked.

"Throwing the ball with Rocky. Actually, I'm throwing it. He's retrieving it," he said with a low, deep chuckle that made her insides tingle.

"The kids and I just drove through Dairy Queen. We were wondering if we could stop by. They have something they want to ask you."

Ten minutes later, Jason was presenting Grizz with a vanilla milkshake that had obviously suffered on the drive over.

"Mom said she remembered vanilla was your favorite flavored milkshake," Jason said, handing over the tall cup. "You know, from when you used to be married to her."

59

Ginny, 2002, Fort Lauderdale

I watched as Grizz froze while retrieving the melting milkshake from Jason's hand. I saw him swallow, and his eyes met mine. Grizz may have been a man of few words, but he was never a man without words. He was without them now.

I proposed he put the milkshake in the freezer to let it harden up a bit. Without saying anything, he did as I suggested, then seated himself in the overstuffed chair in his living room. Jason, Mimi, and I sat on the couch. Mimi spoke first.

"Mom explained to Jason and me that you two were married a long time ago, and how after you went to jail, she married our dad."

"My dad," Jason said.

Mimi looked at her brother. "He was my father, too, Jason. Mom explained that."

"I know, I was just trying to tell James I know that part, too. I didn't mean to hurt your feelings, Mimi." He looked at her with wide eyes, and she gave him a smile and a quick hug.

Grizz swiped his hand down his face. He took a big breath and sat on the edge of the chair. I could see uncertainty in his eyes as he looked to me, then back at the kids. I nodded for Mimi to continue.

"She thought it was important for us to know we had a family," Mimi said. "We've never had a family before. It's always just been

Mom, Dad, me, and Jason. No grandparents or aunts or uncles or cousins."

I'd recently asked Mimi if she remembered Blue from her childhood, and when she confirmed that she did and had even spoken with him briefly at the hospital, I respectfully asked her to leave his name out of any future conversations. She agreed.

"Aunt Carter and Uncle Bill aren't our real aunt and uncle," Jason explained.

"Anyway," Mimi said, frowning at Jason for the interruption, "we're going to meet our family for spring break."

"And we want you to come with us because it's your family, too!" Jason shouted the last part, his excitement too much for him to contain.

Grizz nodded numbly and excused himself to use the bathroom. I knew he was hiding, but he couldn't stay in there forever.

Ten minutes later, we stood at the sliding glass doors and watched Jason play with Rocky in the back yard. Mimi was sitting on the couch watching one of her favorite television shows.

"I can't believe you told him," Grizz said quietly.

"I couldn't keep it from him. He's going to be twelve this year. He's a sensitive child but not stupid. He's had to grow up awfully quick since Tommy died." I cast him a glance. "I'm taking the kids to meet your father whether you go with us or not. I didn't want to go there with the pretense that we were meeting an old family friend. He is Mimi's biological grandfather, and I don't want to hide that truth. I don't want to hide any more truths, Grizz."

"How did he take it?"

"Jason is an optimist. He was excited to find out they had a grandfather and lots of cousins." Before Grizz could ask, I said, "He understands that they are biologically Mimi's relatives, but he doesn't care. He's excited."

"That's not the part I was wondering about. What did he think about us being married?" he asked, his voice still low.

He didn't have to talk so quietly. Mimi knew everything and had even helped me by pretending to learn these things for the first time along with Jason. She didn't want him to feel like he was the last to know. She had changed so much over the past year and a half. My heart couldn't have been prouder.

"He was shocked. Had lots of questions, as you can imagine."

Grizz nodded.

"But the thing that was most important to him was wanting to know if Mimi knew Tommy loved her as much as he loved him. He was worried Mimi's feelings were getting hurt by finding out Tommy had married me when I was already pregnant with her." Tears filled my eyes. "My child has a huge heart."

"Not as big as his mother's," Grizz whispered.

The question the kids wanted to ask Grizz that day was if he wanted to go with us. After returning from his bathroom break I watched him seriously consider his answer, and after a few moments of silence, he nodded.

Four days later we found ourselves on a road trip.

Jason beamed. "Don't be nervous, James. We'll be there with you when you meet your father for the first time."

After making sure Rocky, Hope, and Spooky were safely delivered into Carter's care, we hit the road. We were miles from the North Carolina border when I noticed Grizz's demeanor change. He looked tense.

I gently touched his arm. "It'll be fine," I whispered. "Have some faith."

We had just crossed into North Carolina. The roads were curvy, and I thought I might be getting a little motion sickness. The scenery was breathtaking. I'd visited this little town the previous winter. It was a different type of beauty then. Leafless trees with stark branches had been splayed against a backdrop of brilliant white snow. It was now spring, and the trees and plants were coming into full bloom and providing a canopy over the narrow road. The air even smelled different here. We saw a sign that said, "Welcome to Pine Creek, elevation 3,800 feet."

We made a left turn at a small coffee shop that had been the original schoolhouse back in the 1800s. The school bell still hung proudly in its small steeple. Before we knew it, we were turning onto a dirt road. We came upon a mailbox that said "Hunter," and we knew to make a right.

The gravel crunched beneath the tires, and we all let out a collective sigh of wonder when we reached the top of the long driveway. Green pastures spread out against a breathtaking view of the mountains. A large two-story cabin sat right in the middle, a red barn in the back. Cars and trucks were lined up on the right side of the property, and people were spread out everywhere. The smell of barbecue drifted through the open car windows.

I spotted him immediately. Like his son, he would be a hard man to miss.

Micah Hunter started walking toward our car, speeding up when Grizz put the car in park. I watched as Grizz hesitated, then slowly opened the door and started to get out. He had just slammed the car door shut when Micah reached him and pulled him into a bear hug.

With his voice quavering and his face buried in Grizz's shoulder, I heard him say, "Welcome home, son. Welcome home."

60

Grizz, 2002, North Carolina

G rizz stiffened as the father he'd never known invaded his personal space and clung tightly to his only child. When he pulled back, he allowed himself to meet the old man's eyes, and what he saw caused him to look away.

Micah Hunter looked at his grown son with a love that was timeless. It didn't matter that they'd never met before today. There was acceptance, joy, and a certain expectation in the man's gaze, and Grizz wasn't exactly sure how he felt about any of it. He could only surmise that Ginny hadn't told Micah everything about him. No. There had to be things he wasn't aware of because he certainly wouldn't be welcoming him with open arms.

Grizz cast a wary glance over at Ginny and then at the people who'd gathered in Micah's yard.

As if sensing his son's discomfort, Micah told him, "My excitement got the best of me, and I planned a pig roast to celebrate, but don't worry, they know they're not allowed to stay. They've already cleaned up from supper and were just getting ready to head out anyway, but hung around just long enough to get a look at you-uns."

Micah called out to those gathered on his property. "I thank you all kindly for being here to welcome my son and his family home."

Ginny was standing next to her children and chanced a peek at

338

their faces after Micah's reference to family. Mimi and Jason were both grinning ear-to-ear.

"But," Micah continued, "like I told y'all when we sat down to supper, this is a bit much for them. For me, too. So we'll save introductions for another time."

Grizz watched with obvious relief as the guests, respecting Micah's wishes, started gathering their families. Smiling parents shooed their children toward cars and trucks as they balanced paper plates covered in tinfoil. A few kids hung back, and it was obvious they wanted to meet Ginny's children. Eventually, they were shuffled off, too.

"How many of them do you think there are?" Jason asked his mother, eyes wide.

She shook her head. "Too many to count."

She'd been watching as an older woman, almost mannish in appearance, seemed to take charge of herding the guests toward their vehicles.

Micah was now making small talk with Grizz, Mimi, and Jason, but Ginny wasn't paying attention. She watched as the older woman said goodbye to the last family and, after slamming their car door shut, made a beeline for Micah.

"Don't you think for one single second, Micah Edward Hunter, that I am going to be sent away before I get to meet my nephew!" the woman said in a loud voice. The conversation stopped as Micah turned to face her. "My late husband was a Jamison, so I have connections to this boy from both sides of my family, and I'm not being run off with the rest of 'em!"

Ginny smiled at her reference to Grizz as a boy.

Micah sighed. "Jamison, Ginny, Mimi, Jason..." He gestured toward the woman who was now standing with hands on hips, her gray hair pulled back in a severe bun. "This is my sister, Matilda, and ever since her husband and my Margaret Mae died, she thinks it's her responsibility to take care of me. Thank the good Lord she doesn't live with me, but I've no doubt she would if I'd allow it."

"I'm Tillie, Aunt Tillie to the four of you," she told the small gathering as she stared into each of their eyes with a look that dared them to call her otherwise. "Now. I want some hugs!"

After Aunt Tillie got her hugs and headed for home, Grizz and Micah carried the suitcases into the house, and Ginny realized the cabin was far larger than it looked from the outside. They walked in through the front door and noticed a staircase on the immediate right that led to a second floor. They walked further into the house and found themselves in one large family room with a tall fireplace on the right side wall. The ceiling was high, and above the massive glass sliders there were trapezoid windows that showcased a spectacular mountain view. To the left was a large kitchen and an island that separated it from the family room. There was a small bath off the kitchen and a hallway that led to a master bedroom.

Standing in the center of the family room now, they looked up and could see an open hallway fenced in with rustic mountain laurel railing.

"Hi, Mom!" Jason waved down to Ginny. She hadn't seen him remove himself from the group and was a little embarrassed he'd run up the stairs uninvited. "You should see the view from up here."

"Jason, please come back down here!"

"His room is up there anyway, might as well let him take a look around," Micah said, smiling.

"Where does that other staircase go?" Jason called down, pointing from the second story open loft to another staircase in the kitchen. It was barely noticeable.

"That's the basement. It has two more bedrooms and two full baths," Micah said.

"This sure is a lot of house for one person," Grizz said to nobody in particular.

"I thought so, too, when I first built it, but Margaret Mae told me we'd be filling it up. Obviously, it didn't happen that way. Almost sold it ten times over, but something told me not to."

He winked at Ginny and told them where their rooms were.

A few hours later, their bellies full and their luggage unpacked, Ginny and Micah were standing on the deck overlooking the expansive back yard. If it could even be called a back yard. Micah's property went on as far as the eye could see and gave the optical illusion that it dropped off before butting up to the mountains.

They watched as Mimi swung lazily in a hammock reading a book. She was now wearing sweatpants and a sweatshirt. Spring in the mountains could still be pretty cool. Grizz and Jason were a little further off. They had set up some tin cans they'd found in Micah's barn, and Grizz was teaching Jason how to use an old slingshot they'd come across on one of the shelves. Ginny could tell that Grizz's posture seemed relaxed. He was enjoying himself.

Ginny had been talking to Micah about the layout of the town. She had met him last year at a diner and was wondering where it was in relation to Micah's property.

"If you'd kept going straight instead of turning off at the old schoolhouse, you'd have run right through the center of town." Micah pointed. "The diner would be on the right, right before you got to the crossroads."

The four-way stop sign was considered the center of town and referred to as the crossroads by the local folks.

They went inside, and Micah started a pot of coffee. Ginny sensed he wanted some alone time with Grizz, and she told him she wanted to take Jason and Mimi into town.

"I'd like to make dinner tomorrow night. I'm pretty sure I remember where the one grocery store is. I passed it the last time I was here," she told him.

"Yes, ma'am. If you make a right at that stop sign and go down just a-ways, it'll be on your left."

THE NEXT FEW DAYS PASSED BY IN A WHIRLWIND OF NEW FACES. IT WOULD be impossible to remember all of the names, but little by little, Grizz's extended family showed up to introduce themselves. Some would drop in with a homemade pie or something they'd canned. Others stopped by under the guise of helping Micah repair some piece of farm equipment or to return a borrowed tool. Eventually, they all came, and it was amazing that the visits never went too long or overlapped into someone else's stay. If she hadn't known better, Ginny would've guessed that Aunt Tillie had made up a secret schedule and passed it out to Grizz's relatives.

Ginny watched in awe as Grizz let down his guard and chatted with his cousins about everything from NASCAR, hunting, and farming to homemade remedies for wart removal and toothaches. Grizz's extended family was full of homemakers, teachers, business owners, farmers, mechanics, professionals. One cousin was a deputy with the local sheriff's office.

It was obvious the people who lived in this tiny mountain town were in no way ignorant of the fast-paced world that surrounded them. They'd seen it and deliberately chosen the quiet solitude and fierce loyalty of family over the noise of the world, and Ginny was moved by their love for one another. How different would Grizz have been if he'd been raised here? She wondered more than once.

"I won't remember all their names," Grizz was telling Micah one afternoon. One of Grizz's cousins had stopped by to borrow machinery from Micah's barn, and he was loading it up in the bed of his truck. He'd brought his two sons, who were off somewhere on the property with Jason. His teenage daughter was Mimi's age, and the two girls were sitting on Micah's porch swing laughing about something. Ginny was inside tidying up.

"Yes, you will," Micah told him, patting him on the back. "Yes, you will."

They were all invited to hear Micah preach that Sunday and, of course, Ginny, Mimi, and Jason went to the service, but Grizz didn't. When they returned, they found Grizz in the barn tending to an injured dog.

"How'd you get your hands on that one?" Micah asked. "I've been trying to get him to come to me for months."

"I don't know," Grizz said. "He just came to me."

After a big breakfast, Micah took them on a tour of the small town. The kids were amazed that Pine Creek only had one school, and it was for children in kindergarten through twelfth grade.

"We only have about two-hundred kids in the whole school, and you're related to most of them," Micah said as he looked at Mimi and Jason.

"Cool!" Jason grinned. "Do you have sports here?"

Ginny saw Micah's face light up as he answered, "Our school has every sport except for football. Don't actually have enough boys in the right age group to make a team, but we have everything else."

Ginny secretly hoped that Micah wasn't getting his hopes up that they might live here one day. She couldn't imagine her children or even Grizz wanting to be removed from the city life they'd all been accustomed to.

She'd been invited to a ladies' night at one of Grizz's cousin's homes. At first, she'd been a little reluctant to go, concerned mostly about questions she wasn't ready to answer. But after some gentle prodding from Aunt Tillie, she decided to accept the invitation. Mimi had been invited as well, but after learning there wouldn't be any cousins her age, she'd elected to stay at the cabin with the guys.

Driving up Micah's driveway on her way home from the gathering, Ginny reflected on the evening and how much she'd enjoyed being around people that accepted her as family. A delicious white chicken chili had been the main course, and the women had played a game called Bunco. She was made to feel at home among the ladies, who had welcomed her without hesitation. Apparently, Micah had a lot of family, and he was dearly loved and respected by everyone. That love and respect was trickling down onto Ginny, and she basked in its warmth. She would've stayed longer but Aunt Tillie announced that there was the possibility of a spring snowstorm, and since Ginny had no experience driving in snow—especially on dark mountain roads— they all thought it best to call it an early night.

Ginny let out a sigh of relief as she pulled up to Micah's cabin. It had started snowing on the way home and, like Aunt Tillie had said, she wasn't used to driving in it. It had been a good call to go home early.

After letting herself in the front door, she felt like she'd interrupted a private moment between Micah, Grizz, Mimi, and Jason. A fire was blazing in the hearth, and they were seated around a large coffee table that held some kind of board game. They all just stared at her.

Jason broke into a wide grin. "Hi, Mom!" Ginny noticed Mimi gently elbow his side, and he told her, "I wasn't going to say anything, Mimi."

"Say anything about what?" She laid her purse and jacket down.

"Nothing," Grizz said. "He was just excited about the snow."

"Yeah, that's it. I'm excited about the snow. We're going to go out in it tomorrow, aren't we?"

"I think we need to get some warmer clothes, or at least the right kind," Ginny said. "We didn't come prepared."

"Write down all your sizes, and I'll have Tillie make some calls. Everything you need will be here tomorrow. Don't need to find a store when we just need to ask some kin to send the right clothes and boots over," Micah said.

"How was your hike today?" Ginny asked, trying not to yawn. She was exhausted.

"Best hike ever," Grizz said, giving the kids a wink.

61

Ginny, 2002, North Carolina

I couldn't help but feel there was some joke I'd missed out on, but the day's activities and the fresh mountain air must've caught up with me. I yawned and excused myself. I wanted to turn in early.

My eyes popped open at exactly 2:47 a.m. I'd gone to bed maybe a little too early and now found myself wide awake. I looked over at Mimi, who was sleeping next to me. I gently pulled the covers back, found my robe, and made my way downstairs.

I was standing in the kitchen making myself a cup of hot chocolate when I sensed him. I didn't turn around, but leaned back into him as I felt his arms come around me. He bent low and softly kissed the side of my neck. My hot chocolate forgotten, I closed my eyes and enjoyed the heat that radiated from him.

"How did you know I was up?" I whispered.

"I didn't. I couldn't sleep and thought I heard someone up here. Didn't know it was you, Kitten."

Grizz had been sleeping in one of the bedrooms downstairs. I was sharing one of the two upstairs bedrooms with Mimi. Jason was across from us in his own room.

I turned around then and looked at him. He looked sexier than I could've imagined or remembered, and I had to swallow my intense and immediate reaction. He was wearing camouflage pajama pants and a dark T-shirt. His hair was tousled, and his normally bright green eyes appeared dark and smoky.

I could tell he read the need in my eyes. He took my face in both his hands and kissed me. Not a small feathery kiss that teased. A kiss that took my mouth, hard and unrelenting with its bold claim of ownership.

I welcomed it and hungrily kissed him back, grinding my body against his. His need was apparent, and I felt my own need making my panties wet.

I pulled back, breathless. "We can't here. Micah is sleeping right down that hallway." I nodded in the direction of the master bedroom. "We need to go downstairs to your room."

He stepped back then and gave me a look that told me he had something to say. I knew what it was, and I responded with a small, knowing smile. I knew I'd surprised him. We hadn't taken our relationship to the next level, and I was grateful he'd never pushed it. But I was now letting him know I was willing and ready—and that I could certainly make my way back upstairs and slip into bed with Mimi long before the rest of the household woke up.

I watched as the vein in his forehead throbbed.

"No," he said quietly.

I shook my head as if to clear it, not thinking I'd heard him right. "Wha...what?"

"No. Not now, Kitten. Not tonight. Not here like this. No," he said again in a voice that didn't sound too confident.

I was shocked and maybe even a little hurt.

"No?" I whispered a little too loudly. "Are you sure, Grizz? Because your mouth is saying no but your pants are saying something different."

He inhaled loudly and looked at the ceiling. He didn't say anything. He finally looked down at me and, letting out a long breath, he shook his head and lightly kissed my forehead.

"Goodnight, sweetheart. I'll see you in the morning," he told me with a frog in his throat.

And then he was gone.

I know my mouth hung open as I watched him walk away. I turned back to the kitchen counter and finished making my hot chocolate with shaking hands.

What had just happened? Or rather, what had not happened?

I carried my mug over to the couch and looked out on the most beautiful scene. Micah's back yard was a blanket of white, and the full moon cast just enough light for it to look almost heavenly. I don't remember eventually setting my empty cup down. I don't remember lying down on the couch and grabbing one of the throw blankets to cover myself.

I woke up the next morning staring into four pairs of eyes looking down at me. They were all smiling, and Jason was almost hopping with anticipation.

"We didn't wake you up, did we, Mom?"

Before I could answer him, he told me one of Micah's nephews was bringing over some of his kids' winter gear for Jason and Mimi.

I shook the sleep from my foggy head and sat up, the smell of coffee finally reaching my nose. I yawned and stretched, all of a sudden very aware that I was in a nightshirt without a bra. I grabbed the blanket and pulled it up to cover my chest. Being the perfect gentleman, I noticed Micah had already looked away.

I stood and grabbed my robe, excused myself to go shower. I poured myself a cup of coffee and was getting ready to carry it upstairs with me when I caught Grizz's eye. I looked away, a little embarrassed by last night's rejection.

A little while later, I told the kids to enjoy the snow while I cleared away the breakfast dishes. Micah's nephew had shown up while I was showering with some spare winter clothes and boots and, surprisingly, everything fit the kids perfectly. Micah, Grizz, and both kids were now digging through the barn for sleds.

Beds made, dishes washed, and one load of laundry later, I stood with a second cup of coffee and watched them in the snow. Micah had set Grizz to work clearing a path to his henhouse. Micah's henhouse wasn't what I'd pictured a henhouse to look like. I'd imagined a small structure surrounded by wire. But Micah's henhouse looked like a small house that, if cleared of its feathered occupants, could probably sleep several people. We'd been collecting eggs every morning. In reality, I'd been the only one collecting them. I thought at first that I wouldn't be able to do it. I had a real fear of disturbing the hens, but after getting the hang of it, I loved it. It was just something different, and it made me happy.

After shoveling a path, Grizz gave me a signal to get a coat on and come outside. I laid down my coffee and grabbed one of Micah's winter coats that he kept on a peg. I had on my own boots. They weren't for winter, but I wouldn't need to be sloshing through snow. I made my way toward the henhouse and realized that Mimi, Jason, and Micah had stopped what they were doing and were walking toward me. I waved and grabbed a basket from its hook. Then, after going inside, I set about checking each hen for eggs.

At one point I stopped and turned around, surprised. The four of them had followed me in and just stood there, watching.

"It's really cold out," Jason said, his cheeks a rosy pink.

I thought it odd that they all needed to follow me into the henhouse, but without giving it anymore thought, I shrugged and went back to collecting eggs.

I reached under one particularly feisty mother and felt something hard. It undoubtedly wasn't an egg.

I pulled it out and looked at the small box in my hand. A box?

"Are you going to open it?" I heard Jason ask.

"Shhhh!" Mimi giggled.

Without turning around, I opened the tiny box, and my hand flew to my mouth. It was a ring.

I turned around and saw Micah, Mimi, and Jason leaned up against the back of the henhouse. They were all smiling.

It was then that I realized Grizz had moved closer and was down on one knee. He reached for my left hand and brought it to his mouth.

Kissing the inside of my palm, he said, "I messed this up once before. I'm not going to make the same mistake."

I held my breath, hopeful and yet fearful of what his next words were going to be.

"Ginny." He swallowed. "Let me say first that I already know I don't deserve you. But, I know there is no one else in the world for me and if you'll have me, I promise you won't regret it. Please give me another chance."

My right hand flew to my mouth. I watched him swallow again before asking, "Will you marry me?"

I started shaking, and tears started to form in my eyes. I thought about Grizz's rebuff the night before, and how I'd finally drifted off to sleep resigning myself to the fact that he was probably right and had saved me from myself. I couldn't see how a future for us could ever be in the cards.

He was still holding my left hand in his large one, and I gently pulled it away and replaced it with the ring box. Avoiding his gaze and not chancing a glance at the onlookers, I ran out of the henhouse.

As I left, I heard Micah tell the kids, "Stay with me. Let him go after her."

I could feel Grizz behind me as I stumbled down the path he'd shoveled. I made it to the house and went in through the side door. I realized I still had the egg basket dangling from my right arm.

"Ginny." He shut the door behind us.

I laid the basket down and started to take Micah's coat off.

"Kit!"

Ignoring him, I put the coat back on its peg. My mind and heart were at war with each other. I couldn't fathom my feelings, so I gave into them.

I turned to face him then. Tears were silently making their way down both my cheeks. I just stood there and looked up at him. I was begging for something, but for what I didn't know.

He pulled me to him, wrapping his massive arms around me. My face was buried in his warm chest. I inhaled the scent that was uniquely Grizz. It felt so normal, so natural. What was I afraid of? His jacket was open and I could feel his heart beating through his shirt against my face.

"Say yes, Kitten," he whispered while stroking my hair. "Give me another chance."

"How?" I asked sniffling. "The kids, our neighbors, people in general? How can we ever carve out a life that doesn't involve our past? How do I marry a man who was executed almost two years ago? How could it ever work?"

He pulled away from me then, took my face in both hands. Bringing his face close to mine he said, "I wouldn't have asked if there wasn't a plan that took all of that into consideration."

I stared at him, my heart in my throat. Words wouldn't come. A plan? What plan?

"You already know I've been in love with you for as long as I can remember, Kit. And the years before you came into my life were nothing but darkness. Please, baby. Please, say yes. Say it's not too late for us."

It was then that we sensed them. Slowly, we turned our faces toward the glass sliding doors that led onto Micah's huge deck. Huddled together against the cold, wearing huge smiles and giving their thumbs-up, were Mimi and Jason. Micah was standing behind them. He wasn't smiling, but I saw the approval and optimism in his eyes.

Grizz gently pulled my face back to his.

"It's okay if you're not in love with me anymore, but maybe you can find it in your heart to just love me."

His eyes were warm, sincere, and hopeful. Was his proposal why he hadn't tried anything beyond kissing me, always being the first to pull back when it seemed as if it could've gone farther? Was this a Grizz I'd never seen?

The man I'd originally fallen in love with used to bulldoze his way over people and their feelings. My first marriage to him was pretty much thrust upon me in the back of Eddie's tattoo parlor in 1975. He was now trying to do it the way he thought would be most respectful of me.

I felt a bubble of emotions rising in my chest and I realized that bubble was ready to burst with newfound hope. I started laughing then.

"Yes!" I shouted, grinning like a fool. "Yes! I'll marry you. I don't know how we'll do this, but yes."

The kids couldn't hear me but obviously had read my lips. They started cheering and dancing. Micah just gave a small nod, and winked at me.

62

Grizz, 2002, North Carolina

It took power he hadn't known he possessed to walk away from her that night in the kitchen. He'd promised himself he wasn't going to fuck up the only thing that still mattered to him.

He hadn't let himself hope for a long time. He remembered Kit sadly telling him at Thanksgiving he might have to settle for crumbs. He'd stifled the urge to tell her he would never settle for crumbs, and sat quietly instead, hoping the patience he'd learned in prison would be to his advantage. And it was, as he saw their lives slowly melding together. Mimi and Jason had started to accept him as they healed after Tommy's death. He still never pushed, just patiently waited for them to find their way. At that point he could only wish that way included him.

He'd actually prayed once to Ginny's God, asking—pleading—for something he didn't deserve. But promising that if he got it, he would do his best to do right by all of them. He also knew it would have to play out perfectly, but he'd heard Ginny say more than once that her God was a God of miracles.

He knew he'd needed a miracle, and as he glanced around the dinner table that night at all of them, at his family, he was pretty sure he'd gotten it.

How it had all worked out so perfectly was still a mystery to him.

Somehow, he'd managed to spend some time alone with both kids during the vacation. If Micah hadn't been around to encourage him, he might not have felt like he was ready to approach the kids. But then when Ginny had gone to Aunt Tillie's to get some canning lessons and he had an unexpected free afternoon hiking with Jason, Mimi, and Micah, he had the chance to lay it all out for them.

The four of them had stopped for a picnic lunch at the summit. And then, before he could talk himself out of it, Grizz told the children he was in love with their mother and that he wanted to ask her to marry him, but he wanted to discuss it with them first. The second he'd uttered the words, he realized he hadn't thought far enough ahead about what he'd do if they didn't give him their support. For a moment, he saw in his daughter's eyes that she'd realized it, too, but then she smiled. She looked at her little brother, waited for him to give his answer first.

"Are you going to move into our house with us?" Jason asked, his tone unreadable and his expression curious.

Grizz wasn't sure why Jason was asking, but he knew he now had to hit them with the second half of his request. And that part wouldn't be easy.

He sighed and looked at Micah. Micah nodded.

Looking from Jason to Mimi, and then back to Jason, he told them, "I can't move into your house, Jason. As a matter of fact, if I marry your mother, it's probably not a good idea for us to even stay in Florida. I'm sorry, but my marriage proposal comes with a part two. I'd have to ask if you and Mimi would be willing to move away from Florida. It would involve changing schools, making new friends. Some big changes, I'm afraid." He grimaced. "And I'd also have to ask that it stay a secret. Just like you've been good about not telling your friends about me, I wouldn't want people to know your Mom is moving away to get married. I wouldn't ask you to lie to people. I'd just ask you not to tell them."

They listened intently, clearly mulling it over.

He leveled a look at Jason. "You know I've been to prison. I don't want that stigma to attach to your mother or either of you kids. I'd want to move away where nobody knows about my criminal record in Florida. I don't want to be a source of embarrassment or shame to any of you."

He'd already had his neck tattoo changed after Jason had noticed it last Thanksgiving, and of course, he couldn't tell the boy his real reason for not being able to stay in Florida. But even if he hadn't been "executed," he realized there was still a lot of truth in what he was telling Jason.

The weight of what he was asking of these children hit him, and his eyes sought Micah's. He could see in Micah's expression that he understood what Grizz was thinking, and Micah raised his hand slightly, indicating for him to wait. They were all silent for a few minutes, and Grizz was seconds away from telling them to forget he asked when Jason spoke.

"What do you think, Mimi?" Jason turned to his sister.

"I want Mom to be happy, Jason, and I think she's happy when she's with him." She nodded toward Grizz, then tilted her head and looked at Grizz sideways, met his eyes. "And I like him. I know you do, too."

"But what about school? All our friends?"

"I'm ready for a change, Jason, and from what I'm hearing about what's going on with you, maybe you're ready for one, too. Maybe it's time for both of us to make some new friends. But I'm not going to tell you what to do. You have to give James your own answer."

Jason bit his lip, nodded. "So where would we move to? Could we move to someplace like Montana? Remember when we went there with Aunt Carter when she was helping rescue those horses?"

"Montana sounds reasonable to me," Grizz said with a wide grin.

"If Mimi says yes," Jason said, casting a hopeful glance at his sister, "then I say yes too!"

"Yes," Mimi shouted, giving a fist pump. There was a round of laughter and Jason immediately started suggesting unique ways for James to pop the question.

Now, sitting around the dinner table with memories of that hike tucked away, Grizz watched as Micah said the blessing. They were all holding hands, himself included, except everyone else had their heads bowed and their eyes closed. He took the time to look at each person seated at the table. When he got to Ginny, he was surprised to see she had her eyes wide open and was smiling directly at him. He smiled back.

"In Jesus's name we pray. Amen. Pass those peas, wouldya, Jason?" Micah asked.

And then there were so many conversations at the table Grizz could barely keep up with them. He listened as Micah explained that the engagement ring on Ginny's finger was one he'd bought for Grizz's mother, Frances, but had never been able to give it to her.

"Just like I knew it was a good idea to hold onto this house, I knew there'd be a good reason to hold onto that ring."

"I'm the one that told James he should put it under Miss Prissy for you to find, Mom," Jason said between bites.

"Thank you for picking the meanest hen out there, Jason. I almost skipped her," Ginny said with a smile.

"So, James, do you want us to call you Jamison now?" Jason asked. "Are you going to change your name to Jamison Hunter now that you know your real dad? When you marry Mom, is she going to be Ginny Kirkland or Ginny Hunter?"

"I can answer that one." Micah held up a hand. "She's going to be a Hunter. I'll take care of the legalities."

Grizz just smiled as he enjoyed his meal and the conversations. There was talk of Montana and Wisconsin. Grizz had made it clear the further away from Florida the better.

"How about Louisiana?" Micah asked, and gave Grizz a knowing glance. Grizz had confided in Micah that he was pretty certain he'd run across Ginny's twin sister living in the state of Louisiana. He also told him that he wasn't sure how or when to actually tell her about it. This was Micah's reminder that it still needed to be done.

"So when are you going to get married?" Jason asked through a mouthful of food.

"Don't talk with your mouth full, Jason," Ginny said. "We haven't even talked about a date. We just know we'll stay in Florida until summer so you can both finish up school and have the whole summer to make new friends and get acquainted with wherever we might end up."

"How about this Sunday?" Micah asked.

All conversation ceased as everyone turned to look at him.

"I can marry you this coming weekend in my church."

"Oh! Uh, we were going to drive home Sunday," Ginny said. "The kids have to be back to school on Monday."

"I'm sure they can take a few more days off," Micah grinned. "I can marry you this weekend, the kids can stay with me, and you two can take a short honeymoon."

"But there's no time to plan anything!"

But then she realized she wouldn't have planned anything big, anyway. It would have to be a small and intimate ceremony. She looked at Grizz and her children, saw that they were all considering it. Maybe…

They decided on a Saturday ceremony and thought the smaller and simpler the better.

Grizz was concerned it might've been a little quick for the kids. And the next morning, when he heard Ginny and Jason talking in hushed tones as he was coming upstairs from his basement bedroom, he stopped to listen.

"We won't get married this weekend if it upsets you, Jason," he heard Ginny say.

Grizz had been right. He'd thought Jason was unusually quiet after dinner last night and had wondered if the boy had had a change of heart.

"It's not that, Mom."

"What is it then?"

Jason didn't answer.

"Is it that it's too soon?"

Grizz didn't hear an answer, so he could only assume Jason was shaking his head.

"Is it that you don't like James?" A pause. "Is it because we have to move if I marry him?" Another pause. Finally, "Jason, I can't read your mind. Please tell me what's bothering you."

"I guess, well—I guess I need to know before you marry James that you still love Dad." Jason sniffled. "And you won't forget about him."

Grizz held his breath as he waited for Ginny to answer. He was shocked to realize that in the past he would never have wanted to hear his woman tell anybody, not even her son, that she still loved Tommy, but something had shifted inside of him. He was changing. He knew what he wanted, needed to hear for Jason's sake. Maybe he was learning the real definition of what it meant to love someone.

"Oh, Jason. Come here, sweetheart. Let me hug you."

Grizz took one more step and could see them. Jason and Ginny had been sitting on the couch. The boy was scooting closer and now had his head buried in his mother's chest, her arms wrapped tightly around him. Her eyes were closed when she answered him.

"Jason, I will always, always love your father. Just because I love James again doesn't mean I never loved your dad. It doesn't mean I will stop loving your dad." She pulled back from him then and grabbed his face in both her hands. Looking into his eyes, she said, "And, no. I will never forget about him. Not only will he always live inside my heart, but I see him every time I look at you, Jason. Every time. And I thank God for that. I thank God that I see him in you."

She looked over Jason's head then and caught sight of Grizz. Had he heard? Would he become jealous and doubt her resurrected love for him? Resurrected love? Who was she kidding? She'd never stopped loving Grizz.

Time stood still as she waited for his reaction. Some kind of sign, anything. She had a hopeful look on her face.

And then Grizz smiled at her. Not a smile that was pasted on for the sake of looking real. His smile was genuine and pure, and it radiated a love she was grateful he was now experiencing. And giving her a slight nod, he quietly walked back downstairs.

63

The next couple of days flew by as we prepared for what could best be described as a shotgun wedding without the actual shotgun. Micah wasn't forcing us to get married, but we knew it was important to him that we did so he could personally perform the ceremony.

We only included one family member whose wrath we didn't want to incur when she eventually found out. And it turned out Aunt Tillie was a blessing in disguise. Micah had held on to Margaret Mae's ivory wedding gown, and Aunt Tillie expertly tailored it to fit me perfectly. Micah handled the paperwork with a well-placed relative in the county clerk's office to help expedite things.

The kids had been invited by some cousins to go zip lining. I was standing on a stool in Micah's bedroom while Aunt Tillie made adjustments to Margaret Mae's dress. She insisted that we be given privacy because the groom wasn't supposed to see the bride in her gown before the wedding. Grizz and Micah's voices floated in from where they were in the kitchen.

"I just think an outdoor wedding might be something special," I heard Grizz tell his father.

"I think your bride might disagree with you," Micah countered.

"Maybe not."

"What's this all about, Jamison?"

Aunt Tillie caught my eye and stopped what she was doing. We both listened.

"Just don't know about getting married in a church, is all."

"Why is that?"

"Don't really know. Thinking it might not feel right for someone like me. You know what I mean."

"You afraid you're going to burst into flames if you go into God's house?" Even though it was a serious discussion, I could hear the teasing in Micah's tone.

"Maybe."

The conversation faded as they walked outside, and I never asked either one about their talk. I knew whatever Micah had told Grizz must have offered some form of consolation, because we were married by Micah in his church, and Grizz didn't burst into flames.

Before we got married, we had some ring shopping to do and Grizz took me off the mountain that day to pick out wedding bands and have Frances's engagement ring adjusted to fit my finger better. Walking hand in hand with him in the next town felt so right it was scary. I was on edge at first, waiting for someone to take in his appearance—his massive size, long hair, and tattoos—and run the other way, but other than a few curious glances, we were barely noticed.

I'd continued to wear my wide gold wedding band from Tommy as a way to hide the ring tattoo. I couldn't remember a time I'd left my finger uncovered for anybody to notice it, including my children. I especially didn't want Jason to see the name Grizz tattooed there, and Grizz agreed. I would select another wide band to cover it. Many years later, we vowed, we would tell Jason the rest of our story, but for now, he was still too young.

We were driving back up the mountain and making our way down a lonely side road when Grizz pulled off into a grassy area. He shifted the car into park and reached over me, unhooking my seatbelt with his left hand.

"I don't know how much longer I can wait, Kit," he groaned. "These past months have been fucking torture."

He pulled me over the console and into his lap, my back up against his door and my feet resting in the seat I'd just vacated. We'd somehow slipped back into calling each other Grizz and Kit when we were alone. Maybe we would always be Grizz and Kit.

I was resting in the crook of his arm and looking up into his eyes when I asked him, "Why haven't you tried to do more than kiss me? Why did you walk away from me that night in the kitchen?"

He nibbled on my bottom lip before answering.

"Because I'm trying my damnedest to do it your way. I want to do right by you. I want to marry you before I make love to you, Kitten. And you have to know now that after we take our vows, you're going to be busy. Real busy. I have fifteen years to make up for."

He lightly caressed my cheek with the back of his hand never breaking from my gaze.

"I know you wanted me that night. I wanted you too, Grizz. I was ready to go downstairs with you. You didn't have to propose."

"Yes, I did, baby." He kissed me then. It was a deep, exploring kiss, and just like that night in the kitchen I felt his erection and became instantly aware of my immediate dampness. His right hand started to make its way down to my breasts, and I felt my nipples stiffen in anticipation.

I arched into his hand, urging him to go further.

He stopped the kiss then and practically tossed me back in my seat.

Before starting up the car I heard him grumble under his breath, "I've been aching for you for so fucking long, honey, I'm afraid my dick's going to fall off before I get a chance to use it."

64

Grizz, 2002, North Carolina

"What's troubling you?" Micah asked.

Grizz had been standing at the altar talking to his father as he patiently waited for Ginny to do whatever it was brides were supposed to do. He nervously tugged at the collar of his white dress shirt and tie.

He looked over at Micah. His father. The man who had accepted him wholly and without reservation. He had been wrong. Ginny had told Micah everything, and yet Micah had still welcomed him with open arms. It was almost hard to believe.

"Having doubts? Cold feet?" Micah asked softly.

"Cold feet? Never. Doubts? Yes. Not about her. Doubts about myself."

"What kind of doubts about yourself?"

"C'mon, Preacher. You know my story. You know what I'm capable of." His lip curled.

"I know I've heard stories about who you were. About Grizz."

"That's just it." Grizz sighed. "I'll always be Grizz. Right now, at this moment, I believe I've changed. But I don't know how long I'll believe it, Preacher. I still get called to that old life. Sometimes it's something as simple as the sound of bike pipes or hearing a certain song, and I feel a pull. At this moment, I'm content to leave it behind, but what if it rears its ugly head down the road? I don't know if I can resist, and if I can't, I don't know what that'll do to Ginny."

Micah looked thoughtful.

"Do you know I think about having a nip of moonshine every single day?"

Grizz shook his head.

"Yep. Every single day I could probably come up with a reason to have a drink. But I don't. It's your choice, Jamison. Simple as that. It's a deliberate choice. And I'm going to give credit where credit is due. My faith gives me strength."

Just then, Aunt Tillie began playing the wedding march on the church organ. Their conversation ceased, and Grizz looked toward the front of the church. He couldn't take his eyes off of her as Jason and Mimi walked their mother down the aisle. He swallowed thickly as he realized he'd never thought she looked more beautiful.

He wanted to do right by this woman. Please, God, let me do right by her, he thought, then realized talking to God was starting to become a habit. That is, if you considered doing something twice a habit.

Mimi was Ginny's maid of honor, and Jason served as Grizz's best man. Before Grizz realized it, the ceremony was over. It had been a blur.

"You may now kiss your bride," Micah told him.

A moment passed. Micah gave a subtle cough. "You may now kiss your bride. I'm addressing you, Jamison."

Grizz realized with a start that he'd gotten through the ceremony never taking his eyes off Ginny's. Even when he'd slid the ring on her finger, he'd done it by feel, not wanting to break from her gaze. He was now legally wed to her, and Micah was telling him it was time to seal their vows with a kiss.

"I hope it's a better kiss than the one you gave her under the mistletoe," Jason's voice chimed in, and they all laughed.

Instead of a reception, the six of them went back to Aunt Tillie's house and ate a feast fit for a king. Aunt Tillie sure knew how to lay out a spread.

Micah took the children back to his house while Ginny and Grizz changed into comfortable clothes and headed for the Great Smoky

Mountains National Park. They'd rented a cabin nestled in the woods just beyond the Cherokee Indian Reservation. Micah told them that if they got bored, there were plenty of things to do on the reservation. Grizz informed him privately that they wouldn't be bored, and it was a good thing the cabin was stocked, because he could personally guarantee they wouldn't be leaving the cabin until it was time to get in the car and drive back to Micah's.

It was dusk when they finally arrived. Grizz carried their small overnight bags. Ginny grabbed her toiletry and tote bag.

He had carried their belongings into the bedroom and laid them down on the bed. Walking back out to the living room, he looked at his bride, who had her arms wrapped around herself.

"Are you cold, baby? Do you want me to build a fire?"

"It is chilly in here, Grizz. Yes, a fire would be really nice."

She watched him walk toward the fireplace, and she suddenly felt shy. There was nothing stopping them now. What if it wasn't as wonderful as she remembered? Worse yet, what if it wasn't as wonderful as he remembered?

She was no longer the twenty-something-year-old she'd been when he was arrested in 1985. She pulled her coat tighter and looked at him. He was squatting in front of the fireplace, jostling the logs with a poker. He was the same Grizz she remembered. He'd already taken off his coat, revealing his outfit of choice was still jeans, a sleeveless T-shirt, and biker boots. His long, thick hair had grown out way past his shoulders. The butterflies in her stomach made their way up to her chest. She could feel them tickling her insides, and her knees felt slightly wobbly.

She cleared her throat, and her voice came out hoarse.

"Umm, I didn't know I was going to be on my honeymoon this weekend. I'm afraid I don't have anything special to wear for you tonight. There just wasn't enough time to shop for something."

He turned around and saw the uncertainty in her eyes. She looked at him with a hopeful expectancy that brought back memories so fierce he felt the weight of them filling up his chest. She had the same look as she did when she'd first led him back to his bedroom in the motel in 1975. A look that said that she wanted to please him but wasn't sure how to do it. His woman.

How could she ever doubt herself?

He stood and gave her a half-smile. "It doesn't matter, Kitten, because I can promise you wouldn't be wearing it for long."

She ran to him then and jumped. He caught her in his arms and kissed her as she wrapped her legs tightly around his waist. He let her down slowly, never taking his mouth from hers.

The need to rip each other's clothes off was overpowering, and they had to will themselves to take it slow. She shrugged out of her coat while simultaneously kicking her boots off. He started to pull his T-shirt over his head when she stopped him.

"No, let me."

They shared a laugh when he had to bend low enough for her to help him out of it.

"Forgot I needed a stepstool."

"We won't be vertical for much longer, Kit," he practically growled, the need in his voice now evident.

She reached for his belt when he stopped her. Slowly, painfully slowly, he started to unbutton her blouse. And when it slipped off her right shoulder, his mouth found the spot between her neck and bra strap. She moaned, leaned into him.

They both went down on their knees then, and he gently laid her back on the plush animal skin rug. Its softness swallowed her up as she gazed at him, her want threatening to overwhelm her. Neither one remembered who removed what, but they were now completely nude, and he was on top of her and kissing her, only breaking away long enough to look into her face.

"I love you, Kit. I've always loved you."

She smiled. "I love you, too."

Then she grabbed him hard by his hair and pulled his face to hers, inviting his deep, sensual kiss. She could feel his hardness between her legs and tried to maneuver his entrance, but he stopped her. After a moment, she opened her eyes and realized that he was slowly pulling back from her. Crouching, he swiped a hand through his long hair.

"What are you doing?" she asked him breathlessly.

She felt her hands unconsciously move to cover her breasts. He reached out and grabbed them, pinning them to her sides.

"Don't, Kit. Don't hide from me."

"You're making me a little nervous." She gave a small laugh, heart pounding.

"Can't I just look at you for a minute? Damn, you're so fucking beautiful."

His eyes roamed over her breasts, saw they were larger, fuller, and the color of her nipples had changed. Slightly darker than he remembered. He almost came just looking at them. The completely flat stomach she'd had before giving birth now had a small rise that showed faint stretch marks, and her hips seemed a little wider. He loved every single thing he saw, and he set about letting her know it by kissing her everywhere, lingering for a long time at each breast. He couldn't get enough of them and reluctantly broke away when he caught her scent making its way up between them.

When he finally made his way down between her legs, she grabbed him again by his hair and told him in a voice that didn't sound like her own, "Not yet. I can't wait anymore, Grizz. I need you inside me now."

"You were always so impatient in bed," he said with a smile. "I can smell you, baby. It's driving me insane. Just one taste, okay?"

How could she say no? She let him have his taste, and her orgasm was swift and powerful. He was now up on all fours, looking down at her. He started to lower himself when she used the softness of the fur rug to slide herself down between his legs.

Taking his hardness in her right hand, she lifted her mouth and tasted the saltiness that had seeped out of him.

"Oh, Kitten, what are you doing?" he groaned, squeezing his eyes shut.

"My turn," she managed to say as she leaned up on one elbow and took him into her mouth. When she could feel him getting close to his release she purposely stopped and teased him with her tongue. When he finally couldn't take it anymore, he roughly slid her back into position and lowered himself between her legs.

He was getting ready to push himself inside her when he stopped. Supporting himself on both elbows, he looked down at her. She looked worried.

"Kit?"

She swallowed and told him somewhat shyly, "It's been a long time for me. I'm not sure how it'll feel. I'm thinking maybe it might hurt a little. Can you go slow at first?"

He hadn't realized he was holding his breath, waiting for an answer, thinking somewhere in the back of his mind that maybe she'd changed her mind. He lowered his mouth to hers and kissed her.

"Of course, I'll go slow, baby. I'll never hurt you. I promise."

He never took his eyes from hers as he slowly and carefully sought entrance to what he'd thought about every single day since losing her over fifteen years ago. His hair was now falling down on both sides of his face, blocking out any light or outside distractions. It provided a small canopy as they found themselves as one for the first time in what felt like an eternity.

Never taking their eyes from each other, he slowly moved inside her. When he had gained full entrance, he looked at her for a signal that it was okay to continue. Her answer was to moan and wrap her legs around him, using them to pull him deeper and encouraging his thrusts.

After, they were silent. The crackling and popping of the fire were the only sounds other than their heavy breathing. The sun had set, and in their haste to unload the car and be together, they'd never turned on any lights. The glow from the fire was all that illuminated them.

"Was it as good as you remembered?" Ginny snuggled into his side, her head resting on his shoulder.

"No," he said gruffly.

He leaned up on his elbow and softly stroked her cheek. A smile lit his face. "It's so much fucking better." After a brief pause, he quietly added, "You're my world, Ginny. You know that, right?" Before she could reply, he corrected himself. "I take that back. Mimi and Jason are my world."

She gave him a questioning look, and he glanced at her lips, then her eyes. "The kids are my world, but you're my universe."

His lips found hers, and when he broke the kiss, he saw a sadness in her eyes. Before he could ask her if something was wrong, she whispered, "I wore it once."

"Wore what, baby?" His voice was husky.

"The bandana."

"I know, Kitten. Carter paged me."

"No. I mean before that. I wore it the same day I realized you were alive." She swallowed before continuing. "I wore it behind closed doors, so nobody would see it. I guess I wore it for myself."

He didn't know why she was telling him this, but he could sense the pain in her voice.

"Don't go there, honey. He would've understood. I know I would have."

Ginny had mistakenly thought their short honeymoon would be nothing but non-stop sex for two straight days, but she'd been wrong. As much as Grizz wanted to spend the majority of his time making love to his bride, he was very aware of the fact that too much too soon might be uncomfortable for her. It wasn't easy, but he paced himself, and they found themselves falling back into the comfortable and happy camaraderie they'd shared in the early years of their first marriage.

"I don't know why you won't let me do it. I used to do it all the time for you," she told him as she sat on the edge of the whirlpool tub, watching him trim his beard.

Without looking at her, he said, "How about because nine times out of ten, you'd mess it up, and I had to shave the whole damn thing off. And don't tell me that sometimes you didn't do it on purpose, Kit."

She didn't say anything, and he looked over. She smiled at him and shrugged her shoulders.

"You said not to tell you, so I'm not saying anything."

"Son-of-a-bitch, it was on purpose!" He started laughing. "If you hate it that much, honey, I'll shave it off."

"I don't hate it, Grizz, I just think it would be nice to see your face clean-shaven once in a while. That's all."

She stood up and kissed his shoulder. "I'm going to see what we have left in the way of food."

A few minutes later, she called out to him, "Hey, I just noticed a CD player. I didn't know the cabin had a sound system. And I can load up to six CDs. We could've been listening to my CDs this whole time!"

"Didn't notice it," he yelled back.

He walked out of the bathroom ten minutes later. It was obvious she'd gone to the car to get her CDs. Music was coming through the sound system, and he could hear "Baby, I Love You," by The Ronettes. He smiled when he realized he still recognized most of her music.

She had her back to him as she stood at the small kitchen stove.

"What are you cooking?"

She turned around then. "Grilled chee—. You shaved it all off!"

She stepped to him and stood on her tiptoes to reach his face, rubbing the smoothness with both her palms. He bent low then to kiss her.

"Did you turn off the stove?"

"Yes," she said.

"Good." He scooped her up in one swift movement and carried her into the bedroom.

A short while later they were physically spent and lying in each other's arms when Grizz decided it was finally time to tell her about the woman he'd met last year in Louisiana. He should've done it sooner, but the time never felt right.

"And you're sure, you're positive it was my twin sister?" she asked him, doubt in her expression. She wouldn't allow herself to get too worked up. The chances of this woman being her twin were pretty slim.

Grizz explained his encounter in further detail. He told her he hadn't seen Delia's note in years and was only going by memory.

"I feel kind of bad for not giving that Bible to you sooner, Kit. Guido had been holding onto it, and honestly, I forgot about it until he reminded me he still had it right before the execution. I told him to keep it just a little longer, then deliver it to Carter's."

He asked her to recount the facts she remembered from Delia's note, and after comparing them to his chance encounter with Jodi, he said, "I was sitting at that lunch counter trying to figure out a way for the two of you to meet when I saw on the television that Tommy had been shot. And even though I left for Florida immediately, you know I kept my distance from you. There just didn't seem like a right time to tell you about her."

"It's okay, Grizz. You're right. This past year has been—well, let's just say it's been a year of too many changes to count. Thinking my sister might still be alive would've felt like too much. Thank you for telling me now, though."

They talked a little more about what they thought the easiest and least disruptive way would be for Ginny to meet the woman who may or may not have been her twin.

But as excited as she was at the possibility, she was more than a little anxious for them to get back to Florida and start making preparations for their future. She would make time to meet Jodi and see for herself, but not until after they figured out their plan.

Grizz soon found himself sitting up, his back against the rustic headboard. She was standing on the bed, straddling his face and pushing herself against his tongue. Her arms were braced against the wall she was facing. Her knees almost buckled when she came, but he caught her and slowly lowered her onto his erection.

After, underneath the covers with her head on his chest, her hand tenderly rubbing his flat stomach, their voices were whispers.

"I'm so glad I found that CD player, aren't you?" She sighed as music from the other room floated into the bedroom.

"What's the name of this song, honey?"

"It's called 'Baby, I Love Your Way.' Peter Frampton sings it." She snuggled closer. "Do you like it?"

"Not really. But I like the lyrics. They remind me of you."

"Isn't it nice making love to music that we used to listen to? Music that we used to make love to? And I bet I have some bands in there you haven't even heard before."

He didn't answer so she looked at him. "Grizz?"

"What, baby?"

"Didn't you hear me?"

"No. I'm sorry. I was just thinking."

"What were you thinking about?"

"I was just thinking that after all these years—"

She leaned up on her elbow and looked at him expectantly. "After all these years, what?"

"That after all these years, your taste in music still sucks."

65

I t wasn't easy saying goodbye to Micah and Aunt Tillie, but they knew we'd already extended our mini vacation, and the kids needed to get back to school. Besides, we would be back.

Before leaving the mountains, I'd confided in my new father-in-law that I was uncertain about Grizz's revelation concerning my twin sister and wasn't sure what to do about it. Especially when I wasn't really letting myself believe it. Our transition seemed complicated enough without adding an unlikely unknown. And truth be told, my emotions were at war. One minute, I could feel the nudge to hop on a plane and go check it out for myself, but then reason would weigh in telling me I'd spent my entire life without knowing her. If it was true, a few more months wouldn't matter.

Micah agreed and told me it was something I should do after we settled. He gently reminded me that he'd patiently waited a year to meet his son after I'd visited him that first time.

"I'm so sorry I put you through that, Micah. I was so distraught when Tommy died, and I was really struggling."

"I'm not telling you this so you can feel bad and apologize, Ginny. I'm telling you because I believe it happened the way it was supposed to. His timing is never wrong."

Back in Florida we immediately returned to our regular routines, deciding that it would be best if we lived apart until after our move. It would be easier to keep our marriage a secret this way so Grizz went back to his house in Laurel Falls and his job on Anthony's landscaping crew and I went back to running my household and making sure the kids kept up with their schoolwork and continued to participate in all of their activities.

I didn't have to drive Mimi around as much as I used to. She'd finally gotten her license, and I would let her take my car when I didn't need it. I'd sold Tommy's car the previous year to a man who'd come up from Miami to buy it for his sister. I could've kept it for Mimi, but at that time I couldn't trust myself not to fall apart every time I saw it pull into my driveway.

The wide gold band that now graced my ring finger looked similar to the one I'd always worn, so I wasn't concerned that it would be noticed. Slowly I started letting my friends know my little vacation during spring break had made me realize I'd wanted to move away from South Florida. I never mentioned there was a man in my life, especially not a husband, just that I thought it was time to start fresh somewhere.

And there was some serious truth in that statement. I'd not grown particularly close to anybody over the years. I had lots of friends through church or the kids' social circles, but I couldn't say they were especially close ones. Of course, Carter and Christy Bear would know the truth. But I was undecided about Sarah Jo. We'd grown almost completely apart since the execution, and she seemed to have distanced herself more since Tommy's death last year. Maybe it was a good thing. I didn't want one more person to know that Grizz had faked his execution. The less who knew the truth, the better.

The kids also began dropping hints to their friends, and if that hadn't been enough, the real estate sign in my front yard definitely let it be known. Grizz had been right about Jason. My son wasn't as naïve as I'd wanted to believe. He would be a teenager next year, and he took the vow of secrecy we'd asked of him very seriously. He knew it was important that our private life stay private. I have to admit, though—I had moments when I was concerned he might slip. But as far as I could tell, he never did.

I had to contact Alec to let him know I wanted to sell Tommy's interest in the partnership and, of course, I would offer it to him first.

He didn't seem surprised that I was finally ready to sell, and he agreed to buy me out fairly. He was surprised when I told him that I wanted to move. But, just like other friends that asked, I had a "go to" answer for my decision to relocate. I told everybody that my children and I fell in love with Montana when we visited years earlier with Carter and that it was a well thought out and carefully planned family decision.

"I don't understand," Alec said over coffee one morning. We'd met at a local cafe to work out some details about the sale. "This is your home. It's always been your home, Ginny. I just can't see you leaving it for a strange place."

I knew his question wasn't requiring a deep soul-searching answer. He was seriously concerned that I may have been making the wrong decision.

"I need a change of scenery, Alec, and so do my children. We're all ready for something different. I need to start over somewhere where the memories aren't so painful."

I was being truthful. It was still difficult sleeping in the bed I'd shared with Tommy for fifteen years. I didn't feel guilty about remarrying. My grief at losing Tommy didn't take away from what I had with Grizz. But I still felt it. I missed Tommy. And so did Mimi and Jason.

He avoided my eyes. "What if I told you Paulina and I aren't going to work out after all? Could you stay long enough to maybe give me, give us, a chance?"

He looked at me, and I know my mouth must've been hanging open. I'm certain I was blushing, but I didn't need to think about my answer. I knew what it was, I just didn't know how to say it. He recognized my discomfort.

"I have it coming. I know what your answer is, and I'm embarrassed for putting you in the position of having to let me down easy. I'm sorry, Ginny."

"No apology needed, Alec." Relief washed over me. I started to get up and gather my things when he asked me one more thing.

"I know we still have some financials to work out with the business, so we'll be talking soon, but will you do me a favor? After you do decide where you're going to move and you get settled, will you stay in touch? Will you let me know you're okay? Can you promise me that?"

I was standing now and looked down at him. I was seriously

pondering how to answer him. Was this the Alec who was sincerely concerned for my welfare, or did I have to worry about him showing up one day? I decided that the best way to answer him was with honesty.

"Alec, moving away, starting new like I want to, means I have to break some ties. Leave some people and relationships behind. I'm sorry."

"Fair enough." He nodded, his small, sad smile said he accepted that boat had sailed and wouldn't be coming back.

TWO WEEKS LATER, GRIZZ AND I FOUND OURSELVES IN A SPACIOUS HOTEL room on the outskirts of a medium-sized city in Montana where we could drive forty-five minutes in either direction and visit several smaller towns. I'd found the Internet was a fabulous resource for everything I wanted to know about these small communities.

I'd narrowed our search to three places that met the entire family's criteria. Mimi and Jason stayed with Carter and Bill while Grizz and I made the long drive to make a preliminary visit. If we liked what we saw, we'd bring the kids back on the next trip.

We'd spent two days visiting the towns on our list and were now discussing it in the hotel's oversized tile shower.

"I like all three," I told Grizz. "I'd really like to bring the kids back and let them visit the schools before they let out for the summer. What do you think?"

I had already washed and was standing back, watching him rinse his hair under the showerhead. His eyes were closed, and water cascaded down his body. Just looking at him sent a familiar and welcomed ache through me.

"Sounds like a plan," he said.

He turned the shower off and used his hands to wring out his long hair. I did the same and reached for a towel I'd hung over the top of the glass door. I bent over and purposely wiggled my butt at Grizz as I wrapped the towel around my head. He slapped me hard on my rear end and opened the door to reach for his own towel.

"A slap isn't what I had in mind," I teased. "And—ouch!"

He smiled at me as he dried off. "C'mon out to the bedroom."

Something occurred to me then. That had to be the third, maybe the fourth time since our wedding that I'd purposely bent over, offering myself to him, and now that I gave it some thought, he'd never once accepted. I knew we'd enjoyed that position years before. What had changed?

"Oh!" I said out loud, raising my hand to my mouth as a possible reason occurred to me.

"Oh, what?" He stood before the mirror, towel-drying his hair.

"I just realized that when I bend over like that, it must bring back some bad memories."

He wrapped the towel around his waist and looked at my reflection curiously as he reached for his hairbrush.

"Bad memories?"

"Yeah, bad memories. You know—of prison. Bending over. You know." I made a motion with my hand. "When men are in prison together, and they want sex, I'm sure it's in the shower, and they have to…" I paused before adding, "bend over. Not that we ever had *that* kind of sex," I stammered, embarrassed. "But the position might be reminiscent of something unpleasant."

I bit my lip and he swung around to look at me.

"Did you have to bend over for someone in prison?" My heart thumped as I waited for his answer. I didn't think I could bear to hear Grizz had been ganged up on and raped in prison.

I don't know what I expected from him, but it certainly wasn't what I got. He burst out laughing. Not a small chuckle. No. He was laughing so hard the towel around his waist fell off.

"What is so darn funny?" I put my hand on my hips.

"Damn, how I love you, woman. No. Absolutely no fucking way did I ever get raped in prison. And before you ask, I didn't do it to anybody, either. I haven't been with anybody else but you since 1975."

The revelation that he'd been faithful to me for over twenty-five years brought me up short, and I started to tell him how moved I was by his admission when he interrupted me.

"And seeing your beautiful tight ass cheeks is not bringing back bad memories. I can fucking guarantee that."

He was still laughing about it as we fell asleep that night.

The next morning, I woke up before he did. His arms were wrapped tightly around me from behind. The digital clock on the nightstand read 7:30 a.m. That was sleeping in for us. The curtains hadn't been shut completely, and a slice of sunshine was cutting through the room. I snuggled in, purposely grinding my backside up against his front, which I knew would get his attention.

I was right.

"You're doing that on purpose," he said in a groggy voice.

"Sue me."

"Did you just say, 'do me'?" he teased.

"No, that's not what I said, but yeah, do me," I laughed over my shoulder.

He scooted back and softly tugged on my shoulder so I'd be lying on my back, but I stopped him.

"No, I don't want to lie back."

"No problem, I'll lie back. Feel free to jump on board."

"No, Grizz," I told him, looking back over my shoulder so I could see his face. "I want you to take me from behind. We used to like making love with me on all fours. At least, I did, and I thought you did, too, until last night in the shower."

Something was up, and I wanted an answer.

He forcefully rolled me over then, and his green eyes grew serious as he looked down at me while leaning on one elbow. His long hair fell onto my chest, tickling it. I raised my hand and softly stroked his heavily tattooed and muscular bicep.

"Why, Grizz? Why won't you make love to me like that anymore?"

"It's not that I don't want to, Kit," he said, his voice sounding even deeper than normal. "I'm just not ready."

"I don't understand."

"I'm not ready to make love to you without seeing your face. I've gone so long without you that I guess I still feel the need to look into your eyes, to make sure you're real. That's all it is, honey. Nothing's wrong."

"Really?" It was the last explanation I'd expected, and I had to admit, it really warmed my heart. Especially coming from him.

"Really," he said softly as he kissed the tip of my nose.

I pushed him away then and threw off the covers. I made my way toward the end of the bed and assumed the position. Catching his eye in the mirror that was hung over every dresser in every hotel room ever, I wiggled my backside at him. He did something I never expected. He bit me right on my left butt cheek. He'd never done that before. It wasn't painful, it just startled me, and I yelped.

"Sorry, Kitten. You get under my skin," he said, his voice low and guttural. "And I've gotta say. I know cussing isn't your thing, but if I remember correctly, you used to make an exception in the bedroom. We used to like that. At least I did, and I thought you did, too." He raised a brow, and I smiled to hear my own words thrown back at me.

I glanced into the mirror and looked into his eyes as he knelt behind me, his hands tightly gripping my hips.

"Just shut up and fuck me," I told him.

66

Grizz, 2002, Fort Lauderdale

The four friends sat on the back deck at Carter and Bill's house. Ginny and Grizz had been sharing details of their upcoming move. After returning from Montana, they'd made a quick trip back with Mimi and Jason and let them visit the schools they would be attending. After deciding that one town, in particular, offered every-thing they wanted, they set about looking at the few houses Ginny had found through her Internet searches.

"So are you buying the house?" Carter took a sip of her iced tea.

"No." Ginny shook her head. "We gave a deposit. We're going to rent for a year while we take our time looking for property. Hopefully, it'll come with a house that we like. If not, we'll probably build."

"Building can be such a pain, though."

"I know, but Grizz loves construction. Remember—he practically lived here when we built this house." Ginny looked over at Grizz and gently caressed his arm. She caught a glance between Grizz and Bill and knew something was up.

"Didn't you? Didn't you love coming here when we built this house?"

He sat up in the patio chair and faced her. "Not really, honey."

"What do you mean, 'Not really?' You were always here!"

He didn't answer, so she looked at him, then Carter, then finally Bill. She felt like she was about to become the butt of some inside joke.

"I had another reason for being here. I was overseeing something. I needed to make sure it was done right."

"Make sure what was done right?" she asked with a curious tilt of her head.

Grizz stood and offered her his hand. She took it and stood up.

"It's easier to show you."

She walked with him as he led her down the deck steps and toward the detached garage with the second-floor guesthouse. She followed him up the side stairs and through the door. They were now in the bedroom where they'd retrieved his telescope the previous Thanksgiving. She looked around the room, then back at him. He walked to the small bedroom closet and opened it.

"Come here," he said.

She walked over and watched as he reached into the closet and opened what she'd always thought was an electrical breaker box. He flipped a switch, and she heard what sounded like some kind of latch releasing and the back wall of the closet slid open.

"A secret room? Really, Grizz?" Her eyes widened.

"Yeah, really." He gave her a dazzling grin. "I originally had it done to be more of a safe house or—what do they call them now? Panic rooms?"

"How considerate of you to create a panic room that I wouldn't know how to find since I never knew about it." She rolled her eyes and tried to stifle a smile.

"I got so complacent after we moved in that I didn't think we'd need it, and obviously we didn't. Then after I was arrested, there was no longer a use for it." He paused. "But it's being used now. C'mon."

He had to duck low to go inside, and she followed him down a very narrow metal spiral staircase. She stood at the base of the stairs, and slowly scanned the room. She immediately knew what she was seeing.

"Bill."

Grizz nodded. "It's where he does all his computer stuff. I already told you I knew him from prison, and that I sent him to Carter for a job. When they fell in love and he moved in, I told him about the room. He was doing so much shit for me, you know, erasing every-thing he could find on me...well, let's just say I wanted him to have a safe place to keep doing it."

"So this is why you agreed to let Carter live here as long as the garage was off-limits. I thought it was because of the cars and your bikes, but it wasn't. You didn't want anybody snooping around the guesthouse and finding this room."

He nodded.

"So where are we exactly?" She looked around as if trying to get her bearings. "I feel like we walked down two flights of steps."

"We did. We're underneath the garage."

She peered around, then glanced up at him, tilting her head. "So you don't like construction?"

He shook his head. "Nope. I kind of hated it. I was only here to make sure this was done right."

She shrugged her shoulders. "Okay. Interesting, but not earth-shattering," she stated matter-of-factly as she turned around and started back up the stairs. Teasingly, she called back over her shoulder, "I think I should insist we build in Montana just to make you miserable."

"Are you upset?" he asked as he followed her up the stairs. His weight caused the metal staircase to shift a little, and she grabbed the railing. He came up behind her and put his hands around her waist.

"No, not at all. I guess I'm just relieved there weren't any dead bodies down here. I didn't know what I was walking into, and you are a man of surprises." She turned then, a concerned expression on her face. "There aren't any bodies buried down here, are there Grizz?"

He gave her half a smile. "No, baby. No bodies. I promise."

They returned to the deck where Carter and Bill were still sitting, except that now, the table was covered with food. Apparently, Carter had made some sandwiches and side dishes and brought out fresh drinks.

"Nice Batcave, Bill. You really are into your computer stuff, aren't you?" Ginny elbowed him as she took her seat at the patio table.

"It's my thing," he said somewhat shyly.

They were eating their lunch when Ginny introduced a topic that had been weighing heavily on her heart, and she wanted, needed, to hear the opinion of those she loved most.

"We've drifted apart, and I can't figure out why, and yet there's something in me that's telling me it's okay, and maybe I shouldn't push it."

She then described what she perceived as the loss of her friendship with Sarah Jo.

"I've tried to get together with her since we came back from

Micah's, not to mention the dozens of times I've reached out in the past year or more, and if I didn't know better, I'd say she's avoiding me."

She didn't notice Grizz stiffen, or the glance Carter and Bill exchanged.

"Well," Carter said softly. "Maybe it is intuition, and you should follow it. People drift apart, Gin. It happens."

"Yeah, but if I hadn't been so wrapped up in Tommy's death and him," she nodded toward Grizz, "I would've pursued her more. You realize—we're moving, and I'm not leaving anybody except you two and Anthony and Christy a way to contact us. I would be cutting Sarah Jo off for good. I mean, other than Grizz, she's my oldest friend. I'm not sure I can do that. Especially without knowing what, if anything, came between us."

She looked at Grizz, saw his jaw tighten. He wouldn't look at her. Before she could ask him what was wrong, the cell phone in her pocket started ringing.

"Excuse me," she said while reaching for it. "I always answer in case it's the school, but in this case," she squinted at the phone, "it's a local number I don't recognize."

She answered it anyway. They watched as she got a surprised expression on her face.

"Stan?"—She put her hand over the mouthpiece and whispered, "Talk about weird timing"—"Yes, Stan, of course, I'll come."

She set the phone down and looked at her husband and friends.

"That was the strangest conversation ever. I don't think Stan has ever called me."

"Why is he calling you now?" Grizz's body posture had changed, and his senses were on alert. He wasn't getting a good feeling.

"Sarah Jo is in the hospital, and he wants me to see her, to talk to her."

"In the hospital?" Carter blinked. "Has she been in an accident?"

"No." Ginny stood up. "She hasn't been in an accident. Apparently, she's been admitted to a psychiatric hospital."

67

Ginny, 2002, Fort Lauderdale

"Thank you for coming," Stan said as he pulled me into a hug.

Stan was a handsome man, always well-groomed and manicured. But today he looked absolutely horrible. It was obvious he hadn't bathed or slept in days. I released myself from his embrace and looked into his bloodshot eyes.

"What's going on?"

He led me into a private waiting room and shut the door behind us. He motioned for me to take a seat, and he took the one across from me. It was obvious Stan had connections and clout, because even though I'd never visited a hospital that specialized in psychiatric care, I knew this wasn't the norm. This room had tasteful and expensive furnishings that rivaled a multimillion-dollar penthouse on the beach.

"I'll tell you what I know or at least what I think I know," he told me, his voice shaky.

I nodded.

"Back when you and Tommy were having problems, I think it was right around the time you moved back home after staying with Carter, Sarah Jo started harping on me about moving away from Fort Lauderdale. And not just away from Fort Lauderdale, but out of the country. I was surprised because I'd had some fantastic offers from outside of the states, and she always turned her nose up at them, insisting she would never leave here."

I stiffened at the mention of my brief separation from Tommy, but didn't interrupt him.

"It was so unlike her, Ginny. Fort Lauderdale has always been Sarah Jo's home, and her insistence felt almost surreal. But, I love her and would do anything for her, so I agreed to start the ball rolling."

I reached for his hand and held it in my own. It was cold and clammy.

"I thought we were closing in on a decision about where to move when Tommy was shot. Then she told me you couldn't bear for her to leave...I'm not blaming you, Ginny." He scrubbed his face with his hand.

"It's okay, Stan, I know you're not blaming me for anything. Go on."

He looked at me with red-rimmed eyes and swallowed. "It was just strange, Ginny. Suddenly, she backed off the move so quickly, the move she'd been adamant about, but I understood because she said she wanted to be there for you. But she wasn't there for you, was she?"

I bit my lip, carefully considering my reply. I didn't know where this was going.

"I noticed we'd drifted apart too, Stan. She was there for the funeral, but you're right. I didn't see much of her before that or afterward. We had an occasional lunch, but it wasn't the same. It was like we were strangers playing the roles of two people who were supposed to be friends. Our conversations were almost scripted. We asked all the right things about our kids and our lives, but it didn't feel right. I've wondered about it myself."

He took his hand from mine then and leaned back in his chair, running it through his short hair.

"It started to get worse after Christmas."

"How?" My curiosity and concern rose.

"I've thought long and hard on this, Ginny. She's been here almost two weeks, and because they don't see any improvement, I'm going out on a limb here. I'm desperate and grasping at straws. Either you'll be the best thing for her or the worst. I honestly don't know, but I'm at the end of my rope."

"What are you talking about?"

"Can I just show you?"

I silently followed Stan down a long corridor. He nodded at a woman at the nurses' station who stood and followed us to a room. There was a door with a tiny clear window. As the nurse was unlocking it for us, I stood on my tiptoes and could see Jo sitting in a comfortable and plush chair. She was clutching a stuffed animal and staring at something not in my line of vision.

I followed Stan in and heard the nurse quietly leave, closing the door behind her.

"Darling, I brought someone who wants to see you. Sarah Jo, Ginny is here."

Sarah Jo slowly looked over at Stan and then me. She smiled, then caught herself. Her smile was instantly replaced with something else. Was it fear? No. It wasn't fear. It almost looked like relief.

She jumped up and ran to me, hugging me so tightly I almost couldn't breathe.

"You won't let him hurt me, will you? You'll protect me, won't you Ginny? You're my best friend, and I know you'll forgive me for every-thing I've done to hurt you. Won't you? Tell me you'll protect me from him. Please, please tell me that, Ginny. Please."

Stan gently unlocked Jo's grip from around my body as I looked at him while answering her. What was going on? Was Stan abusing her or something?

"Stan would never hurt you, Jo. Stan loves you. I don't need to protect you from your husband. You're safe, Sarah Jo."

I almost gasped at her reply.

"Not Stan. I know Stan would never hurt me. It's Grizz! Grizz wants to kill me, Ginny! He's alive, and he's coming after me for all the bad things I did to you and him and Tommy."

68

Grizz, 2002, Fort Lauderdale

He waited with Carter and Bill, hoping Ginny would call or show back up, but she hadn't. His calls to her went straight to voicemail.

He headed back to his house in Laurel Falls and dug out Moe's journal. He'd started to get a little antsy when he'd realized he was on edge about Ginny going to see Sarah Jo. If that call from Stan was about what he thought it was, the journal, along with what Carter and Bill had given him, should help shed some light on things.

All he could do now was wait.

He stood at his front window, arms crossed, and stared out. It felt foreign. He was very private and had always kept his front blinds closed. He certainly never concerned himself with what was or wasn't happening on his street. And there wasn't much to see now. A few cars drove by, and an elderly couple who'd recently moved in down the street were walking their large poodle. He only knew they'd just moved in because he saw the moving van on his way to work one day. He stiffened as he watched their dog squat in front of his mailbox and take a humungous dump. So that's who was leaving those piles of shit. He'd recently had to take a fucking scooper with him to check his mail. It didn't matter now. He wouldn't be living here for much longer, so he'd let it go and let the next renters deal with it.

He watched as the nice girl next door pulled up in front of her house. Rosa cleaned his house and used to grocery shop for him. He'd decided after the one time he'd shown up at Ginny's grocery store that he was wrong to call attention to himself when it wasn't necessary. Besides, Rosa was more than happy to earn a little extra money. He'd leave a list and money for her when she cleaned, and his groceries were delivered by the end of the day. Since he'd been back with Ginny, he'd told Rosa he didn't need her to do the shopping anymore. Ginny always showed up with a bag of groceries. Cooking was one thing they enjoyed doing together. He knew how to cook, but he didn't actually like doing it. He used it as an excuse to sit at the table and stare at her ass while she cooked. He smiled to himself.

Just then, a car pulled in behind Rosa's. Grizz watched her body language change as she heard the car and turned to see who'd parked in her driveway. She seemed to stiffen and pasted on what he was certain was a fake smile as a guy got out of the car and sauntered up to her. Grizz knew the type. What was a quiet, studious, hardworking girl like Rosa doing with a total punk asswipe?

His brows furrowed as he studied the scene. The guy pulled her so close their bodies were touching. Grizz watched as he got in her face, whatever he was saying clearly making her uncomfortable. His sneer was meant to intimidate, and he couldn't hide the fact that he was enjoying scaring the girl.

Grizz used to eat guys like this for lunch. It was almost dinner, and his stomach growled. He was hungry. He was frustrated. Where the fuck was Ginny?

He closed the blinds and headed out the front door.

"Justin, no. Please, Justin! You're squeezing too hard. You're hurting my arm!" Rosa's eyes were wide.

"You can't tell me no. You know that, little bird, don't you? Nobody tells me no."

Grizz could hear the whispered threat as he approached the couple. He hadn't been noticed.

Without missing a beat, he said loudly, "No."

They both turned at the sound of Grizz's voice, and Justin let go of Rosa, his eyes round. She stepped back, and Grizz noticed she was trembling.

"This a friend of yours, Rosa?" Grizz asked when he got to them. He casually leaned against Rosa's car and crossed his arms over his chest.

Justin gave him the once-over, his glance at first hesitant and then replaced with false bravado. He'd decided the big tattooed guy wasn't much of a threat. Besides, all he had to do was make a phone call, and his homies would be on this fucker like stink on shit.

He sneered at Grizz. "None of your fucking business, hombre."

He started to puff out his chest and say something else when Grizz pushed off the side of the car and walked right up to him.

"Which one do you want to eat, *hombre?*" Without waiting for an answer or taking his eyes off the guy, he said, "Go inside, Rosa. It'll be fine. This piece of shit won't be bothering you anymore. Tell your parents not to worry. They don't need to call the police."

She did as she was told, and Grizz heard her front door open and close.

"Which one do you want to eat?"

"What're you talking about, dude? The only thing I'm going to be eating is tiny pieces of your ass when my boys show up later."

"I recognize the ink," Grizz snarled. "I know your boys. I'll give you one more chance. Your choice. Which one do you want to eat? Is it going to be eyebrow, ear, or nose? If you don't pick, I'll pick for you."

"You are totally fucked in the head, dude."

"My choice then," Grizz said.

Before Justin could react, Grizz grabbed him by the throat and ripped the ring out of his nose. He was so stunned, he couldn't react. He howled in pain as Grizz spun him around and held him from behind in a chokehold, forcing him to open his mouth by squeezing his jaw. "You should've said ear. It would've been less painful."

He shoved the nose ring down the guy's throat. "Swallow it."

Grizz whispered something in Justin's ear that made his eyes go wide. He let go of him then and shoved him toward his car, telling him, "And that is why you won't come back here. Am I right?"

Shaking, Justin nodded and fumbled with the car door. He got in and drove away.

Just then, Grizz noticed Ginny pull into his driveway next door. How much had she seen?

69

Ginny, 2002, Fort Lauderdale

I stood in his living room and just stared at him. I'd purposely let his calls go to voicemail and of course, he hadn't left a message. Neither one of us spoke, a tactic he'd taught me. Who would be the first to break?

But I didn't have time for this.

"You go first, Grizz. I have a feeling there's a lot you want to tell me."

"Sit down, Kit." He gestured to his couch.

"I don't really feel like sitting."

"Okay, then. I'll start by telling you the punk next door was abusing Rosa. I stopped him."

I nodded, my concern for Rosa quickly replacing any angst I'd had after seeing Stan and Sarah Jo.

"I know it wasn't the smartest thing to do, especially with us being so close to leaving. But I recognized his ink. I was in charge of them in prison. I just had to mention a code word that had clout and meant he would be dealt with. It scared him off. The last thing he'll do is make trouble. More than likely, he's packing."

I didn't say anything, and looked away, nodding in understanding.

"He was hurting Rosa, Ginny. Scaring her, and hurting her physically. There was a time once when you used to beg me to rescue people like her."

"You're right," I said, sweeping my hand through my hair. There had been too many times to count in our past when I'd used him to intervene on someone's behalf. I had no right to be upset that he was now doing it on his own, without my prompting. If anything, he was showing me that he could have compassion for someone in need. How he handled the situation didn't make me happy; the fact that he felt the need to help Rosa warmed my heart. I couldn't help but smile.

"But, couldn't you have just talked him out of bothering her?" I asked, already knowing the answer. He lived and would die by a code he learned from the streets and the last fifteen years he'd spent in prison. His instinct to extinguish anyone who didn't follow that code was still simmering in him, just below the surface.

His raised eyebrow was his only reply.

Just then, there was a knock at the door, and we both looked at each other. He went to the blinds and peeked out.

"It's her parents."

Please, God, don't let them be here to make trouble, I silently prayed.

Grizz opened the front door, and I could hear two voices talking rapidly in Spanish. I could make out a few words. Thank you. Grateful. An angel from heaven. I doubt I heard that last one right. Grizz had been called a lot of things, and I'd bet my right arm an angel was never one of them. It sunk in—they weren't here to cause trouble. They were here to thank him. I sighed in relief.

Saying goodbye, he kicked the door closed behind him.

"Dinner," was all he said as he carried plates of food, which had obviously been delivered out of gratitude, into the kitchen. The aroma of skirt steak, black beans and plantains was tantalizing, but eating wasn't my immediate concern.

"Dinner can wait." I followed him. "Tell me what you've done or have been doing to Sarah Jo. Tell me why she thinks Tommy's spirit sent your ghost to haunt her?" I pleaded.

He laid the plates on the counter and turned to look at me. He leaned his back against the counter and gave me a level stare.

"I haven't done anything to her. I've watched her since around Christmas, though. I've kept an eye out to make sure she wasn't doing anything to you. Maybe she thought she saw me once or twice. I can't say for sure."

"What?" I tapped my temple with my right hand and shook my

head, trying to grasp what he was telling me. "Why in the world would you think she would do something to me?"

He glanced over at his kitchen table, and I followed his gaze. I didn't recognize it at first, but when I did, I walked to it and picked it up, held it up to him.

"Is this what I think it is?"

He nodded.

"How did you get it? I watched Tommy throw it away, bag it up, and take it out to the garbage cans. Were you outside our house? Were you watching my home?"

My last comment came out in a high-pitched squeak. But he shook his head, confused.

"I don't know about that. Likely *they* were listening then and sent someone to get it. They gave it to me the last time I met them."

"And what could Moe's journal possibly have to do with Sarah Jo, Grizz?"

He grabbed it from me and took my hand, walked me back out to the living room and insisted I sit down. I did. He thumbed through some pages as I watched him.

When he came to a certain page, he handed the journal back to me and said one word.

"Read."

I did. And as I read, I could feel the color draining from my face as I learned about the guilt Moe felt for unwittingly participating in my rape and almost murder. I looked up at Grizz and he immediately sat down next to me, scooting closely so our bodies touched. His warmth was inviting as I relived the horror of that night.

"What does Moe's guilt, about helping to set that night up, have to do with Jo?" I asked in a small voice.

"Keep reading, baby."

I looked down at the page and could feel his eyes as they watched me. He knew the second I read the line, the recognition obvious by my expression. He pulled me close then as I let the journal drop to the floor.

As if sensing a shift in the air, Rocky jumped up from his dog bed and padded over to me. I barely noticed him licking my knee or Grizz's quiet reprimand to go back to his bed.

"I'm not exactly sure what this means. I get it. I mean, it's obvious that Sarah Jo was the Wendy that did this, but..." I wasn't talking to Grizz. I was talking to myself and staring at the wall. I glanced up at him. "Tommy read this journal, Grizz. I never did. I left it up to him to tell me if there was something I needed to know. And he never told me this." My jaw clenched. "If he suspected this, I'm certain he would never have had the heart to tell me Sarah Jo had been behind it all."

I told him what Stan had told me about Sarah Jo's sudden insistence that they move away. It all seemed to make sense now. Sarah Jo's distancing. The awkwardness between us.

"Do you think Tommy is the reason Jo was moving? Is it possible he figured out she was Wendy?"

Grizz nodded. "You just figured it out, and he knew her for years before you did so he would've recognized that term she always used. What did she tell you when you saw her?"

"She rambled, Grizz. She didn't make sense at all. She admitted to doing us all wrong, but she never said what it was."

Something struck me, and I felt my stomach clench.

"Sarah Jo was with Tommy when he died. Oh, Grizz! No, no—please don't let what I'm thinking be true."

I was certain I was going to vomit, and I stood to run to the bathroom. But he grabbed me from behind, pulling me to him and cradling my face in his chest. My stomach still roiled, but the acid making its way up my throat receded.

"Quiet down, Ginny. There's more. I have an answer for you. Carter and Bill gave me something today after you left. It will give you your answers. Let's sit back down, honey, okay?"

I was shaking, but there were no tears as he tugged me back to sit on the couch. I was pretty certain I'd cried enough in the last year to last me a lifetime. The well had finally dried up. Or so I'd thought.

Grizz picked up a cassette tape player that had been sitting on one of his end tables. I hadn't noticed it when I'd sat down.

"Bill had to put this on a cassette tape since I don't know how to work the fucking CD player that's in this house. Besides, I don't think we want to hear this coming out in surround sound. It's going to be hard to listen to, Kit, but it will give you some answers." He peered at me. "Can you handle this, baby?"

I sat up straight, determined not to lose my composure. "Yes," I whispered.

Before he pressed play, he looked at me.

"Carter told me the day Tommy was shot, she watched Sarah Jo interact with you at the hospital. She knew how close you two were, and she felt something was off with Sarah Jo. She told me she tripped and purposely yanked Sarah Jo's pendant off."

I nodded, remembering the incident. "She sent it away with Bill to have it fixed. He returned it later that day, I think."

"Yes, he had it fixed. But he also did something else."

I waited.

"He put a bug in it. He and Carter were able to listen to everything Jo said when she was wearing that pendant."

I felt an icy hand wrap itself around my heart.

"She was wearing the pendant in the hospital room when Tommy died," he added in a soft voice.

"I'm okay. Play it." I recognized the false bravado in my tone.

"Are you sure you're ready to hear—"

"Yes." I nodded and braced myself for the pain that would come with reliving that day. I had no clue what I'd hear from Sarah Jo, but I knew I'd eventually hear my screams of anguish and grief in the background. "Play it, please."

Grizz pressed the button as I reached for his free hand.

I listened as the sounds of the hospital room brought back memories so painful I felt lightheaded and had to will myself not to faint. Hearing the steady hiss of the ventilator that Tommy had been hooked up to caused ice water to invade my arteries. I remembered how I'd made a CD of some of our favorite songs and always had them playing on a portable CD player I'd brought to his room. "Love Can Make You Happy" by Mercy could be softly heard in the background. I squeezed Grizz's hand tighter as the sound of my voice brought me back to the nightmare of that day.

"I'll be right back. Do you want something?"

Then came Jo's reply. "I want you to take a break and know that I won't leave his side until you come back, okay?"

I remembered kissing the inside of Tommy's palm, then walking out of the room. I left him. I turned my back on him and walked out. I was now biting the inside of my cheek so hard I could taste blood.

I listened as Jo's words floated out of the old cassette player and hung in the air. The tone of her voice, a tone I'd never heard, sounded sickly sweet. I'd heard the words sickly sweet used before to describe the smell associated with dead bodies during decomposition. My stomach heaved at the thought.

"Stan and I had just returned from Sydney and were visiting friends in Atlanta when Mimi called me. I was doing what you said,

Tommy. Pushing Stan to interview overseas. But circumstances change, don't they?"

I looked at Grizz. I had my answer. So Tommy had figured out that Jo was Wendy, and he'd told her to leave, probably with the threat that he would tell me about her part in my attack.

"Tommy, do you know how easy this would be for me? All I'd have to do is squeeze one of the tubes on your ventilator and stop the air flow." My breath caught. "Or I could slip a syringe out of my pocket and inject insulin right into your IV. I'd have my back to the nurses, and they wouldn't know what I was doing. You're already being given a certain amount of insulin, so if they ever did an autopsy, which I doubt they will because of the seriousness of your wounds, they'll never look for an insulin overdose. It would be so easy. Too easy."

The tears were back, and my hearing became muffled as my heart-beat quickened, causing the blood to pound in my head. Another tune had come on the CD player. The heartfelt love song, "Follow You, Follow Me" by Genesis, was in stark contrast to the sinister conversation.

"But I won't. Do you know why? Because I'm sorry. And like I told you before, Tommy, I love you, and I love Ginny, and I want this to stop. I want for it all to end."

I heard sniffling then and thought maybe Jo had started to cry.

"I could never hurt you, Tommy. You were my best friend before Ginny came along."

She hiccuped then, and I heard what I thought was the sound of her taking a tissue from a box.

"I wouldn't have told Ginny about the herbal pills you gave her. I never would've let her think you caused that miscarriage. I never gave them to you to give to her with the intent of using it against you. I just wanted to hurt Grizz. Not you and Ginny. I never wanted to hurt you and Ginny." She sniffled loudly. "You have to believe me, Tommy! Seeing you here like this, so vulnerable and coming so close to death, is ripping my heart out. It's not supposed to be like this. I want us to start over. I want to put all the bad memories behind us. You have to wake up, Tommy. I need you to wake up so you can forgive me. Please wake up..." There was a pause, and then she softly whispered, "Grunt. Please."

She started crying harder now, and her sobs were becoming muffled. I could picture her leaning over the bed to hug him, the bug in her pendant pushing up against his body and muting her cries.

My shoulders sagged, partly from relief and partly from remembering the weight of the grief. I bolted upright when I heard the loud and shrill hum of Tommy's heart monitor signaling distress. I asked Grizz to turn it off when I heard Jo's cries for help and her efforts to revive him.

I didn't need to hear any more.

"I remember when he gave me those pills for my morning sickness. I never took them, but I never told Tommy because I didn't want to hurt his feelings." I stared numbly at a piece of art hanging on the wall. It was a vivid abstract I'd not paid much attention to, but now, the loud colors screamed at me.

"I can forgive Sarah Jo for everything that was done to me, Grizz. The rape, the beating, Gwinny, maybe even her attempt to cause my miscarriage. But I don't think I can forgive her for letting Tommy die thinking he caused it."

He didn't say anything.

"Why are Carter and Bill just now giving this to you?" I asked without looking at him. "Tommy's been gone for over a year."

"Carter and Bill never knew about Moe's journal until after you left for the hospital this morning. When I told them, Bill let me listen to this. They didn't say anything sooner because they figured that whatever had happened between Sarah Jo and Tommy died with him. She obviously wasn't there to hurt him. Plus, they heard her grieving afterward and believed it to be sincere."

I leaned into him then and welcomed the refuge his massive arms offered.

"How do you want me to handle it, baby?"

I knew what he meant, and my first thought was to lash out at Sarah Jo, but that wasn't me. Besides, there was no way I'd ever use my grief as a segue for him to go back to his old ways. I may not have been with him for the past fifteen years, but I still recognized that look. There was this anticipation he tried to mask, but I could see it in his eyes. I'd always known that you could take a man off the streets, but you couldn't permanently take the streets out of the man. Even though I didn't want him hurting people, I also realized *that* was the Grizz I'd fallen in love with. The Grizz I still loved.

I swiped my hand through my hair and sat up taller. I needed to concern myself with seeking a way to find true forgiveness. I knew it would come one day, and I prayed that day would come sooner rather than later.

"She's punishing herself," I whispered. "I think that's enough."

I looked up at him then and said five words I'd never meant more.

"Take me away from here."

70

Grizz, 2002, North Carolina

G rizz sat at the kitchen table and filled Micah in on the events of their last month in Florida.

It hadn't been an easy one as Ginny had reached into the depths of her soul looking for the forgiveness she knew she needed to give Sarah Jo. She'd convinced herself the only way to find it would be to make an honest effort toward helping her old friend. It hadn't been easy, but she'd done her best to visit her and convince her Grizz was dead and not haunting her. She wasn't sure if her visits helped, but when it was time to leave, she did so knowing she had done her best in the little time she'd had.

She also knew she would heal from this, just like she'd healed from everything else that had ever bruised her soul.

"It kind of sucks that my wife, who doesn't lie, had to lie in the very end," Grizz told his father as he cradled a mug of coffee. His green eyes stared into Micah's. "She had to reassure Sarah Jo I was dead. She thought it would be the only thing that might help the woman."

Micah's eyes were warm as he reached across the table and patted his son's hand.

"She didn't lie. That man is dead."

They didn't say anything for a few minutes.

"So how long has she had this flu bug?" Micah nodded toward the room in the basement, where Ginny slept. "She hasn't kept any food in her stomach since you got here. A trip to the doctor might be in order."

Grizz nodded. "Yeah, she started throwing up when we hit Georgia. She hasn't kept much down since."

They'd all been invited to go on a picnic in one of the many national forests. Both Mimi and Jason were excited and had gone with the others, but Grizz elected to stay home with Ginny and Micah. She was now lying down in the basement bedroom they shared. Grizz had taken the quiet opportunity to fill Micah in on everything that had transpired since they'd last seen him during the kids' spring break.

"So, any loose ends in Florida?"

"No loose ends," Grizz said. "She sold her share of Tommy's business to his partner. The house sold almost immediately, and the new owners let Ginny rent it back from them until our move. She sold it completely furnished and started packing their personal belongings, shipping their things to a warehouse in Montana."

"If somebody looked hard enough, they could probably figure out how to trace those shipments. Might even be able to ask the schools where the kids' records are being transferred to. Guessing she'll have to have things like her car title transferred. Get a new driver's license. Lots and lots of paperwork." Micah was concerned and Grizz didn't miss the question in his statement.

"That's all being handled by a friend." Grizz didn't have to go into detail about Bill's special skills, and Micah wouldn't ask.

Micah nodded. "I know she drove up in her car, and you drove your car while pulling that 'death on wheels' thing you call a motorcycle. If you want to drive with them out to Montana, you know, in one vehicle, I was going to suggest you leave your car and trailer here, and maybe I'll make a little trip out there for a visit. I can drive there and fly back."

He looked away after he said it. With all the secrecy about their move, Micah wasn't certain if he'd be among the people permanently saying goodbye to the son he'd just found. And he'd never mustered the courage to suggest they move here to live near him. He'd never been a father and didn't know what would be considered pushy. He didn't want to lose the family that God had recently blessed him with.

Grizz took a sip of his coffee and gave his father a half-smile.

"Sounds like a plan, Preacher. But you have to come soon. I don't want to miss out on a whole summer of riding with Ginny."

He saw the relief in his father's face and stood up from the table. He wanted to check on his wife. If she wasn't feeling even a little better, he'd take her to the local doctor.

The kids returned later that afternoon and found their mother sitting on the couch gingerly sipping a cup of tea. Both Spooky and Hope were snuggled up to her, Spooky on her lap and Hope burrowed into her side. Ginny smiled when she thought how well the first leg of this journey had gone. That is, until she'd picked up a nasty stomach bug somewhere in Georgia. She had to let Mimi drive most of the remaining miles to North Carolina.

Both cats shared a crate in her car while Rocky rode with Grizz and Jason in Grizz's Chevelle. Grizz and Micah were now in the kitchen doing some prep work for dinner. She hoped she'd be able to keep down whatever it was they were planning on cooking.

"You know your way around a kitchen," she heard Micah tell Grizz in a surprised tone.

"So do you, Preacher."

Jason was excitedly filling them all in on the day he and Mimi had spent with their cousins.

"It's not just called Sliding Rock, Mom. It is a sliding rock. The water's been running over it for, like, a gazillion years and made it smooth."

"Sounds like you had fun, honey," Ginny said, her voice sounding weak.

Mimi stood to head upstairs to pack an overnight bag. She'd been invited to spend the night with a cousin and wanted to be ready when the girl came to pick her up.

"Before Mimi goes upstairs to pack, can we open Aunt Carter and Uncle Bill's wedding present for you and James?" Jason asked his mother.

Carter and Bill had delivered it to them in the early morning hours on the day they were leaving for their move. Ginny had already turned the keys to their home over to the new owners and had promised to spend their last night having dinner with the Bears. Instead of hitting the road after dark, they'd rented a hotel room where Grizz waited for them. Anthony, Christy, Ginny, and Grizz had all decided that it was in everyone's best interest that the Bear kids never meet him, so he'd waited at the hotel while they ate one of Christy's delicious home-cooked Native American meals.

"I can't believe I almost let you guys leave without giving you a wedding gift," Carter had told Ginny as she'd handed her the neatly wrapped present. "Don't open it, yet. I know you're anxious to get going."

Ginny stared at her friend and asked under her breath, "It's not breathing, is it?"

Carter smiled as she remembered Bill's role in having Spooky, the black kitten, delivered to Ginny and Tommy in what seemed like a lifetime ago. She shook her head.

"Please?" Jason begged, interrupting Ginny's memory.

"It's still in the back of the car, I think," Mimi said.

"I'll get it."

Jason was out the door and back inside carrying the present within thirty seconds. Handing it to his mother, he said, "James should open it with you. It's his, too, Mom."

Grizz dried his hands on his jeans and joined them in the living room. He sat on Micah's coffee table, an old sturdy chest.

"Go ahead." He nodded at her.

By the time it was unwrapped, Micah had made his way to the living room and stood back as Ginny carefully opened the plain brown box. She looked down and smiled, showed Grizz.

"What's in it? What did they get you?" Jason peered into the open container. He looked mildly disappointed.

Grizz and Ginny exchanged knowing smiles. Without taking her eyes from his, she announced, "I think there's a little something in here for each of us. This would be for you, Jason." She handed him a homemade slingshot.

"Cool," he said as he snapped the rubber band that was attached to it.

Ginny handed Mimi a small stuffed gorilla. "I think this little guy can find a home with you. But I'll keep the card that came with it." She carefully removed it from the gorilla's wrist.

Ginny handed the shaving bag to Grizz. "I bet you'll find a use for this, Gri—James."

He winked at her.

She took the Barry White album out last, cradled it to her chest.

"And I'll be holding onto this."

71

Ginny, 2002, North Carolina

I scanned the waiting room looking for Grizz, the news I'd just received still not sinking in.

"That's not possible! Please check again, Tammy," I'd begged of the nurse who was offering me an understanding smile. She was Grizz's second cousin and had been there with her family at Micah's that first day we'd met him. She was also one of the women at the Bunco night I'd attended.

"I'd be glad to check again, Ginny, but I'm pretty sure it's accurate. I'll have the doctor come back in."

I now spotted Grizz in a corner, huddled in conversation with a man I didn't recognize. I almost wilted as I realized his body posture while talking to the man brought on a sense of déjà vu—of when he used to conduct business around the pit. He sensed me staring and looked up. My expression must have startled him because he jumped up, and came to me.

"I'll tell you in the car," I mumbled as I headed for the door, not wanting to make eye contact with anyone in the waiting room.

I was walking so fast his long legs were having trouble keeping up with me.

"Who was that?" I asked a little too sharply when we got outside.

"Merlin Shoup. Ginny, what's wrong? Are you okay? Are you sick?"

He unlocked and opened the car door for me.

I shot him a look, suspicion and fear coursing through me. "What were you talking about?"

He slammed the car door shut and quickly walked to the driver's side to let himself in.

"He asked how long we'd be visiting." Before I could ask why Merlin Shoup was interested in our visit, he added, "He found two hunting dogs that were either abused by the elements or by their owner. The only shelter two towns over wants to put them down. Shoup heard through Micah that I have a way with animals, and he wanted to know if I'd be here long enough to foster them, try and rehabilitate them. Okay? Now tell me what's wrong!"

Oh. I flushed, relief washing over me. I swallowed and chanced a glance at him. I didn't know how he would take the news I was about to tell him. This was certainly going to put an end to the honeymoon phase of our marriage. I was starting to feel overheated and asked him if he would start up the car and turn on the air conditioning. He did, and the radio immediately started blaring "I'm No Angel" by Gregg Allman. Grizz gave me a mischievous smile and turned it off.

"I'm pregnant, Grizz. I'm pregnant." I looked up and focused on the car's roof, afraid to meet his eyes. "I can't believe it. I was certain I was missing periods because I was entering menopause. I mean, I'm in my early forties! But apparently, it wasn't menopause. It was stress, and I was still ovulating. I just don't know what to say. I'm just so shocked at myself for being so irresponsible. I didn't even think to use birth control."

He hit the dashboard so hard I jumped.

"Hot fucking damn! Are we going to have a baby, Kit?"

I looked at him then, and he was smiling so hard I thought his cheeks must hurt. I could only nod. He pulled me close to him over the console of the Chevelle, taking my face in his hands and kissing my forehead, my cheeks, my nose, my chin.

"I didn't think you could make me any happier, Kit. Thank you, baby. Thank you for a chance to raise another child with you. Thank you."

I was still in a state of shock when we got back to Micah's and announced it to the kids. They were more excited than Grizz.

The realities were beginning to sink in. I wanted, needed to let him know what having a baby meant. The responsibilities, the exhaustion, the lack of sleep, the midnight runs to the pharmacy.

But he countered every negative with a positive. I was starting to get butterflies of excitement as I realized he really did want this baby. *Thank you, Lord.* One last thing occurred to me, and I figured I might as well throw it out there.

"You know, people will think we're this child's grandparents."

"Fuck what people will think." Grizz looked at me, still smiling. "Ginny—we're having a baby!"

Later that night, the whole family was sitting in Micah's living room watching "That '70s Show." We were chatting about our move during the commercials. We'd planned on staying at Micah's for just a few more days and were discussing when Micah would be bringing Grizz's car and bike out to Montana when Jason asked, "Do we have to leave so soon? I'm having fun here. Aren't you, Mimi?"

"Huh?" Mimi was curled up in a chair with her nose in a book. She blinked, looked around.

"Are you having fun here?" Jason asked. "I asked Mom and James if we can stay a little longer. I like it here."

"Yeah, I like it here a lot, too." Mimi closed her book. "I'm going to have to say goodbye to cousins who are better friends than I ever had in Florida."

"See? Mimi wants to stay longer, too. Do we need to leave so soon?"

Micah piped up, "Do you need to leave at all?"

The room was quiet, and then both Mimi and Jason started talking over each other as Micah's suggestion that we stay in North Carolina took root.

"I know you mean well," Grizz said. "But nobody knows us in Montana. We're looking to make a fresh start."

"Exactly," Micah said. "Nobody knows you. No family. Nobody to rely on. Nobody that will have your back if you need them to. I know why you want to move, and I understand, but I don't think you realize your anonymity in another state can't protect you like your kin. You weren't raised here, but you are family. And nobody messes with family."

I could see Grizz thinking this over.

"Gri—James, maybe we should at least consider it." I put a hand on his arm.

Truthfully, the thought of the cross-country move in my weakened state seemed like a bit much. And was it wrong of me to admit I liked having a family?

Before Grizz could reply, Micah said something that caused the room to grow quiet.

"You can be Grizz and Kit here. And don't everybody look at me like that. I know those are your nicknames for each other, and not only have I caught you both almost slipping, I hear you when you don't think anybody's listening."

I gulped and looked from Micah to Mimi and then finally to Jason, who to my surprise was nodding and smiling.

"I know he's your big old grizzly bear, and she's your kitten." Micah looked at us pointedly. "You have nicknames for each other. That's fine and dandy, and we don't care. Nobody on top of this mountain cares. Stop acting like you have to hide from your past." He waved a hand toward the kids. "A life you have to hide from is no life at all."

I understood what he was doing, and I appreciated it. He'd explained the nicknames away as simple pet names, but I knew one day Jason—and probably even the baby I was carrying—would know the truth. All the truth.

Micah was right. Living a life in hiding would not be living at all. I believed Micah. I believed in the sanctuary this mountain offered. I could only hope Grizz believed in it, too. I didn't want to leave.

THE NEXT DAY, MIMI AND JASON WERE PICKED UP TO VISIT SOME OF THE places where the movie "Deliverance" was filmed. None of us had ever watched the movie, but after last night's discussion, Micah thought they would enjoy seeing what this area looked like back in the seventies, so he popped in a DVD and pointed out the scenes that were shot nearby. The kids were fascinated by the fact that an entire town was relocated to make room for a lake. I had to agree. Even though I didn't care for the theme of the movie, I had to admit that moving an entire town was pretty interesting.

Aunt Tillie had joined the three of us after the kids left for their day trip, and we now sat around the kitchen table talking about the real possibility of moving here. Every time Micah tried to say something, she'd cut him off.

"Micah can come live with me, and you can have this place," she said in a voice indicating there would be no further discussion on the subject.

"Oh, no!" I said. "We can definitely get our own house. We may be homeless right now, but we're not poor by any means." I didn't think it was appropriate to tell Aunt Tillie that we were quite wealthy.

"Nonsense." Aunt Tillie waved a hand. "This house is perfect for the four of you, soon to be five. Besides—"

"Matilda!" Micah's face was red, and he turned to stare at her. "Is your bun too tight, sister? Will you please for the love of the good Lord, who is my all and my everything, shut up and let me get a word in?"

Aunt Tillie huffed her indignation at the reprimand and nodded when Micah thanked her for shutting her pie hole.

"As my older sister was telling you, this house is perfect for you. I'm tired of taking care of all this property. It belongs to you anyway, Jamison." He glanced at Grizz. "I had everything taken care of after your last visit. It's all yours."

I mulled it over. "If we did move in, couldn't you just stay here with us? It's obviously big enough." I looked at Grizz, and he nodded.

Aunt Tillie folded her arms. "No, because—"

"Matilda!" Micah's voice had grown even more agitated. He turned to me. "I'm used to living alone, Ginny, and this ain't an insult because I love when you're here, but let's just say you can't teach an old dog new tricks."

I heard Aunt Tillie mutter "old dog for sure" under her breath. I smiled.

"And I can't believe I'm saying this, but I think I can get more used to living with Matilda than four people and a new baby." I knew he wasn't telling the truth, and he knew I knew, but he smiled at me. "Besides, honey, this is new for all four of you. You'll need your space."

"That's what I was going to say!" Aunt Tillie said.

Micah rolled his eyes and winked at me.

I wasn't happy with the thought of displacing Micah from his home, but he was adamant. It was settled. Grizz would have Bill take care of getting our things shipped here from Montana, as well as the kids' school transcripts, then erase any electronic evidence. He couldn't erase any hard copies of paperwork, although I had to admit he'd done a great job back in the eighties when he'd personally sabotaged files about Grizz stored on microfiche. But I seriously didn't think anybody would ever go to all that trouble to find us. After all, Grizz was dead, and I didn't have any real ties left undone.

I did have one last delicate request, and I felt a little funny bringing it up, especially since Micah was a minister, and I didn't know if this was considered sacrilegious or not. Aunt Tillie had considered the matter settled and had already left for her afternoon bridge game at the local library.

"Umm, Micah?" I asked.

"Yes, sweet pea," he answered, using his new nickname for me. I could tell he was giddy with excitement that we'd agreed to move here, and to be honest, I felt the same way. It just felt right.

"I guess you know by now we're not what most would consider a conventional family." I cleared my throat. "So I doubt this is a conventional request."

"What is it, Ginny?" Curiosity shone in his eyes.

"Grizz asked me what I wanted for a wedding present, and I told him I didn't want anything, but that's not exactly true."

I glanced at Grizz for reassurance. He nodded at me to continue.

"I wanted him to promise me he'd find a way when we finally settled in our new home." I hesitated. "That—that he'd find a way to bring our loved ones with us."

I could tell Micah was confused. I rushed on.

"I mean, our loved ones that have passed away. Tommy, Ruthie. My mother and stepfather. I can't stand the thought of leaving them in Florida. I can't imagine anyone will ever visit their graves."

I wouldn't meet his eyes and looked down at the table, stretching my arms out in front of me. I nervously twirled my wedding and engagement rings. I was asking for a secret exhumation of not just one or two graves, but four.

I felt Micah's warm hand reach out and grab my forearm, pulling it toward him. I looked up and didn't see disgust or condemnation. I saw tears.

"You have the biggest heart of any person I've ever met, Ginny. It's not as uncommon as you might think. I'm certain we can work something out. I know our family graveyard has plenty of room for some more kin."

I smiled and had to blink back my tears.

"My suggestion would be that we have it done quietly," Micah said. "Leave their headstones where they're at and have new ones made for when we move their remains here."

"Thank you, Micah." I stood to give him a hug. "Thank you so much."

"Family is family, and we take care of our own, Ginny. And if you're our own, then so are they."

EPILOGUE

2007, Fort Lauderdale, Present Day

H e laid back against the cushions of the worn couch and closed
his eyes, letting the rhythm of her motions and the teasing of
her tongue take him to a different realm. He could smell diesel fuel
and grease as it drifted through the open door that separated the
garage from the office.

He should've been grateful Axel had given him a job. After being
released from prison, he'd had the option to work on his father's landscaping crew or suck up to Axel for another chance at car and motorcycle repairs. He had to stay off the law's radar, and it seemed like
blending back into society as a mechanic was a good start. He was
crashing at his older brother, Slade's, house in the guest room until he
could figure out what he wanted to do with his life.

He chanced a glance down at the girl who was furiously trying to
spin magic between his legs. It was working until she felt his stare and
stopped what she was doing.

"You haven't even asked me my name," she said coyly, still
holding his hardness with one hand. She batted her eyelashes and
tried to look away shyly.

He rolled his eyes and roughly shoved her away. They were done.

Not another one. Another one who didn't understand a blowjob
was just a blowjob. Not a fucking marriage proposal. He'd just turned

twenty-three, but he knew the type. How he kept getting tangled up with these women, he didn't have a clue. She would want to talk and connect with him. She'd tell him she understood the depths of his pain and could heal him from the inside out.

So many had wanted to try. So many had been kicked out on their slutty asses as soon as he realized they thought they could be more than just a lay.

There was only one who could've been more. Only one he'd had feelings for.

How many times had he berated himself over the years thinking about how tongue-tied he'd been around Mimi? He'd barely been able to communicate back then, and missed more than one opportunity. By the time he was able to finally tell her how he felt, it was too late. Her mother was moving her away to start a new life in another state.

He remembered how back in 2002 when he was seventeen, his mother had invited Mimi's family over for a final goodbye. Except he hadn't known it was final. He'd thought it was just dinner. Apparently, Mimi's mother, Ginny, had sold their house and had already shipped their personal belongings to their new home. They'd be spending the night in a hotel, starting the long drive to Montana the next day.

He almost dropped his fork mid-bite when he realized they were talking about leaving the very next morning. Everything had been set in motion.

How had this slipped by him? How had he not known? How could he not have heard his parents talking about a cross-country move by one of their closest friends?

There was no way his parents hadn't known about this, he concluded. They had purposely kept it a secret, and he wanted to know why. Being caught off guard like that had pissed him off to no end. As everyone stood in the foyer of his parents' house hugging and saying their final goodbyes, he'd slunk off to his room to fume, beyond angry.

He was throwing darts with his back to the bedroom door when he heard a soft knock. He gritted his teeth. If his mother thought she was going to try to smooth things over, she had another thing coming. His parents were guilty, and he planned on playing judge, jury, and executioner.

He heard the door open and was surprised when he heard Mimi's voice.

"Christian?"

His arm had stopped in mid-throw, letting the dart drop to the floor as he slowly turned around to face her.

She was taking something out of her backpack.

"I never had a chance to give this back to you." She gave him a small smile.

He absently reached for the jacket he'd loaned her so many months ago. It seemed like right after the time he'd driven Mimi home, the contact with the families had died down. He'd patiently waited, even suggesting a few times that his mother call Mimi to babysit for Daisy. Christy said she had asked Mimi, but she was always busy. It seemed they were starting to get their lives back together after Tommy's death, and Ginny had been keeping both her children and herself very active. Bullshit. Ginny was planning a move, and his mother knew it and had purposely started pulling her family back from them.

Christian also knew there had been a slight distancing from the community after Tommy's death. Nothing was ever openly said to the Dillons, but he'd heard Christy telling Anthony that Ginny was upset because she knew there was a subtle buzz in their social circle, that supposed friends were slowly slipping away. Ginny wasn't hurt by it, but she was feeling the sting of the rebuffs to her children. Kids were mean. He wondered now if this had been true.

Now, looking back, he realized it had been his own fault. He should've made an effort to pursue Mimi, not sit and wait for an opportunity to be around her again.

And he had to admit, even if just to himself, that a two-month stint in jail back then hadn't helped his cause. He knew his parents purposely hadn't bailed him out that time like they had the night he was hauled in for resisting arrest—the night Mimi was almost raped. He could recall his father's words when he'd been arrested: "You want to engage in this lifestyle, you need to be prepared for what it might bring. This is for your own good, Christian." Anthony had stared hard at his son then, and Christian had seen in his face what he was really saying but couldn't voice in the police station. "You want to engage in this lifestyle? You want to carry on my legacy? You need to earn it the hard way."

That night in his room, Mimi had looked at him with her big, brown eyes as they both stood clutching the jacket, neither one willing to let go. He slowly tugged, and instead of releasing it, she held on and let him pull her closer. He saw something in her eyes then. He saw recognition. She was realizing at this very moment how he felt, how he'd always felt about her, even though he'd never been able to express himself.

"You have to go?" he heard himself ask her.

She nodded. "I want to go," she said in a soft voice. Her forehead crinkled. "At least, I think I do."

A pause. She looked at him with uncertainty and wonder.

Just then, her younger brother, Jason, poked his head into the room, breaking the spell.

"Mimi, Mom said c'mon." They could hear his footsteps as he ran off.

"The guy that Jason mentioned at dinner, James. Is that why you're leaving? Your Mom is seeing someone?"

"He's part of the reason. I'm glad my mother has fallen in love again. I want her to be happy, and I just don't think she can stay here."

"James who?" Not that he cared. He was just trying to think of conversation to prevent Mimi from leaving, if only for a few more minutes.

"Just James." She looked away.

Christian nodded. He was honestly happy for Mimi's mother and respected her privacy. She was a good woman, and Christian thought she deserved some happiness. But Ginny's happiness was taking his happiness across the country and out of his life.

"Mimi, I've waited too long, and now it's too late." His words were quiet.

She'd finally let go of his jacket, and he now held it in a crumpled ball.

Mimi laid a hand on his arm. "No. It's not too late, Christian. Look —we're going away to start over. Mom doesn't want us connected to anything from her old life. I don't blame her. We're going 'off the grid.'" She emphasized the phrase with air quotes. "But it won't be forever. I know how to get in touch with you, and I will. You'll hear from me, okay?"

"When?"

"I honestly don't know, but I'll figure out a way as soon as I can. I have to go now. They're waiting. It won't be long. Trust me."

She stood on her tiptoes and softly kissed his cheek.

"Mimi," he called after her. She stopped and looked back at him, her hand clutching the doorknob. "Were you disappointed Slade wasn't here tonight? You know, to say goodbye?"

He looked at her, then almost shyly at the floor. The tilt of his head caused his long, black hair to fall over his shoulder and hide the right side of his face. When she didn't say anything, he chanced a glance up, his bright blue eyes in stark contrast to the dark tone of his skin. He wanted to eat his words the minute they'd left his mouth, but then Mimi smiled at him.

"I don't think he knew tonight's dinner was to say goodbye," Mimi said softly.

"You didn't answer my question."

She looked at him a long moment, like she was trying to guess his intent.

"No." She dipped her chin and peered up at him through her eyelashes. "I wasn't disappointed at all."

And then she was gone. That was five years ago.

And he'd waited.

And there was nothing.

He went to his parents, who both told him to leave it alone. They didn't have an address for Ginny in Montana, and even if they did, they wouldn't be giving it to him. He'd finally come right out and asked the last name of the man Ginny was seeing. He'd pestered them to death, even doing his own feeble research online. The social networks proved futile, not to mention that he totally sucked at it. And Mimi had only said her mom was "seeing" a man. Who knows—that could've lasted less than ten minutes. She could be with anybody now. Maybe even nobody.

Days slowly become weeks, which became months and finally stretched out into years, and there was no word from Mimi. She left, and he'd never gotten over her. Never forgotten that he'd seen something in her eyes that night. Something maybe she didn't even know was there. Something he'd wanted to pursue and would have—if she hadn't driven out of his life the next morning.

He was no longer the tongue-tied teenager who couldn't bring himself to ask Mimi out. Now he was a man. A man who knew what he wanted. A man who could finally admit that he'd always been in love with Mimi.

Shaking off the unhappy memory from five years ago, he barely noticed when what's-her-name pouted her way out of Axel's office and slipped out the back door of the garage. It was a Sunday, and the place was empty.

He absently looked around the small room and wondered if Axel had any liquor stashed. He rummaged through drawers and file cabinets until he came to the last one. It was an old metal number that had seen better days, and the drawers gave a loud screech when he opened and closed them.

The last and final drawer didn't contain files. A brown paper bag was sitting on top of something black. Maybe there was a bottle buried in here somewhere. He grabbed the bag, but could tell by its weight that it was full of paper. He wasn't interested and tossed it aside. Next, he came to a black leather jacket. Maybe there was a bottle of booze wrapped in its folds. Christian carefully lifted it out, but it wasn't concealing a bottle either.

He started to put the jacket back when he noticed part of a patch. Was this Axel's old club jacket? Standing up from his crouched position, he grabbed the jacket by both shoulders, stretching it out so he was looking at the back. He studied the patch. It was a sinister skull with devil horns. A naked woman was draped over the top of the skull. She had dark hair and dark eyes. He knew he was looking at an image of Mimi's mother when she was a teenager, but he saw Mimi.

The suppressed feelings from his past started rising to the surface. She had told him to trust her. He'd waited. Trusted. And she'd never come back.

Christian was tired of waiting. He knew he could have someone find her. Yes, he would have someone track her down. Life wasn't fair, and there were too many rules.

He didn't play by rules.

It was no secret that Mimi's biological father, Grizz, had her mother, Ginny, abducted back in 1975. It was no secret that Christian's father, Anthony, had taken his mother, Christy.

He'd grown tired of waiting. It was now time for Christian to take what he wanted.

And he'd always wanted Mimi.

Two Weeks Later
Ginny, North Carolina

I felt Grizz's presence as he walked up beside me, carrying Ruthie. He knew not to interrupt the moment I was having with our son. Once again, Ruthie's twin brother traced each letter in the headstone, proud of himself as he said them loudly and slowly.

"D...I...L...L...O...N." He lay back against my chest and looked up. "You look upside down, Mommy."

I smiled and kissed his forehead.

"Who's ready for our picnic?" I asked as Dillon wiggled around on my lap, his interest already leaning toward what I had packed for lunch.

"Me!" he shouted as he jumped up and ran toward the picnic table, which sat under an outside pavilion.

"Let me down, Daddy!" Ruthie squealed.

She started to squirm, and I could see Grizz was ready for her this time, clasping both of her tiny legs together with his gigantic hand.

"Not until what?" he asked her.

"Please?"

"What else?" His eyes twinkled.

Ruthie puckered her lips and waited for him to lift her high enough so she could press her rosy, pursed lips against his hairy cheek. He grinned and set her down.

"You smell good, Daddy, and your beard itches my lips!"

And then she was off, too, barreling toward her brother.

Grizz reached for my hand and pulled me to my feet. I wrapped my arms around his waist and looked up at him.

"I saw that kick when you picked her up. Still hurts?" I was speaking about a bullet he'd taken in his side back when we'd lived at the motel.

"Only when I get kicked there, which isn't often, so I can live with it."

He pulled me closer and rested his chin on top of my head. We stood like that for a few minutes. Words weren't necessary. I used the quiet moment to reflect on our decision to name our little boy Dillon. We had talked about naming him Tommy, but we realized that honor should be given to Jason, should he ever have a son. I wasn't ready to dismiss how important Tommy had been to me, to all of us. The wedding band I'd worn while married to Tommy had been safely tucked away for Jason to give his bride one day.

Dillon was too little to realize his older brother Jason had a different father, but we knew one day we would tell Dillon our story—and all about the man he'd been named after.

Our quiet moment was interrupted when the twins started shouting in unison, "Jason and Pappaw are here!"

We turned to see Jason and Micah walking up from the rear of the little church. They must have come the back way, as we hadn't heard Jason's truck. Micah now walked with a cane, but it did little to slow him down.

Jason was now seventeen years old and would be graduating high school soon. He had transitioned extremely well after our move here and had made good, solid friends in our little mountain town. He'd grown especially close to Grizz's father. We smiled as we heard Micah grumbling out loud to Jason.

"Still can't believe my grown son thinks it's okay to look like a woman. Long hair and earring." Micah trudged toward us. "If I'd-a been the one to raise him, I'd have pushed that nonsense outta his head a long time ago. What's he going to do next? Put it up in a bun like his Aunt Tillie used to wear?"

Aunt Tillie had died peacefully in her sleep just a year after we'd moved here. We'd insisted that Micah move back into his home to be with us. We were grateful that he'd agreed. He made our family, our home, feel complete.

"Do you have a rubber band or hair tie?" Grizz whispered.

I pulled back and peered up at him. "Don't you dare! You are just going to antagonize him. I'm not giving you a hair tie to put your hair up in a bun."

"Why not?" He batted his eyes. "You never know. It might just start a trend."

"A man bun?" The corners of my mouth quirked. "That'll be the day."

I took my ponytail down and handed him the band. I was secretly enjoying the playfulness he was showing. I loved how easily he'd fallen into a relationship with his father. Even when they agreed to disagree about something, there was always an undercurrent of love and respect.

"Where are my kisses?" Micah called as he approached the kids.

They both ran to him, and I noticed Ruthie elbow her brother out of the way.

"Ruth Frances!" I put my hands on my hips. "Tell Dillon you're sorry and let him hug Pappaw first!"

After giving his Pappaw a kiss and a squeeze, Dillon's interest immediately went to his older brother, Jason. Dillon adored Jason, and I loved how much Jason adored him back.

I reached for Grizz's hand to walk toward our family when I looked up at him. The man bun wasn't looking too shabby on my husband. Actually, it was looking pretty darn hot. I gulped.

We were walking hand-in-hand toward the group when Grizz asked me, "Has Mimi called?"

"No. She's not calling until she gets to Pumpkin Rest. She has almost an hour until she gets there."

Mimi was on spring break from college, and like every spring break for the past few years, she'd spent it at a Christian retreat in the mountains. They weren't allowed to have their cell phones or any link to the modern world. We'd dropped her off the first year, and since we approved of the place and the wonderful people who ran it, we'd let her travel there by herself the last few years.

Not that we had much choice. Mimi would be twenty-two this year and a college graduate. She was an adult. But she would always call us from the last place she could get a phone signal—a tiny little town called Pumpkin Rest—just to reassure us. It consisted of a small grocery store, gas station, pharmacy and diner, all in the same building at the center of a crossroads and very similar to the town we now called home.

We finished our picnic, and I gathered garbage and packed away the leftovers. The kids were in the church playground, and Jason was pushing them on the swings. Grizz and Micah were having a conversation about motorcycles. Micah was speaking in a soft voice and trying to get Grizz to tell him that just because he still rode his bike and we spent an occasional long weekend away from the mountains, Grizz was no longer engaging in anything illegal.

"You don't have to worry, Preacher," I heard Grizz tell him. I looked up, and watched Grizz as he added without meeting his father's eyes, "I've told you before, I like getting away with Ginny on the bike. I'm not breaking any laws by riding."

Grizz must've felt my gaze because he quickly changed the subject by asking me, "When is your foul-mouthed, nutty sister coming back up?"

"You're one to talk," I grinned. Grizz did his best to keep his profanity at a minimum around the kids, but he still slipped a little. Actually, he slipped a lot. I winked at him. "You know you love Jodi. What, not excited about her visit?"

He hmphed and muttered, "Yeah, I'm shit-the-bed excited, Kit. Your sister's visit will be the highlight of my year."

"Stop being such a grump." I playfully tugged on his man-bun which was starting to grow on me. "You love my sister and you know it. She's funny and always good for a giggle or two."

"I don't giggle, Kit."

His expression was so serious that Micah and I burst out laughing.

Micah had just asked a question about Jodi's travel plans when my cell phone rang. Mimi.

"Hey! You're at Pumpkin Rest?"

The connection was a bit crackly, but her voice was strong and sure.

"Yep! I just filled up and am now eating the best homemade biscuit with honey in the world. You'd love it. Then I'm heading for the camp."

"You'll text when you get there? And use the code?" I added.

The camp was so far out of tower-signal range she couldn't make or receive phone calls; however, oddly enough, most text messages went through.

"Yes, Mom."

I could hear the smile in her voice. We had established a code, safe words only Mimi knew. I knew I was overly cautious, but who could blame me after the life I'd lived?

"But after that, you know I have to turn in my phone, so you won't hear from me again for ten days," she said. "I'll text when I'm leaving and, of course, I'll call when the signal improves."

"I know. I just hate not being able to communicate for ten days."

"I'm sorry for that, Mom, but you know how important this retreat is for me. And you and Dad have visited the place. We have this same conversation every year."

The static was increasing, and I knew she must've been walking. I was hearing about every third word, but I got the gist of what she was saying.

"Oh, my gosh!" I heard her exclaim.

"Mimi, what is it? Are you okay?" Grizz caught my eye, his body on immediate alert.

"Yes!" She sounded giddy. "It's fine, Mom. I just ran into a friend! It's..."

I couldn't hear the name.

"Who did you run into, Mimi?" I covered my left ear with my

hand to block out any noise from my end, but already my heart had returned to a normal thud. She'd said it was a friend. Probably somebody she would be seeing at the camp.

"Mimi?"

"I'm here, Mom." There was no indication in her tone that anything was wrong.

"What friend did you run into?" I asked, more calmly this time.

Again I couldn't hear the name she repeated.

"Mom, I'm going to run. I'll text you when I get there. Stop worrying. I couldn't be safer. I love you and Dad, and tell the munchkins I'll have presents for them the next time I come home."

"Okay, honey. I know you'll have a great time and—"

My phone gave three quick beeps, and I knew we'd been cut off. I was sending a text to her when one came through.

Sorry. Awful service. Will text you later. Love you.

I texted back, *Love you too*.

I hadn't noticed Grizz and Micah had stopped their conversation about my sister and had been listening to mine. I explained the conversation, then looked at Grizz sheepishly.

"I can't help it. I'm a mother."

He was sitting at the end of the picnic bench, and he turned so he could pull me down onto his lap. Softly, he kissed the side of my neck.

"You are the most wonderful mother a child could ask for. You raised a beautiful young lady. Just the fact that she would rather spend her last college spring break at a Christian retreat than on the beach tells me that. Never apologize for being a mother, Ginny."

I looked at him and saw not only love but admiration in his eyes. I knew my decision to marry him had been the right one.

I remembered asking him once what had changed him when he came back into my life after I'd worn the bandana. He used to be in such a hurry, so impatient to get what he wanted. And still he'd courted me the second time around with a patience and gentleness I'd never seen from him before.

"I've been given a gift, Ginny," he'd told me.

"A gift? You mean a second chance?"

"Yes, a second chance, but even more importantly, a gift. A gift of time."

"I don't know what you mean."

"Time is the real gift, Ginny, because it's the one thing you can never get back."

We had finally come full circle. Back to the way it was meant to be.

He was my first love. He was a true love. And after all the wandering and searching our hearts had done over the years, we had finally found peace.

We had finally found home.

The End

BONUS EXCERPT

I hope you enjoy this excerpt from *The Iron Tiara*, the first spin-off from the Nine Minutes Trilogy.

Prologue: Naples, Florida

A nthony Bear fumed as he sat astride the riding mower and gazed across the large expanse that was the Chapman property. Their lavish home sat on several acres in the exclusive community of Land and Sea Estates. He glanced down at his hands that were gripping the mower's steering wheel and realized there was still some blood caked beneath his fingernails from earlier that day. He hardly noticed the roar of the mower as he reflected on the events that had transpired over the last few hours.

Three Hours Earlier

WHEN HE'D FOUND OUT THAT MORNING FROM HIS BOOKKEEPER THAT A client was in arrears for almost seventy thousand dollars, he had to reel in anger so intense he could almost feel his blood boiling. After willing himself to calm down, he immediately called his second in command, Alexander, who Anthony called X, to find out how this could've happened. He was almost cooled off when the loud pipes from X's motorcycle announced his arrival at Anthony's business, Native Touch Landscape and Design.

"You know that's Denny's job, Bear. He's the one that collects and squeezes clients when they can't pay," X told him, his blue eyes serious. "And as far as I know, you've never had a problem with Chapman before. He's always paid." X hadn't been referring to the legitimate customers that used Native Touch Landscape and Design. He was referring to the ones that Anthony had other business with: the ones who needed drugs or loans to finance their gambling, drug or other expensive habits.

According to Anthony's bookkeeper, X's observation had been true up until three months ago. Denny either wasn't doing his job or he *was* doing his job and keeping the money for himself. There was only one way to find out.

"Get Denny over to the camp. I'll meet you there," Anthony said in a quiet, but menacing voice from behind his desk.

Camp Sawgrass was a children's camp abandoned in the sixties. It was situated in the Florida Everglades, just southwest of the entrance to Alligator Alley, the long stretch of highway that connected the Florida coasts. It was where Anthony conducted all his darker and more distasteful business.

"He said he'd pay. He's always paid you, boss." Denny gasped for air and added, "They always pay—even when I let them slide!" Denny was sitting in a chair, his hands cuffed behind his back. Blood trickled from his nose and a cut on his forehead.

"Them? Are you saying that you've extended credit before and not just to Van Chapman but others as well?" Anthony asked. He spoke with deadly calm, and his voice was so low, X barely heard him. X stood back watching with his arms crossed. An interrogation like this was something he normally would've handled, but it was obvious Anthony wanted to deal with Denny personally. Seventy thousand dollars was a lot of money.

Denny looked like a deer caught in the headlights. His expression told Anthony it was true, spurring another solid blow to Denny's cheek.

"How much of a kickback do you get from clients for letting them slide on their dues?" he asked the trembling man.

When Denny told him the amount, Anthony punched him in the mouth, breaking off his front tooth.

"That's my money. Not yours," Anthony said. His voice carried an ominous tone. "I'm going to let you go, give you an hour to meet up with Van and bring me back my money. I want Van to get a good look at what I've done to your face."

Denny started to cry. "I can't get your money in an hour, boss. Van went out of town and didn't say where he was going. He told me he'd be back in a few days to settle up with you and everybody else he owes. He's always paid," he sobbed. "He's always paid."

"You let a client who owes me seventy thousand dollars skip town?" Anthony asked, his eyes blazing with fury and his voice now a growl. "A client who owes not just me, but other sharks?"

"Seventy thousand?" Denny asked, tears, blood and snot dripping down his face.

"Are you telling me he doesn't owe me seventy thousand?" Anthony was certain that was the figure his bookkeeper had told him.

"I thought it was seventy-five thousand, but maybe I'm wrong," Denny answered, and then spit a blood-stained ball of phlegm on the floor.

Anthony stiffened when he realized that his bookkeeper had possibly been skimming too. The guy was an accountant for a large corporation who moonlighted by keeping Anthony's books. Was he so hard up for money that he took the chance of mentioning Van Chapman's outstanding loan to Anthony? Or was Denny wrong? Either way, Anthony blamed himself. He'd become too complacent, believing that he'd established himself as a force too powerful to be reckoned with. No one had ever dared to cross him before. But they were obviously doing it now. The more he thought about it, the angrier he got.

"Uncuff him," Anthony demanded.

Less than ten minutes later, X was left with a mess to clean up and a body to dispose of.

"He's dead," X announced after checking Denny's pulse. Even after Anthony inflicted more pain during his nonstop interrogation, Denny never gave up Van's whereabouts. He probably didn't know. *Poor slob,* X thought.

"That's unfortunate," came Anthony's sardonic reply as he headed for the sink.

"What do you wanna do now?" X stood and stared down at

Denny's lifeless body. He inhaled the sharp metallic stench of fresh blood and shook his head.

"I'm getting a lawn crew and heading to Chapman's house," Anthony called over his shoulder as he washed up and stared out the window. He gazed out over the camp yard and let his brain mull over his next course of action. The roar of two motorcycles rolling in interrupted his thoughts. "I saw on this week's schedule that they're not due at his house for two more days, but Chapman moved himself up the work roster." It was to Anthony's advantage that Chapman happened to employ Native Touch to take care of his lawn.

After drying his hands and putting the shirt back on that he'd removed for Denny's questioning, he walked over to where he'd thrown his machete. He picked it up and used Denny's body to wipe it clean. "When you're finished here, make some calls. Put some feelers out. See if you can find Van discreetly." He turned to look at X. "We have no way of knowing if what Denny told us about Van being out of town is true. If other sharks are looking for him, I don't need to tell you that I want to make sure we find him first."

X nodded.

Anthony then looked at what he'd left lying on the floor beside Denny. "Toss that on the grill. It'll be a reminder to the crew what happens to anybody that steals from me," he said as he strode out the door and slammed it behind him.

If it was true that Van was gone, Anthony would use the time to learn more than the little he already knew about the man and his family. If there were weaknesses or vulnerabilities, Anthony wanted to know what they were now so they could be used against Chapman later. His anger at himself started to intensify, but he tamped it down. He'd already blown off enough steam. It was time to get to work.

The smell of fresh cut grass drifted through the air, and Anthony inhaled deeply as Denny's beating and death already became a distant memory. He didn't make a habit of working with his landscaping crews, but he wanted to use the time at Chapman's house to observe. Besides, he didn't consider riding the lawnmower work. If anything, he enjoyed the solitary chore as it gave him time to think.

An annoying fly now interrupted those thoughts. He swatted it away, and then quickly used the rubber band on his wrist to secure his long black hair off his shoulders. Returning both hands to the mower, he went back to mulling over the current situation.

Anthony had met Van once, and only as a formality to let him know who he would be dealing with. A lot of loan sharks tried to hide behind their front men. Not Anthony. He wanted people to see who would be coming after them if they didn't pay. Showing them the man behind the money had always been a useful tool. Until now. And he could almost see why Denny fell into a comfortable relationship with Van. After one brief face-to-face, Anthony knew Van was a typical car salesman. His expensive silk business suits and smooth talking had helped Van move up the corporate ladder and into the bed of a wealthy heiress. Anthony wasn't at all surprised that Van had been able to swindle Denny as well.

Anthony swung the mower around again and gripped the wheel tighter as his knuckles whitened, determined that he would get what was owed to him regardless of the cost. He was in the money business, not the mercy business, and Anthony had no intention of showing mercy to a slimeball like Chapman.

His thoughts were disrupted when he noticed a red convertible Corvette slowly creeping up the long drive. He couldn't tell from that distance who was behind the wheel; all he saw was blonde hair. He purposely steered his mower to the car's obvious destination. He watched the auto curl around the circular driveway, pass the ridiculously large front entry doors and come to a stop on the other side of the ugliest fountain Anthony had ever seen.

As he got closer, he saw a petite, curvy, fair-haired female get out of the car and approach one of his men who'd been weeding along the stone pavers. Anthony brought the mower to a halt, climbed off and walked toward them. The woman's back was to him, and he clenched his jaw when he recognized her body language. He'd mowed enough lawns as a kid on the other coast to know exactly what kind of broad his employee, Lester, was dealing with. She radiated an air of misplaced superiority. Another privileged princess. His jaw was still tightly clenched when Lester stood and laughed at something the woman said. As Lester looked past her, his smile faded when he saw Anthony's expression.

"Sorry, boss. Miss Christy here was telling me something I found amusing," the man said with a worried smile and a Southern accent. Lester was an older man, a Vietnam veteran and alcoholic transient who'd found his way to Florida from Georgia. Anthony had given him a chance, and he'd proven to be a reliable employee. He showed up every morning, the stench of whatever he drank the night before almost dripping from his pores. But Lester showed up, on time, which is all Anthony was concerned about.

The blonde turned around to see who Lester was talking to and her smile faded. With her hands on her hips, her posture stiffened as she stared at Anthony, her lips thin and her expression dismissive. She slowly perused Anthony from head to toe and raised her chin up just enough for him to notice.

"You must be new." The disdain in her voice was as thick as molasses.

There it was. The attitude. The one he knew to expect. Yet her bright blue eyes caught Anthony off guard. He'd never once remembered seeing someone whose eyes rivaled the sky. Not even Alexander's. X's eyes reminded Anthony of ice. Hers, combined with her chin-length straight blonde hair and obvious haughty arrogance, brought back sour memories. Memories of the over privileged and spoiled wives and daughters that used to flaunt their bodies and their fortunes to a young and impressionable Anthony as he worked his first job in Miami on a landscaping crew.

"You live here?" he asked, without responding to her comment. He wouldn't let his eyes travel down her body. He was more than a foot taller than her and could tell without directly looking that she had full breasts that hadn't moved or jiggled when she turned around. Definitely implants. Her nipples were protruding from beneath the flimsy tank top she wore despite the heat. Her white shorts contrasted against her tan skin. *Of course she has a nice tan*, he mused. *It's probably the only thing she does all day. Lie in the sun, lunch at the club and go to back-to-back appointments with masseuses, manicurists and cosmetic surgeons.*

"Not anymore," she replied with a tone of indifference.

His hands balled into fists.

Turning her back to Anthony she returned to her convertible and grabbed what looked like a beach bag out of the passenger seat.

"It was nice to see you, Lester," she said as she walked past the man who'd assumed his kneeling position and was back to pulling weeds from a flowerbed that bordered the driveway. "And thanks for the heads-up!"

Pulling a key from the pocket of her shorts, she opened the front door and went inside, closing it behind her. Anthony heard the click of the deadbolt sliding into place. He returned his gaze to Lester who stood up again and nervously started wiping his hands on his jeans.

He knew his boss would want an explanation. Before Anthony could ask, he answered him.

"She's the Chapmans' daughter. Miss Christy doesn't live here anymore, but she likes to come to the house when she knows they won't be around."

Anthony looked hard at Lester, his eyes full of suspicion. "How did she know they weren't here?"

Lester, realizing that what he'd been doing for Christy may not sit well with his boss, started to fidget anxiously. Then looked away. Anthony was six foot six inches tall, muscular and extremely intimidating. Lester knew from some of the other crew members that even though Anthony ran what appeared to be a legit landscaping business, it was rumored that it was only a front for his illegal activities. Lester had heard Anthony was the leader of what could only be described as a vicious, take no prisoners motorcycle club. They had a reputation for terrorizing the west coast of Florida and for some reason that Lester couldn't fathom, getting away with it. Most of the time.

He gulped and avoided looking into Anthony's penetrating dark eyes. "Whenever we come out here, I page Christy and tell her if her parents aren't home."

Anthony gazed out over the property, taking his time before he asked without looking at Lester, "How do you page her? There isn't a pay phone for miles."

"Miss Christy told me where a key is hidden. I go in the house and use the phone to page her. I use a code so she knows it's me and it means the coast is clear." Before Anthony could reply he quickly added, "I don't touch nothing when I go inside, boss. I swear I don't. And none of the other guys see me do it. I make sure they're not around." He then waved his hand in the direction of the three other men who were off on the property mowing, edging and pulling weeds. "I let myself in when you were mowing out back," he said while staring at the ground.

He cautiously glanced back up at Anthony and was surprised to see him smiling. He'd been working for Anthony for almost eight months and saw him every morning when he clocked in at the landscape office and nursery. He also saw him when he would show up unannounced at different job sites to check up on his crews. And not once had Lester seen Anthony smile. Not once in eight months.

"Show me where the key is," Anthony said in a voice laced with authority. His eyes were steady and cool. "Then tell the crew to pack up and get out of here."

"Sure, boss. But what about you? You won't have a ride. We don't want to leave you here."

"Don't worry about me. I'll have a ride," he replied, giving the Corvette a sidelong glance.

He smiled inwardly as he followed Lester around the side of the house. He watched him retrieve a key from an electrical outlet box that was attached to the stucco exterior wall of the home, well-hidden by shrubbery.

Ten minutes later, Anthony stood with his arms crossed and watched his landscaping crew make their way down the long drive-way. When the truck and trailer turned out of sight, he headed for the front door, spare key in hand. He thought of the woman who'd let herself inside not fifteen minutes earlier and knew that he wouldn't have to look any further for leverage to use against Van Chapman. His leverage had already been delivered. In a red Corvette.

A MESSAGE FROM THE AUTHOR

(Warning: Contains Spoilers)

Thank you for reading *A Gift of Time*. I hope you enjoyed reading it as much as I enjoyed writing it. Yes, this is the final book for what I've always referred to as "the three Gs"—Ginny, Grizz, and Grunt—and I feel confident that I've finished the trilogy by answering all or most of your questions. For those of you who fell in love with one or more of them, you'll be sure to see them in spinoff novels.

Your patience and love for these novels is so humbly appreciated. Thank you, my reader friends. Thank you.

About the real Tommy: It wasn't until I finished this novel that I remembered the "real" Tommy. Tommy was a five-year-old boy who I met on the playground of my apartment complex when I was about fourteen. I was pushing my little sister on the swings when he walked up to us and asked if he could play. I would later discover he was the foster child of a couple who lived above us. He was a quiet and shy little boy, and I wish I could remember what happened to him. We moved away soon after, and it wasn't until I was writing the dedication for this book that I remembered him. Yes, his name really was Tommy. Coincidence? Well, you know what I believe.

About Hope: I cannot tell you how long I have waited to tell the story about Hope, the kitten that ran up Ginny's shoulder. This part of the story was inspired by an actual event that happened to a family friend. I consider it a privilege to make it part of Ginny's experience.

About Tommy/Grunt: I know my Tommy lovers are disappointed. I can promise you that nobody cried more than I did when I wrote about Tommy's death. I'd always intended for him to lose his life, and if I'd continued with the scheming Tommy/Grunt that was in my original manuscript, it wouldn't have been this difficult. I had originally written this character as a manipulative and conniving teenager who grew into an even more manipulative and conniving adult. However, when I decided to go back and tell "young" Grunt's story in Out of Time, I couldn't go through with my original version and had to delete almost half my manuscript to rewrite him. I couldn't help myself. Little Grunt stole my heart. His horrible childhood could have certainly justified some of his actions, but I decided against it. I wanted a character who rose above the dysfunction and abuse he'd suffered. Tommy outgrew his teenage ways and became a loving and caring father and husband, which made it all the more difficult to write what I had to write.

This has always been my story, and you have just read how I always intended it. Yes, some things changed along the way, but the end result is what it was always meant to be.

All my love,
Beth

THE NINE MINUTES TRILOGY PLAYLIST

"The Star Spangled Banner" Jimi Hendrix
"Into The Mystic" Van Morrison
"Sharing The Night Together" Dr. Hook & the Medicine Show
"Layla" Derek & the Dominos
"Follow You Follow Me" Genesis
"Baby, I Love You" The Ronettes
"Run Like Hell" Pink Floyd
"More Than A Feeling" Boston
"Don't Look Back" Boston
"Harper Valley P.T.A" Jeannie C. Riley
"Summer Breeze" Seals & Crofts
"Nights In White Satin" The Moody Blues
"Dreams I'll Never See" Molly Hatchet
"Sweet Talkin' Woman" Electric Light Orchestra
"Hush" Deep Purple
"White Room" Cream
"Baby, I Love Your Way" Peter Frampton
"Magic Carpet Ride" Steppenwolf
"More Than a Woman" The Bee Gees
"I Will Survive" Gloria Gaynor
"If I'd Been The One" 38 Special
"I'm No Angel" Gregg Allman

"Love Can Make You Happy" Mercy
"You've Got Another Thing Comin'" Judas Priest
"Dancing Queen" ABBA

ACKNOWLEDGMENTS

This should be the most exciting part of finishing a novel. For me, it's always the most difficult because I can never seem to find the words that adequately describe the level of thankfulness that I feel. My apologies if I've left someone out.

First, and always foremost, I thank my Heavenly Father. Not just for giving me the ability to write this final book in the trilogy, but for the entire experience that has brought me so much closer to Him. This walk has sometimes been excruciatingly painful, but necessary, to bring me where I need to be in my personal and Spiritual journey. I continue to be amazed at the things He's taught me along the way. And I am grateful for the lessons that I know are still coming.

Jim, Kelli and Katie - Thank you for your unconditional love and understanding while I pretty much put our lives on hold to finish this series. I couldn't have done it without knowing that your love and belief in me was absolute and always positive and just like my protagonist, Ginny, I believe that we can have more than one soul mate. It goes without saying that the three of you are mine. I love you.

And now, in alphabetical order by first name, I give my heartfelt gratitude to the following:

Adriana Leiker and Nisha E. George - The final leg of this journey would not have been possible without the gift of your friendship. I thank God for bringing both of you into my life. I'm beyond humbled and honored that you've never left my side. You've healed my heart during the rough times and laughed and celebrated the good times with me. I can't imagine finishing this book without having both of you in my tight embrace of love and friendship. Thank you, my forever friends.

Adriana Leiker, Anitra Townsend, Erin Thompson, Louise Husted, Mary Dry and Nisha George - Thank you for being the best Beta-readers I could ever hope to have. You aren't afraid to "call me out" and "tell it like it is".

Your honesty tells me that you love me, and you want this story to be the best it can be. I appreciate that more than you could know.

Allison Simon - You are so much more than my formatter. You're the one who's been on the receiving end of finalizing this story each step of the way, and your guidance and patience has been invaluable. I consider it a true honor to call you my friend long after the publish button has been pressed. I love you, Allison.

Amy Donnelly - Thank you for putting the finishing touches on this story. The editing process can be a grueling experiencing, yet you brought light and laughter and talked me off the ledge of panic and despair more times than you know. You have been a true friend and mentor who is always, ALWAYS there when I need you. You own a huge piece of my heart, Amy. 'Really,' Amy...you do! (wink wink)

Donnie Hoffman - Thank you for patiently answering all of my computer questions and keeping me true to the technology that was available in the 1980's. If there are any discrepancies, they are my own.

Jennie Simpson and Jonell Espinoza - My ICU Queens will forever have a special place in my heart for their constant willingness to help me with some of the more obviously difficult scenes to write. They never once made me feel stupid for the numerous questions I would blast at them. They helped me bring to life a very realistic and unfortunate experience for Tommy. If there are any errors or variations from ICU standards, they are due to my creative license. Thank you, my lovely friends. Not just for your help, but for your beautiful friendship as well.

Jessica Brodie - Thank you for being my editor extraordinaire. You take my words and vision and find tremendous ways to improve upon them. Your love, dedication and keen insight bring it all together and make it flow. I love you, Jess.

Judy's Proofreading - I'm so grateful that we found each other. Your sharp eye and attention to detail puts the final seal on this manuscript and gives me the confidence to release it. Thank you, my sweet friend.

Lasse L. Matberg - Thank you for being on this cover and for your kindness along the way. Your good-hearted nature continues to shine well beyond your modeling talents. I am honored that you agreed to be our Grizz. Thank you, Lasse.

Timothy Samora - Thank you for sharing some intimate details of the time you spent in a maximum security prison. I know that I stretched the limits of Grizz's privileges beyond the life you described there, but it was necessary to stay true to his character and this story. All deviations from a real prison experience were a product of my own imagination.

A general shout out and thank you to the friends I've made in the beautiful mountains that I now call home. I respectfully borrowed the surnames of some real friends because they fit so perfectly with this story. My characters are all fictitious and not based on any real persons living or dead.

Last, but never, NEVER least, my readers. Whether you are a reader, a blogger, a fellow author, you are reading this because you've read Nine Minutes and Out of Time. You've patiently waited an entire year for me to finalize this trilogy. Your love for me and this story has brought me immeasurable joy for which I will be forever grateful. Thank you from my whole heart.

ABOUT BETH FLYNN

Beth Flynn is a fiction writer and *USA Today* Bestselling Author who lives and works in Sapphire, North Carolina, deep within the southern Blue Ridge Mountains. Raised in South Florida, Beth and her husband, Jim, have spent the last twenty-three years in Sapphire, where they own a construction company. They have been married thirty-seven years and have two beautiful daughters, an adored son-in-law, and a lovable Pit bull mix named Owen.

In her spare time, Beth enjoys studying the Word, writing, reading, gardening, and motorcycles, especially taking rides on the back of her husband's Harley. She is an extremely grateful breast cancer survivor.

KEEP IN TOUCH WITH BETH

Beth Flynn
P.O. Box 2833
Cashiers, NC 28717 USA
Email: beth@authorbethflynn.com
Website: www.AuthorBethFlynn.com
Facebook Group: Beth's Niners

facebook.com/authorbethflynn

twitter.com/AuthorBethFlynn

instagram.com/bethflynnauthor

goodreads.com/BethFlynn

pinterest.com/beth12870

ALSO BY BETH FLYNN

The Nine Minutes Trilogy

Nine Minutes (Book 1)

Out of Time (Book 2)

A Gift of Time (Book 3)

The Nine Minutes Spin-Off Novels

The Iron Tiara (Book 1)

Tethered Souls (Book 2)

Better Than This (Book 3)

Tarnished Soul (Book 4)